Henry VIII's Secret Daughter

Also by F. W. Kenyon

THE EMPEROR'S LADY

ROYAL MERRY-GO-ROUND

EMMA

MARIE ANTOINETTE

WITHOUT REGRET

NEVER A SAINT

SHADOW IN THE SUN
The Secret of Elizabeth I

LEGACY OF HATE
The Tragedy of Mary Stewart

THE GOLDEN YEARS

MRS NELLY

I, EUGENIA

GLORY AND THE DREAM
The Story of John Churchill, First Duke of Marlborough

THE SEEDS OF TIME
The Story of Arabella Churchill

THE SHADOW AND THE SUBSTANCE
A novel of George Sand

THE ABSORBING FIRE
The Byron Legend

IMPERIAL COURTESAN
The Career of Harriet Howard

THE NAKED SWORD
The Story of Lucrezia Borgia

THE DUKE'S MISTRESS
The Story of Mary Ann Clarke

THE CONSUMING FLAME
The Story of George Eliot

MY BROTHER NAPOLEON
The Confessions of Caroline Bonaparte

PASSIONATE REBEL
The Story of Hector Berlioz

SHADOW OF THE CORSICAN

Henry VIII's Secret Daughter

The Tragedy of Lady Jane Grey

F. W. KENYON

HUTCHINSON OF LONDON

Hutchinson & Co (*Publishers*) Ltd
3 Fitzroy Square, London W1

London Melbourne Sydney Auckland
Wellington Johannesburg Cape Town
and agencies throughout the world

First published 1974

Set in Intertype Pilgrim,
printed in Great Britain by The Anchor Press Ltd,
and bound by Wm. Brendon & Son Ltd, both
of Tiptree, Essex

ISBN 0 09 119620 5

I

It was a stifling afternoon in the unusually hot autumn of 1546 but the nine-year-old Jane shivered involuntarily when the King's eyes fell upon her. He was seated restlessly and uncomfortably in a stout oak chair in which, a few moments ago, two burly but panting pages had carried him into this lofty hall, the presence chamber at the Royal Palace of Whitehall. His scantily bearded face was flushed and blotchy, his heaving dropsical stomach gross. One of the pages set a footstool in front of the chair and upon this the King of England, groaning and cursing, placed a heavily bandaged leg. To Jane, standing before him with her mother, he might well have been a menacing, far from human figure in a nightmare, the menace emphasised by the scorn which flashed in his eyes. He struck terror into all hearts, Jane's mother had warned, but apparently not into the heart of the royal jester who skipped into the presence chamber at that moment, his bells jingling, his jester's cap dipping, and vaulted lightly on to the high back of his master's chair. Perched on the jester's right shoulder was a jackanapes, the smallest monkey Jane had ever seen. The King reached up and twitched its tail, causing it to squeal bad-temperedly. The jester squealed in imitation and said: 'Scratch out his eyes, scratch out bad King Harry's eyes.' The King's hand moved swiftly and surely to the jester's crotch and he squealed again, this time in pain. Satisfied, King Henry pointed a bejewelled finger at Jane and uttered a roar which echoed mightily through the presence chamber.

'By God's precious soul, what have we here,' he demanded, 'a scrawny sparrow to throw to the cats?'

Jane, her eyes on the monkey who was scratching himself in a place which her mother had told her never to scratch, amazed herself by laughing merrily and clapping her hands.

'Such disrespect, child,' her mother reproved.

The girl dropped the King a curtsy. 'May it please your Grace, a sparrow with the heart of a lion.'

'A true Tudor, by God,' Henry commented. 'Fearless as well as disrespectful.'

'I felt some little fear just now,' Jane confessed, 'but your Grace made me laugh.'

'*I*, or the monkey?'

'You, Sire,' she said, sensing that her daringly untruthful assertion would please him.

'You're a little jackanapes yourself,' he chuckled, then went on broodingly: 'Laughter, I vow, drives out fear. I pray that laughter, for you, will always drive out fear, however grave the circumstances.' He glanced up at Queen Katherine who was standing patiently at his side. 'Bring her closer, Kate, closer.'

Jane steeled herself to step forward of her own accord and having done so felt inordinately if tremblingly pleased with herself. Watching her, her mother marvelled that this child, always so meek, had become of a sudden so bold. Had her daughter, or the girl who since birth had been regarded without question as her daughter, the agitated Marchioness of Dorset wondered, discovered within herself not only bravery but the instinctive cunning of many a Tudor? Not that it would be surprising if she had, she having more Tudor blood in her veins than was generally believed.

'So this is our little Lady Jane Grey,' Henry said, taking her hand in a crushing grip. 'How many freckles on your face, child? Have you ever succeeded in counting them?'

'I try to ignore such ugliness,' Jane said miserably.

'Ugliness?' he scoffed. 'In a Tudor freckles add a touch of beauty. My daughter Mary sports a few. In point of fact, freckles apart, you resemble Mary closely, not as she is now, poor woman, but as she was at your age. Have they told you why I summoned you to court?'

'Your Grace wished to inspect me,' Jane replied, sickeningly aware of the stench that emanated from his decaying body.

Tenderly Henry massaged his bandaged leg. 'Belatedly, child, I not having seen you since you were a babe in arms. Puny you were then and puny you still are, but the spirit I sense in you is much to my liking. The intelligence also. Are they schooling you well?'

'I have two tutors at Bradgate,' the girl replied, 'and a writing master calls twice a month to instruct me in the art of writing in a fine hand. I am being taught history and geography, several languages and . . .'

'How many languages?'

'Greek, Latin, Spanish, French and Italian.'

Henry nodded approvingly. 'As with my son Edward, your little cousin.'

Frances, Marchioness of Dorset, caught her breath sharply. Was the King thinking of Jane as a wife for his son and heir? He sought a foreign alliance, she knew, but had failed so far to make any headway in that direction. Jane, then, as a last resort? Henry caught her eyes and, as if suspecting her of wanting this, laughed with an echo of the full-bellied lustiness of earlier days. He was not to know, she thought shakily, that to her it was a frightening possibility.

'What of music?' Henry said, addressing Jane with surprising gentleness.

'I like music very much, your Grace, and am learning to play the lute and the harp, and I am very fond of painting.'

He glanced broodingly at Lady Dorset but continued to address the child. 'Have your parents made you fully acquainted with our relationship, yours and mine?' He lolled back in his chair with half-closed eyes. 'Come, Lady Jane, speak up. Give the King's Highness an account of your family tree.'

'How far back must I go?' Jane asked uncertainly.

'It would take too long,' Henry chuckled, 'if you were to start with Adam and Eve. Begin, then, with your great-grandfather. You had four such forebears, I grant you. I refer to the only one of importance to either of us.'

'He,' said Jane, her voice sing-song as she assembled the facts in her mind, 'was your Grace's father, King Henry VII. He had two daughters. One of them is my grandmother. Her daughter Frances, my mother, married Henry Grey, Marquess of Dorset. My mother is your Grace's niece and I, Jane Grey, the eldest of three sisters, am your Grace's great-niece.'

'Clearly stated,' Henry said, 'but where stand you in the line of succession? Not according to the law of England,' he stressed, 'which, being *my* law, is likely to be changed as the fancy takes me, but according to your closeness, by blood, to the throne.'

Jane, while he watched her drowsily, began to count on her fingers but with her hands behind her back in order to conceal such childish behaviour. There were the King's three children, each by a different mother: the Lady Mary, daughter of the divorced and now dead Katherine of Aragon; the Lady Elizabeth, daughter of Anne Boleyn, the poor creature who, for her sins, had gone to the block, and Prince Edward, son of Jane Seymour, who, whether or not she had sinned in any way, had died a natural death. Jane paused for a moment. There was her grandmother, there was her mother, and there was herself. She hesitated in her counting. Was the King's elder sister Margaret still alive, and if so or if not, what of *her* descendants? Somewhat at a loss, Jane made a tentative guess.

'May it please your Grace, I stand eighth in line of succession.'

'Your grasp of family history is greater than mine,' Henry murmured indulgently. 'Eighth, truly eighth, whether or not it pleases me?'

'At this present moment, truly eighth,' Jane said, faintly but doggedly.

'Ah yes, at this present moment,' Henry pondered, 'no allowance being made for future deaths, natural or otherwise, or marriages and births. What if death were to strike us all, Lady Jane Grey excepted, *at this present moment?*'

'I should become Queen of England,' Jane replied, startled by this astonishing realisation.

Henry opened his eyes fully. 'You would like that, child?'

Jane shook her head decisively. 'No, your Grace.' She wrinkled her brows, recalling a phrase of his. 'By God's precious soul, no.'

'Why not?' he demanded.

Jane hesitated, gripping her hands tightly behind her.

'You would be Queen in name only until you came of age,' he said. 'Is that your reason?'

She shook her head again. 'It isn't pleasant,' she said plaintively, 'to think of so many people all dying at once.'

'Soft-hearted, for a lion-hearted Tudor,' Henry said, his voice betraying unexpected emotion, 'yet I love you for it.' He sighed and closed his eyes. 'Remain a moment longer while I weigh the pros and cons and reach a decision.'

For Jane it was a long moment. She fidgeted, in spite of her mother's warning glance to stand completely still; she shifted her weight from one small foot to the other, and she stared about the presence chamber, really seeing her surroundings for the first time. If everybody did die suddenly Whitehall and all the other royal palaces would be hers. She stared at the wide fireplace and the stone lions on either side of it, each lion reaching up to support the royal arms. Then craning her neck she gazed at the high gilded ceiling and the painted battle scenes that adorned it. The might and splendour of England, she thought, of bad King Harry himself. She stole a quick glance at him, at the grossness of his royal body, and suddenly and uncomprehendingly stark fear gripped her heart. What if the lions were to spring to life and leap out at her? What if the massive ceiling were to come crashing down and crush her to death on the straw which covered the floor? She thought with longing of Bradgate Park, her home in Leicestershire, and wished with all her heart that she had not been dragged away from its comfort and safety, especially from the comfort and safety provided, however impersonally, by her nurse, Mrs Eleyn.

'Niece,' said Henry, opening his eyes and scowling at the Marchioness of Dorset, 'it is my wish that Lady Jane should take up residence at court. Do you, being as strong-minded as any Tudor in existence, object?'

Lady Dorset found herself momentarily and uncharacteristically speechless. It seemed to her that what she feared might now be firmly lodged in the King's mind, Jane to marry Prince Edward, King of England in his father's place when that monstrous old man was called, and none too soon, to face his Maker.

'It is a tremendous honour,' she said faintly.

'Tremendous or not, *do you object?*'

'May it please your Grace, it is not my place to object.'

'Honour or not, your place or not—yes, or no?'

Even with the fear still upon her, Jane grew impatient with her mother and said in a trembling voice: 'The Marchioness of Dorset does not object.'

'Nor you yourself, little lady?'

'Nor I myself,' Jane faltered.

Henry chuckled and grasped her hand again. 'You are now an honoured member of the Queen's household. The Queen, by my wish, is your legal guardian. She will superintend your education, fitting you, perhaps, for whatever high place in the Kingdom it may please God to choose for you.' He groaned as a spasm of pain racked his body. 'To my bedchamber with me,' he commanded the waiting pages.

Jane watched them carry him in his chair from the presence chamber, they lurching under his weight, he cursing them and warning them to handle him gently. In an attempt to ward off the thought that her mother had abandoned her gladly, she tried to feel sorry for Great-Uncle Henry but failed miserably. She was sorry only for herself, and then, in some confusion, angry with herself for having in part encouraged the maternal abandonment by speaking up when she should have remained silent. Children should be seen and not heard, Mrs Eleyn was fond of saying.

'I want Mrs Eleyn,' she told her mother tearfully, remembering that her nurse was waiting at the Dorset London mansion near Whitehall.

'She shall be sent to you within the hour,' Lady Dorset said, 'but as your special attendant, not as your nurse. It is only fitting that you should have an attendant. Your rank at court will be almost equal to that of a princess. Obey the Queen in all matters and remember, especially at table, not to pick your nose or scratch yourself in *any* part of your body. Nor must you belch, yawn or let out any wind, even silently. Is that clearly understood?'

Jane felt an insane inclination to giggle, then she glanced at one of the stone lions and saw it turn instantly into a fox with blood dripping from its fangs. Even worse, its eyes were those of her mother and she suppressed a scream of terror.

'Jane, little Jane,' Queen Katherine said softly.

Jane turned uncertainly and faced the King's sixth wife. She saw a small dainty woman who would have looked even smaller had it not been for her no longer stylish head-dress, a high-pointed hood edged with tiny semi-precious stones. Jane caught a passing glimpse of glossy honey-coloured hair and a white satin kirtle decorated with pearls and glowing rubies. The Queen, she thought, looked young enough to be the King's daughter, even, by the look of *him*, his grand-daughter. Then she found herself gazing into soft hazel eyes, surely the kindest eyes in the whole world. Stooping, Katherine Parr held out her arms, and Jane, no longer uncertain, ran into them and a warm embrace. She had, she knew without question, found a loving friend.

Lady Dorset watched in silence while Queen Katherine led Jane away. They were followed by two of Katherine's ladies and the handful of courtiers who had been present during the audience with the King.

'Frances . . .'

She turned with a start and came face to face with the late Jane Seymour's elder brother whom she had failed to notice in the presence chamber.

'Edward!' she exclaimed. 'You were here the whole time? You heard everything?'

'Everything, Frances.'

Formerly Sir Edward Seymour, of a not very important county family, he had been elevated to the peerage and given the title of Earl of Hertford soon after his sister Jane had become the King's third wife. Frances knew him to be an amiable fellow and, as far as she herself was concerned, an excellent lover of earlier days, but she knew him also to be capable of ruthlessness when ruthlessness would seem to serve his own ends. He was highly favoured by the King, his brother-in-law, and had become a conniving statesman of considerable power. It was widely believed that unless by some mischance he should fall from grace he would become Regent if the King died while Prince Edward was still a minor. He glanced round the presence chamber, ascertained that he and Lady Dorset were the only occupants but was still cautious enough to speak in little more than a whisper.

'Was it not foolish of you to bring Lady Jane to the King's attention?' he said.

'He sent for her, as you must know. What could I do but obey a royal command?'

'And now the child is to remain at court,' Hertford said heavily. 'Do you find it pleasing?'

'I must *appear* to find it pleasing,' she said, 'but you know full well that in my heart I find it alarming.'

Hertford ignored this. 'I wonder if the King will notice that Jane resembles him as much in appearance as Prince Edward does?'

'If so it will please him, that and no more. He has already remarked on Jane's resemblance to Mary.'

'A stranger,' Hertford brooded, 'might well take Jane for what she in fact is, his daughter, not his great-niece.'

'The secret is in safe keeping,' Lady Dorset said, inclined to brood herself. 'Yet the truth will have to be revealed if the King decides upon marriage for Edward and Jane. That is what terrifies me. I could never countenance an incestuous marriage. Nor could you, and to reveal the truth might spell your ruin.'

The truth . . . Lord Hertford pondered, his mind drifting back to the events of nine years ago.

*

'The King warned me before he left for Esher,' the royal physician said, facing Hertford in his apartments at Hampton Court, 'that I would be made to suffer if the Queen failed to give birth to a son. Am I a worker of miracles, my lord?'

'You sound as if you go in fear of your life,' Hertford said, sorry for the man.

'You know the King's temper, my lord, but if the Queen's labour is allowed to continue much longer the danger of losing both mother and child will increase. I suggest the stretching of the Queen's limbs, which is sometimes effective. Failing that, a Caesarean operation. What are your instructions, my lord?'

'Proceed with the stretching of the Queen's limbs and keep me informed of her condition.'

When the physician had hurried away, Lord Hertford walked thoughtfully to the nearby apartments which were at present occupied by Frances, Marchioness of Dorset, whose husband was in Calais. If the Queen gave birth to a living son, all would be well. A son for the King, Hertford thought, a nephew for him, and that nephew destined to be King of England. So badly did Hertford want this that he was prepared, now that the King was absent, to go to extreme lengths if the Queen bore a daughter and if the opportunity presented itself. Frances, his slavish mistress, had given birth to a daughter herself seven days ago, a sickly child not expected to live. Thus she had failed him, but there was still her serving woman, now in labour also in one of the rooms of Lady Dorset's apartments. Happily, one could but hope, the King had seduced her in a moment of drunkenness and had then completely forgotten her.

Hertford paused at Lady Dorset's door, struck by the unusual quietness of Hampton Court. The palace was well-nigh deserted because of the plague which had spread from London. The Queen had been considered too ill to be moved but the King had hurried off to Esher, there to isolate himself. Among those still in residence, courtiers and servants alike, there was much fear and confusion. All in all a fortunate circumstance, Hertford concluded, and entered Lady Dorset's apartments.

'A boy,' she said, when he came upon her.

Misunderstanding her, he took her words for a question and said: 'My sister the Queen is still in labour.'

'I mean a boy for my serving woman,' she corrected. 'I was about to come and tell you.'

Hertford smiled broadly. 'If my sister bears a daughter your woman will have provided me with a rare opportunity. Is it a healthy boy?'

'Healthy enough, but the mother died in labour.'

Hertford looked at her closely. 'You appear to have been weeping, Frances. Surely not because of the death of a serving woman.'

'My daughter Jane died at almost the same moment,' she said bitterly. 'Two miscarriages, a stillbirth and now this.'

'My poor Frances,' he said, and then: 'Is it possible for you to keep everything secret for the time being?'

Lady Dorset laughed mirthlessly. 'The midwife fled because of the plague. My nurse had already fled.'

'Before or after your baby's death?'

'Before.'

'What of your personal staff?'

'They fled early this morning. I am alone with a dead baby and a live one, and a dead serving woman.'

Hertford fingered his beard. 'Do you feel well enough to attend the Queen?'

'If you think it necessary, yes.'

'And valiant enough to remain my ally should a daring gamble be necessary?'

'If by valiant you mean deceitful, yes.'

'Let me see the serving woman's baby.'

A brief inspection was sufficient to confirm the fact that the serving woman had not lied; he was without doubt gazing upon the King's illegitimate son. There was nothing for it, he decided, but to make an ally of the frightened and surely willing physician. Accordingly he brought him to Lady Dorset's apartments, agreed that a Caesarean operation should be performed on the Queen and showed him the serving woman's baby.

'Can you give him an opiate that will keep him quiet until you have performed the operation?' he asked.

A knowing look crossed the physician's face. 'Surely, my lord.'

'And should the Queen's baby be in need also of an opiate, would you be able to give it without drawing attention to your action?'

'Difficult but not impossible, my lord.'

'Lady Dorset and I will be standing by to shelter you from over-curious eyes.'

The physician bowed. 'I can envisage no difficulty.'

There was no need now, Hertford thought, to delay his sister's agony any longer. 'To your work, man,' he said briskly. 'Or do you need the assistance of a surgeon?'

'Fortunately, no, my lord. Physicians, with King Henry our Head of the Church in England, are no longer forbidden to shed blood. Therefore I have no religious scruples and would scorn to employ a lowly surgeon.'

Hertford called for a basket after the opiate had been administered and placed the serving woman's baby in it. Then, when the physician had returned to the Queen, he instructed Lady Dorset to follow him and carried the basket to his apartments, hopeful of successfully completing the plan which had formed in his mind when the King, with his gentlemen and personal guards, had left hurriedly for Esher. His apartments were adjacent to the Queen's and connected by a private inner door. He placed the basket in a closet just within the door and led

Lady Dorset to the room where the Queen was in labour. The physician had already begun the operation with a tearful nurse standing by and two of the Queen's ladies weeping in a corner of the room. The Queen herself was unconscious and lay on a high table. Hertford remembered the King's last brutal-sounding words: 'If there is any doubt, spare the boy's life since I can easily provide myself with other wives.' Hertford smiled grimly. Henry had demanded a boy and, by St Mary, a boy he should have.

Hertford and Lady Dorset moved in behind the physician but were careful to leave him full freedon of movement. He threw aside a small knife and seizing a larger one from the small table close at hand began to enlarge the incision. There was surprisingly little blood. It was almost, Hertford thought, as if his poor sister were already dead. Lady Dorset uttered a strangled gasp and averted her eyes, while the nurse, much to Hertford's satisfaction, fell to the floor in a faint. 'Hurry, man!' he said, but the physician was already dragging the baby out.

'A worker of miracles after all,' said Hertford softly.

He was gazing down, as was Lady Dorset, at a living female baby.

'A son for the King,' he added strongly.

'By the grace of God, a son,' the physician said, and severed the umbilical cord.

'A prince for England,' Lady Dorset said, wondering in God's name how the substitution was to be made successfully under the eyes of the Queen's ladies, even though for the moment they appeared to be paralysed in their corner.

'It is fitting,' Hertford said, glancing down at the still unconscious nurse, 'that Lady Dorset, the King's niece, should take charge of the King's heir. Bathe the Prince, my lady, then bring him to my apartments. Meanwhile I shall summon such lords as have dared to remain at plague-ridden Hampton Court.'

He marched excitedly out, leaving his mistress to bathe the baby and wrap her in a swaddling cloth. Then, with the opiate surreptitiously administered, she displayed the baby briefly to the Queen's ladies while the physician gave his full attention to the now conscious but moaning Queen. The next step was surprisingly easy. Hertford was waiting for Lady Dorset. The baby boy, now recovering from the opiate and yawning, was replaced by the baby girl in the basket, and the basket was secreted again in the closet.

'Fortune has smiled upon us and the King,' Hertford said, and carrying the heir to the throne in his arms marched to the hall of his apartments where a handful of lords had now assembled. 'A son for the King, my lords and brethren. Pray make the ritual examination, lest my eyes should have deceived me.'

Lady Dorset remained behind near the closet and presently, when all was quiet and the Prince had been given into the care of the nurse, she carried the basket to her own apartments, there to be joined by a triumphant Hertford.

'Only one problem remains,' he said, 'the disposal of the dead woman and the dead baby, but I anticipate no difficulties.'

'There is another problem,' Lady Dorset pointed out. 'What is to be done with this living baby, this daughter of the King?'

'How obtuse you are,' Hertford reproached her. 'Would you have me risk eventual discovery by placing her with foster parents? And where is your sense of family responsibility? The King's secret daughter, remember, your secret cousin and my secret niece?'

'You want *me* to take her in place of my dead daughter.'

'What could be better, providing word of her death has not been sent to your husband?'

'It has not been sent.'

'And . . . so?'

'Very well, I shall take her,' Lady Dorset agreed, thinking that perhaps a weapon of future political use was being placed in her hands. 'I shall rear her as my own daughter, and full of milk as I am I shall even suckle her.'

'Half-Tudor milk for a half-Tudor baby,' Hertford joked.

Though cynically amused, Lady Dorset asked a sobering question: 'Can the physician be trusted?'

'I recognise some risk there, Frances. Would he dare to blackmail us? Apart from that, he is a poor frightened fellow, and like a frightened cat is likely to jump in any direction. Let us say that he will die of fright and go to an early grave.'

'And that,' said Lady Dorset, 'will leave us the only two living people who know the exact truth.' She glanced at the hour-old Lady Jane Grey and reached a quick and seemingly necessary decision. 'Pray provide me with a coach and a strong guard. I must leave for Bradgate Park before the King returns to Hampton Court.'

*

'The only two living people who know the exact truth,' Lady Dorset said, repeating her words of nine years ago.

'I agree,' Hertford said thoughtfully, 'that these two children, Edward and Jane, must not be allowed to marry, but I have often wondered if the King would be lastingly displeased if told the truth. I need not stress the fact that Prince Edward, though a changeling, is King Henry's only living son.'

'The risk is too great,' Lady Dorset said insistently.

'True, true. We will speak only if forced to do so.'

'Are you ever troubled,' she asked, knowing it to be a stupid question, 'by the ghost of that frightened physician?'

'No more than you are, dear Frances,' Hertford said impatiently. 'All in all, I doubt if we will ever be forced to speak. The King is not expected to live a great deal longer, assuredly not long enough to see Edward and Jane bedded down. Looking at the matter squarely we have nothing to fear.'

'Have you fallen into the habit of praying for the King's death?' she asked dryly.

Hertford smiled broadly. 'If so, I am not the only person in the Kingdom so engaged. Think, for instance, of the many subjects of the King's Highness who lie in the Tower under sentence of death and their death warrants not yet signed.'

'But you not among them. How safe are you, Edward? And tell me, has the King already named you Regent and guardian of your supposed nephew?'

'He has, privately,' Hertford admitted, 'but he is capable, as ever, of changing his mind.'

'And might well do so, if I told him the truth,' Lady Dorset said, and added with the viciousness of a long-rejected mistress: 'What if I were to bargain with you, dearest Edward?'

'*Bargain* with me?'

'Would you have me prevent you from becoming the uncrowned ruler of England during Edward's minority, or would you, preventing me from preventing it, do something substantial for me, the King's niece?'

'I promise,' Hertford said, hating her despite the physical excitement of her earlier and not entirely forgotten bedchamber rompings, 'to persuade the King to exclude the Catholic Mary and set you in her place in the line of succession.'

Lady Dorset turned up her eyes. 'I thank God, if not you, for small mercies.' And then she laughed with Tudor heartiness. 'You, the Earl of Hertford, and I, the Marchioness of Dorset, are two of the nicest people in this blessed Kingdom of England.'

2

SUMMONED by the King before she could do little more than find a suitable room for Jane Grey and present her with two serving maids, Katherine Parr was coping, as she did three and four times a day, with the King's most pressing need. He lay back on a couch, his head and shoulders supported by well-padded cushions, his ulcerous leg in her lap as she sat before him on a footstool. She had already removed the stained and clinging bandage, causing him as little pain as possible, and was now sponging the suppurating, nauseous ulcers. In this respect she was both physician and nurse, no physician or nursing woman being allowed to approach him while she was close at hand.

'Worse today than yesterday?' Henry questioned.

'Neither worse nor better,' Katherine said carefully.

'You lie, Kate,' he groaned. 'What a sorry pass I am come to. Is there no end to this accursed suffering?'

Trying to assess his ever-changing mood she thought, perhaps, to make him laugh. 'Would you have a surgeon cut off the leg?'

'Could it come to that?' he asked fearfully.

She had said the wrong thing and tried quickly to make amends. 'By St Mary, never.'

He peered at her through narrowed eyes. 'Off with the leg, and off with the phallus too, small use that it is to me these days. Or to you either, Kate.'

'Truly of small use, my lord?'

'Small by fits and starts,' Henry chuckled. 'Do you find yourself pregnant of a sudden?'

'If so, it would not be for want of your Grace's trying.'

'Large then, by fits and starts. And the trying would be all the greater if aided by a machine such as they use, curse them, to hoist me from floor to floor.'

'There are other and more comfortable ways of trying, as the King's Highness well knows,' Katherine said, a shade primly.

Henry reached forward and pinched her rosy cheek. 'You serve me well, sweet Kate.'

'Having been well schooled by Harry of England,' she said, blushing but thinking to please him.

'Give me a son before I die,' he pleaded. 'Edward is sickly. I fear for his survival.'

'If it is God's will a son by me you shall have.'

'God's will, God's!' he raged. 'Mine, Kate, *mine*!'

He fell back on the cushions exhausted, and Katherine, prudently silent, applied the ointment and began to bind the royal leg with a new clean bandage.

'That devil-begotten Francis,' Henry said softly but viciously.

'What new sin has the King of France committed?' Katherine asked mildly.

'Younger than I by three years,' he brooded, 'dying inch by inch of an unspeakable disease, but still able to lead the hunt. Damn him to his popish hell, he'll die leading the hunt, whereas I . . . Kate, Kate, if only you could see me as I was, if only I could stop seeing myself as I was. The curse of it, Kate. Always I see myself as I was. Always.'

Katherine looked at him anxiously and with compassion in her heart. He was growing maudlin with self-pity and lapsing into the senility which these days got the better of him at more and more frequent intervals. If only she could see him as he was? He meant, of course, the full flower of his youth, but she remembered him clearly as he was when she had married him three years ago, she thirty-one, he fifty-three. Gross-bodied then, for sure, but alert and vigorous, and off a year later to conduct the siege of Boulogne, leaving her to rule as Queen Regent. It was only after his return that his health had become precarious and had deteriorated rapidly to its present distressing level. Katherine completed the bandaging and looked at Henry again; he was fingering his beard reflectively and there was a dreamy smile on his lips.

'Francis the lecher,' he murmured. 'I, Harry of England, the veritable saint. Am I not, sweet wife, a veritable saint?'

'Surely, my lord.'

'And the reason? Tell me the reason.'

She answered as she always answered. 'You closed the last of the brothels in London.'

'How many of them?'

'Twelve.'

'And did I not, for your dear sake, banish the royal prostitutes from this and other of my palaces?'

'For my dear sake,' she replied obediently.

'A veritable saint,' he gloated, 'and the spiritual and temporal father of my people.'

'Verily, my lord.'

'All four million of them, Kate.'

A gross exaggeration, Katherine thought. Apart from the secretly practising Catholics, there were the more radical members of the Reformed Church, stigmatised these days as Protestants. Katherine shuddered involuntarily. Many of them, fanatical in the extreme, had already been condemned as heretics and burnt at the stake. Strangely enough the King had numerous Protestant friends and often engaged in theological arguments with them. They were safe, as were their fellow believers, provided they accepted his Six Articles and thus acknowledged his religious supremacy. Nevertheless, as she dwelt on this, Katherine suppressed a wave of fear. She herself, by conviction, subscribed to the New Learning and secretly questioned his supremacy. What would happen to her if he discovered her secret questioning, an attitude that in his eyes would amount to heresy? He was diabolically cunning when, in frighteningly lucid moments, he discussed theology with her.

'Kate,' he said briskly, 'I find myself in need of money. The privy purse is all but empty again.'

Relieved at the change of subject, Katherine said: 'Such money as I possess is yours for the asking.'

Henry chuckled richly. 'For the *taking*, Kate—from a double and twice wealthy widow. Wily of me, you must admit, to marry such a woman.'

It was an old joke. Katherine laughed, as she always did, agreed with him and hoped privately that he would not allow the joke to become too stale.

'And wily of you,' he added, 'to marry two wealthy old gentlemen, one after the other, and wait patiently for God to free you of them.'

'I had no choice in respect of my first husband,' Katherine said, trying to keep asperity from her voice.

'Tell me about it,' Henry said, smiling indulgently. 'I know very little of your past, except that your first husband was Lord Borough of Gainsborough and your second Lord Latimer of Snape Hall.'

Katherine came close to laughing derisively. Henry being the sort of man he was, the sort of king he was, must have made painstaking inquiries into her past before commanding her to marry him. However, obedient as ever, she began by telling him that her widowed mother, Lady Parr of Kendal Castle, had chosen her first husband for her.

'I was not quite fourteen at the time. Lord Borough was fifty-five. I ventured to protest because of his age, but my mother told me that age was of no account if the man concerned was wealthy as well as noble.'

'A wily mother if not a wily daughter. Proceed, sweet Kate.'

Katherine smiled faintly. 'I was terrified but need not have been. Lord Borough was in failing health and was taken gravely ill on our wedding night.'

Henry laughed coarsely. 'Before or after—if you catch the drift of my thoughts?'

'Before, my lord,' Katherine said solemnly. 'He ate and drank too much during the wedding feast and he danced with the abandon of a young man. He was ill again during the journey to Gainsborough. I nursed him and continued to nurse him at Gainsborough. He died just before my fifteenth birthday.'

'Leaving you still a virgin?'

'I fear so.'

'What of your second old gentleman?'

'Lord Latimer was fifty when I married him. I was twenty. My mother was dead. The choice was my own.'

'Because of his position and wealth?'

'Not entirely,' Katherine said candidly. 'He was in vigorous good health and seemed not very old. And he offered me a sure escape from a dull and isolated widowhood in the country.'

'And the danger,' Henry said softly, 'of involvement in religious controversy.'

'The danger passed,' said Katherine, her heart missing a beat.

'Tell me the whole story,' Henry commanded. 'Speak frankly.'

'Frankly, if you insist,' Katherine said, determined now on boldness. 'Lord Latimer was a devout Catholic. He was shocked when you, the King, declared yourself Head of the Church in England. But then, you were a devout Catholic yourself before that event.'

'True,' Henry agreed, revealing no anger.

'Lord Latimer,' Katherine continued, 'was shocked again when you, the King, divorced Katherine of Aragon and married Anne Boleyn. Later he came to London with other Catholic leaders from the North and pleaded with you for the restoration of the Pope's authority.'

'I remember it clearly. Confound his impertinence.'

'He lost heart after the petition was rejected,' Katherine concluded. 'His health failed. He died when I was thirty-one.'

'Three months before I married you,' Henry said, rocking with laughter. 'A pretty scandal *that* caused, sweet Kate.' He was silent for a moment, then went on broodingly: 'One petition I did not reject, by God.'

'True, your Grace. My own.'

Soon after Lord Latimer's death Katherine's uncle, Sir George Throckmorton, a zealous Reformer, had been arrested on a charge of heresy and flung into prison. Katherine had approached the King, had pleaded forcefully and convincingly with him and had obtained her uncle's release. And now, as a result, she, Katherine Parr, was Queen of England, a woman who had cared for, nursed and buried two elderly husbands, a woman whose duty it was to care for, nurse and surely bury a third.

'Those two petitions,' Henry said, staring at her narrowly, 'Catholic on the one hand, Protestant on the other. Where stand you, Kate—squarely in the middle?'

'If the middle means that I stand in the midst of the King's true followers,' she answered quietly, 'then in the middle it is.'

'Enough,' Henry said abruptly. 'We were discussing the privy purse, the empty condition thereof.'

'It comes as no surprise to learn that you are in need of money,' she said. 'You debased the currency but that gave you only a brief respite, and stalemate is the result of your last application to Parliament for additional supply.'

'There is, I grant you, the alternative of Cambridge,' Henry said softly.

Katherine tried not to look at him sharply. He had already seized the revenues of the hospitals and the colleges, with the sole exception of Cambridge, thus impoverishing them sorely. Was he quizzing her slyly? She had saved Cambridge before, and Cambridge was a powerful and often vocal centre of the New Learning. Her intervention had been risky, even though she had pleaded for Cambridge entirely on the grounds of scholarship and intellectual progress. She could think of no comment and waited anxiously for Henry to continue.

'Come now, what say you, Kate?' he prompted.

'Since it pleases you to take, not ask,' she said carefully, 'and since it pleases me to give willingly, or surrender willingly, no alternative of any sort need be considered.'

'Well and skilfully put,' Henry said admiringly, 'even if in your heart you accuse me of blackmail.'

Katherine looked at him guardedly. 'What need is there for the all-powerful Harry of England to resort to blackmail?'

He seemed not to hear and added musingly: 'And even if in *my* heart I accuse *you* of something akin to heresy.'

'Because of Cambridge?' she asked faintly.

'Much more comfortable,' he said, touching his newly bandaged leg tenderly. 'Cambridge? How they rejoiced, those Reformers of Cambridge, when I made you my wife.'

'I, the widow of a devout Catholic?' she parried spiritedly.

Henry swept this aside with a wave of his hand. 'Have no fear. Cambridge shall be allowed to flourish unhampered and, unhampered, shall be watched all the more closely.'

'And I, your Grace?'

'I need you too much,' he said, a whimper in his voice now, 'to accuse you of any sort of heresy, or to listen to any man who might dare to do so.'

Katherine was not entirely reassured. Everything would depend, as everything did depend these days, on his fickle mood of the moment. Nevertheless she murmured a dutiful 'Thank you, my lord,' and was astonished to see what looked like a flash of angry frustration in his eyes.

'I began it all,' he said. 'I have only myself to blame.'

Catching the drift of his thoughts she said placatingly: 'There were Reformers in the realm before you made yourself Head of the Church in England.'

'Heretics, damn them to hell!' he raged, but exhausted again he was tired of the subject. 'What think you,' he asked, 'of our little Lady Jane?'

'A fetching child, from what little I have seen of her.'

'It may please me yet,' he said, a mischievous note in his voice, 'to place her closer to the throne than she is at present.'

'How much closer?' Katherine ventured.

'Fourth in the line of succession.' Then remembering and frowning he corrected himself. 'No, it would have to be second, as things stand at present. Am I confusing you, Kate?'

Katherine shook her head. Though it was not generally known, Henry, immediately after marrying her, had excluded his daughters from the succession and had decreed that any children borne by his new Queen should succeed Edward if that prince should die a minor or childless. Certainly Edward was sickly but not desperately so. It seemed much more likely that she, Katherine Parr, would never bear the ailing King any children. She sometimes reproached herself for not persuading Henry to leave his daughters, whom she had grown to love, in their rightful places, but she was politically ambitious enough to look to her own interests, remote as the possibility was of her becoming a mother.

'I appear to be confusing myself, if not you,' Henry said. 'Jane after Edward only if you remain barren and he dies without issue.'

Katherine smiled brightly but felt a certain indignation. Barren, *she*, at the age of thirty-four? She conveniently forgot that the vigorous Lord Latimer had failed to make her pregnant, even during the early years of their marriage, and concentrated her thoughts on Henry Tudor. He, though not always impotent, was surely sterile. It was surprising that he, reputedly syphilitic since his youth, had fathered any children at all.

'Or should we,' Henry pondered, 'marry Jane to Edward? It would give her the chance of becoming Queen-Consort but no chance of inheriting the throne.'

'Should we throw dice, my lord?'

'Joke if you must,' Henry said darkly, 'but it may well come to that.'

'I suggest that you should bide your time,' Katherine advised, thinking that she, as Jane Grey's guardian, would have a secure position at court in either eventuality, 'and see how your great-niece shapes under my guidance.'

Henry shrugged and ran off at a tangent: 'The allowance necessary to the maintenance of your household will naturally continue.'

'To be paid out of the money I give or allow to be taken?' Katherine ventured laughingly.

'I can think of no other way,' Henry purred, 'but let us regard your money as a loan. You shall be repaid in full, and with interest. Even the same rate of interest as charged by the grasping City bankers. I am nothing if not magnanimous. Can you deny it?'

Katherine could, but she murmured softly: 'Your Grace's generosity is beyond question.'

'There's a scholarly glint in your eyes,' Henry said, thinking himself shrewd.

'Because of your undeniable generosity?' a bewildered Katherine asked.

'By St Mary, no. I am thinking again of the little Lady Jane. Do you aim to make a scholar of her, one such as you were yourself at the same age?'

Katherine already had this in mind, but she said: 'Only if she shows the promise which, I think, can be recognised in her already.'

Henry yawned. 'You see her as you were yourself twenty-five years ago.'

Katherine smiled reminiscently. 'Perhaps, but I have yet to discover if Lady Jane loathes needlework as much as little Katherine Parr did when *she* was nine.'

Henry yawned again. 'I have a mind to question her more thoroughly. She shall sup with us, but privately. See to it, Kate.'

3

THE newly arrived Mrs Eleyn was with Jane when Katherine Parr went unattended to the girl's room. She was a plump woman of thirty and had been employed by Lady Dorset when Jane was little more than a month old. She came of a good if impoverished family and was very conscious of the high standing of the Dorsets whom she regarded as superior in breeding to the Queen. She curtsied dutifully enough but with a challenging look in her eyes. Not given easily to anger Katherine dismissed her cheerily and turned with a smile to Jane.

'You appear to be unpacking,' she said.

Jane nodded gravely. 'My mother sent these two hampers from Dorset House. They contain my clothes and some of my books.'

Katherine peered first into one hamper, then into the other. 'More books than clothes, I see.'

'Books are more important than clothes, Madame.'

'Is that your own decision, child, or your parents'?'

Jane smiled shyly. 'I am very fond of clothes.'

'So am I,' Katherine chuckled, 'fond as I am of books, important as books are.' She reached into the second hamper and brought to light a crumpled length of linen. 'What have we here, Jane?'

'A toilet-table cover, your Grace.'

'Truly?' Katherine said solemnly.

'A toilet-table cover in the making,' Jane amended. 'I had only just begun work on it before we left Bradgate.'

'One hem only,' Katherine commented, 'and as straight, I fear, as a dog's hind leg.'

'Perhaps my eyesight is faulty,' Jane said hopefully. 'I shall never be able to sew properly, alas.'

'A neat excuse,' Katherine murmured, trying not to laugh

and remembering that she had once made the same excuse herself. 'Obviously you have no love of needlework.'

Jane arched her slim fingers. 'These hands of mine,' she said, but not offensively, 'were made to touch crowns and sceptres, not needles.'

'Quite uncanny,' Katherine exclaimed. 'I said much the same when my mother reproached me for hating needlework.'

'You expected, even then, to marry the King?' Jane asked in surprise.

'Not King Henry, or any other king, really. An Italian astrologer had predicted that I was destined to become a great scholar and also a gracious and magnanimous queen.'

'But never a great needlewoman?'

'In time I became at least a competent one, and that is what you must become yourself.'

'If I must, I must,' Jane sighed.

'You are very fond of painting. What of drawing?'

'A good painter must also be a good drawer,' Jane replied, half-suspecting that the Queen was leading her into a trap.

'Can you draw a crown?'

'Surely.'

'A sceptre also?'

'I can draw both, Madame.'

'Then you shall draw crowns and sceptres on this toilet-table cover and ply your needle in some exquisite embroidery.'

Jane sighed resignedly. 'Am I to make an immediate start?'

Katherine shook her head. 'We sup with the King within the hour, privately.'

'I dressed as I am now?' the girl asked anxiously.

'You feel a change is called for?'

'Whatever your Grace decrees,' Jane said, but without subservience.

Katherine studied her new charge carefully. Jane was dressed, as was the fashion, in clothes that were exact copies of those worn by her elders. The hood of her purple satin coat was of French origin, and richly jewelled, while the slashed sleeves, revealing slim firm forearms, reached down to her ankles. Her head-dress, stylishly flat, was placed far back on her head and might well have been a silver halo. The bell-shaped overskirt was a mixture of gold and silver tissue and heavily lined with sable, yet the heaviness of it seemed in no way to trouble the child, as Katherine had already noticed: she controlled it with the ease and aplomb of a grown and elegant woman.

'No change is necessary,' Katherine decided, 'but we can dispense with the coat. The additional weight of it is already making you grow pale.'

'How terrible! Paleness makes my freckles stand out.'

Katherine hid a smile. 'Or has all the excitement made you feel ill?'

'I feel a little sick,' Jane admitted, 'but I'm too empty to be sick.'

'Peckish, then. That is your real trouble.'

'Quite ravenous,' Jane said frankly.

Feeling peckish herself, Katherine took a copper canister from the sideboard, removed the lid and revealed a quantity of tansy cakes that had been set aside for an emergency such as this. Jane fell upon them with childish glee while Katherine, opening one of the sideboard doors, took out a flagon of beer and two silver-bound earthenware mugs. Filling the mugs with the amber liquid she offered one to Jane.

'At Bradgate,' the girl confided, 'we drink beer or ale and eat tansy cakes in the early morning and between meals.'

'We are civilised at court and do likewise,' Katherine said gravely. 'Are the tansy cakes as tasty as those at Bradgate?'

'More so, I think,' said Jane, nibbling approvingly.

'They were freshly fried this morning,' Katherine assured her: 'Eggs and breadcrumbs, green wheat and ginger, and a goodly lacing of butter.'

'Nutmeg is used at Bradgate,' Jane said, reaching for another cake. 'I prefer the flavour of ginger. It goes better with the beer.' She took a sip of beer, then another. 'This is lighter than the Bradgate beer.'

'At court,' Katherine chuckled, 'it pays to keep a sober head.'

'I shall remember that, your Grace,' Jane said thoughtfully. 'Did you eat tansy cakes and drink beer at Kendal Castle when *you* were young?'

'Indeed I did, and there was hot spiced wine as well, in winter. So you know that I was born at Kendal Castle?'

'My mother mentioned it. Your father, she said, was Sir Timothy Parr.'

'Sir Thomas Parr,' Katherine corrected.

'Did you love him dearly?' Jane asked, a note of urgency in her voice.

'According to my mother I did, but I can scarcely remember him. He died when I was four. Do you love your father dearly, Jane?'

'I should like to, your Grace, but we don't see much of him, my sisters and I. He is always so busy hunting and hawking, and visiting Leicester to dine and sup with the mayor, and entertaining all the visitors that pass through Bradgate. Why, there are sometimes as many as two hundred people eating and drinking in the great hall and strolling in the galleries above. Mrs Eleyn says it is right and proper for a father to remain aloof where girl children are concerned.'

'What of your mother?'

'She is almost always aloof too.'

Katherine concluded that Jane had known very little parental love. It was fortunate, she thought, that the King had decided to keep her at court. It was the habit, indeed the well-established custom, of noble parents to send their children, once they reached the age of nine or ten, to reside with even nobler parents and thus gain higher learning and a higher understanding of social procedures. Lamentably there was no family in the land nobler than the Dorsets, and but for the King's intervention Lady Jane Grey would have remained in what might be described as splendid isolation at Bradgate Park.

'Your Grace . . .' Jane said tentatively.

Katherine, too, had heard the sound of trumpets. 'Five o'clock and the first call to supper,' she said, smiling upon her charge. 'Have you any appetite left after the tansy cakes and beer?'

'Yes,' said Jane, 'but if I were at Bradgate I would not be allowed to choose more than three dishes from any one course.'

'How many courses?'

'Four, sometimes five.'

'At court we are more restrained and economical. Three courses only.'

'And, your Grace, how many choices?'

'That you will discover presently.'

Mrs. Eleyn had re-entered silently. 'With your Grace's permission,' she said, glancing at Jane.

Katherine inclined her head. 'Speak up, Mrs Eleyn.'

'Lady Jane,' Mrs Eleyn said, 'pray remember, and I know how poor your memory can be, to take your own knives to the King's table as you do, when you remember, to your father's table.'

A feeling of indignation swamped Jane, and to such an extent that she wondered why she had told her mother that she wanted Mrs Eleyn with her. She was, it now seemed, almost as dictatorial as her mother and, being a servant, unbearably presumptuous. Jane took a deep breath before framing what could be considered a necessary and fitting reprimand. It was odd, quite astonishingly so, she thought, that only a few hours at court had given her, despite her initial fear of the King, a self-confidence never felt at Bradgate.

'Mrs Eleyn,' she said at length, 'you must remember that you are my attendant now, not my nurse. It is I, now, who will give the orders.'

Then in some dismay Jane looked anxiously at Katherine. She had spoken pettishly, even arrogantly. Had she made a bad impression on the Queen, her loving friend?

'It is an indubitable fact, Mrs Eleyn,' Katherine said, sensing the girl's anxiety. 'Where are Lady Jane's knives?'

'In the larger hamper, your Grace,' said a flushed and flustered Mrs Eleyn.

'Then find them at once and give them to your mistress.'

Mrs Eleyn did so—there were three knives, large, medium and small—curtsied and fled hastily.

'Your Grace . . . ?' Jane said, somewhat fearfully.

'What is it, dear Jane?'

'Alas, I fear I spoke to Mrs Eleyn most arrogantly.'

'Alas,' Katherine said solemnly but with twinkling eyes, 'you are, in the King's words, a true Tudor . . .'

'By God,' Jane added winningly.

'By God indeed,' Katherine chuckled. 'You, a true Tudor, are entitled to a display of Tudor arrogance. And what, in fact, does arrogance mean?'

'That one is right,' Jane answered promptly, 'and *knows* it.'

'I, though not a Tudor, except by marriage, can but agree.

But do remember, child, never arrogance for its own sake. Assert yourself, your devilish Tudor self, but only when strictly necessary.'

'Devilish?' Jane questioned thoughtfully.

'A slip of the tongue,' Katherine said hastily, and feeling confident that there was no lurking Tudor devil in this innocent child. 'But in the broad and general sense,' she went on, still hastily, 'we must all be on our guard against the Devil who strives constantly to undo us, especially in our most virtuous moments.'

'Your Grace is a very good Protestant,' said Jane.

'Even as you are,' Katherine said faintly.

'Was it strictly necessary, the way I spoke to Mrs Eleyn?'

'Her attitude being what it was, yes. It is important that an attendant, like a well-trained dog, should evince respect rather than love. But enough! The King awaits us. Remember to curtsy three times, also to kneel, before you take your place at the royal table.'

'Curtsy and kneel to the royal table?' Jane questioned impishly.

'You know quite well what I mean,' Katherine said, trying to sound stern. 'I do hope, Lady Jane, that I shall never find it necessary to box your noble ears.'

Carrying her knives and walking a few paces to the rear, Jane followed the Queen to the dining hall where the King was already seated at a long raised table. Jane appeared after Katherine had paid her respects, curtsied three times, then knelt and waited.

'You shall sit between the Queen and me,' Henry said indulgently.

Jane seated herself, feeling very small in the large chair, and carefully placed her knives alongside the table-spoon that marked her place. In earlier days, she remembered having been told, even spoons had been unheard of, but the King had eventually caused a minor revolution by insisting upon their use, he having been impressed by French table habits. Later he had gone further and insisted on the additional use of knives, but for the sake of royal economy had made it obligatory for the members of his household to bear the expense of personal cutlery. Thus a precedent had been established and the table habits of the court had become those of Bradgate and other great houses throughout the country.

The Lady Mary and the Lady Elizabeth had now entered the dining hall. Turn by turn they curtsied three times and knelt, and then, as if rising from an altar, took their places on the King's left. With an informal wave of his hand and a muttering of her name he presented Jane to them. Leaning forward to peer round his kingly bulk they inclined their heads politely. The Lady Elizabeth, who was thirteen, smiled briefly, but the Lady Mary looked so grim that Jane reached the conclusion that she never permitted her face to crack into any sort of smile. She was thirty, Jane remembered, and still unmarried. That, for sure, was nothing to smile about. She was also a Catholic and that must be very uncomfortable at Uncle Henry's court, even though he had been born a Catholic himself. Jane, with her New Learning upbringing, Jane who had known nothing else, was apt to regard Catholics as archaic curiosities, but she had been taught to practise Christian charity under all circumstances, however pityingly superior one might feel.

While the first course, heralded by a trumpeter, was being served Jane glanced round the dining hall. Courtiers and their ladies were seated at lower tables. Apparently to dine privately with the King was not the same as to dine in private with him; it simply meant that one was privileged to sit sedately at the royal table instead of a table set aside for children. She wondered where her other cousin Prince Edward was, and then learnt from the King, who brought up the subject with the Queen, that the boy was at Hampton Court where he had been sent to recover from an illness.

The first course consisted of five dishes: pease soup, brawn, stewed pheasant, roasted swan and an assortment of sweetmeats. When her turn came, and she found the large tureen in front of her, Jane ladled soup into a deep plate knowing but not caring that it would have a distastrous effect in so far as the letting of wind was concerned. She reached for her spoon but waited like everybody else for the King to start. He glanced down at her, winked, and instead of using his spoon lifted the plate to his mouth. It occurred to her that he was being deliberately naughty, like a little boy, and that made her feel at ease in his presence. After draining his plate and wiping soup from his chin with the back of his hand he belched and tackled the brawn, heaping thick large slices on another plate; then glancing down sideways at Jane he jeaped a smaller helping on her own plate. Watching him and copying him she cut the slices into smaller portions and using a hunk of brown barley bread and her spoon guided the brawn to her mouth. There was as yet no conversation; the King was much to occupied with the serious business of eating. Presently a trumpet call made Jane realise that the second course was about to be served and that she, in a somewhat trance-like condition and encouraged by the King, had eaten all five dishes of the first. That would have been rebellion at Bradgate. She was quietly pleased that she was not supping there this night, and when the King belched again she, in defiance of her mother's instructions, conjured up an unladylike belch herself.

There was more soup, onion this time, with the second course, but Jane resisted it and accepted a helping of stuffed peacock and another of baked rabbit to which the King, as if reproaching her on the score of abstemiousness, added three egg fritters.

'The little sparrow needs building up,' he said. 'Eat heartily, child.'

Jane did her best to comply but when the dishes of the third course were placed on the table she found herself flagging shamefully, and from the almond cream soup, the crawfish and the baked apples selected only a small portion of the latter. She glanced up apologetically at the King but fortunately he had failed to notice, possibly because of the glazed look in his eyes. They had been at table for more than two hours now and Jane was beginning to feel sleepy. At the end of the third hour, when the tablecloth was removed and the bowls of water placed within reach, she roused herself sufficiently to wash her hands. But that was not the end of the meal; pages served platters of caraway-seed wafers and hippocras, a special highly spiced wine which was almost too hot to sip but which Jane found refreshing. The King, after his first sip, shifted heavily in his chair and let out a volley of wind that shook both the chair and the table. Jane repressed a giggle and parted, cautiously but not silently, with a little wind herself.

'Now we feel comfortable,' the King pronounced, 'and in

no mood for weighty conversation. What say you, Kate?'

'In no mood at all,' Katherine agreed.

'And you, Lady Jane?' Henry asked, fondling the girl's shoulder.

'May it please your Grace, in no mood, either, for needlework.'

'At Bradgate,' said Katherine, catching the drift of Jane's thoughts, 'it was needlework, was it not, for an hour after supper?'

'Unless I could think of a good excuse,' Jane said candidly.

'Such as . . . ?' Henry encouraged.

'It pleased my mother,' Jane said, her manner pathetically elderly, 'to see me studying Erasmus's Greek New Testament. I am translating it into English.'

'A worthy means of escaping the chore of needlework,' Henry chuckled.

'It is not very easy,' Jane admitted, 'but I prefer it to needlework.'

Testing her, Henry threw a few swift questions at her in Greek; she replied with some hesitancy but on the whole correctly. Then they began to exchange Latin tags. Katherine listened in amazement. She had translated the Greek New Testament herself but at thirteen, not nine. Jane, she thought, was surprisingly advanced, even more so than the clever Lady Elizabeth. They were old long before their time, these royal and noble children. In many ways intensive education robbed them, as she herself had been robbed, of carefree childhood. They were little adults without the advantage of maturity. Knowledge and more knowledge was crammed into them, but understanding, in any depth at all, was yet to come. Better, Katherine sometimes thought, to be a peasant child.

'No, your Grace,' Jane said, in answer to a question from Henry, 'I have not studied *Assertio Septum Sacramentorum*.'

'Most remiss of you,' he said, pretending to grumble.

'But I do know,' she added hastily, 'that it was written in condemnation of Martin Luther.'

'Written by whom, child?'

'The King's Highness was the author,' she supplied.

Henry bobbed his head, as if vastly flattered. 'Who is Martin Luther?'

'He is a German Reformer,' Jane said, making a great effort to fight off sleep. 'He was born a miner's son and became a priest. He protested against the sale of indulgences and burnt a papal bull in public.'

'And what,' Henry asked playfully, 'is a papal bull? The husband of a sacred Vatican cow, perhaps?'

Jane giggled. 'It is an edict issued by the Pope, your Grace.'

'What more do you know of Luther?'

'He was excommunicated and married a nun. It was very naughty of him.'

'Very,' Henry chuckled. 'What reward did I receive for my theological diligence?'

'The Pope gave your Grace the title of *Fidei Defensor,*' Jane suppressed a yawn and added: 'It means Defender of the Faith.'

'Twenty-five years ago,' Henry said heavily, 'and defend it I still do. In my own country, in my own way. *My* faith, Lady Jane, and England's. The title shall be borne by all who follow me on the throne.'

Jane thought that he sounded angry, but she was too sleepy and too concerned with the state of her stomach to take real notice. She felt bloated and her stomach was making loud gurgling noises which, at first, she thought were coming from the King's own mighty belly. Involuntarily she belched, and then looked apologetically at the Queen.

'At least,' she said, her nose twitching, 'I have remembered not to pick my nose.'

A moment later she fell forward and sleep got the better of her as her head touched the table.

4

JANE woke in something of a panic, thinking at first that she was still at the supper table where, because of her impoliteness, she had been sternly abandoned. But no, she was lying flat on her back in a comfortable bed; it was daylight and through the open window floated the chirping of birds, while from the passage beyond the closed door another sound, too faint for recognition, reached her ears. A dog, perhaps, or a cat? She sat up and stretched, and glanced wonderingly round the room. This was not the apartment where she had been lodged immediately after the King's decision to keep her at court. It was larger. There was a carpet on the floor, not the scented rushes she remembered, and against one wall stood a massive chest of drawers. One such article of furniture had been installed recently at Bradgate. An innovation, her mother had said, but soon to be fashionable, since chests of drawers had met with the King's approval. Jane glanced again at the richly fashioned carpet. Another innovation, she thought, but soon to be just as fashionable.

Fully awake now, she threw back the silken coverlet and sprang out of bed. It was not last night that she had fallen asleep at the King's table but the night before, and she was at Hampton Court now, not Whitehall. She, so sound a sleeper, had very nearly forgotten one whole day. It had started quietly enough, she remembered, with morning prayers in the royal chapel, and then, while she was consuming with Mrs Eleyn a breakfast of bread, meat and ale, one of the Queen's ladies had entered to announce the King's sudden decision to quit the Palace of Whitehall. He had had his fill of London and the too close pressure of state affairs. What he needed and must have was rest and peace at a quieter abode. The court, reduced in size, was to leave immediately for Hampton Court. It had been a short enough journey, a mere twelve miles, but a leisurely and exciting one, the royal party being escorted by the King's private army of a hundred Yeomen of the Guard, and with all manner of people lining the route to shout and cheer, and the more humble of them to kneel reverently.

Another noise caught and held Jane's attention. It came from behind an inner door. Of course, Mrs Eleyn's room. Jane opened the door softly; her former nurse was fast asleep and snoring disgustingly. Jane noted with satisfaction that there was no carpet on Mrs Eleyn's floor, only rushes, and that the room was sparsely furnished. Then she heard again, quite distinctly, the noise beyond the outer door. Snatching up and drawing about her thin body a quilted satin robe, she cautiously opened the door. The jackanapes, the royal jester's little monkey! The creature squealed at the sight of Jane and turned a somersault.

'Catch and hold him, my lady!'

It was the jester now, scampering along the passage. Frightened but determined not to show it, Jane tried to seize the monkey, only to find it evading her grasping hands and those of the jester too. She and the jester gave chase together along other passages and up and down both wide and narrow stairways. Jane gave up the chase when the jester and the monkey were beyond sight and began to fear that she was lost. After several minutes of frantic searching, during which she encountered nobody, she came upon an open door, the door which she felt certain she had left open. Entering breathlessly she failed to see her bed. Her eyes fell upon a large draw-table with the side-leaves drawn fully out at each end. Stacked upon it were a number of oak chairs, some with arms. Similar chairs were piled one on top of another in the centre of the room, and behind them, beneath the window, she espied another chest of drawers. She had entered what was clearly a storeroom.

'I am not hiding, I am invisible,' said a voice. 'How can I be hiding when I am invisible?'

Startled, Jane traced the voice to the chest of drawers and saw that the bottom drawer was open. Then she saw the head of a boy, and moving closer his shoulders and the length of his reclining body. She had come upon him while he was reading a book.

'Go away,' he commanded, and then, sitting up and peering at her closely: 'No, be pleased to remain. You are not as I first thought a serving woman's child. You are surely the Lady Jane Grey.'

'*The* Lady Jane?' she questioned in surprise.

'Your are to be addressed, my father says, as my half-sisters Mary and Elizabeth are addressed. One would think you were another half-sister, not a cousin.'

'Then—then you are Prince Edward?'

The boy inclined his head. 'Surely.'

'Why,' Jane asked, 'are your half-sisters not addressed as princesses?'

'Because they are bastards,' he replied casually. '*Royal* bastards, of course.' He frowned in a not entirely puzzled manner. 'Not bastards *all* the time, and not always both of them at the same time. But they are just now, both at the same time. It has something to do with the will of my father and who he wants to place after me in the line of succession. And that, Uncle Thomas said—but I wasn't supposed to hear—is controlled by the state of his digestive system.'

'Whether or not he is able to relieve himself with a mighty belch,' Jane suggested.

Edward nodded. 'Or the other thing.' But he had lost interest in the subject. 'I come here sometimes to escape from my tutor at this time of morning. Not to hide, to escape. I am very devout but morning prayers are sometimes tiresome. Are you very devout, Jane?'

'Yes, Edward.'

The boy lifted himself out of the drawer but remained sitting on the edge. He was only slightly taller than Jane and inclined to plumpness. His cheeks were very pale—he had been ill, Jane remembered—but his eyes were full of life and deeply penetrating. He appeared, she thought, to be trying to stare her out of countenance.

'Who is Uncle Thomas?' she asked in some confusion.

'One of my mother's brothers, Sir Thomas Seymour. How old are you, Jane?'

'I was born on October 5th, 1537.'

He smiled quite winningly. 'You would set me a little sum. What an easy one! You were nine six days ago. I shall be nine tomorrow and as a birthday treat I shall be allowed to do whatever I please.' The smile faded and he said haughtily: 'I forbid you to boss me because you are seven days older.'

'I shall try to remember,' Jane promised. 'What are you reading, Edward?'

He handed her the book with a hint of defiance in his attitude. She had expected a learned treatise, more than likely in Latin, which he had been set to translate, but no, as the title revealed, it was an account in English of old and not so old marriage customs. Not that Jane was interested in marriage customs but it was at least a change, if a shameful one, from theology and philosophy and history.

'May I read it, Edward?'

'Yes, when I've finished with it myself. Aren't you going to ask me where I found it?'

'Where *did* you find it?' she asked obediently.

He gave her a solemn look. 'Under the King's pillow.'

'Well,' said Jane, looking solemn herself, 'the King knows a lot about marriage.'

'Far too much, he once told me, and at the same time not enough. It is often hard to understand what my father means.'

'As many a man has discovered to his sorrow,' said a rich baritone voice. 'Many a woman, for the matter of that.'

Edward sprang up excitedly. 'Uncle Thomas!'

Sir Thomas Seymour had entered the storeroom silently and was lounging very much at ease just within the door. Jane stared up at him in astonishment and awe. Used as she was to extravagant male attire, never before had she seen a man so richly and glitteringly garbed. He was taller than her father who was considered tall, and so handsome that her handsome father would have looked ugly if standing at his side. He smiled down upon her, and only by remembering who she was and who *he* was, a mere knight albeit the King's brother-in-law, did she restrain herself from curtsying three times.

'I thought you were in London,' Edward said. 'You didn't arrive with the court yesterday. I'm sure you didn't. If you had you would have come to see me immediately.'

'I arrived during the night,' Seymour told his nephew, 'and swiftly, on my own special broomstick. And riding it again this morning I was brought unerringly to this hiding place of yours.'

'It is a secret retreat, Uncle Thomas, not a hiding place.'

'Be that as it may, the court is in an uproar and search parties are scampering in all directions. A little girl is lost and her nurse is mad with hysterics.'

'My attendant, not my nurse,' Jane said primly. 'I no longer need a nurse.'

'My cousin, the Lady Jane,' Edward said, by way of unnecessary introduction.

Sir Thomas Seymour bowed deeply. 'My greetings, Lady Jane, my respects and my undying allegiance.'

'She arrived,' Edward said, 'in time for my birthday tomorrow.'

'And what, dear nephew, do you propose to do in the way of celebrating that important event?'

Edward was much at a loss. He had been told that a special birthday feast, if he asked for one, would have to be restrained and quiet, so that his strength, he not fully recovered from an illness vaguely described as 'growing pains', would not be sorely tried. His eyes clouded. He could please himself, that was the rule, but in what way was he to please himself? He bethought himself of the book which Jane was still holding in her hands. A game, a special game, a game of make-believe, children pretending to be adults, and adults, at least one important adult, pretending to be a child yet at the same time remaining solemnly grown-up.

'You will have to shave off your beard, Uncle Thomas,' Edward said.

'For what reason, Highness?'

'I can't think of any man I know in holy orders who has a beard.'

'Your train of thought eludes me,' Seymour said mock-woefully.

'You shall play the priest, Uncle.'

'I am still in utter bewilderment.'

'I want a marriage game,' Edward said. 'You the priest, Jane the bride and I the groom. It is all written in that book. I shall arrange everything myself and we shall have much fun.'

'But by God's precious soul, what of my precious beard?'

'You may keep it but you must pretend to be beardless.'

'And remember not to stroke this luxuriant growth, the very pride of my life.'

At that moment the monkey, chattering and grimacing, bounded into the room and leapt upon Seymour's shoulder. The jester skipped in and was followed by the Queen and Mrs Eleyn. The jester secured the monkey in a firm grip and darted out with it while Mrs Eleyn, apparently on the point of swooning, fell into a chair.

'Pull yourself together,' Katherine told her sharply. 'Escort the Lady Jane back to her room. Hurry, or you will be late for prayers.'

'It was because of the monkey . . .' Jane said, in part explanation.

'That I have been given to understand. Come, child, hurry.'

Jane preceded her attendant from the room, and Edward, after bowing to the Queen, ran after them, shouting: 'I shall join you in the chapel.' Turning at the door, he addressed Seymour briefly. 'Remember, Uncle, the marriage game tomorrow.'

Katherine was staring in some confusion at Seymour.

'When did you reach Hampton Court, Tom?' she asked, the moment Edward was out of sight.

'During the night, far too late for me to pay my respects either to the King or the Queen.' He glanced slowly round the room and chuckled softly. 'A goodly place, this storeroom, for secret meetings.'

Katherine moved to the door. Seymour's presence was quickly beginning to affect her as it always did, but she struggled, hoping that the struggle would not be apparent to him, to keep emotion under control.

'Wait,' he said softly, his manner as persuasive as ever.

Katherine turned and faced him. 'This is an accidental meeting, not a secret one. Secret meetings—and who can keep a secret at court?—I will never permit. I value your life as much as I value my own.'

'Even more so, dearest Kate.'

'If you insist.'

'And would preserve it jealously until the King breathes his last and freedom of choice is ours.'

'Keep your voice low, for pity's sake, Tom.'

'I am a man of vast patience,' Seymour said, slipping round

her and closing the door, 'but when the King snatched you from me I knew my patience would be sorely tried.'

Katherine knew him, on the contrary, to be a man of vast impatience, but she made no comment. She remembered their first meeting at her Wimbledon house a few weeks after her second husband's death. He had been brought to her attention by her uncle, Sir George Throckmorton, Sir George saying that there was no more zealous a Reformer in England than Tom Seymour. He was two or three years her senior, a bachelor and tantalisingly handsome. He had begun, even at that first meeting, to pay court to her and she had been close to yielding when, as he had just said, the King had snatched her from him. If Henry had been aware of Seymour's courtship he had never given any hint of it. On the whole, Katherine was inclined to think that he was completely unaware of it, otherwise Tom would have been banished from court, not left to come and go as he pleased in the guise of a privileged brother-in-law. Nevertheless one must be careful, doubly careful. It was madness to remain alone with Tom a moment longer, and with this thought in mind she moved again to the door.

'What need is there to hurry away?' Seymour asked, grasping her arm none too gently.

'I shall be late for prayers, Tom.'

'The King is indisposed, as you well know, and will not be present himself. Play the wag for once. Play it for my dear sake.'

Katherine weakened but released herself.

'What,' she asked, remembering Edward's parting words, 'did the Prince mean by his reference to a marriage game?'

Seymour explained and added: 'Fortuitous.'

'And by that you mean . . . ?'

'It may serve to give the King a gentle hint.'

'The possibility of marriage for Edward and Jane is already in his mind.'

'Then it may serve to strengthen that which is already in his mind.'

'I know you to be a devious schemer,' Katherine said dryly, 'but I fail to see what you would gain by such a marriage.'

'I shall try to explain with all clarity, Kate. I understand that Jane Grey has become your ward. Is that correct?'

'It is.'

'And will remain your ward, even when the King dies?'

'If he dies while she is still a minor, yes.'

Seymour stooped and kissed Katherine lightly on the brow. 'And that, dear Kate, will make your fourth husband Lady Jane's joint guardian.'

'I may decide never to marry again,' she said, not without coquetry.

'The King will die long before the children are old enough to marry,' Seymour went on, 'but could he not be induced to issue a royal decree in his will?'

'Induced by *me*?'

'By you, for my dear sake.'

'I still fail to see what it would profit you.'

'The future is fraught with interesting possibilities,' he said airily. 'Edward shows signs of becoming an unswerving Protestant. The Protestant faction, led by Hertford, that amiable brother of mine, will achieve full power when the King dies. We, if we bring about such a marriage, will be in an unassailable position. Think of it, Kate—we, the guardians of the future Queen.'

Katherine shook her head. 'I dare not interfere.'

'*Dare* not?'

'I have enemies at court. Oh, they respect me but they would never hesitate to undo me if it suited their purpose. Apart from that the King changes his mind from day to day, often from moment to moment. There are times when even agreement on my part is enough to make him fly in another direction. And remember this, Tom, the King is not and never will be a Protestant.'

Seymour took her in his arms. 'There's an alternative. What if you were to find yourself with child—would the King accept that child as his without question?' Katherine struggled unavailingly to free herself and Seymour added: 'Would he have any reason to doubt his royal paternity?'

'None,' Katherine admitted.

Still with one arm about her, Seymour reached for the door and turned the key in the lock.

'Tom . . .' she begged weakly.

'Not for the want of trying on my part,' he said softly, 'you shall give the King a son.'

5

ALL was in readiness.

Jane stood waiting in her room for the signal, a trumpet call, that would announce the start of the wedding procession. She wore everyday clothes but had been instructed by Edward, who had held a rehearsal earlier in the morning, to pretend to the point of believing that she wore a white wedding gown such as had been fashionable fifty years ago. She was surrounded by her bridesmaids, five little girls, each pretending to be dressed exactly as she was dressed in order to confuse any demons who might be lurking nearby and thus prevent them from snatching up and carrying off the true bride.

The trumpet call came at last and the bride's two pages, sons of court officials, led the way from Jane's room. Once in the passage they were joined by a dozen or more children, would-be relatives and close friends. The procession reached the store-room, which in imagination was now a chapel, without mishap or the sighting of a single demon. There Jane found the priest, Sir Thomas Seymour, the bridegroom, Prince Edward, and two little boy grooms waiting for her.

'Be pleased to sway on your feet,' Edward instructed his uncle. 'You are supposed to be drunk. This is a village wedding and priests were always drunk at village weddings, even before the ceremony began.'

Seymour swayed on his feet and might well have been a demon in holy orders, Jane thought, except for his great good looks. He muttered a few indistinct words, and then Jane and Edward were making the responses which they had memorised. Katherine had slipped quietly into the room and seated herself at the back to watch and listen. She had received a formal invitation but felt something of an intruder. On the whole she was glad that the King, who had also received a formal invitation, had apparently decided against putting in an appearance. There was something chillingly real about this childish marriage game, and Henry might well have exploded in anger while listening to a solemn Prince Edward promise to take Jane to be his wedded wife, then to Jane promising to take Edward to be her wedded husband. But no doubt he would have laughed, Katherine thought, to hear Jane add in accordance with an old custom to be happy and buxom in bed and at board if Holy Church so ordained.

Turn by turn the children drank the imaginary wine and ate the imaginary sops. Then Seymour said a jumbled version of the Bride Mass of long ago, kissed Edward on the brow and instructed him to transfer the sacred benediction to Jane. Only one thing was lacking and Edward seemed not to have missed it: Seymour had not dared, even while play-acting, to pronounce the children man and wife.

At a signal from Edward, very much the stage-manager, the wedding guests prepared themselves for the game of follow-my-leader, and it was then that Katherine was seen and recognised. There was a hint of consternation, with the children falling to their knees, but Katherine bade them rise and continue with the jollifications.

'I am not at this moment the Queen,' she said. 'A good fairy, if you like, but not the Queen.'

Follow-my-leader was played round the storeroom, as it had been played round churches in earlier days, and then with the arrival of the fiddlers there was a procession to Edward's private dining hall where servants were waiting to serve the birthday-cum-wedding feast. To Katherine it was a sad occasion. Edward and Jane were playing a game but solemnly, without any real childish enjoyment. They scarcely knew how to play, she thought, and the rest of the children, all normally carefree, were tongue-tied and ill-at-ease. Knowing that Henry would soon be calling for her, she slipped away before the end of the feast and found him in what appeared to be a good mood.

'How goes it?' he asked.

'Game though it is,' she replied, 'the children are hardly making merry.'

'Even mock-marriage is a devilish solemn business,' he chuckled. 'Who put them up to it?'

'It was Edward's idea entirely.'

'Edward's, not Seymour's?' he questioned, frowning now.

'Sir Thomas is no more in this instance,' Katherine said carefully, 'than your son's obedient servant.'

'And a priest to boot. Rich, by God!'

Katherine had finished re-bandaging Henry's leg when the jester, always a privileged person, entered without ceremony and darting to his master's side whispered and chuckled in the royal ear. Henry scowled and thrust him away so violently that he fell to the floor.

'They go too far!' Henry shouted.

'*They?*' Katherine asked.

'The children. The bedding down is about to begin. Stop them, Kate, stop them.'

'It is only a game,' Katherine dared to venture. 'There won't be any real undressing. Pretence, your Grace, merely pretence.'

'I have known boys of nine as lusty as grown men,' he said darkly.

'Truly?' Katherine laughed.

'One only,' he amended.

'And he . . . ?'

'Who but bad King Harry of England!' the jester shrieked.

With that Henry's mood changed and he laughed heartily. 'This bedding down is something the King's Grace must see with his own eyes.'

He levered himself from the couch and fell into the chair in which, presently, he was carried from the room. The jester led the way; Katherine followed, praying silently that Henry's good mood would continue. When they entered Prince Edward's bedchamber Jane's bridesmaids were miming the undressing ceremony on one side of the bed while Edward's grooms were doing likewise on the other side. There was a cry of alarm at the sight of Henry but he waved an arm and commanded the children to proceed. They did so with many a cautious glance in his direction, the bridesmaids assisting Jane on to the bed, the grooms Edward.

'Quickly now,' Edward urged, 'the throwing of the stocking.'

The two grooms sat on his side of the bed with their backs to him; two bridesmaids sat on Jane's side with their backs to her. A stocking, supposedly Jane's but obviously not, was handed to one of the grooms; he threw it over his shoulder and hit Jane in the face with it.

'Marriage for you, my lad, within the year,' Edward said, but so solemnly that Katherine felt like weeping for him.

The second groom took the stocking but failed to hit Jane with it. Turn by turn the bridesmaids threw the stocking with equal lack of success.

'You'll die old maids, both of you,' Henry laughed. 'What now, my mighty Prince?'

'The benediction posset cup,' said Edward.

Katherine had been thankful that Seymour was absent but he entered now, still playing the priest, still pretending to be drunk and carrying, shakily, a large silver cup. He offered it to Edward who pretended to drink from the empty vessel before passing it to Jane.

'It is a mixture of curdling milk and wine,' he insisted.

Jane, too, pretended to drink. 'I feel sick in my stomach already,' she said.

'Now the blessing of the bed,' Edward commanded.

Seymour, mumbling a mixture of words, made a pretence of blessing the bed, then miming excellently sprinkled Edward and Jane with non-existent holy water. Finally and unwisely, even defiantly, Katherine thought, he issued the conventional, would-be holy command.

'Be fruitful and multiply,' he said, cocking a challenging eye at the King.

Katherine held her breath and waited, but only for a moment. Henry, his face suffused with sudden anger, uttered a bull-like roar and rose with unaccustomed strength from his chair.

'By God's precious blood, enough!'

The children, with the exception of Edward and Jane, melted away. Seymour hesitated momentarily but decided to stand his ground. Henry, his anger all but uncontrollable, pointed a quivering finger at him.

'Out with you,' he shouted. 'Total banishment, if you show your impudent face at court while I live.'

Katherine half-expected Seymour to laugh defiantly, but he bowed in seeming humility and backed from the King's presence. Unassisted but shakily, Henry dragged himself forward and came to rest with his hands on the foot of the bed.

'Sir,' said Edward, in a low, troubled voice, 'since this is my birthday . . .'

Softening, Henry shrugged heavily. 'Very well. Three months' banishment from court will be sufficient punishment for your favourite uncle, damn him to hell. Now enough of this marriage game, but tell me one thing, is it in your mind to marry the Lady Jane when you are old enough?'

'No, Father.'

'No?'

'I don't want to marry at all,' Edward said, cringing slightly.

'Why not, pray?'

Emboldened, Edward said: 'Not even once, may it please your Grace.'

'It doesn't *not* please me, Edward. You shall marry in due course. It is your bounden duty.'

'Cousin Jane, if you insist,' Edward sighed.

'I do *not* insist. You shall marry, and this is my will, a Habsburg princess.'

His will, Katherine thought, but not the will of the Habsburgs. Negotiations, if initiated, would come to nothing. The Emperor Charles, though nobody had dared to tell Henry, regarded the King of England as a barbarian, a gross and gluttonous islander, and in any case saw little or nothing to be gained from an alliance with a king who had rejected the Catholic faith.

'It wants an hour to supper,' Henry said. 'Birthday or not, you shall spend that hour in study.'

'It is not a punishment, Father,' Edward said, but without humour.

Henry's glance shifted to Jane. 'Nor in your case, Lady Jane. But what of needlework? An hour of needlework before supper, and that, sweet child, is my royal will.'

'I have misplaced my work-basket,' Jane said plaintively.

'You will find it in my inner chamber,' Katherine told her, trying not to laugh.

The good fairy a good fairy no longer, Jane thought, and sighed abysmally.

'Off with you, off with you,' Henry blustered.

Jane slipped from the bed and though sorely aware that she was fleeing from the King's presence succeeded in walking daintily to the door. There she turned and curtsied three times, but a tight little knot of rebelliousness within her breast restrained her from kneeling, whether or not it was expected of her on this occasion. 'Little minx!' Henry roared.

Bent no longer on daintiness, Jane took to her heels and was still running when, breathless and strangely angry with herself, she came upon the Lady Mary. Taken aback she dropped a curtsy, then remembering that she had been given equal rank with her cousins Mary and Elizabeth regretted her instinctive reaction. Yet a moment later, as she stared at the unsmiling Mary, she thought of it as a necessary politeness, a bowing as it were to age, Mary surely being old enough to be her mother. And ugly, frighteningly ugly. Jane caught her breath sharply. A demon at last, belatedly arrived but ready in the dimness of the passage to reach out with claw-like hands and carry off her innocent victim.

'Is anything the matter, child?' Mary asked.

'Highness . . .' Jane faltered.

'I am not entitled to such a form of address,' Mary said dryly. 'In any case you must remember that you are my cousin.'

'I—I shall try, Cousin Mary.'

'We are friends, not enemies; you must remember that too.'

'Friends . . .' Jane pondered.

'Catholic though I am, Reformer though you are.' Mary's voice was even drier. 'Is that what troubles you, Jane?'

A *Catholic* demon, Jane thought, but said hurriedly: 'The King is angry with me.'

'That I cannot believe, dear cousin.'

'The marriage game . . .' Jane explained.

'A childish romp. The King's anger will fade. It usually does, even when the fading comes too late.'

'Is he ever angry with you, Cousin Mary?'

'Not any more, not seriously,' Mary said introspectively. 'Not since Queen Katherine brought me and Elizabeth and Edward together under the same roof. I have much to thank the Queen for. She is a good woman. I love her dearly.'

'So do I,' Jane asserted, feeling a stab of jealousy.

'See,' said Mary, 'I have a present for you. A mock wedding but not a mock present.'

Jane looked up in wonder at her cousin. There was a smile on the face that she had thought would never be permitted to crack into a smile. There was gentleness in it, shattering the ugliness. Perhaps there was some little love too, but whatever it was it seemed to Jane to be a very special smile.

'A present, Cousin Mary?' she said.

As if by the stroke of a magic wand Mary Tudor held in her hands a gold necklace finely wrought and studded with pearls. They were slender hands, not in the least claw-like after all, and reaching out she placed the necklace round Jane's neck and adjusted it securely. Impulsively she kissed the child on the brow and then as if angry with herself turned on her heel.

'We shall meet again at supper,' she said curtly.

Fingering the necklace Jane found her way to the Queen's apartments and discovered on the threshold a slightly built woman attired in a long hooded cloak with the hood partly concealing her face. The thought of demons crossed Jane's mind again but when the woman spoke her voice was low and sweet. It was, Jane thought, a familiar voice; she had heard it before, perhaps at Bradgate.

'You are the Lady Jane Grey.'

'And the Queen's ward,' Jane responded with dignity.

'I seek an audience with her Majesty,' the woman said urgently. 'Can the Lady Jane contrive it for me?'

Jane decided that she could, but at a special price.

'Are you skilful at needlework?' she asked flatly.

'As skilful as any other gentlewoman,' came the surprised answer.

'Then,' Jane said happily, 'be pleased to come with me.'

6

KATHERINE, having been dismissed at last by the King, entered her own apartments with two ladies in attendance and passed through the outer rooms to her inner chamber. Poor little Jane, she thought, had she made any progress at all with her needlework? She opened the door of the inner chamber cautiously but not quietly enough. Jane caught sight of her instantly and looking guilty snatched the toilet-table cover from her accommodating visitor. The woman turned quickly, sprang to her feet and throwing back her hood faced a surprised and startled Katherine.

'Anne Ascue!' she gasped.

The woman curtsied, then fell to her knees, an appealing look in her eyes. Katherine swung away from her in agitation, stepped quickly out of the inner chamber and dismissed her ladies. Returning in further agitation she glanced inquiringly at Jane.

'I remember her,' the girl said. 'She visited Bradgate last year.'

'And now she visits Hampton Court,' Katherine said dully.

'Your Grace and I are friends of long standing,' Anne Ascue asserted. 'I . . .'

'This is our first meeting since your arrest a year ago,' Katherine interrupted. 'It is rash and foolish of you to come here now.'

'I was at my wits' end, your Grace. I need and seek your royal protection.'

'I have no protection, royal or otherwise, to give,' Katherine said miserably. 'You are in grave danger, that I admit, and graver danger still to remain here. The Chancellor is with the King at this moment. You must leave at once, my poor Anne.'

The woman drew the hood about her face. 'I see that I must, heaven help me.'

'How did you gain entry?'

'The Lady Jane . . .'

'Entry to the palace, not to my apartments.'

'One of the Yeomen of the Guard admitted me when I said I brought a message from Lady Dorset to her daughter. It was untrue, but it served my purpose.'

'It is easier to enter than to leave,' Katherine said, and turned to a wide-eyed Jane. 'Can I rely on you, dear Jane, to conduct our visitor safely to her coach?'

Jane sprang up instantly. 'Am I not the Lady Jane? No one would dare to bar my way.' She heaved a deep, excited breath and took Anne Ascue's hand in hers. 'This is more enjoyable than the marriage game.'

Anne Ascue paused to curtsy again. 'God go with you, Madame.'

'And with you,' said Katherine, tears springing to her eyes.

The moment she was alone she fell to pacing the room. What if the Chancellor were to emerge from the King's apartments at this moment and come face to face with Anne Ascue? She tried to tell herself that Anne was sufficiently hooded to avoid passing recognition, but even so a woman so disguised would arouse his always suspicious attention. She regretted having implicated Jane and she accused herself of cowardice, but what protection could she give Anne Ascue without placing herself in jeopardy? She breathed a sigh of relief when Jane returned, breathless and bubbling over with excitement, but her relief was short-lived.

'The poor creature,' Jane gasped. 'She was arrested just when she was entering her coach.'

'Were you seen in her company?' Katherine asked fearfully.

'I think I *must* have been, because he questioned me.'

'*Who* questioned you, Jane?'

'He said he was the Chancellor's secretary.' Jane dropped her voice to a conspiratorial whisper. 'I thought first to say she was a member of the wedding game party going home, but I felt moved instead to say I didn't know her. I said she was a stranger who had lost her way. Wasn't that cunning of me!'

'Surely,' Katherine said faintly.

'Your Grace is trembling,' Jane said. 'It makes me feel all of a-tremble myself.'

Katherine looked at her closely. 'Anne Ascue visited Bradgate, or so you said.'

'Yes, but she was sent away. My father said it was unsafe to harbour her. I think it was something to do with heresy. Is she a witch?'

'Far from it,' Katherine said, looking closely at Jane again. 'I think I must tell you Anne Ascue's story; I think you are old enough to understand, and it will serve as a warning, whatever the future may hold.'

Jane smiled brightly. 'I would rather listen to the story than ply my needle.'

'You shall do both, child,' Katherine said, not inclined to smile herself.

Jane pouted and took up her needle resignedly.

Anne Ascue, Katherine told her, was the wife of a Lincolnshire gentleman by the name of Kyme. He had rejected her because of her religious beliefs and she had reverted to the use of her maiden name. Soon after that she had come to court where Katherine, who had known her as a child, had given her a minor position in her household.

'At that time,' Katherine went on, 'it was my habit, with the King's permission, to discuss and freely interpret the Scriptures with my ladies. Anne Ascue was among them and it was soon seen that she was a fanatical exponent of the New Learning. She was rashly outspoken and fell to expressing certain religious views in opposition to those held by the King. This reached the King's ears. He was in a tolerant mood and would have argued with her, but before he could do so the Chancellor ordered a search of her room and heretical books were found concealed there. Anne Ascue was arrested and thrown into Newgate Prison. She was questioned closely but due to her clever answers was eventually released. She had not at that time denied the King's religious supremacy. That came later, only a short time ago, when she made an open and public denial.'

'And then she came here,' said Jane, sucking her left thumb which she had pricked with the needle.

'Yes, poor frightened woman, but she has been declared a heretic and I can do nothing to help her. Do you understand what a heretic is, Jane?'

Jane frowned over this. 'Our chaplain at Bradgate told me that the Church of Rome regards all people who are not Roman Catholics as heretics. There are heathens too, but heathens are only heretics if they refuse to accept the Roman Catholic faith after they have been told about it.' Jane saw that a little blood from her thumb was spreading on the toilet-table cover and tried to hide it. 'I am very puzzled, your Grace,' she went on. 'The King is not a Roman Catholic, you are not and I am not, and none of us are heathens.' Jane sighed and shook her head. 'No, I do not understand what a *real* heretic is.'

'In this case, Jane, a heretic, real or otherwise, is a person who denies the King's religious supremacy, whether that person be a Catholic or a Protestant.'

'Then *we* are safe,' Jane said confidently. '*We* shall not be thrown into prison.'

'Safe indeed,' Katherine said, and tried to feel as confident as the child.

She repeated the two words under her breath, and with a question mark, when she was summoned a few moments later to the King's presence and bade to bring the Lady Jane with her. The Chancellor, Sir Thomas Wriothesley, was with the King again, an impassive expression on his face, but with, Katherine suspected, the fanatical glint of the heretic-hunter in his eyes. She had never liked him, and he, though he had paid her lip service since her royal wedding day, had never liked her.

'Wriothesley feels a need to question the Lady Jane,' Henry said gruffly.

Wriothesley bowed before Katherine. 'With your Grace's permission, that goes without saying.'

'I can but grant it, Sir Thomas,' Katherine said dryly.

Wriothesley smiled thinly and turned to the child. 'Lady Jane,' he said, his voice softly disarming, 'some little time ago you conducted from the palace a woman who you described as a stranger, a stranger, moreover, who had lost her way. Were you telling the truth?'

'You have no right to speak thus to the King's great-niece,' Katherine interposed.

'Let the child answer,' Henry commanded.

'She *said* she had lost her way,' Jane replied.

'But . . . a stranger to you, truly a stranger?'

'Obviously,' Katherine interposed again.

'I concede the possibility,' Wriothesley murmured, 'but any stranger could bring a message from Lady Dorset to her daughter. What I ask is that the Lady Jane should confide in me and tell me the nature of her mother's message.'

'There was no message from my mother,' Jane said, after a moment's hesitation.

Wriothesley inclined his head. 'I feel bound to agree, but the woman gained entry by asserting that there was. Would you say, you being a clever child, that it was a ruse to gain admission to the Queen's apartments?'

'Enough,' Katherine said, unwilling to have Jane either browbeaten or flattered. 'A ruse, certainly a ruse.'

'A stranger to the Lady Jane, but not, would you say, a stranger to yourself?'

'You are fully acquainted with the woman's identity,' Katherine said impatiently. 'She is not, as you well know, a stranger to me.' She glanced at Henry. 'I dismissed Anne Ascue without listening to her. I could do no less. She came uninvited. She forced herself upon me. *I could do no less.*' She looked directly at Wriothesley. 'Come to the point, Sir Thomas, should you have a point to come to.'

Before he could speak Henry said sharply: 'I grow weary of this unnecessary and insolent questioning. Anne Ascue was dismissed by the Queen; she was arrested by you. Off with you, Chancellor Wriothesley, off with you.'

Wriothesley bowed and withdrew.

'What will happen to Anne Ascue?' Katherine asked Henry.

He glanced at Jane and placed a finger to his lips. 'There is an age-old warning about little pigs and big ears . . .'

Jane saw that he was smiling upon her and said daringly: 'The Lady Jane has tiny ears, may it please your Grace.'

'Tiny and shell-like,' he said approvingly, 'but quick of hearing. The Lady Jane shall withdraw.' Jane turned without a thought of curtsying and scampered from the room. 'What will happen to Anne Ascue?' Henry said, no note of interest in his voice. 'Her fate rests with Wriothesley.'

Always, Katherine thought, Henry was quick to deny responsibility when it suited him to do so.

'And *that* fate?' she asked unhappily.

'She is being taken to the Tower,' Henry said, impatient to be done with the matter. 'She will be held there and questioned.'

'Under torture?'

'Should she prove stubborn, under torture.'

'What need is there of questioning?' Katherine took the risk of arguing. 'She made a public denial of the King's supremacy. There are many witnesses. She has condemned herself. I beg your Grace to let it remain at that.'

'And leave her to burn without the opportunity of recanting?' Henry said, growing fretful.

'She will never recant. I plead for royal clemency. Hanging, not burning.'

'My leg pains me,' Henry said. 'Attend to it, Kate.'

Katherine stood back from him, thinking wildly to defy him and send for a nurse, but prudently she repressed the impulse and began to perform the task which was becoming more and more obnoxious to her.

'What has happened to your gentle touch?' he asked when, seated on the stool with his leg in her lap, she tugged at the bandage. 'You hurt me then, damnably.'

She apologised abjectly. 'My mind was on another matter. I was thinking of the unnecessary torture.'

'Are you afraid,' Henry asked, 'of what Anne Ascue might reveal under torture?'

The drift of his thoughts was clear enough; afraid for her own sake. 'She can reveal nothing of detriment and remain a truthful woman,' Katherine said faintly.

'Truthfulness is only that which is acceptable to the individual. A tortured lie is not a falsehood to a man of Wriothesley's character. He is, whether or not you are aware of it, your greatest enemy at court.'

Katherine was fully aware of it. It was Wriothesley who had tried to prevent her from approaching the King in respect of her uncle's imprisonment. She had told him that when the King had visited York, and she and her late husband had paid their respects, he had commanded her to present herself at court when next in London and to do so without ceremony. And when Wriothesley had still stood in her way she had said: 'You leave me, then, to find my way to the King unaided but not without explanation.' With that, and saying that she was a woman bent on making enemies, the Chancellor had led her to the King's apartments. It was a petty enough reason for antipathy, but there was more to it than that. Wriothesley had been given the task, after her uncle's release, of informing her of the

King's decision to make her his sixth wife.

'One question which my doughty Chancellor will put to Anne Ascue,' Henry went on, 'is of vast if amusing interest.'

'May I ask the nature of it, my lord?'

'He suspects her of aiding and abetting the Queen's Grace in an attempt to turn me into a thorough-going Protestant.'

'I should have no more success in turning your Grace into a Protestant than in turning you back to the faith of Rome.'

'Ah, but have you tried, dear Kate?'

'Your Grace! As if I would dare!'

'In certain circumstances, dare you might,' said Henry, giving her the impression that he was playing with her as a cat would a mouse. 'My memory is apt at times to play tricks on me. What if, during a lapse of memory, you were to have your way with me and bring me to the Protestant persuasion?'

'It would be beyond any powers of persuasion possessed by me.'

'But you would try, by God you would try!'

'It is unjust,' Katherine said shakily, 'to hold against me a suspicion placed in your mind by the Chancellor.'

'A suspicion—merely that? The truth of the matter rests with Anne Ascue.'

'Wriothesley's truth,' she said insistently. 'Not mine, not yours. His, only his.'

'My leg feels a great deal more comfortable,' Henry said. 'There shall be dancing during supper. I myself will even attempt a galliard.' He looked at Katherine quizzically. 'Think you, Kate, that I may thus come close to ending my miserable life?'

'It would be heresy for me to utter such a thought,' she said bitterly. 'If dance you must, my lord, I suggest a pavane. It would be less exerting.'

He nodded approvingly. 'Dignified and stately, and since I feel in a stately mood, a pavane it shall be.'

But his courage failed him, or so Katherine suspected, and his mood changed during supper to one of brooding silence. Mercifully the meal was of shorter duration than usual and ended with Henry being carried away to a further meeting with Chancellor Wriothesley. Was there to be clemency after all, Katherine wondered, or was Wriothesley to be given his head? The Chancellor was given his head and thereafter, day by day, news of Anne Ascue's ordeal reached Hampton Court, Henry himself relating the details while Katherine ministered to his needs.

'The woman has courage,' he said on one occasion. 'Neither screwings nor pinchings have so far brought aught from her but a spate of incomprehensible words. She speaks, she claims, in parables. She refuses, she says, to sing a new song of the Lord in a strange land. What make you of that, Kate?'

'The poor creature is close to losing her reason.'

'But may yet speak the truth. Or would you say that a demented woman is incapable of truthful statements?'

Katherine left the question, if real question it was, unanswered.

'The rack was of no avail,' Henry said, on another occasion. 'All she would say was "Pray, pray, pray." The Lieutenant of the Tower, they tell me, has refused to put her to the torture again. A squeamish fellow, but Wriothesley is made of sterner stuff. He proposes to take the office upon himself and apply the rack with his own hands.'

'Failing him,' said a well-nigh distracted Katherine, 'why not the King's Grace?'

'You think me a brute, by God!'

'It is against the law for the Chancellor himself to administer torture,' she said. 'If he must administer it, and take unholy pleasure from it, a written order from the Lords of the Council must first be issued.'

'The King's Consort,' Henry said playfully, 'is frighteningly well versed in the law.'

'A written order,' she added, 'signed by the King himself.'

Henry scowled at her. 'That a woman should be so handled is not to my liking. The torturing of Anne Ascue shall cease. She would die on the rack before recanting. Wriothesley has failed. She would die in agony before confessing the truth he would wring from her. And die in agony she will, at Smithfield.'

'The stake, your Grace?' Katherine said dully.

'That, my clever Doctor of Law, is indeed the law. But let us spare a little sympathy for poor Wriothesley. He will be mad with frustration and will strive as never before to bring about your ruin.'

'The King standing by, watching?' The words were wrung from Katherine.

'Watching—and waiting to discover who is the cleverer, who the more cunning, who the more worthy of my admiration—the Queen or the Chancellor.'

'Will the Chancellor stand in the crowd at Smithfield?' Katherine asked wildly.

'Who can say?'

'What of the King's Grace?'

Henry looked at her with a hurt expression in his eyes. 'I, with my sensitivity? You shock me, Kate.'

'Have you ever in your life witnessed a burning?'

'Kate!'

'Let me give you an account of what will happen to Anne Ascue . . .'

'In the hope of gaining clemency for the heretic?'

'That and no more. Let her hang, not burn.'

'I refuse to listen.'

But Katherine spoke up with reckless abandon, painting a vivid picture of the scene outside St Bartholomew's Church where the stake would be erected and to which Anne Ascue would be marched in procession along with other condemned heretics. There she would be secured and there she would watch the lighting of the faggots beneath her feet. Her only hope of escaping the full agony would be death by suffocation from the smoke before the flames enveloped her. Katherine paused and saw tears in Henry's eyes. Was he listening, really listening? A hanging, not a burning, she prayed, and waited for him to speak.

'My admiration for you,' he said at last, 'would know no bounds if you were to come to me and tell me that God had blessed your womb.'

He had not been listening, truly he had *not* been listening. She thought of Tom Seymour and prayed that he had not made her pregnant. She would rather die, even as Anne Ascue was about to die, than give Henry the satisfaction of believing her with child by him. 'I see no chance, and this I believe,' she said tensely, 'of God blessing my womb.'

'It would seem,' he said, maudlin now with self-pity, 'that I married a barren woman.'

7

PRINCE EDWARD yawned and looked up from his Italian grammar. The Lady Jane, yawning being infectious, yawned widely herself and looked up from her own identical Italian grammar. It was two months since Jane had become Queen Katherine's ward and the court had returned recently to Whitehall. Since Edward and Jane were the same age and had reached the same stage in their studies, the King had decided that they should continue their studies together under the guidance of the same tutors. Facing each other now across a wide writing-table in the study set apart for them in Katherine's private apartments, they had been set a lesson by their Italian master and left to complete it alone.

'I'm tired of study,' Edward said, yawning again and throwing down his pen.

'So am I,' said Jane, but feeling guiltily that it was an evil thing to say.

'Do you like Whitehall better than Hampton Court, Jane?'

'No,' said Jane, knowing that he preferred Hampton Court himself.

'Hampton Court was my mother's favourite palace,' he said.

'Do you remember her?' Jane asked, to keep the conversation going.

'What a silly question, Jane. She died when I was only twelve days old.'

'Then of course you can't remember her at all.'

'I wish I could,' Edward said, but unemotionally. 'And I wish I could remember being born. You see, it was an unusual birth. Uncle Thomas said it was the only sort of birth that could be predicted exactly. The time of it, I mean.'

Jane puckered her brows. 'Are you asking me a riddle, Edward?'

'No, but *can* you tell me the sort of birth it was?'

'A royal birth, of course.'

'Yes, but it was another sort as well. My mother had an operation, a *Caesarean* operation. Do you know what that means, Jane?'

'No, Edward.'

'They call it that because of Julius Caesar. They cut open his mother's belly with a very sharp knife and lifted him out. That's what they did to my mother, and there was I, Edward, Prince of Wales.'

'Very interesting,' Jane said politely and just as unemotionally.

'My father says it ought to make me a second Caesar,' Edward said, frowning, 'but I don't want to be a mighty warrior, and I don't want to be assassinated either, like Caesar.'

'What *do* you want to be, Edward?'

'I should like to be a Yeoman of the Guard.'

'Because of the uniform.'

'I can't think of any other reason, but I was born to be a king and there's nothing I can do about it.'

'The King's robes are prettier.'

Edward looked thoughtful. 'A bishop's are more dignified.'

Katherine had entered silently and had heard the last few words of the children's conversation. She smiled on them fondly and when, at the sight of her, they rose hastily from their chairs she bade them not to stand on ceremony.

'Would you like to be a bishop?' she asked Edward.

'No, Madame,' he replied, 'but then, you see, I don't care for Bishop Gardiner.'

Nor did Katherine. Gardiner was one of the old Catholics and now enjoyed the King's favour almost equally with the Chancellor. This had caused and still caused her much anxiety. It was Gardiner who had first denounced Anne Ascue and Gardiner who, before she perished at the stake, had questioned her more fanatically than the Chancellor. In him, she realised, she had an enemy as implacable as Chancellor Wriothesley.

'Continue with your studies,' she said, and abruptly left the children.

They resumed the Italian lesson but only for a few moments.

'The Queen, my stepmother,' Edward began, then corrected

himself gravely. 'My *third* stepmother. Anne of Cleves was the first one, and Katherine Howard the second.'

'Do you remember Katherine Howard, Edward?'

'Not very well. She was pretty, I can remember that, but they chopped off her pretty head before I could really get to know her.'

'Poor creature,' Jane sighed, not caring much about the loss of a head here and there when the victims were unknown to her, but then she thought suddenly of Queen Katherine Parr, Chancellor Wriothesley and Anne Ascue. 'It would be terrible,' she said, fear gripping her heart, 'if that happened to your third stepmother. You were going to say something about her. Had it anything to do with executions?'

'It *could* have,' Edward said portentously. 'The Queen is being watched closely.'

'Who by, Edward?'

'The Chancellor's spies, and Bishop Gardiner's spies too.'

'You must be a spy yourself to know about it,' Jane gasped.

'It was accidental,' Edward said haughtily. 'I heard the Chancellor and the Bishop talking privately. It was in the garden. They didn't see me. I kept very still and quiet.'

'What did you hear?' Jane asked urgently.

'Bishop Gardiner has gained the King's permission to seek and find proof of the Queen's heresy. The Chancellor said he would help him, and both said they would set their spies to work. That was yesterday afternoon.'

'I,' said Jane, 'shall become a spy myself.'

'It will make a merry game,' Edward said somewhat condescendingly.

Not only a spy, Jane thought, but the Queen's special protector. A *guardian*, that was what it amounted to; the Queen's ward but her guardian too. But first, and immediately, she must hurry to the Queen and warn her most urgently to be on her guard. Excusing herself and walking on tiptoe, as if to evade any hidden, watching spy, she made her way to the Queen's inner chamber and came upon Katherine in the act of picking up a book from a confusion of books and papers on the floor. 'Your Grace...'

'My most private chamber has been ransacked,' Katherine said, a bewildered expression on her face.

'Did they find anything . . . ?' Jane hesitated, seeking the right word.

'Anything incriminating? There was nothing incriminating to find. To whom were you referring, child, when you said "they"?'

Quickly Jane told her all that she had learned from Edward. Katherine thanked her but warned her not to pit her wits against those of Wriothesley and Gardiner. Jane began to feel important. The Queen was regarding her as a grown woman, and that was very pleasing. She promised to heed the warning but had no thought of abandoning the role she had created for herself. She would try very hard to become an invisible spy and might even be able—an exciting thought, this—to turn herself into a witch capable of casting spells on the wicked Chancellor and the wicked Bishop.

'My manuscript is missing,' Katherine said, having gathered together all the scattered books and papers.

'Is it very important?' Jane asked in a conspiratorial whisper.

'To me it is.'

But Katherine was smiling faintly. The manuscript was a religious treatise entitled *The Lamentations of a Sinner*. She had completed it after many months of writing and intended eventually to have it printed and distributed. She had given expression to some radical religious views but had in no way denied the King's religious supremacy. Indeed, she had been cautious enough to praise him, not insincerely, and felt confident that he would preen himself when reading her words of praise.

'I shall complain to the King about this intrusion of my privacy,' she said angrily.

She went at once to Henry's apartments, which were conveniently next to her own, and found Bishop Gardiner with him. Gardiner bowed obsequiously, and Henry, after casting upon her a stony glance, continued to turn the pages of *The Lamentations of a Sinner*. Katherine made her complaint, paused for a moment, and then thanked Gardiner for having by some happy chance retrieved her stolen manuscript. Henry appeared to have heard neither her complaint nor her sarcasm and after a moment laughed softly.

'Some pretty writing here, Kate. I have done much in the past, you claim, and I deny it not, to banish that monstrous idol of Rome. But the past is gone, and it would seem that with the present about us I have become something of a laggard. I must stir myself and direct my energies to the Church of England. I am exhorted to cleanse and purge that Church in the name of God and to the glory of God. To cleanse and purge it, would you say, of such rascals as Gardiner?'

Katherine merely bowed her head. Henry's voice had changed as he spoke and his mood had become unpredictable. Anger, she suspected, was building up within him; would he vent it upon Gardiner or upon her?

'Small comfort it is to me in my suffering,' he said at last, and viciously, 'to sustain the pratings of a learned wife and, by St Mary, to be taught by her.'

His eyes were on Gardiner and with them still on him he said fretfully: 'The Queen, my wife, will withdraw; the Queen, my wife, will enter my presence only when summoned. Escort the Queen's Grace to her apartments, my lord Bishop.'

Katherine curtsied and said in a stifled voice: 'I am not as yet in need of a guard, even in the guise of an august bishop.'

During the next few days she was called to Henry's apartments only when her ministrations were necessary, and even then others were always present while she attended to the King's ulcerous leg. Gardiner and Wriothesley were often there together, watchful and inclined to smirk. Occasionally Edward Seymour, Earl of Hertford, was present, a look of sympathy in his eyes, she thought, but was it genuine? Was Lord Hertford a friend? Could she trust him? It seemed to her that she could trust no one, with the exception of Hertford's younger brother Thomas, who was still banished from court. Nevertheless he would know, since no announcement had been made, that the King's wife was not yet pregnant.

In an attempt to gain some little tranquillity she took to walking unattended in the privy garden and there, on one occasion, came upon Jane Grey. The child had obviously been hiding, but surprised by Katherine she pretended to be pulling out weeds.

'Jane . . . ?' Katherine questioned softly.

'The gardeners are lazy,' Jane said. 'Just look at all these weeds.' She snatched up one and shook it indignantly. 'This,' she said, 'is Chancellor Wriothesley.' She snatched up another. 'And this is Bishop Gardiner.' She flung the weeds to the ground and stamped on them. 'I should like to do that to the Chancellor and the Bishop.'

'You were hoping to come upon them and eavesdrop,' Katherine said gently. 'Have you forgotten my warning? Go back to your studies, Jane.'

'Prince Edward doesn't want to study this afternoon, your Grace. He wants to play cards.'

'How shocking,' Katherine murmured.

'*And* for money, your Grace.'

'More shocking still.'

'Children are not allowed to play cards at Bradgate.'

'While at court they are likely to be led into evil ways, even by Prince Edward. Go back to him, child. A little card-playing will do you no harm.'

On re-entering the palace Jane caught sight of Gardiner, followed him at a distance and saw him steal into a storeroom similar to the one in which she had discovered Edward at Hampton Court. He was followed a few moments later by the Chancellor who closed and locked the door behind him. So that was it, they considered the storeroom a safer place for private conversation than the privy garden, or possibly it was because the Bishop, as Jane had noticed, had a heavy cold. Quickly she hid behind a curtain, imagined that she had become a witch and cast a spell calculated to turn the Bishop's cold into an attack of the sometimes fatal sweating disease. They emerged from the storeroom at last and Jane heard Gardiner whisper to Wriothesley that he would have more to tell him tomorrow at the same hour.

Jane slipped into the storeroom when they had passed from sight and saw what she had hoped to see, a massive chest of drawers, and then another and another. But not one of them was facing the wall; to hide in a bottom drawer would be to invite quick discovery. She was searching the room fruitlessly for a hiding place when two burly porters stamped in. They looked abashed at the sight of her but she bade them go about their business. Still looking abashed they began to trundle one of the chests towards the door. Could she, she wondered, cast a spell and make them turn one of the others round?

'Wrong un,' said the taller of the two when the chest was in the passage. 'Back with it, an' watch thy toes.'

All but dancing with excitement, Jane willed it that they should replace it with its front facing the wall, but not so close that the drawers could not be opened, and this they obligingly did. Then they tackled a second chest and without injury to their toes trundled it out to the passage.

'Where are you taking it?' Jane asked.

'To the Lady Jane's room,' she was told.

'My attendant shall reward you with tansy cakes and beer,' she said grandly.

The next day, at the same hour, Jane was lying in the bottom drawer of a chest when the Chancellor and the Bishop entered. Wondering if it would be necessary for her to cast another useful spell, she heard them discussing the Statute of the Six Articles and a Royal Commission but could make little sense of their words until they spoke of the Queen and a charge of treasonable heresy.

'The document wants only the King's signature,' Gardiner said.

'Is any difficulty anticipated?'

'In the King's present mood, none. I shall obtain royal assent before supper and give the document into your keeping when we meet on our way to the dining hall.'

Jane scrambled out of the drawer when the Chancellor and the Bishop had departed separately and thought that the most powerful spell in the world was now called for. She played cards again with Edward during the afternoon and longed to confide in him, but the secret was hers to be jealously guarded until she was able to place Gardiner's document in the Queen's hands. She prepared herself early for supper and unattended by Mrs Eleyn, whom she gave the slip, made her way to the gallery through which the Bishop and the Chancellor must pass. The Bishop appeared first; his cold was worse and he suffered a shattering sneezing fit while Jane kept her eye on him. The Chancellor entered the gallery a few moments later; he, too, she noted with satisfaction, had caught a cold. He joined the Bishop and they sauntered through the gallery rubbing shoulders. Jane stole up behind them just as the Bishop slipped a folded document into the Chancellor's hand. *Be pleased to drop it,* Jane commanded him silently. He thrust it into his pocket and stood aside for Gardiner to precede him to the dining hall. Jane, tears of frustration in her eyes, rushed forward with the wild intention of trying to pick the Chancellor's pocket. At that moment he sneezed.

'Bless you, Sir Thomas,' Jane said, eyeing his bulging pocket.

He sneezed again, doubling up as he did so, and the document flew out of his pocket with the speed of a stone from a catapult. A paroxysm of sneezing followed, during which Jane snatched up the document unseen and skipped away with it to the Queen's apartments.

'What is it, Jane?' Katherine demanded at the sight of the girl's flushed and excited face.

Jane presented the document and waited anxiously while Katherine read it.

'Is it your Grace's death warrant?' Jane whispered when Katherine looked up from her reading.

'That,' Katherine said bitterly, 'is yet to come.'

The document contained seven charges of treasonable heresy and an order for a commission to sit and consider them. She glanced at the names of the commissioners. Prominent were Gardiner and Wriothesley; the others were undoubtedly their allies and her sworn enemies. Then she glanced again at the King's unmistakable signature; he, too, was an enemy now.

'How did you come by this document?' she asked Jane.

'I cast a spell, your Grace. I turned myself into a witch and cast a spell. There were other spells but this was the important one. The document fell from the Chancellor's pocket.'

'My thanks to you, Jane,' Katherine said dully, 'but the sooner you turn yourself back into an innocent child the better.'

'I shall say a special prayer tonight, your Grace.'

'Say a special one for me too, Jane.'

'Perhaps one more spell . . . ?' Jane suggested.

Much unnerved, Katherine sank back into a chair. She was trembling now and close to being struck dumb by terror. How could she face the King at supper and sustain the triumphant glances of Gardiner and Wriothesley? Then she remembered that Henry had declared himself too ill to be carried to the supper-table and intended to sup alone in his apartments. Dare she break in on him and, swallowing her pride, plead with him for mercy?

'What in the name of heaven am I to do?' she said, not really addressing Jane.

'When I was very young,' Jane said, feeling very grown-up at that moment, 'I used to cry and get my way by doing so. I think your Grace should weep. I shall weep with you. If we make enough noise the King in his room next door will hear us. It will fill him with pity. I am not casting a spell,' she added hastily. 'I am praying now instead of tonight.'

With tears already in her eyes, Katherine, who rarely wept, found it surprisingly easy to do so. Jane joined her experimentally and uttered the first wail. Katherine uttered the second. Thereafter they wailed and sometimes screamed in unison. Two of Katherine's ladies rushed into the inner chamber and at the sight of the Queen's apparent distress screamed loudly. They were followed presently by the King's jester, who, imitating Henry's voice, demanded an explanation.

'It is clear that the Queen has suffered a terrible shock,' one of the ladies said obligingly.

'Her Majesty is beyond coherent speech,' said the other.

The jester skipped away and very soon Henry sent his personal physician to examine Katherine. He found her prostrate and still weeping, though all but silently now. Shaking his head he returned to the King and reported that the Queen had been reduced by mental agitation to a state of dangerous illness. Suspecting the cause Henry shouted for his chair-bearing pages and was carried to Katherine's inner chamber. Jane eyed him cautiously. Should she cast a final spell or pray silently? Before she could do either Henry leant forward in his chair and snatched from Katherine's hands the document which she had twisted and torn.

'Be of good cheer,' he said, his voice betraying no emotion. 'My heart is filled with pity. You have in the King an affectionate and forgiving friend. Rest well this night and return my visit tomorrow.' He glanced at Jane and so penetratingly that she quaked with fear. 'Little jackanapes,' he said softly.

The next morning, having learnt that Henry had risen early

from his sickbed, a cautiously confident Katherine presented herself formally at his apartments. Three ladies accompanied her and leading the way in what was intended to be a solemn procession was the Lady Jane, carrying in each hand a lighted candle. The King, Katherine was informed, was taking the air in the privy garden.

'To the garden, then,' Katherine said.

Jane, still carrying the candles, led the way to the garden. It was a calm windless morning. The candles flickered and spluttered but remained alight, and this, when the little procession came upon Henry, seemed to cause him much amusement.

'To what shrine are you bound?' he asked, leaning forward in his chair.

Katherine, her ladies and Jane curtsied three times and knelt.

'Surely the shrine of St Henry,' he chuckled. 'Rise, ye worshippers, and, with the wind of religion in the windless air, let us dwell on the subject of religion. Is the saint to be instructed, or is he to instruct?'

Katherine, having resolved on a display of politic humility, said quietly: 'I am but a weak woman, as the King's Highness well knows. I can but defer to the superior judgment of the King who, by God's appointment, is the Head of the Church in England and, by that appointment, stands next to God.'

Henry's face darkened. 'We are not yet dead,' he said, employing the royal, even papal, plural. 'You would at times become a doctor to instruct us, not to be instructed by us.'

'My meaning, like that of all well-meaning women, is many times mistaken,' Katherine said quickly. 'In very truth I would be the last wife in the world to instruct her lord. My only wish has been to tempt forth my lord's ruling on points of doctrine and practice, and profit thereby.'

Henry grunted—in disbelief, Katherine thought—but after a moment of silence he sighed heavily and invited her to kiss him on the cheek.

'We are perfect friends again,' he said, apparently fully appeased.

Jane was the first to hear the sound of marching feet and swung round in consternation to watch the approach of

Chancellor Wriothesley and a detachment of Yeomen of the Guard. She shifted her gaze to the King and saw him flinch as if struck in the face by Wriothesley.

'What now, Sir Thomas?' he asked fretfully.

'I am come to perform my duty, a duty decreed by the King's Grace,' the Chancellor said stiffly.

Jane held her breath. The Queen was to be arrested, even in the King's own presence. Katherine too held her breath but on the whole was confident of a favourable outcome. It was one thing for Henry to order her arrest, quite another for him to sit and watch it carried out. He touched the cheek she had kissed and gave way to a burst of anger.

'Knave and fool,' he said in a terrible voice. 'Rather would I see my Chancellor flung into the Tower.'

Wriothesley fell to his knees. 'Your Grace, I beg of you . . .'

Henry darted a slanting glance at Katherine. 'He has been a very knave to you. Do with him as you will.'

Politic again, mindful of the shadow of Gardiner, Katherine said mildly: 'Sir Thomas is at fault, but it is a fault enlarged by a sorry mistake. I have no further quarrel with him.' She looked directly at Wriothesley. 'Go in peace, Sir Thomas.'

He rose from his knees, bowed low before Katherine and at a nod from Henry retreated with little dignity.

'An end of the matter, would you say?' Henry asked Katherine.

'If the King's Grace so determines,' she said demurely.

Suddenly there was a vague look in his eyes. 'Determines *what?*' he asked pettishly.

Katherine saw that he was beginning to pant and sweat, as if out in the midday sun of high summer. Then, while still sweating, he shivered violently.

'Your Grace . . . ?' she questioned anxiously.

'It is still in my mind,' he said feverishly, 'to have to my bosom a fertile wife.'

Katherine repressed the impulse to say: Even if she would presume in other matters to instruct you?

'My leg pains me more devilishly than ever before,' he said in sudden agony. 'Let them carry me back and send for a dozen physicians. Nay,' he joked hollowly, 'make it a baker's dozen for right good measure.'

He kept Katherine at his side during the rest of the day and grew so feverish that his speech was at times incoherent. At nightfall he demanded to see Jane Grey, giving Katherine the impression that he believed the child had yet to be brought to court by her mother. Jane stole into the sickroom and, fearing that she had inadvertently cast a spell on him, stared at him with a look of anguish in her eyes.

'Dear God in heaven,' Henry gasped, gazing fearfully at the child, 'the ghost of Jane Seymour come to carry me away. I'll not be plagued like this. Out with her, out with her.'

Katherine told herself that Henry was delirious, but she remembered that one of the ladies of the court, formerly a member of Jane Seymour's household, had seen in the Lady Jane a fleeting resemblance to the late Queen. She was firmly convinced, she had whispered, that there was Seymour blood in the child's veins, for it was well known that Jane Seymour's brother, the Earl of Hertford, and Lady Dorset had once been lovers.

'Has the ghost been laid?' Henry asked, his eyes closed, his voice still fearful.

'Truly laid,' Katherine assured him, for Jane had fled in terror.

'Then I shall live,' Henry gasped in relief.

To everybody's amazement he rallied during the night and appeared to be gaining strength as Christmas approached. Then early in the New Year he suffered a serious relapse and Archbishop Cranmer was summoned, but even then Henry refused to believe that death was close at hand. The Earl of Hertford, constantly at his side, was seen to be in full control of state affairs, while many members of the court, including Katherine herself, were forbidden to approach the dying King. It was Hertford who came to Katherine with word of Henry's death and invited her to break the news to the new young King.

Katherine found Edward and Jane together. They were playing cards with adult rather than childish concentration.

'I have invented a new game,' Edward said, at the sight of his stepmother. 'It is called Spite and Malice.'

'Why spite and why malice?' Katherine asked.

'Because one plays unmercifully, with no quarter given,' he

said, smiling innocently. 'Do you find it upsetting, Madame? Is that why there are tears in your eyes?'

Katherine curtsied three times, then knelt. 'Your Majesty . . .'

Edward flung down his cards and sprang to his feet. He was struggling, Katherine saw, not to weep himself. He glanced at Jane as if for support and she, at a gesture from Katherine, curtsied herself and knelt. The first of my subjects to kneel before me, he thought, glancing from one to the other, and raised his head proudly, but there was a pain in his chest and his eyes were burning.

'I shall try,' he said chokingly, 'to be a good king.'

8

'AND so,' Thomas Seymour said, 'the late King your husband named Jane Grey fourth in line of succession. She is now third. The Lady Mary to follow Edward should he die without issue, the Lady Elizabeth to follow Mary should she die without issue, and the Lady Jane to follow Elizabeth should she die also without issue.'

'Thank you for hastening to me with this information,' Katherine Parr said dryly. 'I was in complete ignorance myself. The decision must have been made not long before Henry died.'

'It was, or so my brother Edward tells me,' Seymour said, and added thoughtfully: 'Edward Seymour, the most powerful man in England at this moment.'

They were discussing the late King's will, Thomas Seymour having presented himself without ceremony at Katherine's royal jointure-house in the little village of Chelsea. With her and in her care were the Lady Elizabeth and the Lady Jane. The Lady Mary, wary of the new and entirely Protestant rule, had retired to Hunsdon, one of the three manors given to her by King Henry.

'I am bursting with information,' Seymour said, smiling broadly, 'but my real purpose, as you must surely guess, is a most personal one.'

'I abandoned guessing games when I emerged from the nursery,' Katherine said lightly, 'and I was never very good at them, dear Tom.'

'Your dear Tom,' Seymour chuckled, 'has come a-courting.'

'With my late husband scarcely cold in his grave?' she said, trying ineffectually to sound angry.

'No common grave,' Seymour pointed out. 'He lies snugly in the vault beneath St George's Chapel with his third wife close at hand to keep him company.'

'Be that as it may, we must remember what happened to the frog.'

'The *frog*, Kate?'

'He would a-wooing go. Did he not burst? And in respect of bursting, what of the rest of your information?'

Seymour shrugged resignedly. 'King Henry named sixteen executors and, more importantly, a regency council of twelve. My brother Edward heads that council and is named Lord Protector. In addition he is the new King's guardian and will presently assume the title of Duke of Somerset.'

'And you, also King Edward's uncle, have you been forgotten?'

Seymour bowed sweepingly. 'My wife, when I marry, will rejoice in the title of Lady Seymour of Sudeley. She will also be the wife of the Lord Admiral, a position which her husband-to-be has already assumed. In addition but in a secondary capacity—I stress *secondary*, dear Kate—she will be the Queen Dowager. That, let me add, is the title conferred upon you in the will of your late but not lamented kingly husband.'

Most certainly not lamented, Katherine thought, and murmured, 'It makes me feel quite elderly.'

'Married to me you will quickly regain your lost youth,' Seymour assured her. 'How long do you propose to keep me waiting, Madame?'

'I would marry you immediately, if that were possible,' Katherine said frankly, 'but discretion and patience are called for, and surely the Lord Protector's consent is called for too.'

'Nonsense!' Seymour said hotly.

'How rash you are, Tom. Create a scandal and you may ruin yourself. Even to come here today openly, and to be received by me in private . . .'

'You would deny me the right to visit you?' he asked indignantly.

'The *right*, Tom?'

'So I deem it, by God!' he said, a sulky yet appealing expression on his face.

'I concede the right,' Katherine said helplessly, 'but I do insist on discretion.'

'Secret visits, then?'

Katherine laughed wryly. 'I feel as conspiratorial as a young girl in love with a man disapproved of by my parents. There's a private field path. It crosses a concealed footbridge and leads to the side postern. Come by that route at a prearranged time and you shall be admitted safely and secretly.'

'Early morning or late evening?' he asked boisterously. 'I am in full vigour at either time of day.'

'At any of time of day, in my experience.'

Flattered, he bowed and kissed her hand. 'I shall present myself at the side postern at eight tomorrow morning.' He paused, a cunning expression on his face. 'Permit me to pay my respects to the Lady Elizabeth and the Lady Jane before I go, and let it be known that that was the sole reason for my visit.'

It so happened, however, that Lord Seymour of Sudeley came not at eight the next morning but eleven, and openly, with two gentlemen in attendance. He was charged, he said, to deliver a message from his nephew the King. The Queen Dowager, the Lady Elizabeth and the Lady Jane were to return to court for the King's coronation on the twentieth day of the month.

'Only men attend the coronation of a boy King,' Katherine pointed out.

'You are to be present at Whitehall,' Seymour told her, 'which is a different matter from attending the actual ceremony.'

Katherine returned to Whitehall with Elizabeth and Jane the day before the coronation and was informed that her former apartments had been reserved for her exclusive use whenever she might be summoned to court. Edward came to see her that night and found her in her inner chamber with Jane in attendance. His manner, Katherine thought, was just a little sly as he glanced back over his shoulder as if fearful of having been followed.

'I gave them the slip,' he said, laughing awkwardly.

'My lord . . . ?' a puzzled Katherine questioned.

'As King,' he said woefully, 'I am not permitted informality any more. Not until I am old enough to please myself.'

'Poor Edward,' Jane said.

He looked at her sadly. 'Never again, not even when we are alone together, if that is ever permitted, must you address me like that. The Protector, my Uncle Edward, is very strict. I would much rather have Uncle Thomas. *He* would allow you to attend the coronation, but Uncle Edward was really angry when I suggested it. He won't even allow you to be at the feast afterwards.'

'I expect I shan't feel hungry,' Jane said stoically.

Edward glanced over his shoulder again. 'I must go now, but please remain at court for a few days. I want to play cards with you again, and win, of course.'

Jane caught at least a glimpse of the coronation feast by stealing into the gallery unseen towards the end of it. There was Edward sitting at the royal table between his uncle, the Lord Protector, and his godfather, the Archbishop of Canterbury. His small figure seemed somewhat enlarged by the crown and the coronation robes but his companions still towered over him. As Jane watched from her vantage point in the gallery the Lord Marshal's deputy entered the crowded hall below on horseback and rode this way and that to scatter the lords and gentlemen and make room for the King's champion. He was Sir John Dymock, a splendid knight in armour. Quickly and firmly he established himself before the royal table and in the King's name challenged all disputers to press forward and dispute the King's claim to the throne. There were no disputers, and during the little silence that followed Edward drank to his champion before passing him the cup. Poor Cousin Edward looked very tired, Jane thought, and the crown, which slipped when he leant forward to take back the cup, was surely much too heavy for him. It was really fortunate that he would only be called upon to wear it on state occasions. She slipped unseen from the gallery and on entering the Queen Dowager's apartments came upon Thomas Seymour in the act of backing from Katherine's inner chamber. 'Till tomorrow,' he murmured, closing the door softly. Jane looked at him solemnly when he turned and recognised her; then, because he was so handsome, a fairy prince if ever there was one, she dropped him a curtsy. Seymour responded with a sweeping bow but there was a guarded expression in his eyes.

'The beauteous Lady Jane,' he said, his voice caressing.

Jane repressed a delighted giggle and said severely: 'Should you not be at the coronation feast, Lord Seymour?'

He placed a conspiratorial finger to his lips. 'I have been there from the very beginning, Lady Jane. Do you not agree?'

So irresistible was his manner that Jane said instantly: 'I saw you there myself but a moment ago.'

'You and I are friends and allies,' Seymour said softly.

Katherine emerged from her room immediately after Seymour's departure and looked questioningly at Jane.

'Did I hear voices, Jane?'

'If so, I was talking to myself, aloud,' Jane said.

'The voice of a girl one moment, that of a grown man the next. How very peculiar.'

Jane placed a finger to her lips as Seymour had done. 'It would be very nice if the Queen Dowager could marry the Lord Admiral.'

'My dear child . . .'

'Shall I speak to my cousin the King about it?'

'Is this Lord Seymour's own suggestion?' Katherine asked carefully.

'No, your Grace, but since I cannot marry him myself, and since he and I are friends and allies . . .'

Katherine could but smile at the thought of the nine-year-old girl assuming the role of matchmaker. Should she allow Jane to place the idea in the little King's mind before Seymour brought up the subject himself? It could, perhaps, have splendid results, though on the other hand it might serve only to anger the Lord Protector.

'There is time,' she said, deciding to commit herself in no way, 'for some diligent needlework before supper.'

The following afternoon Jane received a summons from Edward and went formally to his apartments with Mrs Eleyn in attendance. He was waiting in an anteroom, he himself attended by his Uncle Thomas. Jane, remembering the obligatory ritual, curtsied three times, knelt and remained kneeling until Edward bade her rise.

'We shall play cards for an hour,' he said, and led Jane to an inner room, leaving their attendants close at hand if not within actual earshot.

After four or five minutes of silent play Jane began to suspect that her cousin's mind was not on the game. He had declared his intention of winning, and he was almost always clever enough to do so, but after having made several silly mistakes it seemed likely that he would find himself losing.

'Is the King's Grace troubled by state affairs?' Jane ventured to ask.

Edward looked at her frowningly. 'Lady Jane, we must find a wife for my Uncle Thomas.'

'*We!*' she echoed, delighted at the prospect of their being fellow matchmakers.

'By "we",' Edward said solemnly, 'I mean "I". You must learn to accept my use of the royal plural, Lady Jane.'

'May it please your Grace,' she said, looking at him obliquely, 'I have thought of a suitable wife for him myself.'

'The selection and the decision shall be ours,' Edward said sternly; then forgetting his new royal dignity he scampered to the door and flung it open. 'Uncle Thomas, a word with you, if you please.'

Behind his back, when he returned to reseat himself at the card-table, Jane caught Seymour's eyes momentarily and placed a finger to her lips. Edward fiddled with his cards and glancing covertly at Jane seemed to gain determination from the sedate, attentive little figure she presented.

'Do I sense an air of mystery?' Seymour asked laughingly.

Edward turned up a serious face to his uncle and said weightily: 'We, the King's Grace, have reached an important decision. It concerns the future welfare of our uncle, Lord Seymour of Sudeley.'

Seymour bowed low. 'I am all attention, Sire.'

'We have decided, Uncle Thomas, that you have been a bachelor much too long.'

'Even if a gay one,' Seymour chuckled.

Edward treated him to the most severe frown he could conjure up, then he relaxed and dissolved into merry laughter.

'Gaiety is not to be forbidden at my court,' he said, his fine grey eyes sparkling. '*I* am the sovereign, not my sister Mary. And—well—I shall remain a gay bachelor myself for as long as possible.'

'Whereas I,' Seymour sighed, 'am condemned to the dull respectability of holy matrimony. Do I have the privilege of choosing a wife for myself, dear nephew, or . . . ?'

'Uncle Thomas,' Edward said, surveying the formation of cards on the table, 'the Lady Jane is winning and I am very short of money.'

'My own exchequer is in a healthy condition,' Seymour said promptly. 'If I may be permitted . . . ?'

'It's very kind of you,' Edward said gratefully.

'And so, the choice of a wife . . . ?'

Edward remembered who he was. 'We have decided, Lord Seymour, to marry you to our late father's fourth wife.'

Seymour, for all his habitual aplomb, came close to blanching. Anne of Cleves indeed! Why *that* impossible creature? Edward, as far as Seymour knew, had never met her, even though she had remained in residence in England after her divorce from his father who had failed, and with everybody chuckling about it, to consummate that rather comic marriage. Seymour, despite his dismay at Edward's decison, felt like chuckling now. Poor Henry Tudor, playing a hand of cards with Anne of Cleves instead of bouncing in the royal bed with her. 'Only in the event of your winning, my lord,' she was reputed to have said, but Henry, his mind on other things, had played a disastrous hand.

'Our wish is not to your liking?' Edward said, torn between anxiety and royal indignation.

'May I ask the reason for your Grace's decision?' Seymour parried.

'They tell me that the Lady of Cleves is lonely.'

'And in her loneliness plays patience. Would you have me, in that most terrible loneliness of all, the loneliness of a loveless marriage, play patience also?'

Edward frowned over this. 'You and she could play this new game of mine, Spite and Malice.'

'With malice aforethought, and nothing else.'

'Perhaps,' Edward said brightly, 'I should marry you to my sister Mary.'

'For what reason, your Grace?' Seymour asked faintly.

'She is lonely too.'

'A Catholic loneliness.'

'It would be good for England if you could change her religion for her.'

'By St Mary, what if she were to change mine for me?'

'That,' said the little Protestant King, 'we cannot risk. Oh dear, this is a very *difficult* marriage game.'

Jane could contain herself no longer and burst out excitedly: 'With the King's permission . . .'

'Ah yes,' Edward said, 'the Lady Jane has a suggestion of her own. You have our permission to speak, dear cousin.'

'The Queen Dowager,' Jane gasped, and exchanged a quick look of intelligence with Thomas Seymour.

'An astonishing suggestion,' he said, pretending surprise. 'Yet I have long admired the Queen Dowager, from a distance.'

'She has been married three times,' Edward said disapprovingly.

'Your Grace's late father was married six times.'

'Do you *want* to marry my stepmother, Uncle Thomas?'

'Let me speak frankly,' Seymour said, with one of his rare flashes of calculated candour, 'I would have married the Queen Dowager had not King Henry snatched her up himself.'

'Would *she* have married *you*?'

'I can but think so. The New Learning brought us together, and enlightened religion is a solid and lasting foundation for any marriage.'

Edward's eyes revealed his agreement. 'It would be nice,' he said, 'for my favourite stepmother to become my aunt.' He rose from the table and, thinking it the dignified thing to do, paced the room in silence for several moments. 'We want,' he said at last, 'to keep our favourite uncle close at our side. What better way of doing it than by marrying him to the Queen Dowager?'

'When is the wedding to be?' Jane asked excitedly.

'Just as soon as Uncle Thomas wishes,' Edward said generously.

But Seymour was cautious for once. 'We must avoid a scandal, your Grace. The Queen Dowager's reputation must not be sullied a second time by a show of haste.'

'Scandal? A show of haste?'

'Your Grace's father married her scandalously soon after the death of her second husband, or so it was thought.'

'That,' Edward said haughtily, 'was a royal precedent.'

'Of which the Queen Dowager is bidden to take full advantage?'

Edward frowned over this, then smiled cunningly. 'Surely, my lord, but *secretly*.'

Seymour bowed deeply. 'The King's will is law.'

'His pleasure too, dear Uncle Thomas.'

9

'I BID you welcome to Chelsea Palace, dear brother,' Thomas Seymour said, a hint of mockery in his voice. 'It is a gracious act for you, Duke of Somerset, Regent and Lord Protector, to seek me out rather than summon me to Whitehall.'

'I am here to talk to you seriously,' the elder brother said stiffly. 'It is my duty to protest at your living openly under the Queen Dowager's roof and seemingly assuming the role of master of the house.'

'A role to which a husband is fully entitled, my dear Edward.'

'Husband?'

'The Queen Dowager and I were married all but a month ago.'

'A secret marriage.'

'Even so, with the King's full approval.'

'But not with the Privy Council's,' Somerset said sharply.

'Are you suggesting that by scorning the Lords of the Council in a private and personal matter I committed a treasonable act?'

'Joke if you must, Thomas, but it would have been a courteous gesture.'

'Ah, then I am not to be flung into the Tower.'

'Enough, Thomas. The Council has no recourse but to accept your marriage.'

'What of you, the Lord Protector?'

'I can but wish you and the Queen Dowager all happiness.'

Seymour bowed. 'With all forgiven you will naturally feel inclined to pay your respects to my wife and offer her your heartfelt congratulations.'

'Presently, but there are two other matters first. The Council had decided that the Lady Elizabeth shall be removed from the Queen Dowager's household. Admittedly the decision was reached before I was aware of your marriage. Nevertheless . . .'

'The reason for it?' Seymour interrupted tersely.

'It was believed that you were in residence here for the purpose of attempting to bring about a marriage between yourself and the Lady Elizabeth.'

Seymour laughed softly. 'Ah, but not being given to bigamy . . . !'

'Nevertheless, you would control the Lady Elizabeth through the Queen Dowager and that I cannot permit.'

Seymour shrugged this aside. 'You spoke of *two* other matters, Edward.'

'The second concerns the Lady Jane. She is to be returned to the care of her parents.'

Seymour looked at his brother in astonishment. He had made no move, yet, even secretly, to bring about a marriage between his nephew the King and Jane Grey; therefore his brother could have no fear of him in that respect.

'Is this, too, a Council decision?'

Nettled, Somerset said unwisely: 'As yet, merely my own.'

'What possible reason could you have for making such a decision?'

'Merely my own,' Somerset added hastily, 'but at the request of the Lady Jane's parents.'

'By King Henry's will,' Seymour pointed out, 'the Lady Jane is to remain in the Queen Dowager's care until she comes of age or marries.'

'I propose to marry her to my eldest son,' Somerset said.

'It will be necessary first to obtain the Queen Dowager's consent.'

'I recognise no obstacle in the Queen Dowager.'

'I do, by God!'

'You are beginning to lose your temper,' Somerset said mildly. 'You, most clearly, would be the prime obstacle.'

'Am I not the master of the house?'

'I can but think that you have marriage plans of your own for the Lady Jane,' Somerset said, striving not to reveal uneasiness.

Realising belatedly that he had gone too far, Seymour said with a shrug: 'None whatever. The girl is not yet of a marriageable age. Meanwhile I refuse to return her to her parents unless they approach me themselves, and even then I should demand an order-in-council, a necessary one if the late King's will is to be flaunted. Even the present King's, by God!'

'Your attitude is vastly puzzling, Thomas.'

'Even more so is yours. Have you any other matters to discuss, any other orders to issue?'

'Since the Queen Dowager has married again,' Somserset said promptly, 'the jewels entrusted to her by the late King must be surrendered to the Crown.'

Seymour flew into a rage. 'Entrusted? Given, by God, *given*.'

'They are Crown jewels and as such must be returned.'

'Take them if you must, but by force.'

'I shall negotiate with the Queen Dowager privately,' Somerset decided. 'She is, or always was, a reasonable woman.'

'Have you finished?' Seymour asked, his eyes still blazing.

'Finished?'

'A final order, perhaps?'

Somerset considered this for a brief moment. 'I think it wise that you should retire from England until the scandal which this hasty marriage will create has blown over.'

'Hasty? Katherine was not with child when I married her. But, *retire from England?*'

'As Lord Admiral you shall join the fleet at Boulogne.'

'Are you afraid of my continued presence in England?' Seymour asked dangerously.

Somerset sighed and weakened. 'You have the alternative of a sojourn at Sudeley Castle. I bid you good-day, Thomas.'

Sudeley Castle was a property in Gloucestershire which had come to Thomas Seymour upon the death of King Henry and from which he had taken his title. Its former lord, a traitor condemned to death for his misdeeds, had forfeited it to the Crown, and Seymour, the new Lord of Sudeley, had yet to take possession.

'And so to Sudeley we go,' Seymour said, after giving Katherine an account of the Lord Protector's visit, 'and taking with us your portion of the Crown jewels, that I vow.'

Katherine shuddered slightly. 'Tom, I'm gripped by apprehension.'

'Because I insist on your keeping them?'

'No, not that. Sudeley Castle strikes me as an ill-omen. I heard it said that the former lord turned in the saddle when leaving under guard and said, "Ah, Sudeley, thou art the traitor, not I." '

'For no better reason,' Seymour said brusquely, 'than that King Harry coveted the estate. Ill-omens are for children and weak-willed women . . .'

'And pregnant women too.'

'Kate, sweet Kate!'

'There appear to be certain signs,' she said demurely.

'For Sudeley an heir!'

'A little knave,' she teased, 'cast in his father's image.'

They journeyed to Sudeley in state, as if making a royal progress. The Lady Jane had a coach of her own, sharing it with Mrs Eleyn, and, to that lady's disgust, a dog named Pointer. This animal had been given to Jane by the Earl of Surrey, who, during King Henry's last days, had been condemned to death, his death warrant being the last such document signed by Henry. Pointer was so named because she was one of a breed of dogs trained by Surrey, and to everybody's astonishment, to point at game.

'A loathsome animal, my lady,' Mrs Eleyn grumbled. 'Nor is it well trained. It points at everything, even at me.'

'Pointer is not an "it",' Jane said huffily. 'Pointer is a bitch.'

'I am well aware of that, Lady Jane.'

'On the other hand, the Lady Elizabeth's dog is clearly a *dog*.'

'Clearly.'

'Pointer's uncle and future husband,' Jane said. 'That may seem improper to you, Mrs Eleyn, but it is different with animals.'

'Assuredly, but does the Lady Elizabeth approve?'

'It was she who suggested it.'

Jane was quietly pleased that her cousin Elizabeth, travelling in a separate coach, was also *en route* for Sudeley Castle. There had been some doubt, Elizabeth had confided, about her continued residence in the Lord Admiral's household. The Lord Protector had tried to forbid it, but the Lord Admiral, much to Elizabeth's satisfaction as well as Jane's, had, to put it vulgarly, thumbed his nose at his elder brother. Jane had grown fond of her cousin Elizabeth. They were scholastically equal, which Elizabeth, despite her seniority, freely admitted, and they shared an undying admiration for Thomas Seymour, Lord of Sudeley and Lord Admiral of England.

'We are close to our destination,' Mrs Eleyn remarked.

The Sudeley estate, as they entered the undulating outer acres of the park, reminded Jane of Bradgate, but the castle itself, when she caught her first glimpse of it, seemed grimly forbidding and made her think of dungeons, torture chambers and bloody executions. However, she was soon too deep in her studies, which had intensified, to take much notice of her surroundings. Edward's studies had intensified too, as Jane discovered when corresponding with him in both Latin and English. Katherine read Edward's letters to Jane before allowing Jane to read them herself, and Jane's to Edward before dispatching them. The Latin epistles brought out clearly, and to Katherine's satisfaction, the fact that the children were absorbing without question the Protestant beliefs which were now being taught openly and unreservedly. The English epistles struck a lighter note, Edward's including a little gossip about his life at court, Jane's a little gossip about hers at Sudeley Castle. In one of Jane's Katherine learnt that Pointer was not, as Jane had hoped, with child or children by Elizabeth's dog, any more than the Queen Dowager, as had been thought and as everybody at Sudeley had hoped, was with at least one child by the Lord Admiral. Angry at first, Katherine shrugged off Jane's gossip as well as her own disappointment. Few intimate personal matters were hidden from children at any of the great houses; it was carelessness rather than the order of the day, but it did at least prevent furtive listening and sly misconstruction.

Jane had spent more than a month at Sudeley and was approaching her tenth birthday when her father and mother appeared unexpectedly. She was in the middle of a history lesson when they arrived and such being the importance of study she was not called upon to pay her respects until the completion of the lesson. She had rarely thought of her parents during the months she had spent in Katherine's care and feeling timid now entered the Queen Dowager's presence chamber with a would-be arrogant air. Katherine and the Marchioness of Dorset were seated with Lord Seymour and the Marquess of Dorset standing behind their respective chairs. Jane's gaze strayed from one to the other of this group that might well have been a painting by Holbein and from the set look on their faces she wondered if she had interrupted an angry argument. Hurriedly she curtsied and waited apprehensively for somebody to break the silence.

'She would seem to have grown a little,' Lord Dorset said, smiling vaguely.

'Filled out a little, too,' his wife added gratingly.

'Dear Jane is thriving physically and mentally,' Katherine remarked conversationally.

Seymour laughed harshly. 'Tell Lady Jane the truth and be done with it.'

'We are here, child,' Lady Dorset said, 'to take you home to Bradgate.'

'At the express command of the Lord Protector,' Lord Dorset explained.

Jane uttered a little moan of distress and flung herself into Katherine's arms.

'I,' said Katherine pacifyingly, 'have yet to give my consent.'

'And so, by God, have I,' Seymour said, and swung round on Jane's father. 'A word with you in private, Dorset.'

'Whatever you have to say, Lord Seymour,' Lady Dorset said haughtily, 'shall be said in my presence or not at all.'

Seymour bowed mockingly. 'The Tudor temper is irresistible.' He turned to Katherine. 'If your Grace would be kind enough . . .'

Katherine understood instantly and rising led Jane from the presence chamber.

'The will of the late King,' Seymour said ponderously, 'is of more importance to me than the wishes of my brother the Lord Protector. I insist on Lady Jane remaining in the Queen Dowager's care.'

'That is to say, in *your* care,' Lady Dorset said angrily.

'So perceptive of you, my lady.'

'King Henry is dead,' she said needlessly, 'and your brother is in full control. He would marry Jane to his eldest son, and what a splendid match—Jane to be Duchess of Somerset when the Lord Protector has breathed his last.'

'I see that I must be frank with you,' Seymour said. 'I have in mind for your daughter a much more splendid match and one, I can but think, to your liking. Can you envisage Jane living long enough, in the normal course of events, to inherit the throne?'

Lady Dorset gripped the arms of her chair in sudden alarm. 'You plan to marry her to King Edward?' she said in a whisper.

'I have had it in mind for quite some time. Does the very thought of it fill you with awe, Lady Dorset?'

'There are political reasons against it,' she said falteringly. 'The King must marry a foreign princess.'

'My understanding of the international situation rules out the slightest possibility,' Seymour asserted smugly.

'Mine also,' Lord Dorset said, smiling thoughtfully. 'A much more splendid match, as you say, Seymour. I have often dreamt of it myself.'

'Fool!' Lady Dorset said involuntarily.

Dorset looked at her in surprise. 'Surely, my dearest Frances, you have dreamt of such a match yourself.'

Lady Dorset tried to take a tight rein upon herself. 'Truly I have, yet I have always known it to be a vain dream.'

'Neither I nor the Queen Dowager think it vain,' Seymour said briskly, and addressed himself solely to Lord Dorset. 'You understand now why Lady Jane must remain in our care, the Queen Dowager's and mine?'

'Fully, my dear Seymour.'

'And so, we flaunt the wishes of the Lord Protector?'

Dorset turned courteously to his wife. 'My dear Frances . . . ?'

Lady Dorset felt trapped but told herself that Seymour's scheme was one never to be realised. Angry as she was with the Lord Protector for having failed to set her in the Lady Mary's place in the line of succession sne knew that she could trust him not to allow Jane to become Edward's wife.

'My poor Seymour,' she said mockingly, 'you are riding for a fall. Success could only be yours if you first brought about your brother's disgrace and took his place yourself.'

'It may well be that you speak the very truth,' Thomas Seymour said softly. 'You daughter remains, Lady Dorset?'

'She remains,' Lady Dorset agreed. 'But what of your noble head? How long, I wonder, will it remain firmly on your shoulders?'

Katherine came close to uttering a similar remark when, after the Dorsets had departed, Seymour spoke of the plans now forming in his mind for the eventual downfall of his brother. She begged him to move cautiously and he assured her that despite his habitual impatience he would be as patient as a cat in pursuit of a mouse and while playing a waiting game endeavour to gather about him staunch Protestant allies. Accordingly he returned with his household to Katherine's jointure-house at Chelsea, there to await, since Katherine was definitely pregnant now, the birth of their child. 'A son, without the slightest doubt,' he said confidently.

Jane was pleased to return to Chelsea but disappointed, after only a few weeks there, to find her cousin Elizabeth abruptly ordered to a residence of her own at Cheshunt. Elizabeth smiled mysteriously when bidding Jane goodbye and said that doubtless it was all for the best.

'Has the Lord Admiral been mastered by the Lord Protector?' Jane ventured to ask.

'Scarcely that,' Elizabeth said, her smile enigmatic now rather than mysterious.

'Have you misbehaved yourself, Cousin Elizabeth?' Jane dared to ask.

'That is a question,' Elizabeth chuckled, 'which you should pose to the Queen Dowager.'

Jane puzzled over this and then said sorrowfully: 'You are often absent from morning prayers, and the Queen Dowager is very strict about morning prayers. Evening prayers also.'

'Then let us conclude,' Elizabeth said, 'that I have indeed misbehaved myself.'

Jane gave her a solemn look. 'The Lord Admiral has misbehaved himself too.'

Startled but still inclined to laugh, Elizabeth said: 'In what way, Jane?'

'He sometimes gets up too late to go to morning prayers himself.'

'A lazy fellow,' Elizabeth murmured, 'but a true Protestant for all that.'

Following Elizabeth's departure Seymour, often at court, tried to assess the full extent of his brother's hold on the Council. The Lord Protector had already made enemies among the landowners by moving to check the spread of enclosure of common land, and among the more fanatical Protestants through his policy of moderation in religious matters, but he still possessed more friends than enemies. In an attempt to undermine this advantage Seymour, by making use of his considerable wealth, soon had a number of influential if impoverished noblemen in his debt and ready, however unwillingly, to do his bidding. Nor did he neglect his nephew the King; he waited on him frequently, sought to be alone with him as often as possible, flattered him and secretly gave him the additional pocket money denied him by the Lord Protector.

'Uncle Thomas,' Edward said on one occasion, 'I miss the card games with my cousin Jane.'

'I see nothing against further little gambling adventures,' Seymour murmured.

Edward frowned over this. 'The Lord Protector has pronounced against them.'

'You would tell me,' Seymour chuckled, 'that that excellent Christian gentleman has come to regard gambling as a sin?'

Edward frowned again. 'I think his real purpose is to keep Jane away from court. Is it silly of me to think that, Uncle Thomas?'

'It is neither silly nor untrue,' Seymour said lightly. 'The Lord Protector is afraid of your Grace growing too fond of the Lady Jane.'

'I couldn't be any fonder or her than I am now, but I think I know what you mean. Still, if I really did want to marry Jane I should have to wait until I was old enough to please myself, eighteen in fact, and it would be too late.'

'Ah yes, the proposed foreign alliance. Would you dislike such an alliance, dear nephew?'

'It may be necessary,' Edward said indifferently.

The boy was ten now, Seymour reflected, but still far too young for emotional involvement.

'Your last birthday passed without a party,' he said, 'without our little King being allowed to please himself for one day in the year. But your ninth birthday was a merry affair. Do you remember the marriage game?'

'I remember that my father was very angry,' the boy said seriously, 'and pronounced against my marrying Jane. It would be undutiful of me to act against his wishes, even if I wanted to.'

'I shall tell your Grace something in absolute confidence,' Seymour ventured. 'King Henry had a change of heart during his last days but he died before he could make a royal pronouncement. He told the Queen Dowager that he would like to think of you and the Lady Jane living happily together as man and wife, if ever it were possible.'

'If ever it were possible,' Edward echoed gravely.

'That is, if the Lord Protector, or anybody else, should fail to bring about a foreign alliance.'

'Is the Lord Protector aware of this?'

'The Queen Dowager spoke to him,' Seymour lied glibly, 'but he said plainly that he did not believe her.'

'Thank you, Uncle Thomas,' Edward said, still gravely. 'I shall respect your confidence and store your words away in my mind for future reference. And—and I truly promise to find a right suitable husband for Jane, if I can't marry her myself.'

Progress, Seymour wondered, progress of a sort?

'The Lord Protector would marry her to his eldest son,' he said.

'Yes, he spoke of that,' Edward said, a surprising flash of anger in his eyes.

'The King's Grace does not approve?'

'I think,' said Edward, the anger in his voice now, 'that I would rather become a monk than remain a king.'

'A *Protestant* monk?' Seymour teased, puzzled as he was.

Edward smiled faintly. 'Kings are surrounded by intrigue. My Uncle Edward would marry Jane to his son because Jane *could* become Queen some day. If we all died first, I mean—myself and Mary and Elizabeth. I don't care for intrigue, Uncle Thomas.'

'And I, the King's favourite uncle,' Seymour avowed, 'don't care to think of the King, my favourite nephew, either dying or abdicating to enter a monastery.'

'I haven't been really ill for a long time,' Edward said. 'I grow stronger every day. I shan't die and I shan't abdicate. There are so many things I want to do when I have the power to please myself. I don't want to win wars and conquer other countries. I want to see the Protestant faith properly established and—and I want *all* my people to be properly educated.' And he added insistently: 'I shall live to be a very old man, Uncle Thomas.'

'Thus making sure that the Lady Jane never comes to the throne,' Seymour said lightly.

Edward smiled thoughtfully. 'She would make a very pretty Queen Consort.'

'And one of high intelligence.'

'For a girl she is very clever,' Edward said generously. 'I miss her because of that as well as because of the card games.'

'Am I to make a state issue of it?' Seymour asked spiritedly. 'Even at the risk of displeasing the Lord Protector?'

'The Lord Protector has already displeased me,' Edward said as haughtily as he could. 'It is my wish—it is *our* wish that the Lady Jane should be brought to court for a few days by the Queen Dowager.'

'Your Majesty's wish is law,' said a satisfied Thomas Seymour.

10

'You were not at divine service this morning, my lord,' Jane said accusingly.

Seymour looked at her obliquely. 'If that be a sin, sweet child, then I can but plead guilty.'

Jane found herself smiling on him fondly. There was always something very special in his sonorous voice when he addressed her as 'sweet child', something that warmed her heart and made her love him almost as much as she loved the Queen Dowager. Nevertheless she wanted to remind him that she would soon be eleven, sweet still, for sure, but no longer really a child.

'Have you a good excuse, Lord Seymour?' she asked in mock severity.

'A good excuse, my lady? Now let me give some little thought to that. Did I oversleep this morning? Possibly. Did I suffer a bout of forgetfulness? Possibly again. The plain truth of the matter is that my noble knees grow stiff and sore from kneeling day after day without respite. What of your own noble knees, dear Jane?'

'I use a softly padded hassock,' Jane said, trying not to giggle.

'Even so, would you not care, on occasion, to play truant with me?'

'My cousin the King would not approve. He is very strict. The Queen Dowager would not approve either.'

'The King is far away in London,' Seymour tempted, 'and the Queen Dowager is indisposed.'

'It would not be honest to deceive them because of that,' Jane said, unwillingly feeling disappointed in him.

'I stand corrected, Lady Jane,' Seymour sighed.

Jane inclined her head gravely. 'Will the Queen Dowager's baby be born very soon, my lord?'

'If a normal birth, very soon indeed.'

'I prayed for a boy this morning,' Jane said earnestly. 'I shall pray for a boy again this evening.'

'And I with you, sweet child,' Seymour volunteered.

'That makes me very happy.'

'You forgive me, for not being honest?'

'I could forgive you anything, my lord.'

Seymour had come upon Jane playing with her dog in the courtyard of the castle and had thought her a lonely figure, yet she was clearly self-possessed and not pining for the companionship of other children. Almost always in the company of adults, and immersed in her religious and secular studies, she was becoming more and more a little adult herself. Other children would surely bore her, with the exception of Edward, himself equally advanced for his years. All political scheming apart, Seymour concluded that the marriage he intended come what may to bring about would be eminently satisfactory to both parties.

'How long are we to remain at Sudeley?' Jane asked, as they strolled across the courtyard together, the dog Pointer bounding ahead of them.

'We shall return to Chelsea as soon as the Queen Dowager is well enough to travel,' Seymour replied.

Urged by Katherine he had retired discreetly to Sudeley a second time, and again as an alternative to being dispatched to Boulogne after an attempt, discovered by the Lord Protector, to form a secret party in the House of Lords. He had come close to over-reaching himself, Katherine claimed, but this he refused to believe. She had even feared that he would be thrown into the Tower, but here he was at liberty breathing in the country air of Sudeley, an innocent enough occupation to mask his plans for the raising of a private army.

'Pointer is pointing,' Jane said suddenly.

'So she is, but not at me.'

'She's pointing at Mrs Eleyn.'

Seymour glanced round the courtyard. 'There's neither sight nor sound of that excellent woman.'

'Pointer always points before she can see her.'

'An amazing animal.'

'It's because she can *smell* her.'

'It must be an unpleasant smell. It seems to be making the delightful bitch angry.'

'Mrs Eleyn,' said Jane, 'smells like a baked apple, and Pointer doesn't like baked apples.'

'Nor do I, Lady Jane. I was obliged to eat too many when I was a child. But here indeed comes Mrs Baked Apple herself.'

Jane's attendant was flushed and breathless. She all but fell when she curtsied, then with an air of belated dignity she made her not unexpected announcement.

'My lord, my lady, the Queen Dowager is in labour.'

From that moment on Jane had the feeling that she was in full control of the Queen Dowager's household, and since nobody, least of all the Lord Admiral, made any attempt to thrust her into the background the feeling took a firm grip upon her imagination. Placing herself in Katherine's anteroom at the head of the ladies and the maids of honour, she was the first to receive from Huyck, the physician, the news of the birth of a daughter and hastened, when Katherine's chaplain would have assumed the task, to convey this news to Seymour.

'A daughter?' he said broodingly. 'So much for your prayers this morning, sweet Jane.'

'It is God's will, my lord,' she said earnestly. 'You must go at once to the Queen Dowager and you must tell her that you are not angry with her.'

'The Lady Jane's will, this order of yours,' he said, a smile twitching at the corners of his mouth, 'or God's?'

'One must not laugh,' Jane said severely. 'It is God's will, but mine also.'

'I can but obey the combined force of His will and yours,' Seymour said, pretending to cringe in fear. 'As for anger, I could no more be angry with the Queen Dowager than with you.'

'Truly, my lord?'

'Truly, my lady.'

Satisfied, Jane began to skip ahead of him to Katherine's apartments, but after a moment realised that skipping was for young children only and slowed down to a dignified pace, as if taking part in a religious procession. Presently she was allowed to hold the baby in her arms for a few moments and later to carry it to the suite of rooms which had been prepared for it along the lines of a royal nursery. She wrote that night to her cousin the King, giving him a detailed account of the momentous event and assuring him that his stepmother had suffered no ill-effects from her ordeal.

'Here at Sudeley', she wrote importantly, 'we are all proud of her Grace, I, the King's loving and obedient subject, in particular.'

But within a few days Jane was writing again to say that a blanket of gloom had fallen upon Sudeley Castle, the Queen Dowager having awakened that morning in a feverish and delirious condition which was causing Dr Huyck much concern. He was very good at delivering babies, she wrote, but when one caught even an ordinary cold it had to run its course despite his ministrations. Begging Edward to send one of the court physicians to Sudeley, Jane dispatched her letter that night by special courier.

Katherine's condition deteriorated during the night and the delirium was more pronounced when Jane stole into the sickroom after her morning devotions in the chapel. Unnoticed in a room crowded with the Queen Dowager's ladies, no longer feeling that she was in control, Jane hid in a secluded corner and began silently to pray again for the Queen Dowager's speedy recovery. Seymour appeared presently and ordered the ladies to leave him in peace with his wife, but Jane, still unnoticed, remained hidden in her corner.

'Kate, dearest Kate . . .' Seymour said, bending over Katherine.

'Have I been delirious, Tom?' she asked in a low but normal voice.

'Strange ramblings from time to time, I must admit.'

'My mind is clear now, perfectly clear. I want you to make me a solemn promise, Tom. If the worst happens Jane must be sent back to her parents.'

Jane was horrified, but when Seymour responded with 'It shall be as you wish,' she suspected that he was only humouring the sick woman.

'A further promise, Tom . . .'

'And that?'

'I beg you to put all thought of court intrigue from your mind. It torments me to dwell upon what happened to the former Lord of Sudeley.'

'You have my solemn word,' Seymour said.

'Are you humouring me, Tom?'

'If so, in the belief that the worst will never happen.'

'To you, or to me?'

'To neither of us.'

'Dear Tom, your foolish optimism melts my heart. Please send my chaplain to me . . . No, no, not to pray and pray. I want to make my will. All that I possess is yours, and the fact must be clearly stated.'

'All—including the jewels given to you by King Henry?'

'Are they or are they not Crown jewels?' Katherine asked.

'They are yours, Kate, yours.'

'Do with them as you will,' she said wearily, and closed her eyes.

When Seymour had gone Jane crept to the bedside and, thinking Katherine to be sleeping, kissed her lightly on the brow. Katherine opened her eyes immediately.

'Jane, darling . . .'

'Please tell me you are feeling better,' Jane begged.

'Much better,' Katherine said, hopeful of deceiving the child if not herself.

'Then there's no fear of my being sent back to my parents.'

'*Fear*, child?'

'I should be miserable at Bradgate, and—and there would be nobody here to make sure of the Lord Admiral going to morning and evening prayers.'

'An important consideration,' Katherine said solemnly.

After a lengthy and tiring session with her chaplain Katherine's straying thoughts turned again to Jane and what best to do for her welfare. That the girl would be miserable at Bradgate, where she had known little or no real love, seemed obvious, but she must be protected at all costs from the fear-inducing schemes of the man who would use her, not for her own dear sake but his. With this in mind she sent at once for Jane's ever-trustworthy attendant.

'Mrs Eleyn,' Katherine said urgently, 'it is my wish that the Lady Jane should be returned to her parents at Bradgate.'

'Immediately, your Grace?'

Katherine shook her head on the pillow. 'I want her close to me till the end. Immediately afterwards, Mrs Eleyn.'

'A wise decision, if I may presume to say so,' Jane's attendant said gravely.

'You suspect my reason, Mrs Eleyn?'

'If it be the fear of the Lady Jane being implicated, young as she is, in court intrigue, then indeed I do suspect your Grace's reason.'

Katherine shuddered slightly. 'I emerged from the nightmare of delirium trembling for the dear child's life.'

'An unreasoning fear, your Grace,' Mrs Eleyn said soothingly.

'As all nightmare fears are,' Katherine tried to agree.

'I have already taken the liberty,' Mrs Eleyn said briskly, 'of sending word to Bradgate. The Marchioness of Dorset will presently be informed of the situation here at Sudeley and will take steps, I feel confident, to ensure the Lady Jane's safe return to her family.'

'For that I thank you,' Katherine said.

Jane returned to the sickroom after evening prayers and found it crowded again. She took shelter in her corner and listened wide-eyed to Katherine, who had fallen back into delirium. She cried out once that she had been badly handled, and when Seymour protested that he had done her no hurt she mistook him for his brother the Lord Protector. Badly handled, she said, because of the jewels. They were hers, she asserted, not the property of the Crown, and nothing would induce her to surrender them. 'You would take them from me, Somerset, and give them to your wife, and for that reason we have this attempt to poison me.' One of her ladies, having missed Katherine's reference to Lord Protector Somerset, uttered a moan and cried, 'The Queen Dowager has been poisoned!'

Exhausted, Jane fell asleep in her corner and discovered there by Seymour at midnight was carried by him to her bed. It was the same the next night and the next, and it was Seymour who came to her room to wake her on the eighth morning after the birth of Katherine's baby.

'The Lady Jane must be very brave,' he said, bending over her.

Not fully awake, she looked up at him uncertainly. 'My lord . . .'

'I find that I must leave at once for London,' he went on. 'In my absence the Lady Jane will assume the role of mistress of Sudeley Castle. It would seem that I am speaking deviously in order to deliver a shattering blow with the utmost gentleness.'

'The Queen Dowager is dead,' Jane said dully.

'She died during the night, an hour before the physician sent by the King made good his appearance. It is my bounden duty to convey the sad news to the King personally.'

'Yes,' Jane whispered, 'yes.'

'It is my wish, and surely the King's,' Seymour continued, 'that the Queen Dowager should be given a royal funeral. Should I be delayed in London the Lady Jane will naturally be the chief mourner. The fortitude thus expected of her will not be lacking.'

'The Lady Jane will be brave,' Jane said, and turned her face into the pillow.

'Weep, sweet Jane, and feel not ashamed of your tears,' Seymour said, touching her lightly on the shoulder. 'They will bring you some small relief.'

But Jane, accusing herself of hard-heartedness, found tears beyond her, even when she knelt at the side of the embalmed body which lay in state in the great hall of the castle. Numb with grief, she felt that she was no longer part of this world, and she had lost all sense of time when precise instructions from King Edward reached Sudeley. It was indeed to be a royal funeral and with the service conducted entirely in accordance with Protestant requirements.

The Marchioness of Dorset arrived from Bradgate on the eve of the funeral and was brought at once to Jane by Seymour's steward. She complained angrily about the state of the roads and told Jane that she had suffered a hundred miles of acute discomfort.

'But it is my duty to attend the Queen Dowager's funeral,' she said querulously, 'after which you shall return with me to Bradgate.'

'I am the mistress of Sudeley,' Jane said lifelessly. 'I must remain here until the Lord Admiral returns.'

Lady Dorset laughed mockingly. 'The *mistress*, dear God in heaven?'

'The Lord Admiral so appointed me.'

'Jokingly, I'll be bound.'

'He was fully serious, Madame.'

'Things have reached a sorry pass when Tom Seymour would flatter a girl not yet eleven,' Lady Dorset said scathingly. 'Do they all obey your orders here at Sudeley?'

'Without question,' Jane said, not having thought to issue orders.

'You have scarcely grown in stature since last I saw you,' Lady Dorset exploded, 'but you have grown mightily in arrogance.' She paused for a moment, remembering the truth of the girl's birth and the arrogance of her real father, then hurriedly she went on: 'We have the Lord Admiral to thank for it. I shall tell him so the moment he returns from London.'

'He has been detained there,' Jane said.

'By which you mean he will not be present at the funeral tomorrow?'

'It will break his heart, but he will not be present.'

'The insufferable Seymour was born without a heart to break.'

Anger began to stir in Jane's breast. 'That is a cruel thing to say, Madame.'

'Pray refrain from arguing with me,' Lady Dorset commanded. 'Since the Lord Admiral will not be present it is my duty to take his place as chief mourner. It is also my right, I being the late King Henry's niece.'

'*I* am to be chief mourner,' Jane said, surprising herself by her firmness.

'Incredible presumption,' Lady Dorset raged.

'It is the Lord Admiral's wish,' Jane said. 'And the King's wish too. He expressed it in the instructions he sent for the funeral.'

Lady Dorset hesitated, then shrugged. It would serve no good purpose to flout the boy King's wishes, even though she felt sure that they had been inspired by Seymour himself in a further attempt to ingratiate himself with Edward. She could imagine the touching little scene at Whitehall, Seymour saying, 'Your Grace's favourite stepmother, the Queen you loved so dearly, and your Grace's favourite cousin who loved her just as dearly.' *Cousin*, by God!

'Katherine Parr was your guardian, Jane,' she conceded. 'It is right and proper that you should be her chief mourner. I am prepared to take second place myself, in this instance.'

But her sense of humour being what it was she took second place in all instances, saying sarcastically when deferred to by anyone, 'You must ask the Lady Jane, Mistress of Sudeley Castle.' She perpetrated this whim so frequently that Jane, who had at first cringed inwardly, began to feel pity in her heart, as if she were the parent and Lady Dorset the child.

'Madame,' she said after supper that night, 'you have had a long and tiring day. Truly you should go early to bed.'

'As the Mistress of Sudeley wishes,' Lady Dorset said, in a final attempt at sarcasm, and went in seeming obedience to her room.

At two o'clock the following afternoon Seymour's steward, who had taken care of all arrangements, informed Jane that the funeral procession was assembling in the great hall and invited her to take up her position. Jane thanked him and attended by Mrs Eleyn followed him to the great hall. She was dressed entirely in black, as was Mrs Eleyn, who held her mistress's long velvet train. At a signal from the steward six hooded gentlemen raised the coffin on to their shoulders and a band of ushers, heralds and torch-bearers preceded them from the great hall in the direction of the chapel. A royal canopy, decorated with Tudor and Seymour arms, was raised above Jane, and under it she walked slowly behind the coffin. Very soon she became conscious of the weight of her velvet train which, to her, emphasised her slightness and smallness in this long procession of adult mourners. Lady Dorset, with Jane's train-bearer ignored, came next and knew a moment of compassion for Jane; a funeral procession was necessarily slow, but the poor child, hampered by her train, was obliged to take a guarded little skip from time to time to keep up with the pall-bearers. Following behind Lady Dorset, and walking in solemn dignified pairs, were the Queen Dowager's ladies, maids of honour and gentlewomen of lesser degree. All this death pageantry, Lady Dorset thought, for her late uncle's sixth wife and the Lord Admiral's first.

On entering the chapel and taking her place in a pew behind the diminutive chief mourner, she glanced about her in astonishment. The walls of Sudeley chapel had been covered in black cloth, while hanging in every direction were more heraldic banners than she had ever seen at even the most royal of royal funerals. It was perhaps fitting. They were all paying their last respects, not simply to the wife of the upstart Lord Admiral but to the woman who had been fortunate enough to save her head by outliving that monstrous Henry Tudor, the eighth of that name. In a sense it could be regarded, religiously, as a joyous celebration, an initial pronouncement of a faith which Henry himself would have rejected. The service was even more Protestant than Lady Dorset had expected. The lesson was read and the psalms were sung in *English*, and the Queen Dowager's almoner, once a Catholic priest, preached a sermon which was an entire rejection of the old religious ways. From time to time she nodded and smiled approvingly. By command of the young new Head of the Church, this service proclaimed the completion of the religious revolution. Protestantism rather than Henry VIII's English Catholicism now reigned supreme. So satisfied was she that she became over-generous when, as tradition demanded, the mourners gave alms to the poor of the district who stood in little expectant groups at the chapel door. Regretting it almost immediately afterwards she spoke harshly when, back in the castle, she found herself alone with Jane.

'We leave for Bradgate early tomorrow morning. Instruct Mrs Eleyn to make all the necessary preparations for you.'

'Mother, I *must* remain until the Lord Admiral returns.'

'In the hope, no doubt, that he might persuade me not to remove you.'

Jane hung her head. 'Yes.'

'It is not fitting, child, that you should remain in the household of a lecherous widower.'

'Madame . . .'

'No arrogant arguments, please. You are well aware that it was the Queen Dowager's wish, her *dying* wish, that I should remove you.'

Defeated, Jane looked at her mother stonily. 'I shall take Pointer with me.'

'Pointer? Oh yes, your dog, but there are dogs aplenty at Bradgate.'

'Pointer is a special dog. She—she is my only friend, now.'

But there was the Lord Admiral, Jane thought, while her mother looked at her in disgust, and there was her cousin the King too, but nobody on earth could ever take the place of

Katherine Parr. She fought back the tears that welled up in her eyes; not having been able to weep before, it would be humiliating to do so now in front of her mother.

'It has just occurred to me,' Lady Dorset said, 'that you made your first official public appearance today. On the whole you acquitted yourself well. I am inclined to feel proud of you. I can only hope that the nature of it was not an evil omen.'

II

'AND what, Uncle Thomas,' the young King asked while taking supper alone and informally at Whitehall with the Lord Admiral, 'is to happen to the Lady Jane?'

'I have received word from Sudeley,' Seymour replied, 'that she has been removed by her mother to Bradgate.' He paused for a moment, then confident that he had in his nephew a sympathetic ally went on sadly: 'It is a sorry blow to me, I having grown to love the child so dearly.'

'Jane will not be as happy at Bradgate as she was at Sudeley,' Edward said, unintentionally helpful.

'That is a concern uppermost in my mind,' Seymour sighed.

'Had you thought to keep her with you?' Edward asked, frowning slightly.

'Indeed I had, and indeed in accordance with the Queen Dowager's dying wish.'

Frowning again, the boy said gruffly: 'It is scarcely right and proper that my cousin should remain unchaperoned in your household.'

Taken aback as he was, Seymour said quickly : 'I see nothing against my retaining for her benefit my late wife's maids of honour.'

'Even so, Uncle, is any one of them old enough for the responsibility?'

With impatience all but getting the better of him, Seymour said resourcefully: 'Would your Grace approve if I were to bring my aged mother out of retirement and place her at the head of my household? Or more to the point, at the head of the household within the household, that of the Lady Jane?'

Edward's face cleared at once. 'That would be a very good solution.'

Only partly satisfied, Seymour said: 'There remains a stumbling block, the Marchioness of Dorset. I must tell you that she was much against the Lady Jane remaining with the Queen Dowager after your father's death.'

'Lady Dorset is an arrogant woman,' Edward said. 'I shall write to her about the Lady Jane's future welfare and you, Uncle, shall send the letter to Bradgate for me.'

'Better still,' Seymour decided, 'I shall play the royal messenger and deliver it personally to Lady Dorset.'

He returned to his London house in Seymour Place that night with the letter in his possession, and curious as he was about the contents refrained from breaking the royal seal. Awaiting him was a courier with a message from his steward. Agents sent to Sudeley by the Lord Protector and supported by the written authority of the Privy Council had seized and carried away the controversial jewels. Late as the hour was, Seymour returned in a temper to Whitehall, knowing his brother to be in residence there, and caused that gentleman to be roused from his sleep.

'I still insist that they are Crown jewels,' Lord Protector Somerset said, equally angry himself.

'Had I been at Sudeley,' Seymour raged, 'they would never have been surrendered.'

'Your retention of them would have meant . . .'

'A pitched battle,' Seymour interrupted, 'between my men and yours.'

'You are a child in the nursery playing imaginary games of violence,' Somerset said wearily. 'Had you retained the jewels you could well have faced a charge of theft. And, mark you well, a most serious charge, the theft of royal property.'

'I suspect you of regretting my absence from Sudeley,' Seymour sneered.

'Why so that?'

'You were thus deprived of placing out of harm's way a dangerous rival.'

'You speak rashly, as usual. Boastfully, too. Go home, Tom. Leave me in peace and remain, if you can, in peace yourself. It is a petty matter, pettily exaggerated on your part.'

Seymour brooded over this on his way back to Seymour Place. Petty in his brother Edward's opinion but not in his own; the jewels could have been broken up and sold at great profit in France, thus providing him with additional money for the coming rebellion against the authority of the Lord Protector, a rebellion that had now become a fanatical obsession. Still, there were other ways of raising money and the fortune willed to him by Katherine would soon be at his disposal. He slept well that night, being able to do so under all circumstances, woke refreshed the next morning and spent a hectic day discussing tentative plans with the more intimate and trustworthy of his allies, chief of whom was Sir William Sharington, Master of the Mint. Two days later he started out at dawn for Bradgate attended by a detachment of private guards and riding hard reached the Dorset estate in the early afternoon. Greeted by Adrian Stokes, the Dorsets' steward, he learnt that the Marquess and Marchioness were visiting Leicester but that the Lady Jane, being somewhat sickly, had remained at home.

'Is she confined to her chamber?' Seymour asked.

'Yes, my lord, with Mrs Eleyn in attendance.'

'Pray inform Mrs Eleyn of my arrival.'

But it was Jane herself who came to greet him, a woebegone figure with an air of solitariness about her.

'Sickly, truly sickly?' Seymour asked shrewdly.

'I am accused of sulkiness rather than sickliness,' she said, smiling faintly.

'And the truth of the matter?'

'Sulkiness, my lord,' Jane admitted.

'Is it possible, sweet Jane, that you are pining for Sudeley?'

She looked at him gravely and said in a low, almost toneless voice: 'I am conscious in my heart of your lordship's many kindnesses and great goodness. They were of a nature equal to those of the Queen Dowager. In my loneliness at Bradgate I have no means of recompense.'

Touched, Seymour said cheerily: 'Take heart, Jane. It is the King's wish that your parents should return you to my care, whether I reside at Sudeley, London or even the Scilly Isles.'

'The Scilly Isles?' Jane asked in astonishment.

'I have bought them with, let me whisper in confidence, piratical thoughts in mind.'

'*Piratical?*' Jane gasped.

'A snug and safe retreat for a lord admiral turned pirate. Does the Lady Jane fancy the role of a pirate queen?'

'You are joking, my lord,' Jane laughed, and more cheerful now said: 'In my parents' absence I shall give immediate instructions for the Lord Admiral's comfortable accommodation here at Bradgate.'

Jane's parents, with her two younger sisters and the usual large party of attendants, returned from Leicester in time for supper. Lord Dorset greeted Seymour affably enough, but Lady Dorset, suspecting the reason for his visit, received him coldly. During supper, with Jane placed beyond earshot with her sisters at a separate table, Seymour presented the King's letter. Lady Dorset read it in silence, then she passed it to her husband, her manner suggesting, Seymour thought, that in so confiding in him she was conferring upon him a signal honour.

'A mere request,' Dorset said, frowning over it, 'not what might be regared as a royal command.'

'To me,' Seymour said smoothly, 'a royal request and a royal command are one and the same thing.'

'It would, perhaps, be unwise to take the risk of offending the King,' Dorset mused. 'And his interest is, to say the least, promising.'

'By which you mean . . . ?' Lady Dorset questioned harshly.

Dorset gave her an oblique look and turned to Seymour. 'Have you made any progress in persuading the King to look upon Jane as his future wife?'

'To a certain extent, yes.'

'The Lord Protector would never permit it,' Lady Dorset said flatly.

'My brother, I do assure you,' Seymour told her, 'will be dealt with adequately when the time is ripe. My aim, and I intend to achieve it, is to wrest from him the guardianship of the King. And, I scarcely need add, with the King's own approval. When all is said and done I am, as all people know, the King's favourite uncle.'

Disturbed as she was by the ring of conviction in his voice, Lady Dorset said with full Tudor haughtiness: 'Until the time is ripe, my lord, and I doubt if it ever will be, Jane remains at home.'

'To sulk, I fear, and become unmanageable,' Dorset sighed.

'So speaks the master of the house,' Seymour said brightly.

'This,' Lady Dorset cried, 'is a fruitless argument. I am prepared to yield only if the Lord Protector is seen to be in full agreement. He would marry Jane, please remember, to his eldest son.'

'With or without her father's consent?' Seymour asked.

'With it, naturally,' she asserted.

'You feel inclined, under your wife's direction, to grant it?' Seymour asked Lord Dorset.

'It is a matter which calls for careful thought,' Dorset replied uneasily.

'You should grow a beard,' Seymour said.

Dorset fingered his smooth plump chin. 'A *beard*, Seymour?'

'Also a moustache,' Seymour added, staring at Dorset's indeterminate upper lip. 'They might possibly give you the appearance of firmness and put some manly heart into you. However, I see that I must produce from my sleeve a master card, reluctant as I am, or was, to play it.'

'I, too, possess a master card,' Lady Dorset said impulsively.

'Indeed, my lady?' Seymour asked in surprise.

But quickly she regretted her words. She would only reveal the truth of the King's birth, and Jane's, if Seymour's marriage plans were seen to be successful.

'Come,' Seymour said, 'you hold me in fearful suspense.'

'You clearly plan rebellion,' she said quickly. 'What if I were to go to the Lord Protector and tell him as much?'

'My poor good woman,' Seymour laughed, 'my brother has already taken my measure, yet he, like you, has only suspicion to guide him. As for my own master card, are you aware that I have lent much money to your impoverished husband? I see that you are not. Would you have me foreclose, or would you rather, in your own need, have me make a further substantial loan?'

'In my *own* need?' Lady Dorset asked huffily.

'You are able, then, to liquidate the debt yourself?'

Lady Dorset rose shakily from the table. 'You would have me sell Lady Jane, but expect no pity from me when the Lord Protector signs your death warrant.'

'Fratricide is not in my brother's nature,' Seymour said, and laughing confidently rose from the table himself and strode to Jane's. 'Sweet Jane,' he whispered, after kissing her hand, 'the pirate captain has boarded the galleon named Bradgate with the greatest of ease and is ready and able to carry you off.'

Jane blushed with pleasure but said gravely: 'To the Scilly Isles, my lord?'

'No, my lady. To Sudeley for a few days, then to London to see the King.'

12

'DEATH by boiling,' Edward said, 'is no longer a punishment for high treason or any other sort of crime.'

'How terrible to be boiled to death!' Jane exclaimed.

'That is what I thought myself. I said as much when I was allowed to attend a council meeting. The Lords of the Council debated my objection and came to a unanimous agreement. I signed the recision order this morning. It was a penalty brought in by my father but I thought, for once, to act against his will. I discussed it first with my godfather, Archbishop Cranmer. We prayed together and he said that God had pronounced that there should be no more boilings.'

'I shouldn't like to see anyone boiled to death,' said Jane. 'Not even that terrible enemy, Bishop Gardiner.'

'He,' said Edward, 'has been arrested and lodged in the Tower, never to be released.'

'I'm so glad,' said Jane.

King Edward and the Lady Jane were playing cards, sipping ale and eating tansy cakes, and now and again Edward tossed a tansy cake to Jane's dog, that animal having been brought to court in defiance of old Lady Seymour's ruling. Thinking of this now Jane heaved a sigh. The Lord Admiral's mother, who was, of course, the Lord Protector's mother also, was almost always an amiable and respectful chaperon, but it did seem ridiculous that a chaperon should be considered necessary. Still, Jane decided, one should try to feel philosophical about it; it was Edward's wish, and what could one do but submit with a proper grace to the lightest wish of the King of England?

'Tansy cakes are not very good for Pointer, your Grace,' she said, without intending to sound complaining. 'They will make her fat, and fat dogs are lazy dogs.'

'She relishes them, Lady Jane,' Edward said indulgently. 'You must permit me to spoil her whenever you bring her to court.'

Jane played another disastrous card and looked at him slyly. 'Should you not say "You must permit *us* to spoil her"?'

Still feeling indulgent Edward laughed ruefully. 'I can't use and don't want to use the royal plural *all* the time. It would be silly and pompous, 'specially on informal occasions. I was feeling above myself when I insisted on it just after I became King.' He frowned momentarily. 'Perhaps I mean, dear Jane, that I was feeling uncertain of myself. But I'm older now and, well, more *sensible*.'

'Not a great *deal* older,' Jane suggested.

'*Considerably* older,' he stressed, giving her a mock-haughty look. 'There's a big difference between being not quite eleven, as I was a month ago, and being rather more than eleven now. Don't you agree?'

'Yes,' she said feelingly. 'You are in your twelfth year, and so am I. It is more important to put it that way, Cousin Edward.'

'It is, for a *king*,' he agreed just as feelingly, and playing his final card said, 'Ha . . . !'

'You have won again, Edward. You almost always do.'

'Do you mind very much, Jane?'

'No,' she said, after a moment's consideration. 'You see, I almost always win when I play cards with old Lady Seymour, and she is said to be a very shrewd card-player.'

'What of Uncle Thomas?'

'I think he *lets* me win.'

'Are you truly happy to be in his care again?'

'Truly, but it does make me feel guilty at times.'

'Guilty? Why that, Jane?'

'It was the Queen Dowager's wish that I should be returned to my parents after her death.'

Edward looked at Jane in surprise. Uncle Thomas had claimed the very reverse. He remembered his exact words. He had thought to keep Jane with him 'in accordance with the Queen Dowager's dying wish'. Why had Uncle Thomas lied? Probably because he had grown to love Jane dearly, but it was wrong to lie, especially for selfish reasons. And why, for that matter, had the Queen Dowager wanted Jane to return to her parents while knowing, as she must have known, that she would not be very happy with them? An indefinable uneasiness began to trouble the boy. Grappling with it, he remembered a warning issued by the Lord Protector: 'Beware of the hidden duplicity of the Lord Admiral.' It had angered Edward at the time, yet he knew his elder uncle, strict as he was, miserly as he was when it came to royal pocket money, to be a just and fair-minded man.

'Jane, are you quite sure that the Queen Dowager wanted you to be returned to your parents?'

'Quite sure, Edward.'

'Did she speak to you about it?'

'No, to the Lord Admiral,' Jane replied, regretting that she had made any reference to it. 'I was in the room but unseen.'

'Did she give any reason for it?'

'No, Edward.'

'Was she delirious?'

'I must speak the exact truth,' Jane sighed. 'She was not delirious. Before, and later, but not then.'

'Did Uncle Thomas promise to carry out her wish?'

'Yes, but I think he was only humouring her.'

'*Dishonestly*, Jane.'

'Perhaps he truly believed her to be delirious,' Jane suggested hopefully.

'Perhaps,' Edward agreed, but the uneasiness was still upon him. 'Did the Queen Dowager speak of her wish to anybody else?'

'To Mrs Eleyn, or so my mother told me.'

'Is Mrs Eleyn in attendance today?'

Jane nodded unwillingly. 'She is waiting in the anteroom. Must you really question her, Edward?'

'You sound afraid of my doing so.'

'I'm only afraid of something terrible happening to the Lord Admiral.'

'That,' said Edward, trying to feel wise and elderly, 'is what we must do our best to prevent. Please bring Mrs Eleyn to me, Jane.'

But when Mrs Eleyn entered, curtsied the required three times and knelt he found himself so much at a loss for words that he had difficulty in commanding her to rise. It was one thing to talk freely with Jane, to question her, quite another to confront her attendant, obsequious as she was, with what was after all a delicate and intimate family matter. He remembered that he was in his twelfth year, that he was the woman's sovereign lord and King and that it was his duty to discover the exact truth.

'Madame,' he said at length, 'it is our command that you should tell us all you know of the Queen Dowager's dying wishes.'

'In respect of the Lady Jane?' Mrs Eleyn asked shrewdly.

'That in particular,' Edward said, feeling grateful that she should prove so helpful. 'Be pleased to speak freely.'

'Her late Majesty did me the honour of confiding in me, your Grace,' Mrs Eleyn said importantly. 'It was her wish that the Lady Jane should be returned to her parents immediately after her death.'

Edward inclined his head. 'It would not have been right and proper for the Lady Jane to remain unchaperoned in the Lord Admiral's household.'

Sensing uncertainty in the boy's voice, and more concerned than ever for Jane's welfare, Mrs Eleyn said quickly: 'That was not the Queen Dowager's reason, your Grace. If I may make so bold as to say so, the Queen Dowager was afraid of the Lady Jane being implicated in court intrigue.'

'Court intrigue?' Edward echoed, his voice rising shrilly. 'The Lady Jane is a mere child.'

Jane looked at him indignantly. She was older than Edward by seven days; he had no right to refer to her so condescendingly. But quickly she repressed the urge to reproach him. It would very nearly be an act of treason in the presence of a lowly attendant, and she had promised at their first meeting not to boss him because of her older status.

'The Queen Dowager,' Mrs Eleyn said, 'was referring to the aims and ambitions of the Lord Admiral.'

Edward smiled, then laughed quite merrily. 'You may withdraw, Mrs Eleyn.'

Mrs Eleyn curtsied and withdrew with careful backward steps.

'Why did you laugh, Edward?' Jane asked crossly. 'Or is it impertinent of a mere child to ask?'

'It would be impertinent, even in a Queen Consort,' he chuckled.

'What do you mean by that, Edward?'

'I feel sure that Uncle Thomas wants to make you my Queen Consort.'

'And that is a *laughing* matter!'

'No, Jane, of course it isn't. I was laughing because I could see nothing sinister in such an aim.' Edward paused, then went on soberly: 'Perhaps there is, if the Queen Dowager was so concerned about it. Oh dear, my mind wasn't very clear or I wouldn't have laughed at all. It would mean the Lord Admiral setting himself up in opposition to the Lord Protector. Court intrigue, you see. I don't like it, Jane.'

'Nor do I,' said Jane. 'It really could be dangerous for the Lord Admiral.'

Edward looked at her slightly askance. 'There's something else I don't like. I don't like to think of you being used for anybody else's sake but your own.'

'The Lord Admiral's sake—is that what you mean, Edward?'

Hidden duplicity, Edward thought, and said unhappily: 'He would have much power at court if he succeeded in making you my wife. He being your guardian, I mean. It seems to me that that was why he took you back from your parents.'

'No,' Jane said loyally. 'He did it because he loves me so much and wants me to be happy.'

'You have a very nice nature, Jane,' Edward said generously. 'I hope you are right.'

'I know I am,' Jane said urgently.

'I wonder,' Edward mused half-teasingly, 'if Uncle Thomas has a different aim in mind. I wonder if he is waiting for you to grow up and then marry you himself.'

'Edward!' Jane gasped, and found herself blushing.

'What fun to think that I may have to give my Cousin Jane to my Uncle Thomas and make her my aunt,' Edward chuckled.

Not amused but remembering her place, Jane said formally: 'Do I have the King's permission to withdraw?'

'Surely.'

Jane rose, curtsied and walked with exaggerated dignity to the door. Turning she called: 'Pointer! Come!' But the dog, always so obedient, remained unresponsive at Edward's feet. 'Pointer!' she repeated sharply, upon which the dog, by no means a lap-dog, scrambled on to Edward's lap.

'She has taken a fancy to me,' Edward said happily.

'To the tansy cakes, more than likely.'

'It seems like love to me,' Edward said, 'but try again.'

'Pointer!' Jane commanded shrilly.

'Hopeless,' said Edward, with the dog snuggling closer.

'The King's Grace may keep her,' Jane said, trying not to sound hurt. 'She will surely stand guard and protect him if protection is ever necessary.'

'Is it a very great sacrifice?' Edward asked, eyeing her anxiously.

'It would have been, once. I thought her my only friend after the Queen Dowager died, but of course there was the Lord Admiral and—well . . .'

'And?' Edward insisted.

'My cousin the King,' Jane gasped, and fled.

Mrs Eleyn found her young mistress unusually silent during their coach ride back to Seymour Place. Not that Jane was ever a chatterbox, but there was a brooding quality about this particular silence that caused Mrs Eleyn to apologise hurriedly for having answered the King's questions in words which might have been hurtful to Jane.

'You were forced to speak up,' the girl said stiffly.

'And truthfully, my lady, without any exaggeration.'

'The Queen Dowager must have been delirious when she confided in you,' Jane said, not really wanting to continue the conversation.

'No, my lady, I swear it.'

'The Lord Admiral can do me no harm.'

'He could, perhaps, do himself a great deal of harm.'

'Then we must keep watch and try to protect him,' Jane said vaguely, her mind still on Pointer's desertion.

'My sole concern is the Lady Jane's welfare,' Mrs Eleyn avowed warmly.

'For that I thank you,' Jane responded politely.

On reaching Seymour Place she learnt that the Lord Admiral was closeted in his inner private chamber, but knowing herself to be a privileged person she sought him out immediately, intent on telling him about her loss. With him, and somewhat startled by her precipitous entry, was Thomas Wriothesley, a man she still regarded with childish loathing. Quickly recovering his aplomb, he rose and bowed, bade Seymour *au revoir* and departed jauntily.

'The Lady Jane appears to be in some distress,' Seymour said, eyeing her curiously.

Pointer momentarily forgotten, Jane said urgently: 'Sir Thomas Wriothesley is a dangerous man, my lord.'

'Let us give him his proper title,' Seymour said lightly. 'He is the newly created Earl of Southampton. But . . . *dangerous*, dear Jane?'

'He was the Queen Dowager's enemy. He tried to ruin her before King Henry died.'

'Only to be foiled,' Seymour chuckled, 'by an astute little person by the name of Jane Grey.'

'I shall foil him again,' Jane asserted, 'if he tries to ruin the Lord Admiral.'

'Your loyalty and concern touch me deeply,' Seymour said softly, 'but we have nothing to fear from the former Lord Chancellor. An enemy once, that I agree, but now a firm friend.' He paused, looking at Jane speculatively. 'You study history among many other subjects, but what do you know of history in the making?'

'Very little,' Jane admitted.

'You are old enough, sweet Jane,' he went on, his voice at its most sonorous, 'to be made acquainted with the various rulings of the Privy Council. Indeed, your high position in the land calls for it. You may yet become Queen, either in your own right or through marriage.'

'Court intrigue frightens me,' Jane said.

'The future Queen of England may safely leave court intrigue and all its fascinating dangers to the Lord Admiral.'

'*Safely?*' Jane faltered.

'Most surely, if one thrives, as I do, on fascinating dangers.'

'What,' she asked flatly, 'has turned the Queen Dowager's enemy into a friend?'

'The fact, for one thing, that the Lord Protector has made an enemy of him.'

Jane looked at Seymour in despair. 'By—by creating him an earl?'

'The earldom came first, and flatteringly. It was followed swiftly by the Lord Protector forcing him to surrender his seals of office. He had spoken up rashly against the establishment of the Protectorate. However, he is still a member of the Council and may yet prove useful to us.'

'*Us*, my lord?'

'The King, the Lady Jane and the Lord Admiral. On the other hand he doubtless thinks that I may yet prove useful to him. Privately I am inclined to believe that in spite of his opposition to the Protectorate he would like to be Lord Protector himself.'

'And you, my Lord Admiral?' Jane asked, dwelling fearfully on Seymour's undoubted opposition to his brother.

'It was disappointing that King Henry named my brother instead of me,' Seymour said candidly. 'But enough of state affairs and court intrigue. The Lady Elizabeth has issued an invitation. The Lady Jane is to spend a few days with her at Cheshunt.'

'That will be nice,' Jane said apathetically.

'What, the invitation is not to your liking?'

'I am very fond of my cousin Elizabeth,' Jane said, a sob in her voice, 'but her dog would remind me too much of Pointer.'

'My dear Jane, you will surely take Pointer with you to Cheshunt.'

'I can't, my lord. She fell in love with the King this afternoon and refused to leave him.'

'In short,' said the ever-resourceful Seymour, 'she pointed on your behalf in the right direction.'

Jane smiled bleakly. 'When am I to leave for Cheshunt?'

'Tomorrow morning. I shall write presently to the Lady Elizabeth and entrust you with my letter. Give it into her keeping as unobtrusively as possible.'

'Do you mean *secretly*, my lord?'

Seymour eyed Jane obliquely. 'I have in mind for your cousin a marriage that would not be to the Lord Protector's liking, whatever her own attitude might be. There may well be spies in her household. Secretly it is, then, for her sake as well as mine.'

Chaperoned by old Lady Seymour, attended by Mrs Eleyn and travelling under the protection of a detachment of Seymour's personal guards, Jane reached Cheshunt Manor with Seymour's letter secreted between the pages of Katherine Parr's book, *The Lamentations of a Sinner*, which Seymour had recently caused to be published. She presented the book the moment she was alone with Elizabeth and feeling guiltily cunning said that she had marked a special passage with an equally special bookmark.

'It is a present from the Lord Admiral,' she added.

'The book or the bookmark?'

'Both,' Jane said faintly.

Elizabeth opened and read Seymour's letter in Jane's presence and to Jane's astonishment fell to giggling like a child, she a mature young woman of fifteen.

'You may tell the Lord Admiral,' she said, 'that the husband he would choose for me may yet meet with my own approval.'

There was a skittishness in her cousin's demeanour that aroused in Jane an uneasy suspicion, a suspicion that lingered in her mind during her entire stay at Cheshunt. Whatever the subject of conversation might be Elizabeth succeeded in turning it, always neatly, to the affairs of the Lord Admiral, the most handsome man in England, she asserted, and surely, now that he was a widower, the most eligible. She seemed to Jane to be encouraged in this by her governess, Mrs Ashley, and encouraged on one occasion quite suggestively. She and Elizabeth were playing cards with Mrs Ashley who, to wind up the evening, made a pretence of telling fortunes. Jane's she said, was too difficult to read in the cards but Elizabeth's, the latter having drawn the King of Hearts, was crystal clear.

'A handsome husband, soon to make his appearance,' Mrs Ashley predicted.

'And whom does this particular King of Hearts resemble?' Elizabeth asked coquettishly.

'Gifted as I am with second sight,' Mrs Ashley said, 'I can but see in this pretty picture not a king but a certain dashing admiral.'

Jane felt like bursting into tears. Edward had been joking when he had suggested that the Lord Admiral was waiting for her to grow up, but she had been inclined to take him seriously and indulge in romantic dreams. She had, of course, been stupid, she reprimanded herself, and if, as seemed clear now, Elizabeth wanted the Lord Admiral and he wanted her, she must out of loyalty wish them well.

'Draw another card, Jane,' Elizabeth invited. 'Perhaps your future is not as difficult to read as Mrs Ashley thinks.'

Jane drew a card and without looking at it passed it to Elizabeth's governess.

'The immediate future is clear enough,' Mrs Ashley said, after making a pretence of deep thought. 'I see the Lady Jane in the guise of a royal messenger.'

'And that she is,' Elizabeth said, giving Jane a significant smile.

'And that I am,' Jane agreed, remembering Elizabeth's message to the Lord Admiral.

'The bearer of a present also,' Elizabeth added.

'Ah yes,' said Mrs Ashley, 'I had quite forgotten the shirt which your Highness has embroidered so skilfully and with such loving care.'

Jane looked down carefully at her hands. 'The Lord Admiral will be flattered.'

'Silly child,' Elizabeth laughed. 'The shirt is for my brother the King.'

'I shall deliver it with great pleasure,' Jane said, feeling ridiculously relieved.

On reaching Seymour Place the next afternoon she found the Seymour household in considerable confusion. Servants were wringing their hands and some of them were in tears. Seymour's steward appeared and while glancing in concern at Jane addressed himself to old Lady Seymour.

'Madame,' he said gravely, 'the Lord Admiral was arrested not an hour ago and carried away to the Tower.'

13

Followed by Mrs Eleyn, Jane entered the King's inner chamber at Whitehall and found the Lord Protector with Edward. After curtsying and kneeling they rose when bidden to do so and waited anxiously. Courteously the Lord Protector offered Jane a chair, leaving Mrs Elcyn to place herself dutifully behind it. During the silence that followed Jane's anxiety grew apace. It was a week since the Lord Admiral's arrest and as yet she had been given no reason for it. Twice she had attempted to see Edward privately but each time she had been turned away by his tutor, Sir John Cheke, even though accompanied by old Lady Seymour. And now had come this imperative summons to Whitehall, issued she could but think by the Lord Protector, a summons demanding the presence also of Mrs Eleyn. Anxious as she was, Jane looked at Edward with a lively curiosity, and then at Pointer who was lying at his feet and taking not the slightest notice of her.

Edward cleared his throat and said rather hurriedly: 'The Lord Protector wishes to ask the Lady Jane and her attendant some questions concerning the Queen Dowager's illness.' He glanced at his Uncle Edward and added stiffly: 'We, the King, have not the right to interfere in Council matters but we have insisted on the questioning taking place in our presence. A Council matter but in part a family matter also.'

'I concede the point, your Grace,' Somerset said equably.

Edward inclined his head. 'Please be as brief as you can.'

Somerset studied Jane carefully for several moments, noting that her resemblance to the late King Henry, supposedly her great-uncle, was just as marked as ever. He had never regretted the deception, the successful replacement of Jane with Edward, for had it not been practised, had Jane been acknowledged as Henry's third daughter, the first daughter, Catholic Mary, would be on the throne today. Or would she? There could have been a rising against her, even bloody civil war. At least there was peace in the Kingdom, and that peace he intended to preserve, whatever his brother Thomas might be planning.

'Lady Jane,' he said, addressing the girl who in reality was his niece, and speaking gently, 'it will doubtless pain you to speak of the Queen Dowager's death, but speak of it we must. You were present not long before the end. So was Mrs Eleyn, so were the Queen Dowager's ladies and other members of the household at Sudeley. Certain charges have been made. It is claimed that the Queen Dowager said, "I have been badly handled." Is that correct?'

'I—I think so, my lord,' Jane said, straining to remember the details of the scene she had witnessed.

'Mrs Eleyn?'

'Those were the Queen Dowager's exact words, my lord.'

Somerset turned to Jane again. 'Did the Queen Dowager make any reference at that time to the Lady Elizabeth?'

'No, my lord.'

'Mrs Eleyn?'

'I have no recollection of any such reference, my lord.'

'It is inferred,' Somerset said, 'that she believed herself to be badly handled in respect of the Lady Elizabeth. Have you any reason to think so yourself, Mrs Eleyn?' Mrs Eleyn, looking confused, remained silent. 'Are you aware,' Somerset pressed, 'of the reason for the Lady Elizabeth's removal to Cheshunt?'

With Mrs Eleyn looking more confused than ever, Jane said: 'The Lady Elizabeth misbehaved herself.'

'In what manner, Lady Jane?'

'She was often absent from morning prayers.'

'Most remiss of her,' Somerset said solemnly, and turning again to Mrs Eleyn prompted insistently: *'Mrs Eleyn?'*

Casting upon Jane an apologetic look, Mrs Eleyn said in a low voice: 'The Lady Elizabeth was absent from morning prayers in order to romp in a state of undress with the Lord Admiral.'

'You witnessed such rompings, Mrs Eleyn?'

'Indeed I did, my lord, and so, on one occasion, did the Queen Dowager. If I may be forgiven for saying so, the Lady Elizabeth is, or was, a shameless hussy. For that reason she was removed from Sudeley.'

'Badly handled, then,' Somerset sighed, 'by both the Lady Elizabeth and the Lord Admiral.'

Jane glanced appealingly at Edward and, catching her eye, he quickly voiced her own thoughts. 'It was shocking behaviour but not a crime against the state. Surely the Lord Admiral should not have been arrested because of it.'

'I fear I must tell you,' Somerset said, 'that the Lord Admiral has been accused of bringing about the Queen Dowager's death by the administration of poison.'

'An infamous charge,' Edward said hotly.

Infamous, Somerset thought, but the truth was often infamous. His over-ambitious brother had paid court to Elizabeth before marrying the Queen Dowager, a fact only recently made known to him. The early-morning rompings had followed and now, with the Queen Dowager dead, he was, as Somerset knew from his spies at Cheshunt, paying court to Elizabeth again.

'The charge has been made, your Grace,' Somerset said, 'and must be investigated. It is claimed that the Queen Dowager herself spoke of poison after saying that she had been badly handled.' He glanced momentarily at Jane, then addressed himself to her attendant. 'Can you substantiate this claim, Mrs Eleyn?'

Mrs Eleyn remembered the scene clearly but fearful of harming herself by describing something that would be offensive to the Lord Protector she said hesitantly: 'I believe poison was mentioned by the Queen Dowager.'

'Can you remember her exact words?'

'I am trying to, my lord.'

Jane had remembered the scene clearly now and sensed Mrs Eleyn's reason for hesitancy. A poor miserable creature, she thought pityingly, but she herself, the King's cousin and third in the line of succession, was not afraid to speak up boldly and truthfully.

'Sir,' she said, looking steadily at Somerset, 'the Queen Dowager was delirious. It was clear to everybody. It must have been clear to the wicked person who has made this infamous charge. The Queen Dowager said that she had been badly handled. The Lord Admiral was very distressed and said he had done her no hurt.'

'Not even in conjunction with the Lady Elizabeth?' Somerset asked dryly.

Riled by his tone, Jane said: 'She repeated that she had been badly handled because of the jewels, and she mistook the Lord Admiral for you, the Lord Protector, and she said: "You would take them from me, Somerset, and give them to your wife, and for that reason we have this attempt to poison me." '

'Preposterous!' Somerset exclaimed, though he knew that his wife had coveted the jewels and had failed to hide the fact from the Queen Dowager. He glanced at Mrs Eleyn. 'Madame, does the Lady Jane's memory serve her accurately?'

'I believe so, my lord, but the Queen Dowager was indeed delirious.'

Edward sprang to his feet and addressed his uncle mockingly. 'It was you, my Lord Protector, not the Lord Admiral, whom the Queen Dowager accused of attempting to poison her.'

'The poor woman was delirious, your Grace.'

'That we concede,' Edward said condescendingly, 'and we trust that the Lords of the Council will act wisely and release the Lord Admiral with all speed from the Tower.'

Somerset bowed. 'Your Grace's words shall be made known to them at the next meeting of the Council.'

'I beg you,' Edward said, his manner gracious now, 'to call them together immediately.'

Somerset bowed again. 'It shall be as your Grace wishes.'

Nevertheless it was ten days before the Lord Admiral returned, a free man, to Seymour Place. Jane hastened to pay her respects the moment she heard of his arrival and found him flushed with anger. He had gone straight from the Tower to Whitehall to see the King, he told Jane, but on the Lord Protector's orders had been refused admission to Edward's private apartments. He had tried then to gain entry through the privy garden outside Edward's bedchamber, only to find his way blocked by guards.

'You see how necessary it is for me to gain control of the Council,' he said wildly.

It was frightening, Jane thought, to hear him talk like that and while doing so stare beyond her as if unaware either of her presence or identity. Presently, after pacing the room for several moments, he grew calmer, smiled in his old easy manner and asked Jane how she had fared at Cheshunt.

'The weather was very pleasant,' she said guardedly.

'And the Lady Elizabeth equally so?'

'She was most hospitable.'

'You gave her my letter?'

'I did, my lord.'

'What was her response, sweet Jane?'

'She giggled,' said Jane, trying not to sound disgusted.

'That and no more?'

'She bade me tell you that the husband you would choose for her may yet meet with her own approval.'

Seymour looked closely at Jane. 'You must suspect that I have myself in mind.'

'Yes, my lord.'

'Would the Lady Jane,' he asked jocularly, 'approve of my marrying the Lady Elizabeth?'

'If you so wish it,' Jane said stolidly.

'But not clandestinely, by God no!' He was suddenly wild-eyed again. 'Another reason for my gaining control of the Council. If Elizabeth were to marry without the consent of the Council she would forfeit all claim to the throne. Control of the Council I must and will have.'

Jane looked at him sadly. She had been thinking of a romantic elopement, the Lord Admiral and the Lady Elizabeth, but the Lord Admiral wanted Elizabeth only because of her closeness to the throne. There was no romance in him, handsome and dashing gentleman that he was. Inadvertently Jane remembered her mother's words, her remark that he was born without a heart to break, but hurriedly she cast this memory from her mind. He was her dear and good friend; she must, whatever happened, remain loyal to him.

'Jane,' he said, apparently in control of himself again, 'do you still have free access to the King?'

'I go to court only when summoned. You know that, my lord.'

'True, but could you not present yourself on some pretext or other?'

'I brought from Cheshunt a present for Edward from Elizabeth,' she said after a moment's thought. 'I forgot to take it when summoned the last time.'

'A good enough pretext,' said Seymour. 'You shall take with

the present a letter from me to Edward. If I were to write to him openly my letter might never reach him.' He paused and smiled winningly. 'Are you still afraid of court intrigue, sweet Jane?'

Jane nodded. 'It is a fear I must conquer for your sake,' she said stoutly.

Two days later Seymour, having ascertained that his brother was absent from court, gave his letter to Jane and this she carried with the present to Whitehall, attended not only by Mrs Eleyn but also by two of the late Queen Dowager's maids of honour. The little party was admitted without question to the privy apartments but detained in an antechamber until Edward's tutor, Sir John Cheke, made his appearance. Jane had always liked him and had studied eagerly with Edward under his direction in what she was beginning to think of as happier days.

'The King will be pleased to receive you,' he said, smiling on Jane in a kindly manner, 'but, by order of the Lord Protector, only in my presence.'

'That I must endure, Sir John,' Jane said with a flash of impishness which caused him to chuckle softly.

Edward received her with a brief smile of pleasure, accepted Elizabeth's present with no show of eagerness and opening it remarked sarcastically, or so Jane thought, that his sister had been unusually diligent.

'It is a very fine shirt, your Grace,' Jane said generously. 'The Lady Elizabeth is better at needlework than I.'

'Whereas,' said Edward just as generously, 'the Lady Jane is better at Latin and Greek than the Lady Elizabeth.'

Blushing with pleasure Jane gave him Seymour's letter saying, 'With the compliments of the Lord Admiral.' Frowning, Edward broke the seal and found not one letter but two. He read the shorter one first. He was urged, as he loved his Uncle Thomas, to copy the second and longer letter, sign it in his capacity as King of England and in that capacity send it to the House of Lords in support of a Bill which the Lord Admiral proposed to present when Parliament next met. He turned to the second letter and with growing distrust studied the words which his Uncle Thomas presumed, dictatorially, it would seem, to put into his mouth. He was to write, if he copied the letter faithfully, that his late father had not intended that there should be a Protector, an assertion which Edward knew to be false. He was also to write that in his own opinion there ought not to be a Protector, and finally: 'Let one uncle be regent of the realm providing the other uncle be given custody of the King's person.' Edward pondered over this. There was a time when he would have preferred to be in Uncle Thomas's custody rather than Uncle Edward's, but now his mind was troubled by unresolved doubts.

'Sir John,' he said, handing the letters to his tutor, 'I seek your advice.'

Sir John Cheke read the letters twice, looked up and shrugged lightly. 'I think I should give your Grace my interpretation first.'

'Please do.'

'I see this as an attempt by the Lord Admiral—or, more correctly, the first step in an eventual attempt—to gain control of the Council. It was not unexpected. The Lord Admiral approached me before his arrest and asked me to ask your Grace to write such a letter. I refused to meddle.'

'That, then, is your advice, that I should refuse to meddle too?'

'It is, your Grace.'

'If the Lord Admiral's Bill is right,' Edward said, 'the Lords will allow it. It is their business, not mine.' He turned with a wry smile to Jane. 'You must be mightily puzzled by all this, Lady Jane, unless you are aware of the contents of these letters.'

'I know nothing of the contents, your Grace.'

'Better that the Lady Jane should remain in ignorance,' Sir John suggested.

'Better, yes,' Edward agreed, and added unhappily: 'Better if I had remained in ignorance myself.'

'Better also,' said Sir John, 'that the Lady Jane should repeat not a word of what she has inadvertently heard this day.'

Jane looked uncertainly at Edward. 'What if the Lord Admiral should question me, your Grace?'

Edward hesitated for a moment. 'You may tell him that his letters were ill-received.' Then, still indecisive, he changed his mind. 'No, that would be unkind. Tell the Lord Admiral that the King cannot interfere.'

To Jane's surprise and relief Seymour remained calm when, questioning her, she revealed this information, and said almost absently that there were those who would poison the King's mind against him. The calmness persisted even when his Bill, the true nature of which Jane was never told, was rejected by the Lords without debate. Thereafter he was often away on seemingly mysterious journeys, leaving Jane to her studies in his London house. When at home he received Thomas Wriothesley occasionally and other visitors unknown to Jane. Finally, with the earlier frightening wildness upon him again, he told Jane one evening to prepare herself for a long journey.

'We shall have with us,' he said excitedly, 'a most illustrious companion.'

'Where do we go, my lord?'

'Where else but the Scilly Isles, my little pirate queen!'

Not quite believing him, Jane asked: 'When do we leave?'

'At midnight.'

Obliged to take him seriously Jane sent for Mrs Eleyn, only to learn that that lady had already received her instructions, as had old Lady Seymour and the maids of honour. She discovered too that several baggage wagons were being loaded and that a large private guard of mounted soldiers was being assembled. It was then ten o'clock and the January night bitterly cold. An hour later Jane watched Seymour leave the house. He was armed with a pistol and the two servants who accompanied him were also armed.

'I am beginning to feel frightened,' Jane confided in Mrs Eleyn.

'So for the matter of that am I, my lady.'

'The Scilly Isles are so very far away.'

'The Scilly Isles?' Mrs Eleyn echoed in disbelief. 'We go to Holt Castle, or so I heard the Lord Admiral's steward say.'

'Perhaps Holt Castle first,' Jane said, wondering where Holt Castle was.

At midnight, with Seymour still absent, his mother said crossly that whatever her unpredictable son had in mind for them all the best place for her was a warm bed. Jane, despite feeling frightened, had fallen asleep in her chair, and roused by Mrs Eleyn allowed herself to be led to her own bed into which Mrs Eleyn, who prided herself on being ready always for any contingency, had placed a warming-pan. Jane slept fitfully to awake at dawn from a dream in which she had seen the illustrious travelling companion in the guise of the Lady Elizabeth, but her cousin, she remembered, had been removed from Cheshunt to Hatfield, another manor house deeper in the country. She was wondering why this had happened when Mrs Eleyn stole softly into the bedchamber.

'My lady ...'

'What is it, Mrs Eleyn?' Jane asked, a strange fear gripping her heart.

'My lady, there is word from Sir John Cheke. The Lord Admiral has been arrested again and taken to the Tower.'

'For what reason?' Jane asked faintly.

'It is believed that he intended to abduct the King. I myself am convinced that he was suffering a serious derangement but that is neither here nor there. He entered the King's bedchamber late last night by way of the privy garden. The guard was negligent of his duty but the dog barked . . .'

'I knew Pointer would always protect the King,' Jane said exultantly.

'I fear, my lady,' Mrs Eleyn said as gently as she could, 'that the Lord Admiral shot the dog. The sound of the shot raised the alarm.'

'Is Pointer dead?' Jane asked in a whisper.

'I fear so, my lady.'

'The Lord Admiral killed Pointer,' Jane said dully, and began then to hate Seymour as much as she was capable of hating anyone. '*He killed her*.'

When the news of Seymour's second arrest reached Bradgate, Jane's parents came up to London and removed her from Seymour Place to Dorset House. Later, she was told, they would take her back to Bradgate with them, whether or not the Lord Admiral regained his freedom.

'Not that he has any hope of that,' Lady Dorset assured her.

'I can't believe that he intended the King any harm,' Jane said apathetically.

'No physical harm,' said Lady Dorset. 'He meant, we suspect, to hold him in Holt Castle, bargain with the Lord Protector and so gain control of the Council. Perhaps one should spare him some pity. He was clearly out of his mind.'

While Jane was still at Dorset House Edward summoned her to court, persuaded Sir John Cheke to absent himself and spoke to her without any thought of formality.

'I would gladly forgive Uncle Thomas for attempting to abduct me,' he said, 'but that is not one of the thirty-three charges he will face when brought to trial.'

'He killed Pointer,' said Jane. 'I shall never forgive him for that.'

'Nor shall I,' Edward said, 'but I wish that was all that can be held against him. He formed a secret party and planned a rising against the Protector. He . . .' Edward broke off and said wryly: 'I am trying to be a king much older than one in only his twelfth year. Do you feel any older than that yourself, Jane?'

Jane sighed deeply. 'I feel older than my mother.'

'Uncle Thomas,' Edward continued, 'had fortified Holt Castle and had formed an alliance with pirates in the Scilly Isles. He had set up cannon foundries in the country and through the Master of the Mint had raised enough money to keep a small army in the field for a month. All this was revealed after his arrest by the Earl of Southampton.'

'A false friend,' said Jane, no longer really caring, then remembering her dream she asked: 'Was the Lady Elizabeth to be abducted too?'

'Nobody can be sure of that. Uncle Thomas visited her secretly after she was removed to Hatfield Manor. She was taken there to be further out of his reach. Southampton suspects that one of his schemes was to marry her and place her by force on the throne. Nobody can be sure of that either. Elizabeth has been questioned, but unsuccessfully. All she would say was that Uncle Thomas was a man of much wit but little judgment. She said it as if he were already dead.'

Hating Seymour as she did, Jane asked fearfully: 'Will he die, Cousin Edward?'

'If he is found guilty,' Edward said chokingly, 'there is only one penalty.'

Lord Seymour of Sudeley was not brought to open trial. The Privy Council debated the issue in Edward's presence and voted unanimously in favour of an Act of Attainder. The Lord Protector formally asked Edward for leave to proceed and Edward, knowing that Seymour had friends in both the Lords and the

Commons, uttered a rehearsed command: 'We perceive that you require only that justice be done, and we beg you to proceed.' Seymour appeared before a committee of both Houses, admitted to some of the minor charges levelled against him but defiantly refused to admit to any of the more serious ones. The Bill was then brought before the House of Lords and read three times without a single dissenting voice. The House of Commons asked for and received more evidence but out of a gathering of four hundred only twelve members said 'Nay'. The Bill was passed and sent to the Crown with the request that justice should be done.

Meanwhile Lady Dorset had taken Jane to Bradgate Park. Lord Dorset, now sporting a half-grown beard, remained in London to safeguard himself against a possible charge of having aided and abetted the Lord Admiral. With no such charge brought against him he came to Bradgate towards the end of March, little more than six months after Katherine Parr's death, with news of Seymour's execution.

'The Council,' Dorset told his wife and Jane, 'sought royal permission to proceed with the required debate without further troubling the King or the Lord Protector. The Lords of the Council considered it too heavy a burden for the nephew and the brother to bear. A unanimous decision was reached. The Lord Protector signed the death warrant. Justice was done. The Lord Admiral was plainly guilty of high treason.'

'Were you present at the execution?' Lady Dorset asked, her tone of voice making Jane shudder.

Her husband inclined his head. 'I felt it my duty so to be.'

'Did you enjoy it, my lord?' Jane asked on a high note.

'Hold your tongue, child,' Lady Dorset said, and asked, again in that sickening voice, 'Did Seymour die bravely?'

'He died without flinching,' Dorset said, 'though not at the first stroke of the axe. But let me quote the words of the Archbishop: "He died as he lived—dangerously, irksomely, horribly. Whether he be saved or not, I refer that issue to God. In the twinkling of an eye God may save a man and turn his heart. When a man suffers two strokes of the axe it might well be that between the two he finds repentance."' Lord Dorset sighed lightly. 'If Seymour had succeeded the Archbishop would have been careful to say the same of his defeated brother.'

'Be that as it may,' Lady Dorset said, intensely if secretly relieved at the failure of Seymour's marriage plans for Jane, 'the Lord Admiral was a wicked man. The realm is well rid of him, and so are we.'

Close to hysteria now, Jane said: 'You gave me into his care.'

'His wickedness was unknown at that time,' Lady Dorset said quickly.

'Why did you give me into his care?' Jane asked.

It was Dorset who told her. 'Can you not guess, child? It was thought that he would eventually have sufficient influence to marry you to the King.'

'We were misguided,' Lady Dorset said, and added perversely: 'With Seymour dead you are of no further use to us, in that or any other direction.'

14

ROUSED from a deep sleep, Edward sat up in confusion to find a shadowy figure, unrecognisable in the light of a single candle, approaching his bed. Steadying himself he wondered if he were still asleep and dreaming the old recurring dream of the night his Uncle Thomas had broken into his bedchamber from the privy garden. Edward listened intently but there was no warning bark from Pointer.

'Your Grace . . .'

'Sir John!' Edward exclaimed, recognising his tutor's voice.

Relief stilled the rapid beating of his heart. No harm would come to him from the always kindly Sir John Cheke. Then sadness touched him; Pointer was dead and the man who had killed her had gone to the block seven months ago. High treason or not, one could still weep for Uncle Thomas. Would one be called upon to weep also for Uncle Edward some day? Staring up at Sir John he remembered a dream in which the ghost of Uncle Thomas had whispered: 'He sealed his doom when he signed my death warrant.' But superstition was not to be tolerated, Edward told himself sternly, in a Protestant king.

'What is amiss, Sir John?' he asked.

'I must warn your Grace to prepare yourself for immediate departure from Hampton Court.'

Fully awake now, Edward remembered that he was not at Whitehall, as he had thought on waking so suddenly, but at Hampton Court. None too happily he recalled the reason for it. The Lord Protector, troubled by opposition within the Council and by a rising in Norfolk, had issued a proclamation in the King's name, summoning all loyal subjects to Hampton Court for the King's defence. *My* defence, Edward thought; Uncle Edward had meant his own.

'Where do we go, Sir John?'

'Windsor Castle, your Grace. Windsor is thought to be safer than Hampton Court, and the castle is being fully fortified.'

Lord Protector Somerset had already departed for Windsor. Edward himself left Hampton Court soon after midnight on horseback. At his side rode Sir John Cheke. They were surrounded by gentlemen of the household and guarded in addition by a company of five hundred men. Edward, armed with a small sword, felt as if he were going to war, but who was the enemy? He reached Windsor in the chilly dawn of a late October morning. He was feverish and the cough which had troubled him intermittently during the autumn had returned. They put him to bed but he was too exhausted after the hectic ride through the night to sleep and rose soon to wander unattended on an inspection of the castle. There was very little furniture in any of the rooms and very little food in the kitchens. Depressed by the forbidding atmosphere and shivering with cold, he went back to his bed. Somerset waited on him presently and told him that wagons loaded with all the necessities would soon arrive.

'Are we to withstand a siege, my lord?'

'We must at all events be prepared for one, your Grace.'

'What,' Edward asked, 'has brought us to this sorry pass?'

'The King is ill and must rest,' Somerset said evasively.

But Edward, feeling a surge of rebellious indignation, was unwilling to be denied an answer. His mind amazingly clear despite the fever, he remembered the outline of events which Sir John Cheke had given him from time to time.

'Uncle Edward,' he said informally, 'is the war with Scotland part of the trouble?'

'Perhaps the greater part of it, Edward.'

'You won a great victory at Pinkie Cleugh,' Edward pointed out.

'That was not the end of it,' Somerset said sourly. 'The Scots have the support of French money and men, and have improved their position. I can make little headway while Parliament refuses to grant me much needed subsidies.'

'You are accused,' Edward said, not unkindly, 'of squandering money on personal things.'

'So say the ass-heads in Parliament *and* in the Council.'

'Unjustly, Uncle?'

'Unjustly!' Somerset said angrily.

But this Edward knew to be untrue. His uncle, since his father's death less than three years ago, had acquired as many as two hundred manors at the expense of the Crown; and now, a very rich man, was causing to be built in London a palace for himself. Adjacent buildings, including two chapels, had been demolished to provide much of the stonework. St Margaret's would have suffered the same fate had not the people of Westminster risen in anger and attacked the workmen with pikes and bows. This reminded Edward of other more serious revolts arising out of religious discontent and a resentment in some quarters of the introduction of the new Prayer-book. He spoke of this, asking Somerset if that too was part of his present trouble.

'You must know that it is,' his uncle replied, 'but would you have me withdraw the new Prayer-book?'

'Never,' said Edward, the fervent Protestant, 'but I would not allow the new ministers of religion to hold secular offices. I think it wrong, for instance, that a clergyman should have been made Master of the Mint.'

Ignoring this Somerset said quickly: 'The revolts were put down. That is all that need concern us now.'

Put down, Edward refrained from reminding him, by the Earl of Warwick. Edward himself had been present when Warwick had come to court to demand of the Lord Protector a just reward for his officers and men and recompense for the families of those who had died in pitched battles in Norfolk and elsewhere. Somerset's flat refusal had infuriated Warwick, but growing calmer he had said the real fault lay with him and his fellow Lords of the Council, since they and they alone had bestowed so much power on the Lord Protector. A scarcely veiled threat, Edward thought now.

'Uncle, is Warwick suspected of forming a secret party?'

'He and other members of the Council are known to meet secretly.'

'Is it against him that Windsor has been fortified?'

'Yes,' Somerset said briefly.

'Are we to do nothing but remain here and wait for the attack?'

Somerset seemed not to have heard. Edward, his mind growing hazy now, looked up at him uncertainly. He had changed startlingly during the last few months, had grown rapidly older. He was thinner in the face; his eyes were often vacant, as they were now, and his hands often trembled, as they did now. Too much power and the troubled result of it, Edward thought with a flash of insight, was not the real cause at all.

'Uncle,' he said, a shrill note in his voice, 'does Uncle Thomas's death lie heavily upon your heart?'

Somerset heard and came quickly to angry life. He wanted to shout, 'He was not your uncle, *I* am not your uncle.' Slowly he grew calmer. What good would be achieved by revealing to Edward the truth of his birth? If he were of age and in full possession of kingly power it could be used in a blackmailing attempt to preserve one's own power. Or could it, successfully? The virtuous Edward might well abdicate in favour of the next in the line of succession and that, Catholic Mary being Edward's immediate heir, would destroy the New Learning which he, Somerset, had done so much to establish. Or perhaps Edward would name Protestant Elizabeth and naming her cause outright civil war. A thought full of irony crossed Somerset's mind. Mary and Elizabeth were still regarded as illegitimate by many people, whereas the only true illegitimate was the boy who sat upon the throne.

'Uncle . . . ?'

'Does his death lie heavily upon your own heart?' Somerset asked harshly.

'It does, but I was powerless to help him.'

'Whereas I . . . ?'

'Could you not have pardoned him?'

'Had he pleaded with me, yes. But there was a conspiracy to keep him from me. And from you.'

'He would not have pleaded,' Edward said, tears running down his cheeks. 'He was too proud.'

Thereafter, with the sweating sickness getting the better of him, Edward was barely conscious of those who anxiously surrounded him. When not sleeping he was hazily aware of the royal physicians, the nurses and a figure whom he thought was Archbishop Cranmer one moment, Sir John Cheke the next. And then, waking one morning with a clear mind, it seemed to him that he had spoken unkindly to his Uncle Edward.

'Pray send for the Lord Protector,' he instructed one of the nurses.

But it was his godfather, Archbishop Cranmer, who came and, kissing him on the brow, said how thankful he was that the King's Highness was showing every sign of speedy recovery.

'Not in the least do you resemble Sir John Cheke,' Edward remarked.

'Speedy recovery indeed,' the Archbishop murmured.

'Godfather,' said Edward, 'I sent for the Lord Protector.'

'Alas, he is not within reach.'

'By which you mean . . . ?' Edward said, alarmed by Cranmer's tone.

'The Lord Protector is held under guard and will shortly be removed to the Tower of London. Had God not helped in his mercy the Lords of the Council the country would have been brought to ruin and you, the King, might well have been slain.'

'By my uncle, the Lord Protector?' Edward exclaimed. 'He has never harmed me. Nor would he ever do so. Has the castle been taken by his enemies? Am I a prisoner here? Please tell me the truth, Godfather.'

'As you wish, dear Godson,' Cranmer acceded. 'The Lords of the Council assured the Lord Protector that no harm was intended him, that their sole purpose was to guard with all jealousy the Proctorate. He in his turn agreed that certain changes in the Government were necessary. The Lords came out to Windsor in a body and there was great rejoicing.'

'The Earl of Warwick among them?'

'Foremost among them.'

'And then, Godfather . . . ?'

'The Duke of Somerset allowed his personal and private guards to be replaced with the usual royal guards. I myself advised him to do so, otherwise he could have been accused of the treasonable act of holding the King by force here at Windsor. Thereafter the royal guards obeyed Warwick instead of Somerset.'

'Has Warwick made himself Lord Protector?'

Cranmer shook his head. 'That title was becoming largely hated. He will be known as President of the Council, and also as your Grace's new guardian.'

'With your blessing, Godfather?' Edward asked bitterly.

'I have no choice but to accept the change,' Cranmer said tonelessly. 'Nor have you, my son.'

Realising this, Edward said: 'If my uncle the Duke cannot be accused of a treasonable act, for what reason is he to be held in the Tower?'

'Other charges will be formulated, among them the misappropriation of Crown property.'

'Whatever the outcome,' Edward said tensely, 'I shall never permit the signing of his death warrant. I may be only in my thirteenth year but surely I, the King, have some say in the affairs of my kingdom.'

'Surely,' Cranmer murmured placatingly.

'I want to see the Duke before they take him away.'

'That would be unwise, your Grace.'

'It is our royal wish,' Edward said heatedly.

Cranmer shrugged and departed, and within the hour Somerset entered the young King's bedchamber with a royal guard on either side of him.

'Withdraw!' Edward ordered the yeomen imperatively.

They did so instantly, all but falling over each other in their haste. This caused Edward to laugh, though wryly, and bidding Somerset to be seated he looked at him covertly. He was shaking as if suffering the ague and there was a pathetic dullness in his eyes. Edward had thought to apologise for having spoken unkindly to him earlier and he had felt pity for him while listening to Cranmer, but now, to his innermost dismay, he felt moved only to anger.

'I am fallen near as low as the Lord Admiral,' Somerset said in a whisper.

Edward controlled his anger. 'Could you not have saved yourself by making peace with Scotland?'

'That I cannot say, but I had thought to bring it about through marriage.'

'Marriage, Uncle?' Edward questioned sharply.

'The King of England and the little Queen of Scotland, and so, an indestructible union of the two countries.'

Edward remembered that such a marriage had once been contemplated for him by his father. He had often wondered about Mary, the little Queen of Scotland, a cousin in the same degree as Jane Grey, but younger than Jane. She was—he made a quick calculation—no more than seven at this moment. Her grandmother, his father's sister Margaret, had married James IV of Scotland. Mary was the daughter of their son James V who had been fatally wounded at Solway Moss, a battle lost to the English. He had lived long enough to learn that a daughter, his only child, had been born; and Mary, that daughter, had come to the Scottish throne when only six days old. Edward found it sad to think that a war was being fought in his name and hers, when England and Scotland, if only through the ties of blood, should be living together in peace.

'I have nothing against such a marriage, Uncle,' he said eagerly.

'Only by invading France and snatching the Queen of Scotland from the French could it be brought about,' Somerset said helplessly. 'She has been sent to France. She is to be reared at the French court. She is already affianced to the Dauphin. There can be no Scottish alliance for you now. Nor can there be a French one.'

'No,' said Edward, no longer caring. 'We are at war with France too. Must I really marry, Uncle Edward?'

'In the course of time duty will demand it of you,' Somerset said apathetically.

'Will the choice of a bride for me be Warwick's now?'

'Apparently.'

'I shall speak to him about an English bride,' Edward said thoughtfully but without enthusiasm. 'I shall suggest my cousin Jane Grey.'

'By God's precious blood, no!' Somerset came to life sufficiently to exclaim.

'I cannot understand why you should object so strongly,' Edward said in surprise. 'The Lady Jane is a Tudor like myself, and a staunch Protestant. Such a marriage would be acceptable to my Protestant subjects.'

'I wanted the Lady Jane for my son,' Somerset said quickly but in a subdued tone. 'I still want her for him.'

'Warwick may want her for *me*.'

'It is not my aim for you or for England.'

'My dear Uncle,' Edward said, not intending hurtfulness, 'you have not the power, now, to say yea or nay.'

Somerset rose wearily from his chair. 'I have no power at

all,' he said, his cheeks quivering, 'except the power to throw myself upon your mercy.'

Edward bowed his head and remained silent. It was Warwick's mercy that the fallen Lord Protector must seek, not his.

Later that day he watched from his window the departure of Edward Seymour, Duke of Somerset. There was a strong guard in evidence but placed at a discreet distance from the main party, a company of three hundred lords and gentlemen. His uncle the noble captive, Edward reflected, being carried in triumph to the Tower of London. He caught a glimpse of his new guardian, the victorious Earl of Warwick, and then a glimpse of Jane's father, the Marquess of Dorset. Very much hand in glove, it seemed, the Earl and the Marquess, sitting their horses side by side. Edward overcame a momentary resentment. Second only to Warwick, Dorset was the most influential and respected Protestant lord in England. Once, and only a short time ago, the most influential, if not the most respected, had been the Duke of Somerset. Protestant quarrelling with Protestant, Edward thought indignantly, religion never sacred where self-interest was concerned. He saw them, the Earl and the Marquess, exchange gleeful smiles, and that added anger to his indignation.

'Your Grace . . .'

Edward swung round. 'What is it, Godfather?'

'Within two or three days,' the Archbishop said, 'the King's Highness will be well enough to travel to London.'

To Whitehall, Edward very nearly asked sarcastically, or to the Tower? His anger still upon him he said impulsively: 'My uncle the Duke, whatever his sins may be in Warwick's eyes or yours, must and shall be pardoned.'

Cranmer, he saw, was too taken aback to speak.

'We demand it,' Edward said, with a finality that left the Archbishop still speechless.

15

'AND so,' John Dudley, Earl of Warwick concluded, 'I pardoned the wretched Somerset.'

'Coerced, one might say, by his Highness the King,' the Marquess of Dorset remarked.

Warwick, never quick to take offence, especially where a valued ally was concerned, laughed pleasantly. 'The King is growing up more rapidly than we might have expected. He was old before his time, even at nine, and is older still in his thirteenth year. It is not my wish to antagonise him, not at present, where his closest kinsman is concerned. I have even allowed Somerset a seat on the Council and restored some of his confiscated property. Let him wallow in a feeling of security. Real power will never be his again, whatever move he may make. He will be watched closely. I can bide my time.'

'Surely,' Dorset murmured admiringly.

Warwick, a welcome visitor, was newly arrived at Bradgate Park where he proposed to spend two or three days discussing both political and religious moves, and for the additional purpose of conversing with and assessing the truth worth of Dorset's eldest daughter Jane. He touched lightly on the latter subject now.

'It is near on a year,' he said, 'since the Lady Jane was taken back into your care. Is she happy to be in the bosom of her family again?'

'At Bradgate,' Dorset said sharply, 'the girl is known as Lady Jane, that and no more.'

'I begin to suspect that she is not entirely happy, my dear Dorset.'

'She returned with an extremely arrogant manner,' Dorset said indignantly. 'She was shockingly spoilt by the Queen Dowager, by the Lord Admiral, even, earlier, by King Henry. I suspect her of regarding herself as a royal princess. However,

Lady Dorset and I are taking steps to tame her, to put a bridle on her when, for three years, she ran free and unrestrained.'

'Take care,' Warwick warned lightly, 'that you do nothing to offend the King. He plays with the idea of marrying her. True, he blows hot and cold, but the inclination is sometimes uppermost in his mind.'

'Also in yours?' Dorset asked eagerly.

'As yet I am uncommitted.'

'It is an old ambition of mine,' Dorset said dreamily. 'And it was my reason, as you may have guessed, for my returning Jane to Tom Seymour's care after the Queen Dowager died.'

'It was one of his wild schemes, as I well know.'

'One thing I beg of you,' Dorset said hurriedly, 'breathe not a word of the King's inclination to my wife until the match is made and contract sealed.'

'Why so that?' Warwick asked in surprise.

'On the surface she would appear to favour such a match, but I know her to be set against it.'

'You amaze me, Dorset.'

'I admit to much puzzlement myself.'

'A matter of jealousy, would you say?'

Dorset's face cleared. 'She is, I grant you, a jealous woman. Jane placed before her in the line of succession, for example. Jane, if Queen, or even Queen Consort, demanding obedience of her. I do agree, jealousy is the only possible explanation.'

Warwick rose late the next morning after a night of drinking and gambling in private with Dorset and several gentlemen of the neighbourhood and was informed that the Dorsets and most of their household were hunting in the park. Learning also that Lady Jane had remained behind to study he decided against joining the hunting party and sought out the girl in her room. Seated at the writing table with her was Mrs Eleyn. Warwick sensed a certain amount of confusion at his unexpected appearance. What looked like a small cascade of papers fell beneath the table when Mrs Eleyn sprang to her feet. The girl herself reached for a book and waited without a word while her attendant curtsied and withdrew.

'It seems that you prefer scholarship to hunting,' Warwick remarked.

Jane looked at him closely, wondering if sarcasm was intended. 'I was forbidden to join the hunting party,' she said. 'But I do indeed prefer to study Plato than to hunt. It is no real punishment, my lord.'

'For what are you being "punished"?' Warwick asked, smiling broadly.

'I find that a difficult question to answer,' Jane said, deciding implusively to confide in him. 'Perfection is expected of me in all things. I expect it of myself and strive for it, but my striving is seldom satisfactory to my parents.' She paused, feeling momentarily guilty. 'It is disloyal of me to speak thus,' she said. 'I beg you to forget my words.'

Warwick inclined his head. Wondering what conversational move to make next he strode to the window and looked out across the rolling acres of the park. He caught a distant passing view of the hunting party and listened absently to the baying of the hounds and the music of the hunting horns.

Jane stared at his back resentfully, but her resentment was directed against her parents, not her cousin the King's new guardian. In no way did it seem possible to find favour in their eyes, not even in simple things such as eating and drinking, speaking or keeping silent, dancing or making music. Her mother was far worse than her father, always sharp in her tauntings and heavy with her jewelled hands when slapping in a fit of rage. Even her younger sisters, the skittish Katherine and the pitiful hunchbacked Mary, were ranged mockingly against her. There were times, Jane thought, when she believed herself to be in hell. Study was her only true escape, and the gentleness and understanding of her tutor, Mr Aylmer, the only blessing.

Still staring at Warwick's back she wondered if she was to find in him a sympathetic friend. She had caught occasional glimpses of him at court but had never before conversed with him. She knew him to be a man of fifty, the eldest son of Edmund Dudley who had been executed early in Henry VIII's reign. Nevertheless the son, this Earl of Warwick, had found favour in Henry's eyes, had been ennobled by him and had held the offices of Lord Admiral and Master of the Horse. His wife had borne thirteen children, seven of whom had survived. He turned from the window as Jane dwelt on this and smiled in a kindly manner. For fifty, which was really old, he had a smooth brow and the rosy cheeks of a countryman. Stylishly dressed, he wore the new male fashion, a tall starched ruff, and the even newer fashion, a padded doublet designed to resemble close-fitting armour. His drooping moustache and twin-pointed beard were a work of art and far neater than her father's now luxuriant if uncontrolled growth.

'Tell me about your religious studies,' he invited.

'They are supervised by my tutor, Mr Aylmer, and by my father's chaplain, Dr Haddon,' Jane said gravely. 'They have reached the stage where I must master Hebrew in order to study the Old Testament with greater accuracy. My faith is founded in the Bible and strengthened through comparing the classics with Protestant beliefs.'

'Have you at any time doubted the Protestant faith?'

'Never, my lord. Each new study convinces me that it must triumph over the old faith.'

'Well said, Lady Jane.' Warwick's voice was warmly approving. 'I hear that you are in correspondence with certain learned German Reformers.'

'With Henry Bullinger in particular, my lord. My father began the correspondence but was too busy with other matters to continue it. He assigned the task to me.'

Warwick too was in correspondence with Bullinger, once a lecturer at Cambridge and now one of Dorset's honoured pensioners. Bullinger had written recently in praise of Lady Jane, praise arising out of what he had heard of her from others and out of the contents of her adult-seeming letters to him in Latin. He found that the knowledge gained by her study of the Scriptures and the classics came close to equalling his own. 'In truth', he had written, 'I do not believe that among the English nobility, even for many ages past, there has risen a single individual who, in the highest excellences of talent and judgment, has united so much diligence and assiduity in the cultivation of philosophical pursuits.' Thinking of these words now Warwick decided that Jane Grey was one of the most outstanding of the precocious and studious young Protestants of the day, but he hoped that she was not in danger of becoming a priggish bore. 'It is incredible', Bullinger had also written, 'how far she has advanced already, and inspiring to contemplate to what perfection she will advance in the years before her, for I am confident that she will complete what she has begun, unless she be diverted by some calamity of the times, such as the untimely accession of the late King Henry's daughter Mary.' A calamity indeed, Warwick thought, and remembered Bullinger's closing words: 'I hear talk among persons of consequence that this most noble virgin is to be given in marriage to the King's majesty. If such an event should take place, how happy would be the union and how beneficial to the Church!'

If, Warwick thought, *if* . . . He felt confident that he could bring the union about himself, but there was the young King's health to be taken into account, Edward's last illness had weakened him and he had been slow to recover. True, there was nothing in his condition to occasion serious alarm, though one of the royal physicians had predicted in confidence that the boy was unlikely to live beyond the age of seventeen. Warwick decided to bide his time. If the prediction proved false, then marriage for Edward and Jane; if the worst happened he had an alternative and personally more satisfying plan for the girl who, at present, stood third in the line of succession.

'Do you wish to question me further, my lord?' Jane asked, rendered uneasy by Warwick's lengthy silence.

'For the time being, no.'

Approaching the writing table Warwick stooped to pick up the papers that had fallen earlier. A chuckle rose in his throat. They were not papers, as he had first thought, but playing cards, and near them lay several coins. Chuckling again he placed the cards and the coins on the table. No priggishness here, he thought thankfully.

Jane blushed and stammered, 'Thank you, my lord.'

'Do I observe a certain guiltiness, Lady Jane?'

Jane nodded and fingered the book. 'I should have been studying Plato's *Phaedo*, but the words were beginning to dance before my eyes. It was six o'clock this morning when I began my studies. Mrs Eleyn suggested the frivolity of cards as a restful change.'

'Pray do not be too hard on yourself,' Warwick urged. 'Did you not enjoy the restful change?'

Jane smiled guardedly. 'I admit that I did. I win more often than I lose when playing with Mrs Eleyn; whereas I lost more often than I won when playing with the King.'

'Deliberately perhaps?'

If Jane had not been seated she would have stamped her foot in anger. 'My lord, I did *not* cheat myself into losing because my cousin Edward is King of England.'

'I stand corrected,' Warwick said in mock humility.

Thinking of her attendant Jane frowned and said: 'Mrs Eleyn suggested cards for another reason. She thought it might please my parents to learn that I had indulged in a pastime that is sternly discouraged at Bradgate.'

'Ah yes, but not by them. By St Mary, no.'

'By St Mary, no,' Jane echoed, if somewhat primly.

The Dorsets, Warwick reflected, were heavy and often rash gamblers, even when merely throwing dice. Lord Dorset's chaplain, James Haddon, supported by Jane's tutor, John Aylmer, had pronounced against this sinful habit over-indulged in by the Dorsets and their household. Dorset had grumbled about it last night but had admitted to having given way to the extent of forbidding his household in general to gamble while reserving the right to do so himself in private.

'I shall leave you to your studies,' Warwick told Jane, 'or would you have me recall Mrs Eleyn for another purpose?'

'I am sufficiently refreshed,' Jane said sternly, 'to continue my acquaintance with Plato.'

Warwick bowed. 'I look forward to furthering *your* acquaintance at the supper table.'

'It is the rule,' Jane felt obliged to tell him, 'that I sup separately with my sisters.'

'A rule, I vow,' Warwick said warmly, 'that shall be waived this night.'

And waived, at his insistence, it was. Seated between her tutor and the chaplain, and facing Warwick across the table, Jane cast upon him a shyly admiring glance and began to think that she had indeed found a friend and ally in the most powerful man in England. She glanced at her mother, who scowled at her resentfully, then at her father, who, after the day's hunting and a heavier consumption of ale than usual, was lolling uncaringly over the table with a vacant expression in his eyes. As the meal progressed Jane grew drowsy and was thinking that a day of study was more exhausting than a day of hunting when an argument between her father and his chaplain brought her sharply to attention.

'Gambling, my lord marquess,' Haddon asserted heavily, 'is not only sinful but there are still certain laws in existence which prohibit it.'

'Laws or no laws,' Dorset said, still lolling over the table but with his eyes alive now with resentment, 'the King himself is known to gamble at cards.'

'May God forgive him,' Haddon intoned.

'Out of deference to your holy orders,' Dorset reminded him, 'I have restricted my sinful gambling to the privacy of my inner chamber.'

'My lord marquess,' Haddon said in a conciliatory tone, 'I object not to card playing, only to gambling with the play.'

'I care not whether I win or lose,' Dorset said, causing Jane almost to see a halo hovering over his head. 'But play without stakes is dull beyond endurance.' Jane sighed; she would look in vain for a halo. 'Would you force upon me,' Dorset added spiritedly, 'a game that is cold and lifeless?'

'That I would, my lord marquess.'

'Ass-head,' Dorset sneered.

At this point Aylmer tried to change the subject by describing the game of bowls he had played after the day's hunting. He was a chubby little man of twenty-seven, as full of energy as he was of piety, and, Jane believed, the greatest patriot in the country. God, he was fond of saying, and with absolute conviction, was an Englishman.

'Are you never tempted to gamble on your bowling skill?' Dorset challenged.

'Unlike you, my lord marquess, never.'

'I beg my lord marquess to forbear,' Haddon said, his manner no longer conciliatory, 'otherwise I shall be compelled to preach a sermon of much force this coming Sunday.'

'A public rebuke in my own chapel!' Dorset all but screamed.

'I pray that so stern a duty will not be thrust upon me,' said Haddon, turning up his eyes.

'And *I* pray,' Dorset said heatedly, 'that I shall not be compelled to dismiss you and Aylmer from my service.'

'Dismiss us, my lord marquess, if the devil so moves you. I myself rest content in the sure knowledge that God will never dismiss me from his.'

Jane was forced to restrain herself from springing up from her chair in alarm. To be deprived of the two people who made life at Bradgate supportable would place her in hell without respite. She glanced fearfully from Haddon to Aylmer and saw on each face a look of quiet inquiry. Then she looked as they were doing at her father and to her astonishment saw an expression of almost silly defeat in his eyes. The power of a man of God, she thought, was surely infinite. Dorset shrugged helplessly, then catching Jane's eyes gave himself up to a moment of spitefulness.

'I hear,' he said, 'that Lady Jane indulged in a hand of cards with Mrs Eleyn this morning.'

Haddon turned in his chair and looked at Jane in shocked surprise. She lowered her eyes and, hoping that God would forgive her the sin of deceitfulness, was about to assert that the game had been cold and lifeless when Warwick, miraculously, gave voice to her own unuttered words.

'I came upon the culprits myself,' he said, 'but the game, God bless them, was cold and lifeless.'

'The devil it was!' Dorset exclaimed in disgust.

Jane raised her eyes and looked at Warwick with gratitude in her heart while praying hastily that God would forgive *him* for *his* deceitfulness. Then feeling a need for the privacy of her room she begged to be excused. Her father glanced at Warwick, as if for instruction, and then at his wife who was too greedily occupied with a chicken leg to take any notice at all.

'A long day of study,' said Warwick, making Jane feel that she and the King's guardian were very much at one in their thoughts, 'can be as exhausting as a long day in the hunting field.'

'You may withdraw, Jane,' Dorset said gruffly.

Warwick rose from his chair the moment Jane rose from hers and came round the table to her side. Stooping, he bowed ceremoniously and taking her small hand in his kissed it as if kissing that of a queen.

'Tomorrow,' he said, 'we shall play cards together, coldly and lifelessly. Meanwhile, sleep well, Madame.'

Jane found his unexpected and heavily stressed form of address both flattering and impressive. Not yet thirteen, she would only be entitled to it when, at fourteen, she reached what was regarded as full maturity. She curtsied, but feeling some confusion addressed him incorrectly.

'You are much too kind, my lord duke.'

'The Lady Jane,' Warwick chuckled, 'is not mistaken in her astute prediction.'

16

'UNLESS I am much mistaken,' the Lady Mary said, after formal greetings had been exchanged, 'you were fourteen a week ago, Madame.'

Jane looked at the King's elder sister suspiciously, but there was nothing in her expression to suggest that she had used the now obligatory form of address other than sincerely.

'Ten days ago, to be be precise,' Jane's mother said, giving scarcely a thought to the fact that Jane had been born seven days after the acknowledged date. 'It was a happy occasion, Cousin,' she added grudgingly.

'I well remember my own fourteenth birthday,' Mary Tudor said, harshness in her deep mannish voice. 'Important as it made me feel, as a woman, the event was marred by the shadow of divorce that hung over my mother.'

Jane's mother sighed as if in sympathy but was careful to hold her peace. The uttering of a single word that might, even mistakenly, be regarded by her Catholic cousin as controversial could well be dangerous at this stage, or at all events impolitic. Mary, at her brother the King's request, had issued the invitation, but had she done so willingly? It was Edward's wish that friendly family relations should be established between his immediate heir and Lady Jane, third in the line of succession. The Duchess of Suffolk, for that was what the Marchioness of Dorset had recently become, was intent herself on friendly relations with Mary Tudor, solely because the King's sickly condition suggested the near-certainty of Mary, with all that her religion implied, coming soon to the throne.

'I must compliment you, Cousin Frances,' Mary said, 'on your husband's elevation.'

'My heartfelt thanks, Madame,' the new duchess said, and

came close to tittering. 'I have yet to grow accustomed to being a duchess instead of a marchioness.'

Mary smiled thinly. The title had become vacant through the deaths of two of the former Lady Dorset's male relatives but would not have been inherited in the normal course of events by her husband. It had been bestowed, with the King's tacit approval, by the man who had replaced the fallen Lord Protector and who, at the same time, had bestowed upon himself another dukedom. He, John Dudley, Earl of Warwick, was now the new Duke of Northumberland. It seemed clear to Mary that Jane's father had been rewarded for services rendered to the man whom she herself regarded as a mortal enemy. Must she, she wondered, regard the Duke of Suffolk as a mortal enemy also? And what of his daughter Jane? One must strive for compassion. Jane, fourteen or not, a woman or not, still had the look of a child. A learned child, none the less, but that learning, Mary thought bitterly, entirely and so mistakenly Protestant.

'My dear Jane,' she said, repressing the bitterness, 'I see that you are wearing the present I gave you when you first came to my father's court.'

Jane fingered the necklace self-consciously, she having worn it at her mother's insistence. She remembered Mary's unexpected kindness at that time, yet a kindness never again repeated. She glanced covertly at her cousin and thought that she had aged much more than five years. Mary at thirty-five had a face that was drawn and sallow, far more so than Jane's memory of her at their last meeting soon after King Henry's death. Was it, Jane wondered, because of the strain of her unremitting fight to remain a Catholic and practise her faith despite the Protestant opposition initiated by Lord Protector Somerset? She seemed even shorter in stature while being narrow above the waist and enlarged to a dropsical extent below it. She wore a bright red wig to cover, if gossip was correct, an almost bald pate. Both Dr Haddon and Mr Aylmer constantly referred to her as Jezebel, but that, if appearance alone was a guide, was surely ludicrous. She looked more like a man than a woman, and resembled her late father to an almost frightening degree.

'When did you last see my brother the King?' Mary asked Jane.

'It was on St George's Day at Greenwich, Madame. I go only rarely to court. It was in fact my only visit since my removal to Bradgate.'

'Did he appear to be in better health?'

'He looked frail,' the Duchess of Suffolk answered for Jane, 'but he was in high spirits.'

Mary herself had seen her brother once only during the same period and the occasion had not been a happy one. Reluctantly and angrily she had journeyed from her Essex manor to appear before the Privy Council at Whitehall. The religious quarrel had flared up again, Mary having ignored the Act of Uniformity by permitting Mass to be said in her private chapel here at New Hall Manor. She remembered the scene in the council chamber, her brother a silent witness, the Lord Chancellor the Council's spokesman. She was told that the celebration of Mass, openly or privately, could be suffered no longer. 'My soul is God's,' she had retorted; 'I will not change my faith, nor will I dissemble my opinions with contrary doings.' She was then warned that she was not a king to rule but a servant to obey the laws. Obdurate herself, she had held the young King's eyes steadily and said: 'I am the King's true servant and sister, ready to obey him in everything except in matters of religion.' Only the presence in London of the Emperor's ambassador had saved her. Should she be further molested in the exercise of her religion, he had declared publicly, he would leave the country, and that, as everybody knew, would be tantamount to a declaration of war. Somerset, still at liberty, still a member of the Council, had waited on her before her return to New Hall and had complimented her on what he termed her victory. Thinking of this now she asked Jane another question.

'Was the Duke of Somerset present at the St George's Day festivities?'

'Yes, Madame.'

'Did the King show him any favour?'

'They laughed and joked together,' Jane said, recalling the scene at Greenwich. 'The Duke told the King that according to the legend St George drew his sword and ran the dragon through with his spear. "Tell me, Uncle," the King asked, "what did St George do with his sword?" The Duke replied that he struck off the heads of all the wicked barons. The King laughed and the Duke laughed, there being so many of the Lords of the Council there within earshot.'

Mary could but smile. A double meaning without doubt, whether or not her brother had taken it seriously. She had given much thought of late to the former Lord Protector and wondered now if he had any hope of regaining his old position. That he was planning secretly to oust the new Duke of Northumberland was already known to her. He had approached her, offering her his full support provided she gave him hers. She felt nothing but contempt for him. How could an unremitting enemy become of a sudden a sincere friend? He sought only to protect himself in the event of her brother's untimely death. It had crossed her mind that her two cousins, mother and daughter, might be in league with Somerset but that, considering their close association with Northumberland, was a preposterous thought. She regretted having mentioned his name and changing the subject asked Jane if she had seen the Lady Elizabeth lately.

'No, Madame,' said Jane. 'I last saw her before the Lord Admiral's death.'

Mary looked at her closely. 'His execution must have grieved you sorely.'

'He killed the King's dog, Madame. The dog I gave to the King.'

'A childish reason for hating Lord Seymour,' Mary reproved.

Nettled, Jane said: 'I did not say that I hated him.'

Mary shrugged. Seymour would have married Jane to Edward. Had she been left with a feeling of frustration? Somerset had been and still was against such a match, though heaven alone knew why. And what of Northumberland? He too, it would seem, was against it, since he, apparently, was keeping Edward and Jane apart. However, there was still Edward himself to be reckoned with and it was no secret that he was very fond of Jane. Not that he could as yet choose a wife himself; nor, for that matter, could he be forced to marry against his will. It was believed by many that she, his immediate heir, would survive him, sickly as she was herself. If he too believed it, Mary thought sardonically, it was patently clear that he must marry soon and beget an heir in order to prevent his Catholic sister from inheriting the throne.

'I trust,' she said, addressing her cousin Frances formally, 'that you and Lady Jane will enjoy your stay at New Hall. I live a quiet life. There will be no hunting, no card playing, no dice throwing. No excitement such as you enjoy at Bradgate.'

'It will make a pleasant and restful change,' the Duchess of Suffolk said dryly.

Feeling tired, as she so often did these days, Mary excused herself and as if at a prearranged signal Lady Wharton, one of the ladies of her household, appeared silently. She was a large dignified woman, entirely humourless, and much inclined to take her duties seriously. She suggested immediately that the visitors might like to inspect the walled garden which the Lady Mary, when well enough, took pride in cultivating herself.

'The Lady Mary,' she explained as they entered the garden, 'has imported many rare plants and has succeeded in naturalising them. The rarest are of Spanish origin.'

'As was the Lady Mary's mother,' the Duchess said brightly.

'A sufficient reason for the Lady Mary's intense interest,' Lady Wharton said sternly.

A large part of the garden had been converted into an aviary. Fascinated, Jane gazed upon a bewildering and colourful collection of parrots and parakeets, love-birds and other birds which she was unable to identify.

'Just as the Lady Mary's sainted mother was fond of monkeys,' Lady Wharton said informatively, 'and the misguided and unfortunate mother of the Lady Elizabeth fond of dogs, so is the Lady Mary fond of birds.'

'I like dogs myself,' Jane ventured, and wondered, while deciding that she did *not* like Lady Wharton, if she would be stigmatised as both misguided and unfortunate herself.

'I prefer cats myself,' Lady Wharton said stoically, 'but cats, these birds being so precious, are not permitted.'

They returned to the house by way of Mary's private chapel, Lady Wharton being piously determined to give the Protestant visitors, the perhaps redeemable heretics, a glimpse of the holy splendour of a real chapel. Pausing abruptly before the altar, and very nearly causing Jane to fall over her, she curtsied to the Host.

'If the Lady Mary is present,' Jane said, a flash of impishness getting the better of her, 'I see no sign of her.'

'Nor,' said a surprised Lady Wharton, 'do I.'

'Why, then, did you curtsy, Madame?'

The poor ignorant Protestant, Lady Wharton thought, and said: 'I curtsied, as I always do, to Him that made us all.'

'In point of fact,' said Jane, still in the grip of impishness, 'you curtsied to something that was made by the baker.'

Lady Wharton uttered a low gasp of horror at this arrant Protestant blasphemy. 'May God forgive you, Lady Jane, for such terrible wickedness.'

She curtsied to the Host again, then knelt in silent prayer, leaving the Duchess of Suffolk to hurry Jane away.

'What caused you to say such a dreadful thing?' she demanded.

'I think,' said Jane, after a moment's reflection, 'it was because the Lady Mary thought me childish in my reference to poor Pointer.' She looked at her mother curiously. 'You don't sound very angry, Madame.'

'Under different circumstances I would have been obliged to laugh,' the Duchess admitted, 'but angry I am. We are here to establish friendly family relations but I fear you have made a lifelong enemy.'

'In Lady Wharton? Surely she is of small account.'

'Your stupidity is beyond belief,' the Duchess said despairingly. 'Lady Wharton will tell the Lady Mary, and the Lady Mary will never forgive you.'

Jane hung her head. 'I shall apologise,' she said contritely.

'Do so, however fruitlessly, at the first opportunity.'

The first opportunity arose at the supper table, but so grim a silence did Mary Tudor maintain that Jane remained silent herself. From time to time Mary cast a baleful look upon her but for the most part addressed herself manfully to her meal and ate as voraciously as Jane had ever seen Great-Uncle Henry eat. Finally she flung a spoon across the table, aiming at Jane but missing her, if only narrowly.

'Madame,' she rasped, 'were you sent by my brother the King for the express purpose of insulting me?'

'Madame . . . ?' Jane faltered.

'Or, more to the point, for the express purpose of insulting my faith?'

'Your Cousin Jane,' the Duchess of Suffolk said hastily and

unwisely, 'has, I fear, a wry sense of humour.'

Mary gave her a contemptuous glance. 'I am not disposed to laugh where faith is concerned—mine or yours, misguided as yours at present is. You were born a Catholic, Madame. Indeed, England was a Catholic country at the time of your birth. When did you change, and why? Did you consider it politic to make the change?'

'I was inspired by the conviction that the New Learning was irresistible,' the Duchess said firmly. 'There was nothing politic about it. Your late father, permit me to remind you, was never a Protestant. I, and others, were in some danger until the day he died.'

Mary turned furiously on Jane. 'What of you, Madame?'

'I have known no other faith than that in which I have been reared,' Jane said.

'Nor have I,' Mary said, 'and I am many years older than you. Such is my conviction that I would go to the block for my faith.'

'As I would for mine,' Jane said staunchly.

Mary looked at her young cousin broodingly now, rather than angrily. 'God grant that you will never be called upon to make good your words.'

'Nor you yours,' Jane felt compelled to retort.

17

'AND so,' said Edward, struggling to keep all personal feeling from his voice, 'my uncle, the Duke of Somerset, has been arrested again.'

'He can only blame himself,' the Duke of Northumberland assured him, betraying in no way the satisfaction he felt. 'An unholy combination of Somerset the Protestant and your sister Mary the Catholic would have been disastrous to your Grace's reign.'

'And to *yours*,' Edward said with some asperity. 'Have you any proof that they were conspiring together for my overthrow?'

'Suspicion in this case is proof enough.'

'You arrested him on mere suspicion—he my uncle and closest living kinsman?'

'It is a charge that will not be pressed,' Northumberland said smoothly. 'There are other more substantial charges, charges that he has no hope of denying.'

'You have kept me in complete ignorance of them,' Edward said wearily.

'You were ill, your Grace. It was thought unwise to trouble you.'

'So very considerate of you,' Edward said, irony getting the better of him.

Northumberland studied the fourteen-year-old King as unobtrusively as possible. His eyes seemed to have become unnaturally enlarged in a face that was still pale and drawn. He was recovering, though more slowly than on the previous occasion at Windsor, from an attack of the sweating sickness. It was believed that it had been brought on by his having become overheated during a hunting party in which, deserting study for sport, he had indulged too violently. The illness, though often enough fatal, was not regarded as alarming in this instance, and even the physician who had predicted an early death was more optimistic now. The King, in many respects a manly boy, had outgrown his strength and would be susceptible to bouts of illness during adolescence. The physician admitted to having suspected a trace of consumption earlier but was inclined to believe now that he had been mistaken.

'Please state the more substantial charges,' Edward said, 'or am I to be kept in further ignorance?'

Northumberland bowed. 'Briefly, the Duke of Somerset is charged with assembling an army in the North for the purpose of marching on London. That in itself is a treasonable offence. He is further charged with plotting my death and the deaths of all the Lords of the Council who stand firmly behind me. Finally he is charged with planning to raise the City of London during an innocent-seeming banquet to be given by him for all the responsible lords, gentlemen and citizens. He was arrested on the eve of that banquet which was to have been held at Somerset House, a palace, need I stress, which he caused to be built at the expense of the Crown.'

'I must thank you for confiding in me,' Edward said stiffly. 'Is the result of the trial a foregone conclusion?'

'We can but wait and see, your Grace.'

The trial took place while Edward, at Northumberland's insistence, was resting at Hampton Court. Somerset was acquitted of one charge but found guilty on the others of felonious treason. Northumberland brought this news to Hampton Court and found Edward at the butts practising archery.

'The sentence is death,' Northumberland said unnecessarily.

Making no comment Edward aimed carefully and watched the arrow hit the white.

'Well aimed, my liege,' Northumberland applauded.

'You aim to aim better,' Edward said impulsively, 'when you shoot off my uncle's head.' Northumberland flinched but Edward found little satisfaction in his discomfiture and asked quickly: 'When is he to die?'

'The Lords of the Council have yet to decide upon a date.'

'I, at least, will not be called upon to sign the death warrant.'

'For that I thank God, your Grace,' Northumberland said, trying to assess the boy's attitude. 'I spared him once when he had not brought himself into such grievous danger. Would you have me spare him a second time?'

'Ah, you defer to me. You seek, however unnecessarily, my royal approval. Or am I mistaken?'

Northumberland remained uneasily silent, leaving Edward to thank God himself that he would not be called upon to sign his uncle's death warrant. It was perhaps fitting, he thought, that Uncle Edward, having signed Uncle Thomas's death warrant, should now find his own signed by the man who had replaced him. *Fitting?* Edward quickly reproached himself. It was not for him, even for one moment, to assume the role of God. 'You *do* defer to me?' he said insistently.

Northumberland smiled faintly. 'Are you not the King?'

'That, my lord duke, is no answer.'

'Year by year I defer increasingly to the King's Highness.'

'That is still no answer.'

'Somerset must die, your Grace.'

'And will, whether I say yea or nay.'

'Surely.'

'Year by year . . .' Edward mused, thinking of the time when he would come of age. 'May I never be called upon to sign your death warrant, Northumberland. And meanwhile may no other person be called upon to assume that duty in my name.'

Northumberland shuddered involuntarily and noticeably.

'What,' Edward said, 'has the future ghost of my uncle already crossed your future grave?'

Northumberland recovered himself quickly. 'I am moved always, your Grace, by the need to preserve for you and your heirs the Protestant faith.'

'My Catholic sister is my immediate heir, if I need remind you of that sobering fact.'

'You need not,' Northumberland said feelingly.

'I shall surely outlive her,' Edward said confidently, 'and beget a son to follow me on the throne.' He blushed, and angry with himself for doing so blushed all the more. 'Young as I am,' he said in an attempt at boastfulness, 'I could beget one if you arranged an immediate marriage for me.'

'Truly, your Grace?'

'Truly,' Edward said hotly. 'I beg you not to make fun of me.'

'Nothing is further from my mind,' Northumberland avowed. 'One would not dare to make fun of a Tudor in a matter so important to the maintenance of Tudor pride.'

Gratified, Edward said: 'Since you defer to me increasingly, may I then enjoy the realisation of one small personal wish?'

'And that?' Northumberland asked curiously.

'It is eight months or more since I last saw my cousin, the Lady Jane. One might suspect that she is being kept deliberately from my court.'

'If so, your Grace, not by me.'

'Then by whom?'

'If by anyone, the Duchess of Suffolk.'

'For what possible reason?'

'I have often wondered. The only possible explanation is that she is jealous of her daughter's position.'

'And because of that treats her harshly,' Edward said indignantly. 'Has always done so.' And with a flash of his father's humour he added: 'Must I send Suffolk to the the block and marry the mother instead of the daughter?'

'So . . . marriage for the King's Highness,' Northumberland said lightly.

'The Lady Jane is old enough,' Edward said, wrinkling his brow, 'but I have yet to make up my mind. The Lady Jane is in her fifteenth year. To what extent has she changed since St George's Day? My father brought her to court when she was nine for the purpose of inspecting her. I must do the same now before deciding whether or not to establish her safely, securely and permanently at *my* court.'

'We are grown somewhat pompous,' Northumberland chuckled.

'That,' said Edward, chuckling himself, 'is our royal privilege.'

The question of a royal marriage, Northumberland mused, was a matter for the Council, yet if Edward was capable of begetting a son, or even a daughter, and if he lived long enough to do so, it would be a sure way of preserving the Protestant succession. It might even be a better way, or at all events a safer way, than his alternative scheme which could be fraught with danger.

'Christmas is close at hand,' he said jovially. 'It will help your

Grace in your convalescence to enjoy some little merry-making at Greenwich.'

'Enjoy?' Edward asked, thinking of his condemned uncle.

'I regard it as a necessary distraction from state affairs.'

'And Greenwich is well removed from the Tower,' Edward said soberly. 'I fully understand. Very well, Greenwich and merry-making. My principal guests shall be the Duke and Duchess of Suffolk and the Lady Jane.'

'What of the Lady Elizabeth? By all accounts she is conducting herself with propriety at Hatfield and is addressing herself assiduously to her studies. I, not being Somerset, see no reason for keeping her in disgrace any longer because of her intrigues, never fully substantiated, with the late Lord Admiral.'

'You would make a friend of her,' Edward said shrewdly but not accusingly, 'because of her religion and her place in the line of succession.'

'That I would, your Grace, but the decision is yours.'

'She is said to be in bouncing health,' Edward commented, 'and would surely enjoy Christmas merry-making far more than the Lady Mary.'

'You have your immediate heir in mind also?' Northumberland asked carefully.

'She was always kind to me,' Edward said, 'and has defied me only in religious matters. Christmas is a time for families to gather together and forget their differences. I shall write to the Lady Mary personally.'

'A royal command or a brotherly invitation?'

'The latter,' Edward said generously.

Thinking that this might propitiate Mary's supporters, those at all events who were not over-fanatical, Northumberland raised no objection and went on to suggest the appointment of a Master of the King's Pastimes to superintend the festivities at Greenwich. When Edward had agreed to this with a hint of boyish enthusiasm Northumberland presented him with a large purse heavy with gold.

'The King's Highness,' he murmured, 'is surely in need of extra funds to cover the inevitable incidental expenses.'

Edward thanked him graciously. Northumberland's generosity, he reflected, was greater even than Uncle Thomas's had been, but one must not be deceived by it. Uncle Edward, always niggardly, had at least refrained from stooping to what might be regarded as bribery. Nevertheless it was heartening, ill as one sometimes felt, to know that Northumberland would seem to believe that the King's Highness would live to assume full kingly power. Or was he, a man who like many a noble lord gambled heavily at the card-table, merely gambling on the main chance?

No longer feeling gracious, Edward said gruffly: 'You must give the Lady Mary a Christmas present also.'

'What does your Grace suggest,' Northumberland asked brightly, 'a diamond-studded crucifix?'

Edward could but laugh and feeling happier wasted no time in writing his letter to Mary. She accepted his invitation, saying in her brief letter how happy she was to be asked rather than commanded, and reaching London before the court was ready to move to Greenwich took up residence at her rarely used town house, St John's, once the property of the Knights Hospitallers. From there, on a cold but sunny morning, she set out by coach to pay her respects to her brother the King at Whitehall. Riding with her, though not at her own instigation, and sometimes hindering her passage was a growing throng of Catholic supporters. Northumberland, warned of her impending arrival, was at the palace gates with a band of Lords of the Council to greet her in the King's name. Her coach, with the horses now removed, was being drawn by stout burghers, a display of loyalty to the Catholic heir not anticipated by Northumberland. All but deafened by the cheering of the throng, he thought wryly that he had miscalculated when agreeing to Mary Tudor's visit and he wondered, not without superstition, if he was being given a glimpse of a future that he wished to prevent. He dismissed the thought angrily; Mary Tudor must not and would not be allowed to come to the throne.

'The King awaits your Highness,' he said, after greeting her with false cordiality and assisting her to alight.

'And my many friends also?' Mary asked in her mannish voice.

Northumberland bowed. 'Are they not, as we are, Madame, his Majesty's loyal subjects?'

Bested but unwilling to admit it, Mary allowed him to

escort her to the presence chamber. They were followed by her attendant, Lady Wharton, several members of her suite (a large and imposing one, Northumberland noted) and the Lords of the Council, many of them smiling in a sickly manner. The presence chamber was overcrowded with courtiers and their ladies, among them the Duke and Duchess of Suffolk and Lady Jane Grey. Edward was seated in a throne-like chair wearing what he called his second-best robes which he reserved for state occasions less important than the opening of Parliament. Mary curtsied three times and was about to kneel when Edward, springing up, forbade her to do so.

'It gives us great joy,' he said formally, 'to receive our sister and heir.'

Mary kissed his hand. 'And I much happiness so to be received.'

Edward offered her his arm. 'Let us mingle with the court. If there are any here with whom you are unacquainted, pray let me present them.'

'I am well acquainted with my cousin Jane,' Mary said dryly when Jane, flanked by her parents, stood uncertainly before her.

'A disastrous acquaintance at the last meeting,' the Duchess of Suffolk said woefully.

'Madame,' said Jane, addressing Mary in a low voice, 'I beg you to accept my apology for causing you to lose your temper.'

Mary laughed unexpectedly. 'As arrogant, this cousin of mine, as any Tudor, living or dead. None the less, lose my temper I did, and for that I must strive to forgive myself. I was in poor health at that time and easily ruffled. To make amends I bring you a present, Jane. Lady Wharton shall give it to Mrs Eleyn.'

'I am overcome with gratitude,' Jane said demurely.

Mary turned to Edward. 'Our cousin's present, like mine for you, must not be opened until Christmas morning.'

'You shall receive yours from me on the morning itself,' he said, 'but I am hard-pressed to think of a suitable one.' He remembered Northumberland's suggestion and choked back the laughter that bubbled up in his throat. 'Something frivolous, perhaps.'

'Royal clemency is all that I ask of the King's Highness,'

Mary said gravely. 'Not, however, on my own behalf but on behalf of one of the many prisoners languishing in the Tower.'

Northumberland, within earshot, stiffened and stepped forward. 'With the King's permission, Madame,' he said quickly, 'I must state that the Duke of Somerset, unless he begs for clemency himself, will receive none.'

'Somerset's fate is no concern of mine,' Mary said. 'A traitor and self-condemned. I seek clemency for Bishop Gardiner.'

Edward, as surprised as Northumberland, looked at his sister indignantly. Gardiner, the old Catholic favoured by his father because of lip-service to what was sometimes called the Henrican faith; Gardiner who had plotted and schemed to bring about Katherine Parr's disgrace, even her death; Gardiner, never a Protestant, who after her actual death had been arrested on a charge of heresy for preaching a sermon in near-praise of the old faith. His life had been spared but he would never be released while a Protestant monarch sat on the throne.

'Do you regard him as a martyr?' Edward asked Mary.

'That I do, your Grace.'

'It would be a pity,' Edward said, glancing at Northumberland, 'to deprive him of that distinction.'

'Well said, your Grace,' Northumberland applauded softly.

'I am trying to remember,' Mary said angrily, 'that I have always loved my brother dearly.'

'And I that I have always so loved my sister,' Edward said sincerely but unmoved where Gardiner was concerned.

Mary curtsied. 'This is a brief visit, your Grace, but even brief ones are apt to weary me.'

Edward inclined his head. 'You have our permission to withdraw.'

Northumberland escorted Mary Tudor back from the presence chamber to the gates of the palace. The same burghers were waiting to take again the place of the horses and the crowd of cheering supporters seemed to have grown even thicker. Many of them, Northumberland suspected, were hirelings not necessarily paid by Mary Tudor herself, but even so, perhaps even more so, they represented a dangerous element and must be controlled by force of arms if necessary.

'I fear,' Mary said, as he assisted her into the coach, 'that illness will confine me to my bed during the festivities at Greenwich.'

'A vast pity, Madame,' Northumberland sighed. 'The Archbishop is to preach the Christmas sermon. It was hoped by the King that you would not refuse to hear God's word.'

'From the lips of a renegade who has recently taken a wife?' Mary questioned indignantly.

'I admit that at sixty-two Cranmer should have known better,' Northumberland joked. 'The truth of the matter, however, is that he married a Lutheran woman in Germany all of twenty years ago, has only now admitted it and brought the good creature to England.'

'He feeling it safe to do so! But shame on him, shame on him!'

'Safe to do so indeed,' Northumberland said. 'Priestly celibacy is no longer the law of the land.'

Mary was shaking with anger. She had more than one reason for hating Archbishop Cranmer. Ordained a Catholic priest twenty-eight years ago, he had found favour in her father's eyes by suggesting that the validity of the King's first and, to her, only true marriage should be debated in the universities of Europe. Appointed Archbishop of Canterbury in 1553 he had declared her parents' marriage null and void and had crowned Anne Boleyn, Elizabeth's deservedly ill-fated mother.

'God's word!' she burst out. 'By my faith, Northumberland, I do not know what they call God's word these days. It is not the same as in the days when my father was a true son of the Church. What you mean by God's word is not the same, I vow, as what I mean.'

'What I mean, Madame, and what the Archbishop means is the same as what the King himself means.'

'Enough!' Mary said, and smiling thinly made a sweeping gesture with both hands. 'A sad day, Northumberland, if this joyous crowd should become a righteous and angry mob.'

'Madame,' Northumberland retorted instantly, 'do you warn me or yourself?'

Mary's eyes darkened. 'The Duke of Northumberland is not lacking in intelligence. Let him arrive at the answer without comment from me.'

18

'WHAT,' Edward asked Jane, 'were the disastrous circumstances of your meeting with my sister Mary at New Hall Manor?'

Jane stared beyond him across the river and in an all but expressionless voice gave him the facts plainly and without exaggeration. Then she looked at him obliquely, wondering anxiously if he was angry with her because of her inexcusable rudeness. He remained silent, his face revealing nothing of his thoughts, and turning stared across the river himself. It was Christmas Eve. They were standing together beneath a canopy in the royal barge, the Tower Wharf far behind and Greenwich in sight. At Edward's command they were isolated from their attendants who stood, not incuriously, at a respectful distance. He was wearing a long and bulky fur cloak, a fur cap and fur-lined shoes. To Jane he had the appearance of a Russian bear, except for his fine-featured, once chubby but now rather thin face. She had thought him frail and ill at her brief encounter with him in the presence chamber at Whitehall, but now, if only because of the biting December wind, his cheeks had a healthy, rosy complexion. Swathed in furs herself she wondered if she too looked like a Russian bear.

Edward, his shoulders shaking, swung round on her and said sternly: 'It was a wicked remark you made to Lady Wharton.'

'I was sadly amiss,' Jane said contritely.

'I am doing my best,' said Edward, 'not to laugh.'

'Your Grace . . . ?'

Trying to sound stern again he said: 'That you very nearly fell over Lady Wharton there before the altar must have been a most amusing sight.' He frowned at the thought of Mary's illicit altar and went on broodingly: 'The Lady Mary has a powerful friend in the Emperor. It angers me that because of him she should be permitted to flout the Act of Uniformity, even in private. It is a case of winking the eye or risking war with Germany.'

'You have never wanted war,' Jane reminded him.

'Not even a holy one. If only I could bring Mary to see the error of her ways. It is because I love God and have much affection for her that I would destroy her obstinacy.'

'There is little you can do,' Jane ventured.

'There is nothing, except to prevent all possibility of her coming to the throne.' Remembering his reason for bringing Jane to court he submitted to an irritating fit of shyness and said hesitantly: 'How funny you look. I can only see your face but . . .'

'I can only see yours,' Jane interrupted, then quickly apologised for her rudeness. 'Your Grace was about to say . . . ?'

'It is a face that I don't quite recognise. You have changed much, Cousin Jane, since last St George's Day.'

'For the better, I pray, I having become a woman.'

'And,' he said, feeling gauche, 'a handsome one.'

'Handsome?' she questioned, unconsciously coquettish.

'Pretty,' he amended.

In relief he saw that the rowers had shipped their oars and that the barge was being tied up at Greenwich Wharf. Courteously he helped Jane ashore and gave her into the care of her father who, with Northumberland and Archbishop Cranmer, was waiting to welcome the royal party. Suffolk, having been acquainted by Northumberland with Edward's frame of mind, gave the boy a searchingly cautious look, then Jane a similar look. Both of them, he thought with satisfaction, seemed to be unnaturally flushed. He glanced at Cranmer and he, in Northumberland's confidence also, nodded approvingly. Then arm in arm the layman and the cleric followed in the wake of the royal party.

'Progress, my lord duke?' Cranmer questioned, sounding ridiculously arch.

'One can but think so, my lord archbishop.'

'Since my godson must marry in the interests of the realm,' Cranmer pronounced, 'how happy the circumstance if he is blessed with a Protestant wife, and one of his own choosing.'

'Amen to that,' Suffolk murmured.

At supper Edward's guests at the royal table were confined to Jane and her parents, Northumberland and his wife, Archbishop Cranmer and the newly arrived and at first silently watchful Elizabeth Tudor. Jane sat on the King's right, a distinction regarded by all present as significant, Elizabeth on his left.

'Did you enjoy a pleasant journey from Hatfield, Madame?' Edward asked his sister after the first course of five dishes had been served.

'Pleasant enough, your Grace,' Elizabeth responded without enthusiasm.

'May your stay at your birthplace be a happy one,' he said graciously. 'Do you find your room comfortable?'

'More comfortable, though I have no memory of it, than when I was born in it,' Elizabeth said dryly.

Edward raised his eyebrows. 'So, they have lodged you in the Chamber of the Virgins.'

'I thought it a fitting gesture, your Grace,' Northumberland said softly.

Edward looked at the President of the Council suspiciously. Was sarcasm intended, Northumberland having in mind the scandalous rumour that Elizabeth had lost her virginity to the late Lord Admiral? If so, Edward was not ready to be amused. Seeing Elizabeth for the first time since her removal from Katherine Parr's household, he was remembering how much he had loved her when they had played together in the nursery, she his senior by four years. He was remembering too the declaration of her birth which lay in the royal archives. It had been prepared before her actual birth by her over-confident mother, Anne Boleyn, one sentence reading: 'Whereas it has pleased Almighty God in his infinite mercy and grace to send unto us a Prince . . .' How long, he wondered, before his father, in a fit of anger, had added the two letters 'ss'? One must feel compassion for Elizabeth because she had not been born a prince.

'Madame,' he said, turning to Jane and battling with a return of the shyness that had attacked him earlier, 'I must compliment you on the prettiness of your gown.'

Jane, having felt self-conscious about her new and unaccustomed finery, experienced a little glow of pleasure. It was her father, not her mother, who had insisted on 'some little brightness in Lady Jane's attire', and it was her tutor who, as if voicing her mother's disapproval, had protested in shocked tones. Such rich adornment and a glittering array of jewellery, he had said, were unbecoming in a maiden professing godliness. That the King should approve, he being full of godliness himself, the Duke of Suffolk had said, was all that would matter. Should he disapprove, then Jane would have no recourse but to resume the uninspired and uninspiring colourlessness of the normal garb forced upon her by the Duchess. But Edward did indeed approve, Jane thought happily, and thanked him warmly for the compliment he had paid her.

'Your appearance, Madame,' he said, feeling and trying to sound gallant, 'brightens my court.'

He turned in his chair, trying not to stare too obviously at Jane. It was not only her face that he did not quite recognise now but her whole entrancing person. The low-cut gown revealed the swelling of breasts that he had never noticed before. Had they grown magically since St George's Day when scarcely her neck had been visible because of a high dowdy bodice of dark grey brocade? It was a slender neck, adorned now with a string of richly glowing pearls. He drew in his breath sharply, acutely conscious of an exciting warmth in his loins never before experienced except in dreams. Hurriedly he raised his eyes to Jane's brow fully revealed in all its smoothness by the placing of her white satin head-dress. She held his eyes for a moment, then dropped hers modestly. Commendable, he thought, but infuriating. He wanted to reach out and touch her in a way that he had never wanted to touch anyone before. Not quite in control of himself he took her hand unsteadily in his and kissed it.

'We shall have a merry time this Christmas, Madame,' he said, and as if to deceive all present he turned from Jane and kissed his sister's hand. 'What say you, Elizabeth?'

'As merry as we can make it,' she said, suppressing a yawn.

Cranmer and Suffolk exchanged sly glances. Progress and more progress? Northumberland looked on indulgently but the Duchess of Suffolk, knowing what they were about and trembling at the thought of the unwanted duty which seemed to lie ahead of her, scowled and choked on the meat which she spooned furiously into her mouth.

'Northumberland,' Edward said, flinging back his chair, 'let us have music and dancing. It is the King's pleasure that he should dance the galliard with the Lady Jane.'

'The pavane would be less exerting in your Grace's present state of health,' Cranmer warned.

'The galliard, the galliard!' Edward insisted imperiously.

He offered Jane his arm. Northumberland rose and bowed before Elizabeth. Suffolk approached the Duchess of Northumberland in like manner while the Duchess of Suffolk cast upon Archbishop Cranmer a challenging glance which prudently he chose to ignore. The musicians played the opening bars and at a gesture from the King courtiers and their ladies rose obediently from the lower tables.

'The pavane,' Edward whispered to Jane, 'is much too slow and stately for the young and healthy.'

But the galliard, aways a lively and energetic dance, was soon too much for him. He felt a sharp pain in his chest and a weakness in his legs which he tried stubbornly to ignore, even when Jane, aware of his distress, whispered diplomatically that his manly strength was bringing her to the point of exhaustion.

'Shame on you,' he gasped, and fainted.

A physician, hurriedly called, revived him with pungent smelling salts and then, though he protested angrily, he was carried from the dining hall in a chair, rather in the manner of his late father. Northumberland followed, gained the physician's assurance that all the King needed was a good night's rest and returned to inform Jane that by royal command she was to open her Christmas presents with Edward and Elizabeth at an informal breakfast on the morrow.'

'I, the much-needed chaperon,' Elizabeth remarked.

Northumberland hid a smile. 'Morning prayers before breakfast,' he reminded her. 'As for the meal itself, informal as it is expected to be, the King's tutor will be present as well as your own attendant and the Lady Jane's.'

'Even at the ripe age of eighteen,' Elizabeth said spiritedly, 'I am still not considered responsible.'

Northumberland bowed. 'It is a cross, Madame, which you must bear with fortitude.'

Unaware that the physician had given him a sedative, Edward woke almost too late for morning prayers. Remembering the exciting Christmas breakfast that lay ahead he came close to regretting the need of the habitual early-morning devotions. He fretted and fumed in his private pew and, when at last release was his, hurried to his private dining room with Sir John Cheke in attendance. He was waiting impatiently in his place when Elizabeth and Jane, followed by Mrs Ashley and Mrs Eleyn, joined him.

'Laggards!' he admonished, and impatient still forbade them to curtsy. 'We shall open the presents before eating. Be seated, be seated.'

Elizabeth and Jane placed themselves on either side of him at the table and their attendants removed themselves to a smaller table beyond earshot to await his demand for breakfast. Quickly sorting the presents which were heaped in front of him he distributed them according to the various inscriptions.

'The Lady Jane shall open hers first,' he said generously.

Jane found that Edward, whom she had expected to give her some scholarly tome, had selected a paste pomander, a little ball on a silver chain to be worn round the waist, the ball filled with delicate French perfume. She thanked him warmly.

'Frivolous,' he said, 'but it will go well with your new fashionable clothes. What has the Lady Mary given you?'

Jane opened Mary's present and found a bracelet to match the necklace which Mary had given her five years ago. It was a nice gesture, Jane thought, and was overcome with mortification.

'Pretty,' said Edward.

'Alas,' Jane confessed, 'I neglected to find a present for Cousin Mary.'

'No matter,' Edward said airily. 'What has Elizabeth given you?'

Jane opened her third present and found a pair of jewelled gloves. Then Edward, still placing generosity before impatience, commanded Elizabeth to open her presents. He had given her a comb-case set with pearls, Jane had given her a dozen fine handkerchiefs and a highly polished steel glass and Mary had given her a brooch set with rock rubies round an agate.

'Now!' said Edward, and fell upon his own presents.

From Jane he found a miniature of herself, from Elizabeth

a small portrait of *herself* and from Mary a copy of the book which their late father had written in condemnation of Martin Luther.

'Mary would jog my memory that my father was once a Catholic,' he said angrily. 'Knowing that she is fond of birds I had thought to send her a sweet-singing lark . . .' He broke off, laughed with religious spitefulness and said softly: 'Instead I shall send her an illuminated copy of the treatise I wrote two years ago, my denial of the supremacy and infallibility of the Pope.'

'A matter of tit for tat,' Elizabeth commented.

'Now,' said Edward, 'let us tackle a hearty breakfast.' He was looking at Jane as he spoke and suspecting silent disapproval asked gruffly, 'Is anything amiss, Lady Jane?'

'I was thinking of the sweet-singing lark,' she said quietly. 'Would your Grace permit *me* to send it to the Lady Mary?'

Edward flushed quickly but not angrily. 'In the King's name, Cousin Jane?'

'If the King should so wish it.'

'By which you mean,' Edward said softly, 'if the Lady Jane should so wish the King to wish it.'

'Yes,' Jane admitted, holding his eyes steadily and lovingly.

A lesson in compassion, he thought, and felt deeply ashamed. He would never weaken in religious matters where Mary was concerned and he really ought to be angry with Jane, but a deepening love shattered even the beginnings of anger.

'No,' he said, not caring if he was exhibiting a weakness unwarranted in a king, 'send Mary the bird in your own name. I shall withhold the treatise and give it to you.'

'Thank you,' Jane said. 'I shall treasure it.'

'And treasuring it,' Edward said proudly, 'pray remember that I wrote it without the aid of any living person.'

'It must, for sure, have been heavenly inspiration,' Elizabeth murmured.

'Hold your tongue, Sister,' Edward said angrily.

'Sarcasm was not intended, your Grace.'

'Your very words are an admission of it.'

'I stand corrected,' Elizabeth said unrepentantly.

Edward shrugged and laughed. 'I must find a husband for you to put a bridle on your Tudor tongue.'

'That no man will ever do,' Elizabeth avowed, and glanced at Jane. 'And for yourself a wife?'

Edward blushed and called loudly for breakfast to be served. Later in the morning he summoned the Master of the King's Pastimes and discussed with him the festivities which were to begin immediately after the Archbishop had preached his Christmas sermon, but eager as he was to indulge in a continuing day by day round of merry-making he was preoccupied with thoughts of Jane. Her compassionate attitude had impressed him deeply and it seemed to him, more and more strongly as the festivities continued into the New Year, that it was the deciding factor. Finally, but with some trepidation, he summoned Northumberland to a private audience and after an exchange of formal greetings fell uneasily silent.

'Your Grace is about to inform me,' Northumberland said knowingly, 'of the satisfactory outcome of your royal inspection of the Lady Jane.'

Rendered bashful by this frontal attack Edward said hurriedly: 'My uncle the Duke still languishes in the Tower. Hints have been dropped of royal clemency, should he ask for it.'

'He was invited to ask but did not ask.'

'Had he done so, would it have been granted in my name?'

'Since he did not ask, why beggar the question, your Grace?'

'You knew his pride would prevent him from asking.'

'True, true.'

'And so without any risk at all you sought to win favour in the eyes of his friends and supporters.'

'Your Grace's innate perception will never cease to amaze me.'

Trying not to feel flattered Edward asked: 'Must he suffer much longer in the Tower?'

Northumberland looked at Edward covertly: 'The Duke of Somerset died on Tower Hill this morning.'

Edward grasped his hands tightly behind his back. 'Bravely?' he asked, trying to assume an air of indifference.

'Bravely enough.'

'Did he speak first?'

'He adjured the onlookers to accept the will of God and yield obedience to the King and his Council. Afterwards there were many who pressed forward to dip their handkerchiefs into his blood.'

'To them he died a martyr,' Edward said, turning away.

'Your Grace . . .'

Edward swung round on Northumberland. 'Am I,' he asked bitterly, 'to announce, on the same day, my decision to marry Lady Jane Grey?'

'The affairs of the quick,' Northumberland said, 'are of greater importance than the soon-to-be-forgotten affairs of the dead.'

'Very well, Northumberland. Pray inform the Duke of Suffolk that I seek the hand of his eldest daughter.'

Northumberland bowed. 'A King does not seek, he commands.'

'Joyfully, on this occasion,' Edward said. 'I shall issue the command myself. Inform the Duke of Suffolk that the King's Highness is waiting to receive him in private audience.'

But to Edward's surprise it was his cousin Frances, Duchess of Suffolk, who, after an irritatingly lengthy delay, came in her husband's place. She curtsied and knelt and on being bidden to rise was shaking so greatly with agitation that he invited her to be seated.

'Are you aware, Madame, of my reason for requesting your husband's presence?'

'I am, your Grace,' Frances said faintly. 'It may seem that I am a domineering woman but it is I, your cousin, your Tudor cousin, who should be consulted in this family matter rather than my husband.'

'A consultation was not intended,' Edward said, feeling sorry for the man who was always weak where his Tudor wife was concerned. 'A decison has been reached. It is for you to obey that decision.'

In spite of her agitation Frances came close to bristling with anger; then she consoled herself with the thought that Edward's kingly arrogance would receive a well-deserved blow when she revealed to him the truth of his birth. Her eyes narrowed. Need she really reveal it? Now that Somerset was dead the secret was hers alone and the horror of incest seemed not to matter very greatly. Why, then, deprive herself of the satisfaction of ridding herself of the troublesome Jane and at the same time seeing the girl, her apparent daughter, become the King's Consort? On the other hand, and she shuddered at the thought, if she allowed the marriage to take place her immortal soul would surely be cast into the fires of hell.

'Madame . . . ?' Edward questioned impatiently.

'It is a high honour,' she faltered, and burst into tears.

'Tears of joy?' Edward asked uncertainly.

'No, your Grace, tears of sorrow. You cannot—in desperation I must betray a trust and speak the truth—you cannot marry your sister.'

'What nonsense is this?' Edward demanded.

'Your half-sister. It amounts to the same thing where marriage is concerned. Jane is your half-sister. You could no more marry her than Mary or Elizabeth.'

Edward looked at her in stunned silence for a moment; then in a low, horrified voice he said: 'You mean, Madame, that you and my father—that is, you and your uncle . . . ?'

Frances had not contemplated such a charge being made but it was a likely enough assumption on the boy's part. She denied it hotly, saw that he accepted her denial and feeling more kindly towards him snatched at the opportunity of sparing him from being told that he was a changeling.

'I took Jane,' she said, 'when my own daughter of that name died within a few days of her birth and reared her in her place. I took her,' she added for good measure, 'at your father's command and he swore me to secrecy.'

'Who was Jane's real mother?'

'A woman of no consequence,' Frances said, thinking that Jane Seymour had been a woman of considerable consequence.

'Is your husband aware of the deception?'

Frances shook her head. 'He was in France at that time. I am the only living person aware of it, apart from yourself.'

Edward remembered his father's anger when he had come upon them during the marriage game. It was an understandable anger now. He remembered, too, that Uncle Thomas had said that his father had changed his mind, but clearly Uncle Thomas had lied. And it explained, he thought, why his father had placed Jane after Elizabeth in the line of succession. Nevertheless it was a sorry blow and he wanted desperately not to accept the Duchess of Suffolk's story.

'Can I really believe you?' he asked, almost pleadingly.

'Why should I lie, your Grace? Would I not, in normal circumstances, like to see my daughter married to the King of England?'

'Yes, I must believe you,' he said bitterly, 'and—and thank you.'

He had more to thank her for than he knew, Frances thought, and said with a harshness that grated on him: 'With your Grace's permission I shall remove Jane to Bradgate.'

'Yes, that would be wise, but I beg you to treat her gently. Nay, Cousin Frances, I command you to do so.'

Frances withdrew and presently Edward sent for Northumberland, not quite knowing what to say to him. He was certain of only one thing, he must respect the Duchess's confidence. Or *must* he? It would at least give him some joy to acknowledge Jane openly as his sister. Then it crossed his mind that the Council, if told, might hasten to remove Jane from the line of succession. No one, not even Jane herself, he decided, must be told the truth.

'Northumberland,' he said somewhat lamely, 'I have changed my mind. That is to say,' he added, attempting imperiousness, 'we, the King, have changed our mind.'

Northumberland studied him in silence for several moments. During the festivities Edward's health had improved and he had gained a very nearly robust appearance. Now, of a sudden, he seemed to have shrunk in stature and his cheeks were unnaturally flushed. He moved across the room looking pathetically like an old man and all but fell into a chair. Was his uncle's execution the cause of this incredible change, or had he been upset by the Duchess of Suffolk?

'May I ask if the Lady Jane's mother is in some way responsible for your change of mind?' Northumberland asked carefully.

'In no way at all,' Edward said, surprised and pleased by his unexpected resourcefulness. 'I remembered in time that my father pronounced long ago against my marrying my cousin Jane. My father's will is still law to me.'

Northumberland accepted this philosophically. Jane Grey might yet be of greater use to him in another capacity, if the King's apparently improved health had deceived both him and the royal physicians. And looking at him now one could but believe that it had.

'Is the Princess Elizabeth of France still unmarried?' Edward asked.

'She is, your Grace.'

'And peace has been made with France. My father had her in mind for me. The negotiations came to nothing. Let them be re-opened, Northumberland.'

'It shall be as you wish,' Northumberland said, with no intention of allowing such a marriage to take place.

'Your acquiescence is gratifying,' Edward said. 'It almost makes me believe that I am eighteen and have reached my majority.'

Looking to the future where his personal schemes were concerned, Northumberland said softly: 'Once you have entered your sixteenth year it may be possible to change the law.'

'Possible? How so?'

'By Act of Parliament, but we must move cautiously, you the King and I the King's chief minister, and bide our time.'

Edward sprang up excitedly, then collapsed into his chair again, looking more flushed than ever. Withdrawing quietly, Northumberland summoned a newly appointed physician, the celebrated Cardona of Milan, and sent him to administer to the King. An hour later Cardona waited on Northumberland with an unexpected diagnosis.

'Measles, my lord duke, and clearly a serious attack.'

19

'HEALTH and long life to the King's Highness,' Frances, Duchess of Suffolk said, drowsy after a heavier consumption of food than usual. She raised her silver-bound mug of spiced wine and added tipsily: 'May his royal progress bring him more honour than any enjoyed by his late, monstrous and regrettable father.'

The others at the supper table—Jane, Aylmer, Haddon and the favoured steward, Adrian Stokes—raised their own mugs and murmured: 'The King.'

'God bless and keep him,' Haddon added.

'From gambling,' Frances commented, casting upon that most Protestant cleric a baleful look.

Jane did her best to suppress a bored yawn, then reproached herself for feeling bored. It was her fifteenth birthday and much to her surprise her mother had decided to give her a special party with strolling players brought in to perform and with music and dancing to follow the performance. Frances, aware of Jane's surprise, had refrained from telling her that, however much it went against the grain, she was obeying Edward's command to treat her gently. Not that gentleness called for merry-making, but Frances herself was bored, she not having been invited by the King to accompany her husband on the royal progress of the northern counties. She glanced bleary-eyed at Stokes and very nearly giggled. He was younger than her husband by five or six years, more manly and, as she knew from experience, a great deal more vigorous. There was one sure way, now she came to think of it, of relieving any sort of boredom, and she began to wish with Tudor impatience that the supper party could be brought to a speedy conclusion.

'It is to be hoped,' Dr Haddon ventured, 'that the royal progress will not prove too rigorous for the King.'

Frances scarcely cared. The King, but only because (on the

wrong side of the blanket, as it were) she had helped to make him so. She had not seen him since last Christmas at Greenwich. He had scarcely recovered from his attack of measles when he had been laid low by smallpox, the dread disease first suffered in England by his father nearly forty years ago. But Edward was said to be in excellent health again and fit, according to Northumberland, to embark on a lengthy royal progress. Her thoughts flew off at a tangent when she saw Jane yawning widely. What a stir it would cause if she, the supposed mother, were to announce that it was not Jane's birthday but the celebration of the birth of that other Jane whom she had replaced. She checked the thought in midstream. Northumberland had hinted during his last visit to Bradgate that Jane might be of paramount importance to him, to her parents and to England if the King should die prematurely. He had spoken in riddles beyond her comprehension but his tone of voice had impressed her and left her expectant. But of what? A yet to be revealed Northumberland-inspired miracle? Northumberland, she reflected, more in resignation than resentment, had rapidly become a greater dictator than the late Somerset. She must warn him to take care lest he should overreach himself and follow her one-time lover to the block.

'Jane,' she said sharply, 'wake up or the performance will be wasted on you.' And clapping her hands she called loudly: 'Let the players be brought in.'

The performance was interrupted almost immediately by the arrival of the Duke of Suffolk. He and his attendants, it seemed, were the advance party of the royal progress. The King, weary after much travelling and finding his quarters at Leicester cramped and uncomfortable, had accepted Suffolk's invitation to rest for a few days at Bradgate Park.

'His acceptance fills me with new hope,' Suffolk told his wife eagerly.

'The King will never change his mind about Jane,' Frances said, in something of a temper because his return had foiled her plan for a merry night with Adrian Stokes.

'Negotiations for the hand of the Princess Elizabeth of France are under way,' Suffolk admitted, 'but progress is slow and the French ambassador has yet to reveal any real enthusiasm.'

The main party of the royal progress reached Bradgate an hour later. Edward entered the courtyard leaning heavily on the arms of two physicians and was taken immediately to the apartments that had been hastily prepared for him.

'The King's condition is worse than I believed,' Suffolk said when he and Northumberland were alone together. 'Even the short journey from Leicester has taken its toll. The royal progress should never have been embarked upon.'

'The King was eager to make it,' Northumberland said mildly. 'I myself suggested that it might be much too strenuous.'

'Could you not have prevented it?' Suffolk asked, speaking mildly himself.

Northumberland shrugged lightly. 'I permitted it for the purpose of discovering to what extent the King's strength could be tried.'

'There are some who would regard such an attitude as diabolical,' Suffolk ventured.

'More than likely, if told, but since you, my dear Suffolk, are my only confidant . . .'

Suffolk laughed awkwardly. 'I make no accusation. A royal progress, however strenuous, could scarcely endanger the King's life.'

'Scarcely, but it could hasten the inevitable end of that life.'

'Inevitable?' asked a startled Suffolk.

'Rest assured,' Northumberland said dryly, 'I did not consent to the royal progress with that aim in mind. I need the King alive if not healthy until my plans for the preservation of my government and the Protestant faith are fully prepared. The King is suffering from consumption, a fact revealed to me by the physician who examined him before we left Leicester. It was supected once before. There is no doubt about it now. The King will not be told. Nor will anyone else.'

'You have already confided in me.'

'For the very good reason that I need you in the Lords to rally all possible support on my behalf.'

'I was unaware that you were in need of support,' Suffolk said cautiously.

'Let me confide in you fully,' Northumberland said bluffly. 'When Parliament meets after Christmas a special Bill will be presented, a Bill which will allow the King to attain his majority immediately.'

'At fifteen instead of eighteen. Why that, Northumberland?'

'In order that he can make a will, legally, incontrovertibly, and in it name your daughter, the Lady Jane, his immediate heir.'

Suddenly Suffolk was shaking with excitement. 'My daughter to be the next monarch! Incredible!'

'And, I would say, within the space of a year.'

'But my dear Northumberland, would the King consent to signing such a will?'

'Persuaded by me, yes.'

'I do trust you are not being over-confident.'

'Over-confident or not, Suffolk, there will be no persuasion on my part unless you first consent to your daughter Jane marrying my son Guilford.'

'Lord Guilford Dudley to be Prince Consort,' Suffolk commented. 'A neat scheme, one which I should have suspected of a man who was never altruistic.'

'Do you agree to it?' Northumberland asked impatiently.

'Gladly, but what of my wife?'

'By St Mary, Suffolk, you must learn to assert yourself where that woman is concerned.'

Suffolk smiled in a sickly manner. 'She will have to be told, unless you plan a secret marriage.'

'Secrecy could be dangerous. The marriage must be open and above board, and with the King's consent. But I run ahead of events. Meanwhile, keep your counsel, Suffolk.'

'You have my word, my solemn word,' Suffolk promised.

Edward remained at Bradgate until his birthday which he insisted should be celebrated informally. He ate sparingly during the birthday feast and took no part in the dancing. He felt rested but knew that any exertion would tire him sorely. He tried to assume an attitude of indifference toward Jane and was relieved, though experiencing a feeling of frustration, when it became evident that she was being prevented by the Duchess of Suffolk from being alone with him. On one occasion when he found Jane looking at him in a bewildered and hurt manner he felt an urge, quickly suppressed, to tell her the truth and welcome her as the sister she was. During the dancing he watched her dance the galliard with Northumberland's fourth and only unmarried son, Lord Guilford Dudley, a fair-haired, graceful youth a year or more older than Jane. Edward had grown to like him, even though young Dudley was not over-given to scholarship. He glanced quickly from Northumberland to Suffolk who were seated at table with him and saw them exchange fatherly nods of approval. Jane for Guilford Dudley, Edward thought bitterly, not for him, yet it would be a suitable alliance and a splendid opportunity for Jane to abandon a name never rightly hers for that of Dudley. Feeling inordinately noble he took Northumberland aside later that night and asked him if he proposed to marry his son Guilford to the Lady Jane.

'With your Grace's approval, yes,' Northumberland said, gratified that Edward should be the one to broach the subject.

'I shall make it a royal command if you so wish it.'

To egg him on Northumberland said thoughtfully: 'The Council may well prefer a more important marriage for the young woman who is presently third in the line of succession.'

'Am I to be baulked?' Edward asked pettishly.

'Not in the long run, your Grace. Let us say no more about the subject until Parliament has debated the question of reducing your majority by three years.'

'Satisfactorily debated?'

Northumberland smiled engagingly. 'I can but think so. The Bill, initiated by me, will give the lie to the claim, the most unjust claim, that I, the King's chief minister, am an uncontrollable dictator.'

'Pray call Parliament soon,' Edward said, and wondered why he should feel of a sudden that all matters, important and unimportant, needed the urgent attention of his full kingly power. Looking at Northumberland searchingly but trying to keep anxiety out of his voice he said: 'Are you keeping anything from me, Northumberland?'

'In matters of state,' Northumberland said glibly, 'I hide nothing whatever from the King's Highness.'

'What of my state of health?' Edward asked tensely. 'I want the truth, Northumberland.'

'If you are anxious about your health,' Northumberland said unhurriedly, 'let me assure you that you are suffering only from exhaustion brought on by too much exertion after the childish disease of measles and the commonplace disease of smallpox.'

'Many people die of smallpox,' Edward said lugubriously.

'And many survive it, as you did, as your father did and as I did when much the same age as you.'

'I have not dared to look too closely in my steel glass,' Edward said, only partly consoled. 'Vanity is a sin, that I believe, but is my face as pock-marked as yours?'

'Far less, and when the time comes for you to sport a beard the marks will be even less in evidence.'

'I do hope,' Edward said, 'that the Lady Jane will never suffer from smallpox.' And then, abruptly, he issued a command. 'We begin our journey to London at daybreak tomorrow.'

'If your Grace,' Northumberland ventured, 'would like to see the Lady Jane privately before we leave Bradgate . . .'

Edward hesitated for a moment, strongly tempted. 'No, Northumberland, no.'

Jane, with her mother, her two sisters and their attendants, was in the courtyard at dawn to bid the King godspeed. She had first thought that he had come to Bradgate, not because of the state of his health, but because it was her birthday, but his formal attitude had given the lie to that. She should, of course, have known better than to dream of a sentimental gesture on his part, he having failed to write to her during the months that had passed since she had last seen him at Greenwich. She curtsied, as did the others, when he approached the family group, but he seemed not to notice her own curtsy, even though she was standing slightly apart from her mother and sisters. What, she wondered, was amiss? Was he troubled by the need to marry a foreign princess? But even if he was, why should that bring about such a hurtful change in him? She caught his eyes at last and tried to hold them steadily, but quickly he turned to her mother and uttered a few formal, meaningless words of farewell. Jane watched him enter the royal coach, stumbling a little as he did so, and still watching saw him lean out and wave his white-plumed cap to all in general. There was a fanfare of trumpets, the horses were whipped up and the coach rolled out of the courtyard.

'A retinue of two hundred or more,' Jane heard her mother

grumble. 'Had the King remained longer we would have been brought to the edge of bankruptcy.'

'You must apply for a royal grant,' Jane felt stung to say.

'More to the point,' Frances said acidly, 'I must marry my three daughters to wealthy noblemen.'

Attended by Mrs Eleyn, Jane went early to morning prayers, and then, reproaching herself for having found little consolation on her knees, she made her way to her room, the thought of breakfast with her sisters unbearable. Thinking that for once she would be unable to lose herself in any form of study she saw on her writing table a basket which, to her astonishment, moved as she approached it. Removing the lid she found within a little black dog of perhaps six or seven weeks old. Attached to its neck by a silver chain was a brief note in the King's unmistakable handwriting.

'Pointer could never be replaced,' she read. 'Hence this different breed, the spaniel I found in Leicester. His name is Rex. He has the same warm brown eyes as the Lady Jane. Her birthday was not forgotten.'

Jane re-read the unsigned note and glowed with happiness. She might be forced to marry at the convenience of her parents but her heart would always be Edward's.

20

'GUILFORD DUDLEY?' Frances, Duchess of Suffolk questioned sharply.

'I can think of no one more suitable for Jane,' her husband said, squaring his shoulders and remembering what Northumberland had said about the need to assert himself where Frances was concerned. 'He is, need I remind you, the favourite son of the most powerful man in England.'

Frances's eyes narrowed. So this was her husband's reason for expressing urgency when summoning her from Bradgate to London and instructing her to bring Jane with her. And then, exasperatingly enough, he had delayed a full day before giving any sort of explanation.

'I waited on the King yesterday immediately after reaching London,' she said. 'How long is it since he was at Bradgate? Six months or more. His appearance shocked me then. It shocked me a great deal more yesterday. Is he dying?'

'Who can say, Frances.'

'I want the truth,' she said in a voice she used when berating a servant who had displeased her.

'The King is dying,' Suffolk admitted reluctantly. 'Northumberland sought the opinions of six physicians a week ago. The King is not expected to live for more than a few weeks. That was the joint decision. Apart from the physicians, who are sworn to secrecy, only Northumberland and I, and now you, are aware of it. I think the King is aware of it in his heart, poor lad, but he must not on any account be told.'

Having listened impatiently Frances said in disgust: 'Fool, fool! When the King dies and the Lady Mary comes to the throne Northumberland will be ruined. He will be fortunate if he keeps his head on his shoulders. And you would marry Jane to his son. Fool, fool, fool!'

Suffolk sighed, squared his shoulders again and said pleadingly rather than assertively: 'Bear with me for a moment, Frances. I have Northumberland's permission to confide in you fully. The King is now of age by Act of Parliament, and that has placed a valuable weapon in Northumberland's hands.'

'Or in the King's, if Northumberland should displease him.'

'The King has come to rely on Northumberland, to lean on him, to trust him implicitly.'

'More fool he.'

'Pray allow me to continue,' Suffolk said plaintively. 'Northumberland, for very sound reasons of his own, has meanwhile thrown dust in everybody's eyes by *appearing* to relinquish much of his power. Also by pleading ill-health, the task master, he told Cecil, who would whip ambition out of any man.' Suffolk paused and chuckled. 'He even told Cecil that he was now the faithful servant who, according to that old Italian proverb, was in danger of becoming a perpetual ass.'

'I have one such servant myself in the person of my noble husband,' Frances said without amusement. 'But proceed, my own perpetual ass, proceed.'

Suffolk looked at her with ineffectual balefulness. 'Northumberland has even thrown dust in the Lady Mary's eyes by assuring her that he regards her truly as heiress presumptive . . .'

'Presumptive, not apparent?'

'The Lady Mary has been led to believe that the King will marry Elizabeth of France and through her continue the dynasty.'

Frances interrupted again with a ribald laugh. 'Has she also been led to believe that the ailing King is capable of bedding down with any wench?'

'Be that as it may,' Suffolk said, trying to sound severe but merely smiling faintly, 'Northumberland has sworn to her that his only desire is to serve her, and through her England, should she come to the throne.'

'Catholic or Protestant England?' Frances jeered. 'The Lady Mary was never a fool. She would have our Protestant dictator on the rack in the twinkling of an eye, and whether or not he confessed his apostasy fling him into the fires of Smithfield. In the name of God, or the Pope if you think it necessary, come to the point, if you have a convincing one to come to.'

'The King,' Suffolk said huffily, 'is to be persuaded to make a will in which the Lady Mary and the Lady Elizabeth will be set aside and Jane will be named his immediate heir. But Jane must marry Guilford Dudley first, and soon, Frances, soon.'

Instantly and unguardedly Frances said: 'Jane has every right to be so named.'

'An arguable point,' Suffolk said weightily. 'And what of the late King Henry's will?'

'That is obviously to be set aside,' Frances said hastily, and to counter suspicion where no apparent suspicion was in evidence added unctuously: 'What I mean is that King Edward has every right to name her, she being more worthy, religiously, than even the Lady Elizabeth.'

When it no longer mattered Suffolk asserted himself strongly. 'No more need be said, Frances. I have already accepted Northumberland's offer and he is at Whitehall at this moment informing the King of the betrothal.'

'On the assumption that the King will grant royal permission.'

'Leaning on Northumberland as he does . . .'

Any doubts that Frances might have harboured were dispelled when later that day Jane, looking palely determined, confronted her parents in her father's private retreat, a richly furnished room, that of a scholar in appearance, with well-filled bookshelves and rolls of manuscripts but, incongruously, an array of pistols, swords and riding whips.

'Madame,' Jane said, addressing her mother, 'I have received a letter of congratulations from the King.'

'Ha!' said Frances.

'He wishes me well in my coming marriage with Lord Guilford Dudley.'

'Most gratifying.'

'Madame,' said Jane in a low but determined voice, 'I do not want to marry Guilford Dudley. I do not, and I shall not.'

'By God's precious blood . . . !' Frances gasped, and for the moment was bereft of further speech.

Jane flinched but stood her ground. She had resigned herself after last seeing Edward at Bradgate to the fate of taking a husband chosen for her by her parents, but the thought of Guilford Dudley revolted her. She had met him for the first time at

Bradgate during the royal progress. He was handsome, that was undeniable. And he was charming enough, if one cared to listen to boastful tales of high success in hunting and jousting, but his lack of scholarship, his pronounced contempt for it, appalled her.

'Recovering her voice Frances said wrathfully: 'Your impertinence and arrogance are beyond belief. No other daughter in this age, or any earlier age, has dared to challenge the will of her parents.'

Jane remembered a story often told and said quickly: 'There was Mary Tudor, your mother, Madame, and my grandmother.'

'And . . . so?' Frances demanded, remembering the story herself.

'She refused to marry the King of France.'

'Successfully?'

'No,' said Jane, regretting that she had mentioned that particular Mary Tudor. 'She conceded defeat when her father agreed that if the King of France should die while married to her, as he did, she would be allowed to choose a second husband herself, and did.'

'Are you, at fifteen,' Suffolk tittered, 'already dreaming of a second husband?'

Frances gave him a scathing look. 'The point of this historic story is that Mary Tudor conceded defeat only after her father had thrashed her so soundly that she was to remember the pain of it until she died. She wept and pleaded but in the end she submitted.'

'I,' Jane said stolidly, 'am neither weeping nor pleading.'

'That, you wretch, has yet to be vouchsafed.'

'Frances?' Suffolk questioned, giving Jane the impression that he had turned into a wounded bird and was flapping his wings helplessly.

Frances glanced at him pityingly, then she lunged at Jane and boxed her ears ringingly. Not satisfied with that she seized a riding whip, flung Jane over a footstool and exposing her buttocks attacked her viciously. Suffolk stood by, cursing first his daughter for her disobedience, then his wife for her cruelty. Jane steeled herself not to weep or plead but there were scalding tears in her eyes when, abruptly, Frances ceased her onslaught. 'Get up,' she said curtly and flung the whip aside.

Jane rose, never so humiliated in her life, and asked coldly: 'Are you exhausted, Madame?'

Frances glowered at her in silence. She had thrown the whip aside because Jane, turning her head, had looked up at her and she had seen on the girl's face the devilish Tudor look which she had seen so often on the late King Henry's face. It had frightened her. It was almost as if Henry Tudor had been brought back to life in the spirit of his secret daughter. When Jane was on the throne, Frances thought grimly, they would all be faced with difficulty after difficulty, whether or not the girl was told the truth of her birth. Blood, particularly Tudor blood, would always tell.

'Exhausted?' she said at last. 'My patience is.'

'I have often dreamt,' Jane said, never having thought of this before, 'that you were not my real mother. I could wish with all heartiness that that were the very truth.'

Startled but recovering herself quickly, Frances said: 'The King has expressed his royal approval of your betrothal to Guilford Dudley. That is tantamount to a royal command. As you love the King you must humble yourself and obey.'

'As I love the King . . .' Jane echoed.

'Take heart,' Suffolk interposed, 'if you have a virgin fear of marriage you will be given time to accustom yourself to your new situation. There will be no immediate consummation.'

'No?' Frances questioned.

'*No*,' said Suffolk with surprising firmness.

'For that I am grateful,' Jane said, 'but I think there must be some doubt in your mind about the family usefulness of this marriage.'

'*Doubt?*' Frances demanded sharply.

'An unconsummated marriage is the more easily dissolved.'

'You argue with true Tudor shrewdness,' Frances said with reluctant admiration.

Doubt, yes, she reflected, but only in association with the doubt in her own mind about Edward's attitude to Jane, he knowing a half-truth about her birth, when asked to name her his immediate heir.

'Jane,' Suffolk said quite gently, 'you will marry Guilford Dudley if for one reason only. You will marry him because the King so wills it.'

Jane, though still rebellious, bowed her head. 'The King so wills it.'

It was announced the next day that the marriage was to take place within a week, and to forestall a charge of undue hastiness it was further announced that the betrothal had been arranged privately six months ago. At the same time two other marriages were to be solemnised, Jane's younger sister Katherine marrying Lord Herbert and Northumberland's daughter Katherine marrying Lord Hastings. Jane laughed cynically when told. Northumberland was marrying his son to her, a Tudor, and his daughter to Hastings, a Plantagenet, while her father was marrying young Katherine to Herbert, the son of one of Northumberland's most wealthy and influential supporters. She resolved then that if she outlived Edward, Mary and Elizabeth and became Queen she would do her utmost to shatter the stranglehold of self-seeking family dictatorships.

She was first informed that the three marriages would take place at Sion House in Isleworth, the most impressive of Northumberland's three London palaces, but was later told while Mrs Eleyn was busily and importantly assembling her wardrobe that they would take place at Durham House on the Strand which was of easier access for the ailing King who had expressed a wish to be present. Jane shrank from the prospect of being married in her beloved Edward's presence, but at the last moment his physicians declared that the air of London was too stifling for him and he was removed to Greenwich.

'So the poor King will not be present after all,' Mrs Eleyn remarked when presenting for Jane's approval a gown of gold and silver brocade.

'A sad pity,' Jane said, masking her relief but at the same time wondering anxiously if Edward was as seriously ill as she was beginning to suspect. 'Are there not too many diamonds and pearls sewn into the bodice?' she asked quickly.

'For the King's cousin and the third in the line of succession,' Mrs Eleyn simpered, 'there are by no means enough.'

On the morning of May 25th, which happened to be Whit Sunday, Jane went by barge from Suffolk Place, formerly known as Dorset House, to Durham House with the Duke and Duchess of Suffolk and the more important members of their household in attendance. She wore the gold and silver wedding gown to which Mrs Eleyn had added more diamonds and pearls, and her hair, released from its formal severity, hung about her shoulders with threadings of tiny seed pearls.

During the service in the private chapel she centred her gaze on the altar-front which had been sewn with pearls on a crimson background. She tried to play her part with dignity but a feeling of unreality was growing upon her and scarcely did she notice the resplendently dressed Guilford Dudley who stood at her side waiting with boyish eagerness to place on her finger the blood-red ring which would make her his wife. She stared at it after he had done so and wondered, with very little interest, if she should regard the colour as an omen of catastrophes to come.

The triple service was followed by a feast which would have put any of the late King Henry's to shame, even in his heyday of eating and drinking; and then, with the feast continuing hour after hour, by masquerades and dancing. Jane endeavoured to show a polite interest but all she could think of was Edward in his sickbed at Greenwich, and with the feeling of unreality more pronounced than ever stared unseeingly at the rich tapestries of the dining hall, the hangings of cloth of gold and the Turkish carpets.

'Come, Lady Guilford,' she heard her mother say commandingly. 'We return to Suffolk Place, your maidenhead unbroken.'

'Am I first to bid my husband *au revoir?*'

Frances chuckled richly. 'Not unless you wish to see vomit on your bridal gown. They carried him away, he retching pitifully. He is not yet man enough to hold his food and liquor.'

Nor I yet woman enough, Jane thought, to minister to him.

21

'It has been your Grace's firm intention for some time,' Northumberland said, 'to exclude the Lady Mary from the succession, but by what alternative in the event of your not begetting a child of your own?'

Edward shifted uneasily in his bed and pretended not to have heard. He had passed a more comfortable night than usual and was scarcely feverish this morning but there was no longer any doubt in his mind, though everyone denied it, that he was close to death. In the event, he thought bitterly, of his not begetting a child of his own . . .

'Your Grace?' Northumberland prompted.

'Sir,' said Edward, rushing off at a tangent, 'I hear that your son Guilford made himself disgustingly ill at the wedding feast.'

'So it was first thought,' Northumberland explained, 'but others were reduced to a like state. The cause was food poisoning. One of the cooks was at fault.'

'Food poisoning, not poisoned food?' Edward said querulously.

'The latter was at first suspected by the Spanish ambassador who himself succumbed, but the careless cook confessed to having served a twice-cooked dish that he had intended to throw away. Your Grace . . . ?'

'Very well,' Edward sighed. 'All I want and long for is release from this miserable life but the question of the Lady Mary must indeed be resolved. And quickly. That I do most thoroughly understand. It was never my intention to *exclude* her, only to forestall her accession. That is the very truth and you know it, Northumberland.'

'If the Lady Mary comes to the throne . . .'

'Wait, wait! I have not the right to set aside my father's will.

I must accept it, loathsome as one aspect of it is to me. The Lady Mary, the Lady Elizabeth and then the Lady Jane.'

'If the Lady Mary comes to the throne,' Northumberland persisted, his voice full of well-calculated horror, 'she will by force re-establish popery, whatever the cost in blood.'

'Is there no way of restraining her?' Edward asked miserably. 'A special Act of Parliament?'

'She could no more be restrained than you could have been in firmly establishing the Reformed Church, the *Protestant* Church. Are we, your Grace, to see destroyed in the twinkling of an eye all that you have created in the name of God and would, in God's name, preserve?'

'My father's will . . .' Edward protested weakly.

'Certain aspects of consanguinity must be set aside,' Northumberland said unctuously, 'when the glory of God and the welfare of the nation are sorely endangered.'

Growing feverish again, Edward shuddered violently. 'The glory of God . . .'

'Were your Grace to do otherwise,' Northumberland said, thinking to frighten the young King with a hint of hellfire to come, 'there is the expectation after this life, which is short, of holy revenge at God's dreadful tribunal.'

Edward shuddered even more violently. 'The Lady Mary shall not succeed.'

Satisfied, Northumberland said: 'Never could I face God's dreadful tribunal myself if she were permitted to do so.'

'And so,' said Edward, 'the Lady Elizabeth.'

Prepared for this Northumberland said: 'A Protestant, yes, but not as devout as one could always wish. Nor is that my fully considered objection. The Lady Elizabeth must in time marry, and whom can she marry but a foreign prince? Thus she would consign herself, and England, to foreign influence. Her husband would establish his own line, he would abolish all ancient rights and immunities. How many generations of foreign rule, your Grace, before the very name of England disappeared?'

'I thought that neither Mary nor Elizabeth could marry without the Council's consent, or that if they did so they would lose all claim to the throne.'

'That ruling applies only during your Grace's lifetime.'

'Then I must exclude Elizabeth also,' Edward said, yet with a feeling of rebelliousness. 'There remains, if I should honour in part my father's will, the Lady Jane.'

His voice trailed away and remembering what the Duchess of Suffolk had told him of Jane's birth began to feel that he should not have spoken. And yet, did she not, as his secret half-sister, have a greater claim than a mere cousin? And yet again, he thought, an *illegitimate* half-sister.

'The Lady Jane has all the virtues required of a Protestant queen,' Northumberland said, but feeling cunning, not wanting to sound in too ready agreement, he added ponderously: 'It is not for you to honour *in part* your father's will but to make one of your own. If you were to name the Lady Jane there would then be the Duchess of Suffolk to consider.'

'How so that?'

'Before making a will of your own your late father's must be rendered null and void. That could occasion certain arguments in respect of blood. The mother would seem to stand before the daughter. She could argue that she had prior claim.'

The mother, Edward thought—the irony of it. He tried without humour to imagine the expression on Northumberland's face if he were told that of mother and daughter only the mother had a true claim.

'If your Grace so wishes it,' Northumberland said, 'the Duchess of Suffolk shall be invited to relinquish her claim.'

'Summon her to Greenwich,' Edward decided. 'The task is mine, as King and the Duchess's cousin, not yours as chief minister.'

Northumberland bowed. 'As your Grace wishes.'

'Wait a moment longer,' Edward commanded. 'Do you press most heartily for the naming of the Lady Jane?'

'I press only for your Grace to consider again and again, and to remember that kings must out of very duty protect their subjects and defend them from injury. Should they fail to do so, how can they stand before the judgment seat of God and receive the reward of everlasting life?'

'Would you alarm me anew?' Edward asked reproachfully. 'And pray answer me this: was it in your mind when you married the Lady Jane to your son that she should be named my heir?'

'Indeed it was,' Northumberland replied frankly.

For the good of England, Edward wondered, or the good of the Dudley family? He felt uneasy to the point of indignation, yet Northumberland's continued rule seemed more vital than ever. Mary or Northumberland, that was what it really amounted to until Jane, if named, came of age. Then he smiled faintly.

'You may find,' he said succinctly, 'that the Lady Jane has a will of her own.'

'That indeed I may,' Northumberland said, not for a moment believing that the girl would ever give him any trouble.

'Bring the Duchess of Suffolk to Greenwich with all speed,' Edward instructed.

Later that morning he learnt from a gentleman of the Privy Chamber that it was being said in London that he, the King, had died mysteriously and that his death was being kept from the nation by Northumberland. Edward rose shakily from his bed, commanded his attendants to dress him and with Northumberland at his side began to walk through the galleries of the palace, his intention being to appear in public view in the grounds where little knots of sightseers had gathered. He faltered before reaching the main entrance and was carried back to his sickroom. He tried again during the afternoon, with the same result, but thought to issue a curt order before being carried away. 'Northumberland, have me lifted to one of the windows.'

This was done, and presently he heard the sound of cheering rising from the grounds below.

'We still have a king in England,' he said, and was moved from window to window to give the impression that he was walking freely. 'Enough,' he said at last, and close to exhaustion was helped back to the royal apartments, there to be told that the Duchess of Suffolk had arrived and was awaiting his pleasure. 'I shall receive her privately,' he said, 'but first let me catch my breath.'

An hour later Frances was ushered into his presence. Slightly revived after a nauseating dose of medicine, he was seated at his desk and at the sight of her amused himself wryly by affecting a judicial attitude, his elbows on the desk, his chin in his hands. All he lacked, he thought, was a long beard, grey in colour.

Formal greetings over, Frances seated herself at his command and studied his face in surprise. He still looked ghastly but appeared to be somwhat improved since her last meeting with him before he left Whitehall for Greenwich. Perhaps the royal dying would be a lengthier business than she had been led by her husband to believe.

'It would be a simple matter, Cousin Frances,' Edward said, after telling her what he expected of her, 'to issue a royal command, but out of family feeling I invite you to relinquish your claim of your own accord.'

'In favour of my supposed daughter?' she questioned satirically. 'It surprises me that you should have brought me here, knowing what is known only to you and me, to subscribe to a lie.'

Edward pressed his chin more heavily into his hands. 'Confusion is apt to overwhelm me these days. I have considered the problem again and again since this morning, but not with a clear mind. The Lady Mary must be set aside but must the Lady Elizabeth be treated in like manner? She presents certain *possible* dangers but are they as alarming as I first thought them? I reached an ill-considered decision. Mary shall be excluded in favour of Elizabeth.'

'Your Grace . . . !' Frances protested, struggling to control her ever-fiery temper.

'You would rather I left the Crown to you?' he asked with exaggerated politeness.

'Far rather, by God!'

'You are much too old, Cousin Frances.'

'I am a year younger than the Lady Mary,' Frances gasped. 'Your rudeness is insufferable!'

'You forget yourself, Madame,' Edward said coldly. 'It is either the Lady Elizabeth or the Lady Jane, but how can I, knowing what I know, perpetuate a lie by naming the Lady Jane? How can I, knowing what I know, name an illegitimate halfsister?'

'If the full truth were known,' Frances said, her temper beyond all control, 'it would be clear to all that you have not the right to name anyone. If the full truth had been known from the beginning the Lady Mary would be Queen of England at this moment.'

'You add confusion to confusion,' Edward said, staring at her and seeing a woman who, to him, had lost her senses.

'The Lady Jane is *not* illegitimate,' Frances went on, frightened now but unable to restrain herself. 'I told you only a half-truth before. I misled you in order to spare you pain. Unnecessary pain, it seemed at the time. But now . . .'

'Jane not illegitimate?' Edward said, watching his cousin's face dance grotesquely in front of his eyes. 'She, my father's daughter by a woman whose name you failed to reveal to me?'

'May God forgive me,' Frances said, 'I must reveal it now. Jane's mother was Jane Seymour. *Jane Seymour,*' she stressed, 'your supposed mother.'

Edward fell back in his chair and watched the grotesque dance continue.

'My *supposed* mother?' he asked, on a note of hysteria. 'Have you been sent by the devil to torment me?'

'I see that I should not have spoken. I should have left you in peace to name the Lady Elizabeth.'

'Peace, Cousin—if you are my cousin? What peace did I know before you spoke? I command you . . . Have I the right to command? I command you to tell me everything that up to now you have withheld from me.'

Speaking in a low voice Frances gave him a faithful account of the events that had taken place on the day of his birth and Jane's at Hampton Court. He listened without interruption, a feeling of disbelief gathering in his breast, and when she had finished he hammered the desk with his clenched fists.

'This is a fabrication, Madame. You would induce me by it to name the Lady Jane.'

'I spoke only because I lost my temper,' Frances said, 'but I would for sure prefer you to name the Lady Jane and have the world know me as the mother of the Queen. In truth she stands before me in the line of succession.'

'A fabrication,' Edward repeated, but weakly.

'I am prepared to write a confession and sign it.'

'Unsupported by anyone, the Duke of Somerset being dead.'

'*And sign it,* as God is my witness.'

'And so,' Edward said, obliged at last to believe her, 'I have never had any right to the throne. I am an impostor.'

'You are the late King Henry's only living son.'

'Bastard son. I—I must abdicate.'

'I begin to lose patience with you,' Frances said stoutly. 'Were not your half-sisters Mary and Elizabeth declared bastards by your father?'

'Their mothers were married to him.'

'As was Jane Seymour, the Lady Jane's mother,' said Frances, pouncing on this. 'And she, Jane, was never declared illegitimate by him.'

'He knowing nothing of her existence as his daughter.'

'His *legitimate* daughter, your Grace. There must be no talk of abdication. The secret must remain ours and ours alone. As you love England you must not abdicate.'

'As I love England . . .' Edward sighed.

'Only by remaining King can you assure the Protestant succession.'

Edward straightened up in his chair and steadied himself by grasping the edge of the desk. 'A reign of short duration,' he said, his voice quivering, 'and abdication of a sort close at hand.'

'My poor dear cousin . . .' Francis said, a modicum of pity in her heart.

'And Jane is healthy, Madame?'

'Slight of build but strong, stronger than any of your father's other children. Strong in heart, too. And great-hearted in her faith.'

'How you do long to be known as the mother of the Queen of England,' Edward said, but without sarcasm. 'You may withdraw, Madame.'

Frances curtsied three times, knelt for a moment and then withdrew, leaving Edward to send for Northumberland.

'I shall leave the Crown to the Lady Jane,' he said wearily. 'Prepare a will for my inspection.'

Northumberland bowed. 'I take it, your Grace, that the Duchess of Suffolk, who passed me in one of the galleries without a word, has agreed to relinquish her claim?'

'Obviously,' Edward said, realising that that issue had been forgotten.

'A noble woman,' Northumberland murmured.

'Of that there is no doubt, if only by birth,' Edward said dryly.

He retired to bed and remained there, scarcely conscious of the passing of time, while discussing and rejecting one draft will after another. Finally, after suffering the first of a series of haemorrhages, he dictated a will entirely of his own devising and having recovered from the effort was helped to a writing table in his bedchamber. Seated there in a heavy fur-lined dressing-gown, despite the unusually oppressive heat of the June day, he copied the will slowly and painstakingly. It was a lengthy document in which he described his sisters, Mary and Elizabeth, as illegitimate and therefore 'disabled' to claim the imperial crown. Standing at his side, watching and correcting, Northumberland sighed in relief when Edward came to and copied the one important clause. The Crown was herewith willed, he wrote, to the Lady Jane and her heirs male. He laid down his pen and with his head on one side listened intently.

'Do I hear thunder, Northumberland?'

Northumberland had heard it too. 'Well to the north, your Grace. The wind is from the west. The storm will not affect Greenwich.'

But the sky was darkening rapidly and a flash of lightning heralded another and closer roll of thunder.

'Is the Lady Jane still with her parents?' Edward asked.

'In so far as I know,' Northumberland said lightly.

'It surprised me to learn that she had returned with them to Suffolk Place after the wedding feast.'

'Ah . . .' said Nothumberland, giving the boy a quizzical look.

Edward fingered the will and returned Northumberland's look in kind. 'Whether at your behest or Suffolk's, it is surely safe, now, for the consummation of the marriage.'

The will was yet to be made law, but Northumberland anticipated no trouble from the Lords of the Council or from the Chief Justice and his fellow law-officers.

'Surely,' he said jovially.

Safe indeed, Edward thought, for Jane to conceive and bear a future Dudley king, but before he could put this ironic thought into words vivid lightning illuminated the room and thunder shook the foundations of the palace.

'The Lady Jane,' Northumberland said when he could make himself heard, 'shall join her husband at Durham House tomorrow.'

'I wish them all joy,' Edward said stiffly.

'As I do,' Northumberland responded, the thought in his mind, unnecessarily cautious as it might seem, that Jane should remain in isolation at Durham House and be told nothing of the King's will until the King was dead.

Heavy rain was falling now and a whirlwind was shaking the palace. He went to the window and staring out at the storm saw a tree struck by lightning. He thought for a moment of the Lady Mary and wondered what she might think to say of the storm in connection with, to her, an infamous will. 'It is a great sign,' he imagined her saying, 'of the avenging justice of God.' Better, he thought, repressing an unwanted shudder, to feel cynical than superstitious.

22

JANE lay tensely in the marriage bed waiting for her husband to join her. The storm of yesterday had returned but with much less violence. Even so, she had suffered a drenching when being brought by her mother from Suffolk Place to Durham House by barge. 'Happy is the bride that the rain rains on,' Frances had misquoted but Jane had refrained from correcting her. A bride was supposed to be happy with the sun shining on her, a corpse at burial in the rain. A corpse, she thought, that is what I am, an unburied corpse lying in a bridal bed. She stirred at the sound of prankish laughter then grew more tense when the door was flung open and Guilford Dudley was carried into the chamber on the shoulders of two young roistering friends. Unceremoniously they stripped him of his night attire and flung him naked into the bed at her side.

'Be fruitful and multiply,' they chanted in unison, and punching each other ran from the candlelit room.

'Charming horseplay,' Guilford said tentatively, and stretched out his long legs.

Be fruitful and multiply . . . Jane repeated the words silently. They reminded her of the marriage game that Thomas Seymour had organised for her and Edward on Edward's ninth birthday but this, six years later, was no game. Then she remembered King Henry's explosive anger and wished with all her heart that he could be present now to shout: 'Enough, by God's precious blood, enough!' But no, she thought, he would applaud heartily and give utterance to one of his lusty jokes.

'My father,' young Dudley said, not turning to look at Jane, 'bade me remind you of an old exhortation. You are, if it pleases you, to be happy and buxom in bed and at board.'

'If Holy Church so ordains,' Jane completed in a whisper.

'He said nothing of that, sweet Jane.'

She flinched at his would-be endearment and questioned quickly: 'If it pleases me?'

'My own words, not my father's,' he said gruffly.

'That is considerate of you,' Jane said, refusing to warm to him.

'A mere figure of speech,' he said, feeling that in part he had denied his manhood. 'Yet still do I want you to be happy at Durham House.'

'We are to live here, have no establishment of our own?'

'Who can say? Perhaps we will be given Sion House. Yet if we live long enough, if we outlive the others, and they die without issue, all the royal palaces will be at our disposal.'

'Is it for that remote possibility,' Jane asked, feeling no real anger in her corpse-like condition, 'that this marriage has taken place?'

'I can think of no other, but I do pray, sweet Jane, that we will come to love each other.'

An even more remote possibility, she thought, and making further conversation to delay the inevitable said indifferently: 'I think I prefer Durham House to Sion House.'

'I find it hard to decide,' Guilford said, and went on to reveal a seriousness she would never have suspected in him. 'Durham House, like Sion House, was once the property of the Duke of Somerset. He seized it when it had been promised to the Lady Elizabeth. It reverted to the Crown after his execution. My father seized it then. Who, and under what circumstances, will be the next to seize it? The Lady Mary on behalf of one of her Catholic bishops?'

'This,' Jane said unwittingly, 'is strange talk in a bridal chamber.'

'Nervousness was getting the better of me,' Guilford said, and cursed himself for his weakness in admitting it. 'Do you likewise feel nervous?'

'I feel nothing,' Jane asserted.

'What,' he demanded in sudden indignation, 'do I make so ugly a husband that you feel *nothing*?'

'Not ugly,' Jane said, trying to feel charitable.

'How then do you see me?' he asked, well used to praise.

'I see you,' she said, failing to feel charitable, 'as your father's tool.'

'Yet possessing,' he boasted, 'a ready one of my own.'

'To whom do you refer?' Jane asked in all innocence.

'That you will presently discover,' he said, thinking that a hard night's work lay ahead of him. He sat up and gazed down at her impassive face. 'You have yet to ask me how *I* see *you*.'

'Pray tell me,' Jane said politely.

'If you were to smile I would say—God help me, what *would* I say, since I have yet to see you smile? I must content myself with quoting, and in full agreement, the words of the Spanish ambassador before he fell a victim of food poisoning.'

'Better before than during or after,' Jane said dryly.

Guilford laughed and began to feel more at ease. 'He desscibed you as short, not too thin and very prettily shaped. Clearly he could see you, as these Spanish gentlemen can see women, fully clothed but naked.'

Jane, the would-be corpse, felt that she was blushing from head to foot and said sternly: 'Pray proceed.'

'He spoke of your sparkling eyes, yet I see no sparkle in them now. He spoke too of your arched eyebrows, darker in colour than your hair, and of your well-made nose, whatever that may mean, except in the sense of it being a Tudor nose, and of your rich red lips which, he asserted, were made for kissing.'

'Did he make any mention of my freckles?' Jane asked hurriedly.

'He found them entrancing, as do I.'

'The French ambassador was present,' she said even more hurriedly. 'Did *he* make any comment?'

'Yes, but for a Frenchman he was strangely restrained. After conversing with you he . . .'

'Conversing with me? I have no recollection of it.'

'Converse with him you did, and he reached the conclusion that you were quick-witted and wise beyond your sex and above your age.' He bent and brushed his lips across her brow. 'I myself am far more taken with your sex than your age. And please believe, dear virgin wife, that I am not without experience. I have bedded down with many a wench and still remain unscathed.'

'Unscathed?'

'I come to you free of the pox.'

'With which ambassador do you mainly concur?' Jane asked, not entirely for want of something better to say.

'The gentleman from Spain. I had already remarked myself on the madness-inspiring attractiveness of your freckles, to say not a word of your lips that were made for kissing.'

Insincere flattery, Jane thought, but strangely heart-warming. She tried to remember, and thus steady herself, the letter she had been writing to Bullinger when her mother had dragged her to Durham House, a letter in which she had expounded new thoughts on Plato's *Phaedo*. Surprisingly enough intellectual concentration was difficult, particularly when Guilford kissed her on the lips and she found herself responding in the manner of making a new and entrancing discovery about herself.

'Are the Tudor freckles merely on your face?' Guilford asked, and with youthful eagerness tore off her nightgown.

'That is for my husband to discover,' Jane said shakily.

'I can find none anywhere else,' he said, after a prolonged search of her breast and abdomen.

'Listen,' Jane said, conscious only of the heavy beating of her heart.

He raised his head for a moment. 'A sudden stillness. The storm has passed.'

'Truly passed?' Jane asked faintly.

He moved roughly over her. 'To be buxom in bed and at board,' he reminded her, 'but what do we care about board?'

'To my knowledge,' Jane said, even more faintly, 'the word buxom has four meanings: yielding, gay, lively and jolly. Which do you prefer, my lord?'

'The storm having passed and a greater one before us,' he said, thrusting suddenly, 'the one most likely to shatter with pleasure your scholarly maidenhead.'

*

The law-officers, headed by Sir Edward Montague, the Chief Justice, had been hastily assembled in the King's bedchamber. The Privy Council, every member of which was terrified of the Lady Mary ascending the throne, had accepted Edward's will but the law-officers had expressed grave doubts about the validity of that will. And so Northumberland, in a furious temper, had brought them to Greenwich to make known to the King the legality of their legally minded objections.

'Pray repeat your last statement, Sir Edward,' the King said, his voice, weak as it was, expressing great impatience.

'It would be treason,' the Chief Justice said, 'to make or execute a deed in accordance with your Grace's requirements.'

'Treason!' Edward expostulated.

'Without an Act of Parliament,' the Solicitor-General interposed, 'such a deed would carry no validity. The Statute of Succession passed by Parliament before your father's death is still in force. That statute can be altered only by the passing of another.'

Edward tried to rise to a sitting position in the bed, failed to do so and was then supported by an attendant on either side of him. Could Parliament be assembled speedily? Not speedily enough, he was convinced of that, but even if it could he lacked the strength to sustain the rigours of a state opening.

'I will hear of no objections,' he gasped. 'I command you to proceed.'

'We cannot,' the Chief Justice said unhappily, 'without placing ourselves in danger of a charge of high treason.' He approached the bed and fell to his knees. 'I have served your Grace and your Grace's most noble father these nineteen years,' he said beseechingly. 'I am a weak old man and without comfort.'

'Proceed, proceed,' Edward tried to shout. 'The deed must be executed at once, at once. It can be ratified later by Parliament.'

'Spare me, your Grace, spare me,' the Chief Justice begged.

Northumberland drew his sword and said in a terrible voice: 'Traitor!' He swung round on the others. 'Traitors! I will fight any man in my shirt who dares to flout the King's wishes!'

The Chief Justice rose shakily, his eyes on Northumberland's sword, and feeling of a sudden inspired said thoughtfully: 'We will prepare the deed on two conditions . . .'

'Name them, name them!' Northumberland roared.

'The first condition, that we be given a commission under the Great Seal to draw up the deed; the second, that we likewise be granted pardon under the Great Seal for having done so.'

Northumberland's eyes narrowed. 'I will have no man in better case than myself, by God!'

Edward fell back on the pillows. 'A pardon shall be issued for all who sign,' he said in a whisper. 'Prepare the deed, and quickly.'

And then, coughing uncontrollably, he suffered another haemorrhage.

*

'The shame has passed,' Jane said, stretching her limbs and laughing softly.

'Shame?' Guilford Dudley said in frank amazement. 'You actually felt shame?'

'In very truth I did, the first night.'

'But now—truly passed?'

'Did I not admit it?' And laughing softly again she added: 'Shame on my Tudor blood.'

'By which you mean, since you laugh and blush rosily . . . ?'

'My Tudor blood my Tudor undoing.'

'A remark which I would take, if so minded, as a slur on my Dudley manhood.'

'So take it, if it pleases you,' she challenged.

'And chastise you for it?' He flung back the sheet, turned her over on to her stomach and then gasped in astonishment. 'Jane, these scars. How did you come by them?'

'Perhaps I should say that my husband began by beating me into submission.'

'Never that,' Guilford avowed. 'Why have I not seen them before?'

'Your interest was taken with another view of my noble body.'

'True, but they are not long healed. Come, the truth, sweet Jane.'

'My mother has a heavy hand. It was she who thought to whip me into submission.'

'If you are ever Queen,' he said with heavy humour, 'and the Duchess of Suffolk is still alive, you must fling her into the Tower, the deepest dungeon thereof.'

'Is there a dungeon, however deep, strong enough to hold my mother?'

'I, the Queen's husband, shall devise one.' He frowned and went on seriously: 'If you are ever Queen . . . What, then, will my title be? Prince Consort? *King* Consort? The latter would be preferable.'

'Whatever the title,' Jane said with unconscious hauteur, 'it could never make you King.' And teasingly she added: 'At the most I shall turn Lord Guilford into a royal duke.'

*

Edward had been carried into the audience chamber beyond his sickroom and was seated now at the table upon which the deed lay. Slowly he signed his name and then, one by one, the Lords of the Council, his godfather the Archbishop, the judges, the Officers of the Household, the Knights of the Privy Chamber and the Sheriffs, a hundred in all, appended their signatures. The dying King was carried back to his bed and the company dispersed, leaving Northumberland and Suffolk alone.

'And now . . . ?' Jane's father asked.

'The taking of the Lady Mary into custody. Three hundred horse are held in readiness for the task.'

'That alone,' Suffolk said uneasily, 'is not sufficient to fill me with confidence.'

'I have reached an agreement with the French ambassador. I have, if necessary, the promise of French support.'

'France is a Catholic country.'

'Religion has little meaning when I am prepared to sell both Calais and Boulogne. As for money, I have raised a forced loan from the City of London bankers. For the rest, my troops are stationed at strategic points throughout the country and the fleet is ready to do my bidding. If you envisage even the possibility of successful opposition from Mary Tudor you are the greatest ass-head in the realm.'

Flushing, Suffolk said: 'Did you notice the King's fingers?'

Northumberland shrugged. 'A trace of gangrene. The King is all but moribund.'

'There is talk of poison, Northumberland.'

'Supposedly administered by me?'

'I make no charge,' Suffolk said hastily. 'You need the King alive.'

'*Needed*, until a few moments ago,' Northumberland said cynically.

'And now?'

Northumberland refrained from answering, and Suffolk thought: The longer he lives the more dangerous our position will be.

'The haemorrhages have ceased,' he said. 'He may yet recover.'

'With gangrene setting in? A well-tried treatment has stopped the haemorrhages. An alleviation, not a cure.'

'Are you referring to arsenic?' Suffolk asked.

'Surely.'

'Small doses only, I trust.'

'I am not a physician,' Northumberland said acidly.

'I can but believe that the royal physicians would be most cautious,' Suffolk said, giving Northumberland an oblique look.

'You know as well as I, damn you, that my personal physician is in charge these days.'

'Assisted,' said Suffolk, 'by a female quack.'

'One of high repute.'

'If he has allowed her to be over-zealous . . .'

'Enough,' Northumberland said. 'If she has been over-zealous she will, while making the King more comfortable, have done no more than hasten, mercifully, the inevitable end.'

*

Jane, roused from sleep, found Mrs Eleyn bending over her and believed for a moment that she was at Bradgate and late through oversleeping for morning prayers. Then she remembered and reached out to touch her husband, only to find his place in the bed empty. Full memory flooded back; Guilford had been summoned by his father to Greenwich the night before.

'Madame . . .'

Jane glanced beyond Mrs Eleyn and saw the somewhat massive figure of her mother-in-law, the Duchess of Northumberland.

'Is anything amiss?' Jane asked, her thoughts directed instantly to the ailing King.

'You are to prepare yourself for removal to Sion House,' the Duchess told her.

So she and Guilford were to be given Sion House, Jane thought, but why should her mother-in-law wake her early in the morning to impart such information? She looked closely at the Duchess, a woman to whom she had never felt drawn. Oh, she was a worthy enough creature, a devout and God-fearing Protestant, but she was even more domineering than her own mother. She smiled now, quite mysteriously, Jane thought, and bade Mrs Eleyn withdraw.

'Something *is* amiss,' Jane said. 'Has the King taken a turn for the worse?'

The Duchess hesitated. King Edward, having prayed for death for several days, had died at dusk the night before, but she had been instructed by her husband not to say a word of this to her daughter-in-law. Out of sheer political necessity the King's death was to remain a secret for the time being, and Jane, who might spread the story, was to be kept in ignorance until held securely at Sion House.

'It is the King's wish,' she said, obeying her husband's instructions to the letter, 'that you should repair to Sion House. Once there the King's further wishes will be confided in you and you will, I need not add, render implicit obedience.'

'It is not for my mother-in-law to remind me of my duty to my cousin the King,' Jane said haughtily. 'Am I to leave at once for Sion House?'

Angered, the Duchess of Northumberland remembered, but only narrowly, that she stood in the presence of the Queen, even if the arrogant girl had yet to be told and proclaimed.

'No,' she said tersely. 'You are expected for the moment to hold yourself in readiness.'

Jane inclined her head. 'As the King so wills.'

But what indeed, she wondered, did Edward will?

23

SION HOUSE was originally a monastery founded by Henry V and as such it had remained until seized along with other church property by Henry VIII. Somerset himself had seized it during the days of his indisputable power and then, after his execution, the boy King had allowed Northumberland to seize it, the seizure being known legally as a royal grant. As a monastery it had resembled a prison and in that respect it had remained unchanged. High walls enclosed the gardens and only from a small terrace set in one of them could a view of the outside world be obtained. Here on the evening of July 9th Northumberland and Suffolk stood together watching the arrival by barge of Jane and her sole companion Lady Mary Sidney, one of Northumberland's married daughters. They were received by the officers of Northumberland's household and passed quickly from sight. Suffolk turned to Northumberland and asked him if Jane was still in ignorance of King Edward's death.

'Out of sheer necessity, yes, but she shall be told now.'

The protracted secrecy had troubled Suffolk. It had seemed essential, certainly, that the Lady Mary should be secured before a public announcement was issued, but that bold venture had resulted in failure and secrecy could be maintained no longer. Where, he wondered uneasily, was Mary Tudor at this moment? She had been warned and had fled; he had been told no more than that. In what direction had she fled, and was she rapidly gathering about her an army of loyal supporters?

'Come!' said Northumberland.

Suffolk shrugged and in silence accompanied him to the great hall of Sion House where Jane and her companion awaited them. They looked forlorn, Suffolk thought, in the vast emptiness of the lofty chamber, the repository of tapestries and other costly treasures filched from many a church and chapel during the dissolution of the monasteries.

Northumberland bowed briefly. 'Madame . . .'

'I am come,' said Jane, 'to hear the wishes of my cousin the King.'

'The King,' Northumberland said with brutal frankness, 'is dead.'

Jane uttered a gasp of disbelief. She had been told, while holding herself in readiness at Durham House, that a banquet was to be held at Greenwich in celebration of Edward's recovery.

'When did he die?' she asked after a moment of stunned silence.

'On the evening of the seventh.'

'Then he was already dead when I was told to hold myself in readiness. For what reason did you think it necessary to deceive me?'

Northumberland swept this aside. 'You are here, Madame, to learn the King's wishes . . .'

But Jane, scarcely hearing him, had fallen to her knees and was sobbing convulsively. Northumberland watched impatiently while Suffolk and Lady Mary Sidney did what little they could to comfort her. She was still on her knees in an agony of grief when the Lords of the Council and all the other subjects who had signed the deed filed into the hall and placed themselves in a semicircle before their Queen-elect.

'Madame!' Northumberland said sharply.

Jane rose, rejected her father's offer of support and looked squarely at her father-in-law.

'The King's wishes, sir.'

'As President of the Council,' Northumberland said, 'I do now publicly declare the death of his most blessed and gracious Majesty, King Edward VI. All present here are overcome with grief, yet we take comfort in praising King Edward's goodness and prudence, and for having prayed God to defend the realm from the popish faith and to deliver it from the rule of his evil sisters. In no manner did he wish them to be his heirs, he being in every way empowered to disinherit them.'

Jane felt herself trembling and waited apprehensively for Northumberland to continue.

'The King, Madame,' he said after a deliberately lengthy pause, 'named you, the Lady Jane, his heir to the Crown of England. This declaration which I now make has the approval of all the Lords of the Council, a majority of peers and all the judges of the land, and is confirmed and ratified by Letters Patent under the Great Seal of England. There is nothing wanting but your Grace's grateful acceptance of the high estate to which Almighty God has advanced you.'

Almighty God or Almighty Northumberland? He made it sound like the latter, Jane thought, and remained silent while, at a gesture from Northumberland, the gathering knelt, acknowledged her as their Queen and swore allegiance. Trembling all the more, she dwelt on Northumberland's reference to Mary and Elizabeth as Edward's evil sisters. Evil? He meant Mary in particular. She was misguidedly a Catholic, surely that, but never evil. And was she not, by the will of her father, Edward's rightful heir?

'Your Grace . . .' Northumberland prompted, impatient again.

'I am stunned and stupefied,' Jane said. 'This honour that you would thrust upon me is not one that I had thought to anticipate. It fails to please me and moves me only to declare that the Crown is not my right while the Lady Mary and the Lady Elizabeth are still alive. The Lady Mary is the rightful heir.'

Staring at her in disbelief, Northumberland remembered Edward's warning: 'You may find that the Lady Jane has a will of her own.' Only with difficulty did he succeed in controlling his rising anger. His will was greater than hers. He and he alone had made her Queen; it was an obligation which she must be forced, and fully, to accept.

'You do wrong to yourself and to your house,' he said sternly but persuasively. 'And what of your faith? Would you deny it and so doing deny God? Would you reject God's will as expressed in the dying wishes of your cousin King Edward? Would you, Madame?'

In an agony of doubt Jane capitulated. 'I feel a great insufficiency,' she said, faintness all but overcoming her, 'but if that which is given me is legitimately mine, I pray God to grant me the grace to govern in His name for the good of the realm.'

Govern? That, Northumberland thought, was richly arrogant in a girl not yet sixteen. And yet he needed her, his little figurehead, and must tread with a certain amount of caution until he was fully established himself.

'God bless and save Queen Jane,' he intoned.

But his words, in which she might have suspected irony, were lost on her. Faintness and nausea got the better of her and she collapsed unconscious at his feet. When she recovered she found herself lying in a bed in the would-be royal chamber that had been prepared for her. A newly arrived and anxious Mrs Eleyn was in attendance, and it was Mrs Eleyn who told her that she must stir herself to be well enough for tomorrow's important ceremony. She would be called upon, in accordance with tradition, to travel in state by royal barge to the Tower of London, there to be presented with the keys of the Tower in the presence of her court, the Lord Mayor of London and the city fathers.

'Watch and pray that ye enter not into temptation,' Jane quoted wildly: 'the spirit is indeed willing but the flesh is weak.'

'I know not what to make of your words,' Mrs Eleyn faltered.

'I have little understanding of them myself,' Jane said in utter confusion. 'So ill do I feel that tomorrow's ordeal is more than I can face.'

Fearful that the Queen was in danger of nervous collapse, Mrs Eleyn spoke to Northumberland and he quickly sent his personal physician to examine her, minister to her and put new heart into her. He, Scurrah Jones by name, was recognised as one of the most highly skilled physicians in the land, he being more than ordinarily versed in astronomy as well as physiology, and capable always of getting the better of an academic adversary when it came to rhetoric, logic and geometry.

'Your Grace,' he said, swaying on his feet as he was wont to do when embarking upon a learned lecture, 'you are undoubtedly the victim of a bout of ill-humour, but precisely which of the four humours is at fault we have yet to discover.'

'Sir . . . ?' Jane questioned, staring up at him blankly.

'Madame,' Scurrah Jones continued weightily, 'man, by which I also mean woman, by which indeed I mean the human body, male or female, is compounded of four humours. We have, for example, blood, phlegm, yellow bile and black bile. A diagnosis is reached by a careful study of the patient's complexion. Is it sanguine, is it phlegmatic, is it choleric or is it melancholic? When one or other of these four humours is unbalanced, then we have illness.'

Jane laughed hysterically and flung herself back on the pillows.

'One would say at this moment that your Grace's illness, your Grace's complexion being choleric, is a disturbance of the third humour. However, there is always room for doubt, the more so in this interesting case because your Grace's complexion would seem to change from choleric to melancholic even as I speak. An examination of the royal urine is called for. I have with me a urine flask. I shall turn my back respectfully while your Grace, assisted by the good Mrs Eleyn, makes valiant effort to provide for me a sample.'

Mrs Eleyn took a firm grip of the neck of the flask which, of clear glass, was large enough to resemble a container designed to house the choicest of French wine. Jane, laughing hysterically again, complied to the best of her ability and the flask was handed back to the physician.

'Copious,' he said, and held it close to one of the candles. 'And a little too thin,' he added. 'Do we have water in the bowels? That I most gravely suspect. The simple remedy of blood-letting is indicated. Simple, do I say? Simple indeed when one considers that the moon is now in its third phase. I suggest the application of leeches rather than the opening of a vein. Leeches are costly, for sure, but we are treating the Queen of England, not a poor ignorant peasant. I have with me a canister of choice and blood-hungry leeches. With your Grace's gracious permission . . . ?'

Leeches were applied immediately and more at intervals during the night, and all were removed in a bloated condition at dawn. Jane had slept fitfully and woke in an irresolute state of mind. Scurrah Jones inspected more urine and pronounced her much improved and fit, with God's help, to play her queenly part in the day's ceremonial activities. Once again Jane capitulated; she was beginning to feel that she had no will of her own.

'The complexion is just a shade melancholic,' he said, 'but this, your Grace, is not a melancholy occasion.'

'That I concede,' Jane said listlessly.

He then prescribed a light breakfast of brawn and ale, to be followed as a medicine by a small measure of spiced wine. At first Jane refused the offering, then feeling surprisingly ravenous ate and drank with relish, and was told that her complexion was now more sanguine than melancholic. Since sanguine meant hopeful as well as bloody she tried to take heart from his words, received her newly appointed ladies and allowed Mrs Eleyn and three maids to dress her. Her clothing and jewellery had already been decided upon by Northumberland. The Tudor colours of white and green were paramount in her kirtle and bodice, both threaded with gold, and her white coif was a mass of diamonds and rubies, emeralds and pearls. Northumberland himself appeared to inspect his puppet queen when she was fully dressed and waiting to be escorted to the royal barge.

'Chopines,' he said imperatively.

'Why chopines?' Jane asked, remembering that they were clogs of French origin with bulky high heels.

Northumberland pursed his lips. A vast crowd would be abroad to watch the new Queen's progress. Few of them had ever seen her, still fewer had heard of her, except as a remote cousin of the late King Edward. There were already mutterings against her in the streets of London, or so his agents had informed him. Who was this Jane Grey, Catholic and Protestant alike had asked, to replace King Henry's elder daughter? Was he to present them with a tiny figure, shorter by several inches than Mary Tudor? Finery and jewels were not enough.

'Sir . . . ?' Jane pressed.

'The Queen,' Northumberland said crisply, 'must look every inch a queen.'

'And four of those inches made of wood,' Jane commented dryly.

Chopines were found and placed on her feet, and in haste the hem of her skirt was let down in an attempt to cover them.

'Where is my husband?' she asked belatedly.

Lord Guilford Dudley emerged from the shadow of his father and gallantly offered her his arm. He too wore Tudor colours, and for some strange reason Jane found herself resenting it. She very nearly asked if he himself was in need of chopines, but his tallness was impressive without their aid and the lusty firmness of his white and green encased thighs made her tremble with longing.

'This is a day I had never thought to come upon us for many a year,' he said, and laughed excitedly.

'Nor I,' Jane said.

'*King* Consort?' he whispered insistently in her ear.

'My lordly husband is over-confident,' Jane retorted, surprised at the sudden vehemence of her words.

A string of barges lay waiting in the river, and in the first Northumberland was rowed away in the direction of the Tower. Jane boarded the royal barge and remembered that it was in this same barge that she and Edward had made the journey from Tower Wharf to Greenwich the Christmas before last. But it was Guilford Dudley who stood at her side now, Guilford the would-be King Consort. Why, she wondered, did she feel so rebellious? This feeling remained with her until the salute of a hundred cannon announced her arrival at the Tower where the Lieutenant of that fortress was waiting to receive her. Behind him stood the Duke of Northumberland wearing a black velvet surcoat trimmed with sable and, most prominently, his blue Garter ribbon, that highest honour of knighthood bestowed upon him by the late King Henry. Behind them both stood a detachment of Yeomen of the Guard, the sun of a calm windless day glinting on their axes. The Lieutenant offered Jane the keys of the Tower, but Northumberland, asserting his authority, snatched them from him. Feeling rebellious again and wondering if he thought to be offering her the keys of the Kingdom of Heaven, Jane accepted them from him and allowed him to lead her towards the royal apartments.

'Where are the dungeons?' she asked, never before having been in the Tower.

'Beneath,' Northumberland replied angrily. 'Well beneath.'

'To be entered,' she said, feeling an urge to taunt him, 'by way of Traitors' Gate.'

The royal apartments in the White Tower were crammed with courtiers when she entered them with Guilford Dudley possessively at her side. Shepherded by Northumberland they passed through to the presence chamber. There the Lieutenant directed Jane's attention to the glittering Crown jewels, selected from them the crown and invited her to take it.

'I have not yet demanded it,' she said hesitantly.

'Your Grace,' he said gently, 'I beg you to take it with no fear in your heart.'

But while she still hesitated Northumberland seized the crown and removing her coif placed it on her head. She thought of Edward at his coronation feast, he wearing this same crown. It had slipped a little, she remembered, but she felt the grip of it on her own head and the unmoving firmness of it. A sign, she wondered, that Edward would have been pleased?

'Another crown shall be made to crown your husband,' Northumberland said.

'I, the King Consort,' Guilford cried exultantly.

'No,' Northumberland said in a whisper loud enough for Jane to hear, 'King—King to reign equally with Queen Jane.'

Appalled, Jane said tensely, 'Let us not squabble in public,' and dismissed from the presence chamber all but Northumberland and her husband. Then she sank into a chair and struggled to make plain sense out of the confusion of her thoughts.

'*Squabble*, your Grace?' Northumberland questioned harshly.

'I suspect,' Jane said slowly, 'that it was you who caused the King to name me his heir. With that already in your mind you first married me to your son. Now you would have that son crowned King of England. Queen I might be, but Guilford Dudley King? Never!'

'Not even by Act of Parliament, Madame?'

'Neat,' young Dudley chuckled. 'I shall be King by Act of Parliament. I am prepared to control my impatience and wait for the Queen to call her first Parliament.'

'A Bill to that effect will never be presented,' Jane said, surprising herself by her firmness.

'Never?'

'Not by me.'

Longing to box her ears Northumberland said cajolingly: 'I suggest that you should retire to your inner chamber and weigh the pros and cons calmly before reaching a final decision. It would even be wise for your Grace to sleep on the matter.'

'My inner chamber, here at the Tower?' she asked in surprise.

'Queen and court are now in residence,' Northumberland said. 'Tradition demands it.'

'I will never change my mind,' Jane said.

'Sleep on it, Madame,' Northumberland urged.

'And alone, alone,' Guilford Dudley shouted, and rushed from the presence chamber laughing mockingly.

Jane removed the crown from her head and held it out for Northumberland's inspection. 'Would you have me reject this symbol of power?'

'Your Grace!'

'No,' Jane said, 'if it is really mine I must do my duty rather than attempt to thwart you. Call back my husband.'

Northumberland did so, but with Guilford was his mother and she who had always pampered her favourite son was shaking with anger. Before Jane could speak she heard herself abused with a spate of obscenities that would have made even a Thames fishwife blush.

'My son shall deny you his husbandly servicing,' the Duchess of Northumberland concluded on a note of triumph. 'You like it, I'm told, and enjoy it madly. Deprivation will settle the matter.'

'By St Mary it will,' Guilford chuckled.

Jane froze in horror. The Duchess had spoken truly, except that it would not settle the matter. To have liked, to have enjoyed madly . . . but had there been love in the physical ecstasy? Guilford had said: 'I pray, sweet Jane, that we will come to love each other.' If he had meant it then, all he wanted now was a crown.

'If this crown is really mine,' she said, 'I will gladly make my husband a royal duke.'

'I will be King—King!' Guilford raged.

'Enough!' Northumberland interposed, accepting out of necessity what he regarded only as a temporary defeat. 'Queen Jane has yet to be proclaimed.'

'Proclaimed or not,' Guilford threatened, 'she sleeps alone this night.'

'And many a night to come,' Jane told him, trying to keep disgust and loathing from her voice.

Before Northumberland could issue orders for a public proclamation he was called to the council chamber and presented with a letter from the Lady Mary. In it she said simply and briefly that having heard of her beloved brother's death she assumed without doubt that the throne was now hers, and she commanded Northumberland, President of *her* Council, to prepare for her royal reception at the Tower of London. Her messenger refused to reveal her present whereabouts, upon which Northumberland resisted the temptation to have him forced by torture to do so and calling together the Lords of the Council drafted out a reply to Mary's letter. Confident that he had placed his daughter-in-law securely on the throne, he demanded that the Lady Mary should submit herself to the will of her Sovereign Lady, Queen Jane, and promised in Jane's name to grant her any service that might preserve the common state of the realm. The final draft of the letter was signed by Northumberland and the Lords of the Council and dispatched at once to Mary. This done, Northumberland bethought himself of Jane's proclamation and issued the necessary order.

Mrs Eleyn was among the crowd when the heralds, the first of many to repeat the proclamation in other parts of London, made their appearance at the Cross in Cheapside at seven o'clock that night. It was July 10th, the first day, by official proclamation, of the new Queen's reign. There were three heralds and one trumpet, and they were received in silence. The Lady Jane, the silent crowd was told, had that day entered the Tower of London as the rightful Queen of England. Standing close to Mrs Eleyn was the drawer from one of the nearby taverns. 'In God's precious name,' the young man asked her, 'who is the Lady Jane?'

The answer came as the herald, speaking in Jane's name, continued: 'We, the Queen, therefore will you to defend our just title, to preserve our rightful possession of the Kingdom and to repel the untrue claim of the Lady Mary, bastard daughter of our great-uncle Henry VIII of famous and undying memory.' The silence continued until the drawer, nudging Mrs Eleyn in the ribs, spoke again.

'God preserve King Harry,' he roared, 'whether he be in heaven or hell. And God preserve the Lady Mary, our rightful Queen.'

A faint cheer rose and Mrs Eleyn, quivering with indignation, said accusingly: 'You, my man, are a Catholic.'

'I was born and bred a Protestant,' he retorted.

He was seized by two well-placed officers of the law and carried away. Surely a misguided Protestant, Mrs Eleyn thought, but hating violence felt sorry for him. He for his pains would stand in the pillory, pinned there by the ears, and would gain release only when those Protestant ears were severed.

'Barbarians!'

Mrs Eleyn turned to the speaker on her left and saw by his dress that he was, as she had suspected by his accent, a Spaniard.

'In your own country, Sir,' she said reproachfully, 'you have the Inquisition.'

'I think not of the loss of English ears,' the Spaniard asserted. 'I think only of the power of the Duke of Northumberland. Power, if he can retain it, is paramount in this island of meat-eating, ale-swilling, pox-infected barbarians.'

Bereft of a fitting retort Mrs Eleyn made her way back to the Tower and the royal apartments, knowing that she would never give the new Queen a truthful account of the common reception of her proclamation. The poor child, she kept thinking, the poor innocent child.

Jane, as it happened, had gone early to bed. The physician, having diagnosed a slight unbalance of her second humour, had prescribed a remedy composed in the main of antimony and was confident that her Grace would enjoy a restful night. Jane did and woke surprisingly refreshed the next morning to take breakfast alone with her husband. His attitude was a mixture of sheepishness and defiance.

'I find myself missing it,' he said, 'even as much as you must be.'

'Which is precious little, my lord,' Jane retorted.

'Regarding the other matter,' he said, not believing her, 'all will be well if, meanwhile, I am granted the right to be addressed as "your Grace".'

'Meanwhile?' Jane questioned.

'I am confident, Madame, that we shall yet be crowned jointly in Westminster Abbey.'

'Your confidence is overwhelming,' Jane said dryly.

Two pages entered and, addressing Jane as 'your Grace' and Guilford Dudley as 'my Lord', began to serve breakfast.

'Wait!' Guilford said sharply.

'Ah yes,' Jane murmured, an undertone of sarcasm in her voice, 'the Queen's husband will henceforth be addressed as "your Grace".'

'And kneeling in the first instance,' Guilford ordered the pages.

'One kneels to the Queen and no one else,' Jane said, and instantly felt as childish as Guilford had sounded.

Breakfast thereafter was a silent meal.

At midday, with Northumberland insisting on it, Jane held court and among others received Bishop Ridley, one-time chaplain to Henry VIII and now Bishop of London. Cautious while Henry was alive, he had become a fanatical Protestant after the accession of Edward VI. He had hastened this morning to the Tower after preaching a sermon at St Paul's Cathedral in support of Jane. Kneeling before her now, expectant of warm approval, he repeated some of his thunderous phrases. Jane listened with growing disquiet, and when it transpired that Ridley had roundly stigmatised the Lady Mary and the Lady Elizabeth as wicked bastards she rose and drew back from him. 'Enough, my lord bishop.'

'It is possible, your Grace,' Ridley said, rising from his knees and eyeing her sourly, 'that I spoke too zealously?'

'How were the words received by the congregation?'

'In silent approval, Madame. One does not raise a cheer in God's holy presence.'

Jane dismissed him and demanding privacy retired with Mrs Eleyn in attendance to her inner chamber. Much troubled she felt instinctively that Ridley had lied or had at best exaggerated.

'Mrs Eleyn,' she said, 'you sought permission to attend the service at St Paul's. Did you do so?'

'Yes, your Grace,' Mrs Eleyn said unhappily.

'Silent *approval*, Mrs Eleyn?'

'Your Grace . . .' Mrs Eleyn faltered.

'You must tell me the truth.'

'Your Grace, there were murmurs of discontent, even of anger, and . . .' Mrs Eleyn's voice trailed away.

'*And?*' Jane insisted.

'Bishop Ridley was hissed and booed in the precincts of the cathedral.'

'And,' Jane said sadly, 'by a Protestant congregation.'

It was then that for the first time Jane began to feel trapped and helpless. She struggled against the feeling and was still struggling when Northumberland called her to take supper with the leading Lords of the Council, the French and Spanish ambassadors, his Grace her husband and her father and mother. It was meant to be a state occasion with musical entertainment and dancing to follow, but the second course of the meal had yet to be served when Northumberland's secretary made his appearance with a newly arrived letter from the Lady Mary. To Northumberland's anger he spoke Mary Tudor's name in a voice audible to all. Even then he would have set the letter aside but Jane had an instruction for him.

'The President of the Council will read the letter aloud,' she said.

Northumberland broke the seal. The letter bore yesterday's date, was addressed from Framlingham Castle in Suffolk and was clearly not a reply to the letter he had sent to Mary in Queen Jane's name.

'Proceed,' Jane said when he hesitated.

'The Lady Mary has caused herself to be proclaimed Queen,' he said with every show of indignation. 'She begs the Council to avoid bloodshed and promises to respect the Reformed Church and the beliefs of its members.'

'And beyond that?' Jane demanded.

'The Lady Mary has the effrontery to affect the royal plural. She says in effect: "We require and charge you, on your allegiance, which you owe to God and to us, and to none other, to cause our right and title to the Crown and Government of this realm to be proclaimed in our City of London." ' Northumberland took a deep sharp breath and concluded: ' "This our letter, signed by our own hand, shall be, in your wisdom, your sufficient warrant." '

In the silence that followed Jane felt that the world, if only the world of the Tower, was closing in on her. She remembered Mary at New Hall Manor, Mary hurling a spoon across the table at her and later saying that she would go to the block for her faith. 'As I would for mine,' Jane remembered retorting. She centred her gaze on Northumberland at whom in another sense Mary had hurled a spoon. There was an indeterminate look on his face, and she fancied, as if in a nightmare, that he was gazing beyond her and seeing not a throne but a scaffold.

'A party of horse,' he said, stirring himself, 'shall advance on Framlingham Castle.'

'With or without our royal permission, my lord?'

'Surely with it.'

Feeling more trapped than ever Jane said tonelessly: 'And so ends the second day of the reign of Queen Jane.'

24

GUILFORD DUDLEY, as if already King, was sitting at the council table with Jane. On their right was Northumberland, on their left Suffolk. It was the morning of the third day of Queen Jane's reign and she was present rather than presiding at her first council meeting. Not entirely the puppet Northumberland would make of her, she thought, glancing round the table at the other Lords of the Council; she would, God willing, strive to the utmost to assert her queenly authority. More than anything else she wanted to believe that Edward would have been proud of her and that she would be able to justify the faith he must have had in her when deciding to name her his heir. Northumberland, President of the Council, declared the meeting open and tabled letters to Charles V, Emperor of the Holy Roman Empire, and the King of France, informing them officially of Jane's accession. She approved the wording of the letters and Northumberland appended his signature; then before more business could be introduced she asked for a report on the state of the City of London.

'The Queen's Highness,' Northumberland said evasively, 'need not trouble her head with such a matter.'

'All,' Suffolk said inadvisedly, 'is relatively quiet.'

'Relatively?' Jane questioned insistently.

'Paid agitators are abroad,' Northumberland said, scowling at Suffolk and silently calling him an ass-head. 'It was to be expected. They are being speedily dealt with.'

'With respect,' the Earl of Arundel said, addressing Jane instead of Northumberland, 'there is one agitator who, paid or otherwise, is yet to be apprehended. He claims to be a friend of a certain tavern drawer who stands at this moment in the pillory. He has written a newsletter in support of the Lady Mary. Many copies have been made and are being circulated. I have one such copy here.'

'Pray let me see it,' Jane said.

Arundel rose, came round the table to Jane's side and, with Northumberland cursing him, presented it. Jane set it on the table before her and read it aloud:

' "To the citizens of London and all inhabitants of this fair land—her Grace the Lady Mary is feared because of her religious beliefs, yet a sense of British justice is stronger than fear and calls for a protest against her loss of the Crown. It is a loss brought about by the machinations of the hated Duke of Northumberland who is answerable to God for his misdeeds. It is asserted and believed that the Duke of Northumberland caused the Duke of Somerset to order his brother the Lord Admiral's execution. Thereupon, it is asserted and believed, the Duke of Northumberland ordered the Duke of Somerset's execution. Thus he ridded himself of King Edward's two uncles, leaving the said King Edward with no close kinsmen to protect him. And so fell King Edward under the influence of a monster who hastened to poison him once he had named Jane Grey his heir. Long live our rightful Queen, the Lady Mary Tudor." '

Northumberland snatched the newsletter from Jane and tore it to shreds.

'If the work of a paid agitator,' she said, 'it has in it the ring of sincere belief.'

'Infused by your Grace's reading,' he all but shouted.

'Such was not my intention.'

'Baseless charges, all of them!'

'But surely . . .' Jane began, doubt gathering in her heart.

Northumberland controlled his rage but spoke contemptuously. 'Education is being thrust upon the common people, Madame. As a result we have this letter from a low fellow, the friend of a drawer of ale, who should never, God save us, have been taught to read and write.'

'In respect of the drawer,' Jane said, intellectually offended, 'royal clemency is called for. Let the man be released from the pillory.'

'It shall be done,' Northumberland agreed, but with a bad grace.

The meeting continued with an account of the disposition of Northumberland's military and naval forces, believed to be formidable, and was on the point of breaking up when Northumberland's secretary entered. He bowed to Jane but without seeking permission addressed himself to Northumberland.

'My Lord President, there is grave news. The Earl of Bath has sent his eldest son to join the Lady Mary at Framlingham. Likewise the Earl of Mordaunt and the Earl of Wharton. Meanwhile Lord Derby has proclaimed the Lady Mary in Chester.'

'Grave news, you call it?' Northumberland jeered. 'Let us wait and call it grave when the axeman has done his duty on Tower Hill.'

Jane rose to dismiss the Council. 'And so ends,' she said, 'my first council meeting on the third day of my reign.'

'*Our* reign,' Guilford Dudley said, speaking for the first time but smiling so charmingly that Jane's heart softened.

They dined with the Lords of the Council, making of the meal a semi-state occasion, Jane and her husband being seated together beneath a royal canopy. Dinner was followed by another council meeting from which Jane, too late, found herself excluded. Her father, his manner placating, brought her state documents to sign and having read them carefully she signed them with still-unfamiliar 'Jane R.'

'Has the drawer been released?' she asked.

'Yes,' Suffolk said lightly, 'leaving behind him his ears pinned to the pillory.'

'So much for royal clemency,' Jane said hotly. 'Dare I show my face in the streets of London at this moment?'

'A trifling matter, Madame, a commonplace punishment. Northumberland will be blamed, not you.'

'But should I not in any case ride through the streets and let the people see their new Queen?'

'They saw you from the banks of the Thames. A further public display is not thought advisable until the Lady Mary has been arrested.'

'Then I remain in the Tower to all intents a prisoner.'

'Scarcely a prisoner,' Suffolk blustered.

'Queen of England, or Queen of the Tower of London?' Jane asked ironically.

Feeling ill, sick at heart rather than sick in body, she refused supper that evening, dismissed her ladies and went unattended to her bedchamber, there to find Guilford Dudley sitting on her bed in naked splendour. Her heartbeats quickened at the sight of him.

'Guilford . . .'

'Madame?' he questioned jauntily.

'Are you here, my lord, with your mother's permission?'

'Not even with the Queen's.' He reached for a beer mug which Jane had failed at first to notice and drank deeply. 'Marriage,' he said, 'is thirsty work. How much ale must I drink before making the Queen pregnant?'

'And thus provide a Dudley son to succeed me,' she said bitterly.

'Let us indeed look to the future, sweet Jane, but what of the present? Is there not in your bed at this moment and soon to be deep in your royal person a King by the name of Dudley?'

'You would take me by force,' she faltered.

'Is force necessary, sweetheart?'

Jane took the beer mug from him. 'No more necessary,' she said faintly, 'than the drinking of ale.'

They were informed during breakfast the next morning that the company of horse sent to arrest Mary Tudor at Framlingham had failed. There had been no fighting; the failure was the result of desertions to Mary. Northumberland called a council meeting that afternoon and again succeeded in excluding Jane. It was her father who came to her afterwards to acquaint her with a decision that had been reached unanimously.

'Your Grace,' Suffolk said formally, 'I am to command the Government forces and raise the country against the Lady Mary.'

'You, not Northumberland?'

'Northumberland considers it his duty to remain in full control here.'

Jane looked at Suffolk in alarm. 'In full control, and I at his mercy,' she whispered. 'Bring Northumberland to me, and all the Lords of the Council with him.'

'You sound as if in fear of your life,' a sorely troubled Suffolk commented.

'I once thought Northumberland my friend,' Jane said tensely. 'How wrong I was! He is an unscrupulous man, mad for power and more power. He would, if unchecked, replace me with Guilford. Am I not entitled to have my father here to protect me?'

'You are, indeed you are,' Suffolk said warmly, 'but the decision has been taken.'

'I have yet to sign your commission. Is it not my prerogative to refuse?'

'By St Mary it is,' Suffolk agreed. 'No one has the power to send me forth without the Queen's approval.'

'Truly?' Jane asked anxiously.

'Approval is expected of you but cannot be forced. Northumberland and the others have sworn allegiance. They could face a charge of treason if they revoked their oath. They can advise, then can argue, they can cajole, but they cannot under the Great Seal command.'

'I am determined to keep you with me,' Jane said.

Northumberland and the other Lords of the Council were summoned. Jane looked only at Northumberland and briefly stated her wishes. His astonishment quickly gave place to an anger so intense that he found it impossible to speak. Jane for her part was shaking with fear but she wondered, as she tried to face him squarely, if she could induce him to believe that the trembling of her limbs was caused by royal indignation.

'You, Sir, must take the field,' she said. 'The task is plainly yours.'

Northumberland found his voice and said with mock modesty: 'Suffolk is the better soldier.'

That he should seem to argue, Jane thought, was an encouraging sign. Or was it? What powers of argument could she muster up against those of a man capable almost always of browbeating the entire Council? There was danger in argument; she had issued a royal command and must stand by it without argument.

'The short and the long of it,' she said, 'is that the Queen's father must remain in the Queen's company.'

'It is not a question of who is the better soldier,' the Earl of Arundel said, coming in an unflattering manner to Northumberland's aid. 'Far rather is it a question of who, in hostile territory, is the more popular figure. Suffolk is less hated, if hated at all, in East Anglia than Northumberland.'

'Plain if unkind speaking,' Jane said, as if in reproof.

'And yet,' said the Earl of Pembroke, coming unexpectedly to her support, 'Northumberland by his experience, his wit and his wisdom is capable of animating his forces while pacifying and allaying his enemies.'

Then Suffolk added his own voice persuasively: 'No man is better fitted than Northumberland to undertake the task.'

'We think it good that you should do so, my lord,' Jane said, and waited breathlessly.

Knowing that he had been driven into a corner, Northumberland bowed, but pointedly he addressed the Lords of the Council rather than the Queen.

'Very well, then go I must, and not doubting your fidelity, my lords, I leave in your custody the Queen's Highness.'

It was an offensive statement, Jane thought, but better their custody than his.

'Pray have your commission drawn up and present it for my approval,' she said. 'I thank you humbly for your obedience and beg you to use your diligence.'

'To diligence let us add duty, your Grace,' he said harshly. 'Within a matter of days I shall bring into the Tower the Lady Mary, captive or dead, like the rebel she is.'

Jane shuddered and said quickly: 'Not dead. No harm must come to my cousin Mary Tudor.'

Northumberland left the Tower immediately after Jane had signed his commission and went by barge to Durham House to gather about him his officers and inspect the Government forces which had already assembled there. With him in addition to his other sons was Guilford, eager to ride forth at his father's side and prove his worth as a soldier, but Northumberland would have none of it.

'The life of a king soon to be proclaimed,' he said, 'is too precious for me to risk in any skirmish great or small. Back to the Tower with you. The Queen is in her husband's keeping rather than her father's.'

Guilford swelled with pride. 'It shall be as you wish, my lord.'

At noon the next day, the fifth of Jane's reign and the fiftieth of her marriage, Northumberland, an impressive figure in flowing scarlet cloak, rode out of London at the head of three thousand foot and two thousand horse. It was a bright clear day, the sun glinting in armour and sword and pike. The streets were crammed with people but neither a cheer nor a curse was heard. An ominous silence, he wondered, or were the people struck dumb with awe at the sight of his invincible army?

'They press to see us,' he said, turning to Lord Grey who rode at his side, 'yet I fail to hear a single voice wishing us godspeed.'

And then out of the silence came a lusty cry: 'The Queen, God save her!'

'Ah . . .' said Lord Grey.

Northumberland looked at him questioningly but held his peace. The Queen, yes, but which Queen—Jane, whom he had caused to be proclaimed, or Mary, who had caused herself to be proclaimed?

25

JANE woke suddenly to find Guilford shaking her by the shoulders.

'Am I late for morning prayers?' she asked.

'You were groaning in your sleep,' he said accusingly. 'It made my blood run cold.'

Jane touched her brow and found it damp. 'I have a terrible headache.'

Guilford peered down at her closely. 'You also have a rash on your face and neck.' He sprang from the bed in alarm. 'Have I caught the disease, whatever it is?'

She studied his naked body only vaguely. 'I can see no rash on any part of you.'

'Even so . . . !' And with that he snatched up a gown and fled to his adjacent dressing room, shouting over his shoulder: 'I shall send Mrs Eleyn to you.'

Mrs Eleyn came bustling in. Jane sat up, but feeling feverish to the point of light-headedness fell back on the pillows. Mrs Eleyn examined her and discovered that the rash extended to her shoulders and chest.

'I shall summon your Grace's mother,' she said, and withdrew in haste.

Frances, Duchess of Suffolk came after what seemed to Jane a lengthy delay and brought with her Northumberland's personal physician. He touched Jane's brow, studied her face and said that the Queen was more than ordinarily troubled by the first of the four humours.

'A further application of leeches is called for, Madame.'

'No,' Frances said decisively. 'I myself have never placed much faith in leeches, and the Queen is clearly weak enough without suffering further loss of blood.'

Scurrah Jones bowed. 'As you wish, Madame. We shall continue with the antimony treatment.'

Frances dismissed him and looked fixedly at Jane. '*Continue* with it?'

'I have been taking the doses three times a day,' Jane said after a moment of confused thought, 'since—since my second day in the Tower. Dr Scurrah Jones insisted on it.'

'Who gives them to you?'

'Mrs Eleyn.'

Frances's eyes narrowed. 'Then they can be discontinued without his knowledge.'

'Discontinued?'

'I have only suspicion to guide me,' Frances said, 'but is my daughter the Queen being slowly poisoned? Is she to be removed in order to make the way easier for that would-be King, Guilford Dudley?'

Appalled, Jane said: 'The doses shall be discontinued.'

'You shall remain in bed for the rest of the day,' Frances decided authoritatively, 'and Scurrah Jones shall not in any circumstances be admitted to your presence.'

Jane sat up again. 'I feel so light-headed my memory is beginning to fail me. When did Northumberland march out of London?'

'At noon the day before yesterday.'

'What news since then?'

Frances hesitated momentarily. 'The Lady Mary has been proclaimed in Norwich. There was a false report that she was there at the time *en route* to Yarmouth in an attempt to escape to France. I know our cousin Mary all too well. It is not in her nature to run away. Eight naval vessels were sent earlier to Yarmouth to prevent a possible attempt. She must have found it heartening to learn that the captains had declared for her, also that she had been proclaimed again at Yarmouth.'

'Where is she now?'

'She is still in residence at Framlingham Castle, the stronghold of her Catholic friends, the Norfolk family. I need not remind you that they have a strong body of armed retainers.'

Memory was flooding back, but there was another question to be asked. 'Where is Northumberland?'

'According to the last report he was advancing on Cambridge. Meanwhile he has requested reinforcements.'

'He must have them.'

Frances, already shaken by a feeling of approaching doom, knew full well that all the troops stationed in and near London might be needed to keep order in the event of a rising in the City.

'The Queen must speak to her father,' she said.

Jane rested during the morning, attempted with small success to eat the meal brought to her at midday by Mrs Eleyn and dozed fitfully until Guilford, braving the risk of infection, disturbed her near supper time. She sat up, feeling surprisingly better, and looked at him curiously.

'You appear to be in a temper, Guilford.'

'My father left you in my keeping,' he burst out, his handsome face flushed with anger. 'The Lords of the Council refuse to believe it. Further, they refuse to accept me at the Council board and, God damn them, they refuse to dine with me—I who am soon to be their King. I may dine in state, they tell me, but alone—alone! This is sheer rebellion.'

'We shall dine in state together,' Jane said placatingly.

Guilford was looking at her closely. 'The rash has all but gone.'

Jane was aware of this but still felt light-headed. 'I shall join you at supper,' she said, and sent for her ladies. They bathed and dressed her, and then at her father's urgent request she dismissed them and received him.

'Two Lords of the Council, the Earl of Pembroke and the Marquess of Winchester,' he said at once, 'have left the Tower for their separate London houses.'

'Desertion?'

'One can but think so. They were expressly commanded to remain here to protect you.'

'No, Father. Northumberland left the Queen's Highness in their custody.'

'A mere figure of speech; indeed, a conventional figure of speech.'

'He also spoke of not doubting their fidelity. Their fidelity to him or to me?'

'To you, Madame. They and many others swore allegiance.'

'Very well. Test their allegiance by inviting them to return to the Tower.'

'I did so,' Suffolk said unhappily. 'They refused.'

'Treason, would you say?' Jane, not quite so light-headed now, made up her mind. 'Have them brought back under guard.'

'Am I to issue the order in my own name?' he asked hesitantly.

'Are you not the acting President of the Council during Northumberland's absence?'

'Well, now . . .'

'Very well, issue it in the Queen's name.'

Admiring Jane's spirit he did so, and when informed that Pembroke and Winchester had been brought back to the Tower he escorted her to the presence chamber to receive them. She was seated on the throne beneath Edward's royal canopy when they entered in the company of the Lieutenant of the Tower. They showed every sign of anger but they knelt before her, if rebelliously.

'My lords, I bid you welcome,' Jane said, as if receiving noble visitors from a distant part of the Kingdom. 'Be pleased to rise.' Then she glanced at the Lieutenant and said firmly: 'Sir John, no person is to leave the Tower without my permission. Furthermore, all the keys must be brought to me at dusk each night.'

'Are we your Grace's prisoners?' Pembroke asked hotly.

Even as she might be regarded as their prisoners, she thought, but said: 'Tell me first why you and Winchester left the Tower in seeming desertion.'

'It had occurred to us,' Pembroke said, a hint of despair in his voice now, 'that if Northumberland were defeated and captured and no immediate word received of it, we would be held here never to escape.'

As she herself would be, Jane thought, and asked: 'Do you fear that Northumberland, with an army of five thousand, will suffer defeat and capture?'

It was Winchester who answered: 'Your Grace, the Lady Mary has raised an army of twenty thousand.'

Jane turned to her father. 'Why was I not told?'

'Simply because I was not told myself,' Suffolk replied querulously. 'Much is being kept from me by Northumberland's secretary.'

'You, the acting President of the Council?'

'Normal council meetings no longer take place, Madame. The

Lords have taken to meeting in little groups, privately, secretly. They are all as fearful as Pembroke and Winchester. They seek ways and means of saving their heads.'

'And you, Sir?' Jane asked searchingly.

Suffolk drew himself up, hand on sword. 'I shall remain with the Queen my daughter, come what may.'

Jane believed him, but she had a sudden memory of him standing helplessly by while her mother attempted to whip her into submission. How long ago was that? A mere two months, yet surely each month a year. Nay, a lifetime. Her head cleared fully.

'Northumberland has yet to give battle,' she said. 'Why then this sad talk of defeat and capture? He has asked for reinforcements. Pray dispatch them with all speed.'

'I can muster no more than six hundred,' Suffolk told her.

'Not even six can be spared,' Pembroke said. 'The City is seething with discontent.'

'Six hundred would be less than useless,' Winchester remarked scathingly. 'Desertions would reduce that number by half during the march, as desertions are now robbing Northumberland of a real army.'

'He has the promise of French support,' Suffolk reminded him.

'Even if the promise were kept, it would take weeks to assemble French mercenaries and bring them across the Channel.'

'Enough!' Pembroke said, and addressed himself to Jane: 'I repeat, Madame, are we your Grace's prisoners?'

She looked at him steadily: 'As Lords of the Council, whose prisoners are you but your own?'

Neat, Suffolk thought admiringly, and grasping his sword again glanced challengingly from Pembroke to Winchester. 'The Queen, God save her,' he said softly.

'Aye, and all of us,' Pembroke said, even more softly.

*

The barge drew alongside the wharf of Baynard's Castle, the Earl of Pembroke's Gothic palace, the most magnificent of all the private palaces on the Thames, and from it stepped the Marquess of Winchester and the Earl of Arundel. Side by side they passed through the water-gate and the spacious formal gardens and entered the palace to be greeted warmly by the Earl of Pembroke.

'I take it,' he said, 'that you left the Tower without hindrance?'

'The guards saluted and allowed us to pass unquestioned,' Winchester said. 'I was not surprised, you having suffered no hindrance yourself.'

'We live in the midst of rapid change,' Pembroke commented. 'After a mere two days the guards have reached the point of ignoring the Queen's orders. The point,' he added sombrely, 'of desperation.'

He led them through the main hall of the palace to what he termed his own private council chamber, a large and lofty room luxuriously furnished and decorated with rich tapestries. Here, with one exception, all the other Lords of the Council had already assembled.

'Suffolk alone is absent,' Pembroke said dryly.

'He was bursting with suspicion and would have joined us,' Arundel said, smiling reminiscently. 'I warned him that if he meant to desert his daughter I would run him through the heart.'

Pembroke laughed and invited the company to be seated at the large central table. No longer laughing he began by telling them what he had withheld from the Queen and Suffolk, that Northumberland had advanced from Cambridge to Bury St Edmunds, a distance of thirty-five miles from Framlingham Castle, and had then fallen back on Cambridge without striking a blow.

'Northumberland is in sorry plight,' Pembroke continued. 'Desertions have reduced his forces to less than a thousand, and the Lady Mary has ordered the Mayor of Cambridge to arrest him. That worthy gentleman is at present in no position to do so, but the end of Northumberland's adventure is close at hand.' Pembroke paused before adding sonorously: 'Need I remind you, my lords and dear brethren, that King Edward's will has not been ratified by Parliament? And need I draw your attention to his father's will? The Crown is due to the Lady Mary and she, by King Henry's will *and* ours, shall have it.'

An uneasy silence followed with all present gazing as if in doubt at the Earl of Arundel who, until now, had been one of

Northumberland's strongest supporters, even though in earlier days Northumberland had caused him to be fined and imprisoned for a time in the Tower. Arundel himself was gazing at one of the tapestries. It depicted a magnificently arrayed king riding in a chariot. Northumberland's son, he thought satirically, his Grace King Guilford? His eyes strayed to another tapestry on the opposite wall, a woman floating on a cloud with a globe of the world raised in her hands. Queen Jane or Queen Mary?

'My lords,' Arundel said at last, 'the Lady Mary shall have the Crown.' He sprang up and grasped his sword. 'This blade shall make her Queen or I'll lose my life.'

'Are there any,' Pembroke asked, 'who would return to the Tower and Queen Jane?'

There was none.

Satisfied, Pembroke proposed, without opposition, that their allegiance to the Lady Mary should be made public with as little delay as possible. Despite this there was a lengthy discussion, it being finally resolved that Mary, the rightful Queen, should be proclaimed in London, that the foreign ambassadors should be informed of this, that Arundel should carry their loyal submissions to Mary before proceeding to arrest Northumberland and that Winchester should make known to Suffolk the undoubted fact that his daughter's reign, if reign it could be called, was at an end.

'We must now give thanks to God for His holy guidance,' Pembroke said, glibly if not righteously.

'Publicly,' Winchester suggested.

'Where else but at St Paul's?' Arundel added.

And so to the cathedral they went in a body and there, at Pembroke's insistence, Mass in the Anglo-Catholic form of the late King Henry was celebrated with not a thought being given to the Holy Communion favoured by his Protestant son Edward.

*

'Your Grace...'

Startled by this unexpected confrontation with Northumberland's physician, Jane signalled to the ladies who were attending her to the dining hall to draw back.

'Sir?' she questioned as arrogantly as she could.

'It is gratifying,' Scurrah Jones said tonelessly, 'to find the Queen's Highness looking so much improved in health.'

'Surprising also?'

'I find it in no way surprising,' he said, a hint of shiftiness in his eyes, 'when the mixture I prescribed has obviously been of great benefit.'

'I have taken not a drop of it since the rash was discovered,' Jane said, and decided against telling him that she had ordered Mrs Eleyn to get rid of it. 'I was tempted to throw it away but thought it better to keep it for your own use.'

'Madame?'

'By the look of you, Dr Scurrah Jones, you are suffering a grave disturbance of all four humours. You shall take the mixture three or more times a day under my personal supervision.'

'Your Grace makes a hearty joke,' he said, looking about him as if in search of escape.

'Is it the same mixture that you prescribed for King Edward?' Jane demanded.

'No, Madame, indeed no.' He had grown very pale.

'Something of greater strength, perhaps?'

Jane watched him as he turned on his heel and fled. Guilty? She had no proof but felt convinced that he had carried out Northumberland's orders to the letter.

Only two people were awaiting her in the dining hall, her mother and her mother-in-law. At dinner there had been two others, her father and her husband. She had been told then that the Lords of the Council were dining privately; it seemed that they would be supping privately also. She wondered idly if Guilford was sulking in his room and assumed that her father was busy with the Lords. Her ladies escorted her to her chair beneath the royal canopy, curtsied and waited for the Duchess of Suffolk and the Duchess of Northumberland to take their places before taking their own.

'Let supper be served,' Jane said formally.

But at that moment Suffolk strode into the dining hall. She saw at once that he was agitated. He faltered once as he approached the royal table, then with a gasp that in no way revealed his feelings he darted round to Jane's side, reached up to the canopy above her and tore it down.

'Father!' Jane exclaimed.

Suffolk was prevented from speaking by Guilford Dudley's hurried entry. He too was agitated.

'The Lady Mary,' he shouted hysterically, 'has been proclaimed at the Cross in Cheapside.'

Then Suffolk spoke. 'Lady Jane, you are no longer Queen. You must set aside your royal robes and content yourself with the life of a humble servant of her Grace, Queen Mary.'

Guilford flung himself to his knees at his mother's side, grasped her hands and burst into tears. Jane looked at him with pity in her heart but felt for herself a vast relief.

'I am far more willing to set aside the royal robes than I was to assume them,' she said. 'The Crown was never truly mine. I relinquish it happily. Be kind enough, Father, to take me home.'

'Home?' Suffolk echoed.

'To Bradgate.'

Suffolk, all forcefulness spent, looked helplessly at his wife. She came instantly to his rescue.

'Take Lady Jane to her apartments,' she instructed Jane's pale and trembling ladies. Then she turned furiously on the Duchess of Northumberland. 'And you, Madame, be kind enough to remove that snivelling monstrosity, that would-be king never weaned by his mother.'

Once Suffolk was alone with his wife in the echoing dining hall he said tentatively: 'Bradgate . . .'

'Fool!' Frances raged. 'If we remove Jane from the Tower we will increase the danger of a charge of high treason.'

'Are we to leave her here a prisoner?' Suffolk faltered.

'Are we held in captivity ourselves?'

'As yet, no. But we must leave before Pembroke can act against us.'

'Immediately,' Frances decided, 'and separately. I shall go first to Suffolk Place. Join me there.'

'But . . . poor Jane?'

'She may, if she wishes, make good her own escape.'

Frances delayed only long enough to collect her jewellery before departing, without a thought of seeing Jane again, by barge for Suffolk Place. Suffolk himself, followed and guarded by his men-at-arms, wandered aimlessly and unmolested to Tower Hill. He felt troubled and was ready to quarrel with himself because of it. He touched his sword lightly and remembered having said that he would remain with the Queen his daughter, come what may. The Queen, but Jane was no longer Queen. Even so, should he attempt an escape to France, taking Jane with him? Few people would recognise her, probably none at all if he dressed her in the clothes of a serving-maid. As for himself, he could shave off his moustache and beard. Yet why run away and thus commit an act of cowardice? And in any case, of what was he guilty? *He* had not placed his daughter on the throne; *he* had not led an army against Mary Tudor. And Jane herself, of what was *she* guilty? Guilty only of obeying the will of her cousin King Edward. It was even on record that she had accepted the Crown unwillingly. Neither Jane nor he had anything to fear.

'Then why,' he whispered for his own ears only, 'am I angry with myself?'

He grew conscious as he walked slowly on Tower Hill of cheering crowds, of the ringing of church bells and of the leaping flames of bonfires. Still he remained unmolested and remembered Arundel saying that he was less hated, if hated at all, than Northumberland. He paused, savouring the memory, and then moving on stumbled over a body lying in his aimless path. Gazing down he recognised the dead face of Scurrah Jones.

'He seized my sword,' someone told him, 'and fell on it.'

Suddenly Suffolk found gathered about him what looked like an ugly, expectant crowd, hemming him in. Quickly he ordered his men-at-arms to throw down their weapons, but he retained his own sword, drew it and flourished it high above his head.

'I am but one man in your midst,' he shouted, little knowing that he had not been recognised, 'but I, one among many, proclaim the Lady Mary our rightful Queen of England.'

He was cheered, but the cheering made no music in his ears. And so ends, he thought, the ninth and final day of the reign of Queen Jane.

26

'YOU abandoned her,' Mary Tudor said. 'That is the long and the short of it.'

Frances, Duchess of Suffolk studied her cousin the Queen with a feeling of uncertainty growing upon her. There was no hint of accusation in Mary's voice; it was expressionless, as was her face, a face that had aged much since their last meeting. It seemed to Frances that the bridge of Mary's nose had flattened and widened, and she had noticed when closer a foul smell coming from the royal nostrils. Moreover, Mary was apt to peer at one short-sightedly. These were all signs, Frances concluded, she having made an avid study of the subject, of congenital syphilis. Poor creature, Frances thought, but unpityingly.

'You abandoned her in the Tower,' Mary continued, 'as did your husband.'

'She could have made good her own escape,' Frances said defensively.

'That you know to be untrue. Scarcely had you left the Tower when the Lieutenant, on Pembroke's order, placed her in the Gentleman-Gaoler's lodgings. You abandoned her and then came to me to plead. To plead for what, Cousin? Her safety, or yours and your husband's, or yours alone? Knowing you, I would say the latter.'

Frances, with only her own safety in mind, made no reply. After two days at Suffolk Place with her husband she had hastened here to New Hall Manor where Mary was resting and holding court before continuing her advance on London from Framlingham Castle.

'Your Grace,' she said at last, 'I came to swear allegiance to my cousin the Queen.'

'Then swear it,' Mary said, her voice still expressionless.

Frances, hating the need to humble herself, fell to her knees and swore allegiance.

'I came also,' she said, when bidden to rise, 'to plead for royal clemency for Northumberland's little innocent victim.'

'No,' said Mary, 'you came to plead with me on your own behalf.' And she added, her eyes empty of any emotion: 'Northumberland's innocent victim, yes. I intend her not to suffer. I intend her no harm.'

'Release shall be hers?' Frances ventured, feeling most virtuous.

Mary laughed suddenly and harshly. 'Strange, is it not, that neither you nor I have referred to the innocent victim by name. "Her", "she", but never "Jane Grey".' She shrugged and said indifferently: 'Having sworn allegiance you are free to go wherever you please. Your husband also. But I doubt if I shall ever receive you again.'

Cursing her cousin silently, Frances curtsied. 'I am now and always at your Grace's service.'

'No,' said Mary, 'at your own, always at your own.'

*

Jane was standing at a window in the Gentleman-Gaoler's lodgings. From this same window she had watched the Duke of Northumberland brought in by his captor the Earl of Arundel; from it she had watched him go to his trial at Westminster Hall and return condemned to death; now, on the morning of his execution, she was watching him walk slowly but firmly to the Tower Chapel where, having renounced the Protestant faith, he was to hear Mass and receive the Sacrament. In renouncing the Protestant faith he had in fact returned to the faith in which he had been born. She had long believed that his adherence to her own faith was a matter of policy, not conviction, for he had once said in her hearing that having seen a new religion begun he had felt the need, run dog, run devil, to go forward with it. She wondered now if his recantation could be viewed in the same light, he hopeful at this last stage of royal pardon.

'My lady . . .'

Jane turned from the window. It was Mrs Eleyn.

'I seek your permission, my lady,' Mrs Eleyn said, 'to leave the Tower for an hour or so.'

Jane shrugged. 'Since you may come and go as you please . . .' Then she looked at the woman closely. 'You would go to Tower Hill?'

Her face red with anger, Mrs Eleyn said: 'But not to dip my handkerchief in Northumberland's blood. *He* is no martyr. Hating him as I do I would see him dispatched to hell.'

'That is not a Christian attitude,' Jane said severely. 'I shall pray for him, and so must you.'

Mrs Eleyn curtsied, scowled and withdrew.

Jane seated herself at her writing table and thought again of a letter she had in mind to write to Bullinger. She had been well provided with books and writing materials, nothing of that nature being denied her. Her rooms, though a prison within a prison, were comfortable enough, and if she felt in need of exercise she was allowed to walk once a day in the Lieutenant's private garden, but no farther. Her attendants had been reduced to four: Mrs Eleyn, two tiring-women and a young page. The Gentleman-Gaoler and his wife were kind and courteous, and now and again she dined with them on the floor below, otherwise she dined with her four attendants. Her husband Guilford had sought permission to dine with her, but visitors, either from within or without the Tower, were not allowed. Guilford, who seemed more and more a stranger to her, was housed in the Beauchamp Tower and was busying himself, she had been told, with the task of carving on his wall a memorial to his unfortunate family. And what, she wondered, of her own family? Her parents had not written to her or communicated with her in any way. All she knew was that they were at liberty and living in seclusion at one of their houses at Sheen. She assumed that they preferred to ignore her existence while she remained in the Tower, a threat, they no doubt thought, to their own safety. She tried to feel no bitterness, but bitterness was sometimes there like a cloud passing slowly across the sun.

She took up her pen and wrote the date. It was August 21st, little more than a month since her father had torn down the canopy. She began by telling Bullinger of Queen Mary's visit to the Tower to hear sung in the chapel the requiem dirge and

Mass for King Edward. Thus Mary had risked arousing Protestant anger but she had compromised, reluctantly it was said, by allowing Protestant rites for the funeral service in Westminster Abbey. Then she had issued a proclamation, to what extent sincerely Jane could not say, in which she stated that she had no mind to compel her people to adhere to the faith in which she herself believed but would be glad if they were reconciled to it. And pronouncing against the use of the devilish term 'papist' on the one hand, the equally devilish term 'heretic' on the other, she begged her good and loving subjects to live together in Christian charity. 'Sincere or insincere?' Jane asked Bullinger. 'I can but think the latter,' and she added, so well schooled was she in anti-Catholicism, that her cousin's Church, as they all knew, was the Whore of Babylon.

The tramping of feet drew her to the window again. Northumberland was being marched the short distance out of the Tower to the scaffold on Tower Hill. It was clear that what Jane regarded as his apostasy had not achieved for him a royal pardon, unless it was to come dramatically at the last moment. She returned to the writing table, finished her letter and then began to compose a long-contemplated deposition for presentation to her cousin Queen Mary. She was frowning over the first few laboured sentences when Mrs Eleyn, flushed and breathless, returned from Tower Hill.

'Well?' Jane asked, setting aside her pen.

'Such a vast crowd, my lady—men, women and children, so many children.'

'As at a country fair. Were they thoroughly entertained?'

'The Duke made a speech, but then they always do make speeches. Tradition demands it. He said that his treason was not altogether of his own devising. He was procured and induced by others, he said, lying wretch that he is—I mean *was*, he being no more. But God forbid, he said, that he should name any man. It was for him to forgive all men. He might have added one woman, his mother, for conceiving him.'

'Mrs Eleyn, please!' Jane felt pained.

'Then,' said an uncontrite Mrs Eleyn, 'he removed his surcoat and offered it to the executioner. That is traditional too, with the highborn. A costly surcoat. The executioner will sell it. After that he continued his speech, saying that he was a wretched sinner most justly condemned. There was a priest with him on the scaffold and he asked that popish fellow to bear witness that he, John Dudley, Duke of Northumberland, had acted freely and truly when receiving the sacrament, and then and there he repeated his confession of faith. There were some suppressed but quite clear boos and jeers, I'm glad to say, but he seemed not to hear and asked the good people of London to follow his example before it was too late and forsake the new doctrine.'

'It was not a matter of policy after all,' Jane decided, 'nor a matter of run dog, run devil.'

'Madame?'

'Or perhaps Northumberland, born a Catholic, was in fear of damnation. I pray God that neither I nor any friend of mine should die in that manner.'

Mrs Eleyn, born a Catholic herself, shuddered involuntarily and went on hurriedly: 'He died bravely enough, Madame. He placed the bandage round his eyes himself and he forgave the executioner, as one always must—poor man, it is his livelihood. Then he knelt at the block and said: "Let me discover how neat a fit this block is for my head." The executioner—he really has had much practice—finished him with one sure blow. He was rich in blood, that wicked duke. It spurted everywhere. Men, women and children swarmed on the scaffold and dipped their handkerchiefs into it.'

'So he did die a martyr,' Jane said in surprise.

'To some, perhaps, though I doubt it. No, my lady, they will sell the blood-soaked handkerchiefs and the men will swill down much ale in the taverns tonight. And that reminds me,' she said, not exactly running off at a tangent, 'your ladyship's stock of ale is perilously low.'

'What of the state of my by no means royal exchequer?' Jane asked, glad of this domestic distraction.

'Low also, I fear,' said Mrs Eleyn, Mistress of the Purse, as so dubbed by Jane in one of her lighter moods. 'Of the ninety-three shillings a week granted by the Queen, less than three are left this week.'

'When is the next payment due?'

'Two days hence. I will gladly and humbly advance a few shillings from my own grant of twenty.'

'Then,' said Jane in would-be gaiety, 'let the ale flow without restraint.'

She wondered if her Gentleman-Gaoler's fee was in arrears. Penniless but for Queen Mary's bounty, she was obliged, it being the practice with prisoners in the Tower, to pay her own way. Master Partridge was in effect her landlord as well as her gaoler. She sent for him at once to discuss this ticklish financial matter but he shrugged it aside and announced with a bow that he had news which he hoped would be to her liking.

'Madame, you have been granted the privilege of taking a daily airing farther afield than the Lieutenant's garden. You may walk, if you wish, in the Privy Garden and also the Queen's Garden. You have been granted what is known as the Freedom of the Tower.'

'And will soon be granted,' Mrs Eleyn predicted, 'the freedom of the whole world.'

*

'Your Majesty, we have a precedent to guide us,' Simon Renard said silkily. 'And are not precedents as sacred to the English as their love of ale?'

Queen Mary looked angrily at the Emperor Charles's envoy. 'You would joke in a matter so serious?'

'No joke was intended, Madame,' Renard said, bewildered by her anger and bewailing the fact that he had little understanding of what passed for a sense of humour with the English. 'It is the Emperor's belief that the more guilty of your enemies should be put to death, as in the case of that arch-traitor Northumberland.'

The Emperor Charles was Mary's greatest ally and she knew that she must listen to his views and advice as conveyed to her by Renard who had become more closely her confidant than any of her ministers. That he was a handsome man, gallantly attentive, was beside the point, or so she deceived herself into believing.

'Pray acquaint me with your precedent,' she said, trying to remember that she was Mary Tudor with a Tudor will of her own.

Renard bowed obsequiously. 'Did not the Emperor Theodosius order the execution of his son Maximus? And why, Madame?

Maximus unlawfully attributed to himself the title of Emperor.'

'I have no son,' Mary said woodenly.

'Your Majesty has a cousin by the name of Jane Grey.'

'I loved my little cousin,' Mary asserted, 'heretic though she is, and that through no fault of her own.'

'*Loved?*' Renard said softly.

'In happier days, yet in these unhappy days I love her still.'

'She accepted the Crown and the title of Queen,' Renard pressed on, his manner grave. 'It can be said that the title was insufficiently proved, but to many it had, and still has, some semblance of foundation. These are troubled times for England. How secure is your Majesty in a realm that is predominantly Protestant? While Jane Grey lives she is a rallying point for those who, however rashly, might rise against you. Power and tyranny sometimes have more force, as was proved however briefly in the case of Northumberland, than *right* and *justice*.'

'Come what may,' Mary said stubbornly, 'I shall spare my little cousin.'

Renard bowed. 'With your Majesty's permission we shall discuss this matter again at a later time.'

When the Imperial envoy had withdrawn Mary read for a second time Jane's deposition. Jane outlined the scene at Sion House when she had been informed of the nature of Edward's will and she repeated the words she had uttered at that time, that the honour that had been thrust upon her was not one she had thought to anticipate. 'It failed to please me,' she wrote, 'and moved me only to declare that the Crown was not my right.' Her fault in accepting it, she continued, was such that, but for the goodness and clemency of the rightful Queen, she could have no hope of finding pardon or any of forgiveness. The poor child, Mary thought, was putting up, perhaps instinctively, a fight for her life. She read on broodingly: 'I trust in God, as I now confess my want of prudence, that infinite clemency be extended, it being known that the error imputed to me was not altogether caused by myself.' Mary set the deposition aside. Nothing, she vowed, would ever induce her to harm Jane Grey.

Renard returned to the attack immediately after Mary had announced the date of her coronation, but he spoke first of marriage and saw at once that the subject was most pleasing to this virgin and to him unlovely Queen. She smiled, she blushed and she gave him the benefit of the coyest of looks.

'There are those,' she murmured, 'who would have me marry Lord Courtenay.'

Renard was well aware of this and had been instructed by the Emperor to stand in opposition to such a match but practising guile and subtlety while so doing in order to avoid arousing Mary Tudor's well-known stubbornness. Courtenay, Renard reflected, was a great-grandson of Edward IV. His father, the Marquess of Exeter, had been executed by Henry VIII and he himself had spent the last fifteen years of his life as a prisoner in the Tower. Mary had ordered his release and had thanked God that she had been able to do so when Northumberland, had he maintained his power, would have sent him to the block.

'A handsome young man,' Renard commented. 'If your Majesty is bent on marrying an Englishman such a choice would be admirable, he being not far removed from the throne.'

'No, not far removed,' Mary agreed.

'There was a move afoot,' Renard said, lying nobly, 'to advance him in opposition to Lady Jane Grey.'

'Am I to marry him,' Mary burst out, as Renard had hoped she would, 'to prevent a similar move being made during my reign?'

'An unpalatable thought in my own mind also,' Renard purred. 'He, whatever his rank, is your Majesty's subject. Would it be fitting, Madame, for you to marry a *subject?*' He paused, concluded from her expression that he had made on her an impression favourable to the Emperor's plans, and added in a humble tone: 'I apologise for my presumption but plead in excuse my confusion in respect of the attitude of the English to their Queen's marriage.'

'The attitude of the *English?*' Mary said broodingly. 'Am I not half-Spanish myself? It becomes increasingly clear to me that my rank, I the daughter of Henry Tudor and Katherine of Aragon, calls for a prince of equal rank.'

'Such a one,' Renard suggested thoughtfully and unhurriedly, 'as the Emperor's son, Prince Philip of Spain?'

'It would make a powerful alliance,' Mary mused, 'and would

hold in check that other ever-dangerous alliance of Scotland and France.'

Satisfied with the progress he had made, Renard said: 'It is the Emperor's dearest wish, should your Majesty wish it yourself, to provide you with a consort who is as well versed in statecraft as he is handsome.'

Mary blushed. 'Being a woman I cannot make the first advance myself.'

'Am I to inform the Emperor,' Renard felt it safe to say, 'that if he were to offer the Prince of Spain such an offer would not be entirely unwelcome?'

Mary gave him an arch look. 'We shall dwell on it, my dear Renard.'

Renard bowed. 'Have I your Majesty's permission to broach again the question of Lady Jane Grey?'

'Surely,' Mary said indulgently.

'Is Lady Jane to remain in the Tower year after year, as Lord Courtenay did?' Renard said, his tone suggesting personal sympathy. 'Is she to remain there, forgotten, until her death? By law she is neither guilty nor guiltless. Should there not be the formality of a trial?'

Mary frowned over this. 'Cruel, I do believe, to leave the poor child in the Tower in an agony of doubt.'

'And she, as you see it, Madame, a guiltless puppet. A trial, whatever the outcome, would serve as a warning to her friends and supporters.'

'Whatever the outcome . . .' Mary echoed. 'In the eyes of English law she is guilty and would plead guilty.' And then what seemed to Mary a pertinent thought occurred to her. 'If I am to pardon her she must first stand trial and be judged guilty. Very well, she and her husband, he who had come to regard himself as King, shall be brought to trial.'

'But not,' Renard warned, 'before your Majesty's coronation.'

'True,' Mary agreed. 'I see good sense in that.'

*

The prisoners had travelled by barge from the Tower and were now walking in grim procession from the water's edge to the Guildhall surrounded by guards. Archbishop Cranmer, arrested soon after King Edward's funeral, led the way. Jane's brothers-in-law Ambrose and Henry Dudley, both having been with their father during the abortive advance on Framlingham Castle, followed immediately behind Cranmer. Jane and her husband brought up the rear. It was their first meeting since Jane had seen Guilford in tears at the news of Mary's proclamation. Now he held his head high and walked with a proud swing of his shoulders. Jane, a tiny figure at his side, was dressed entirely in black, from her satin hood down to her velvet slippers, and from her girdle hung a prayer book. Husband and wife had greeted each other in guarded silence and had yet to exchange a single word.

Cranmer glanced from side to side, noting that halberdiers lined the route. They were there, he knew, to keep back the crowd that had gathered and break up, if the need arose, a demonstration in favour of Jane and her husband. It was November 14th, four months since the end of Jane's short reign, and the feeling had grown in London that Jane and Guilford, innocent young victims of Northumberland's ambition, were soon to suffer, innocently, the full force of Queen Mary's vengeance. It was a different matter where Cranmer and the two Dudley brothers were concerned; they had been fully and openly implicated in Northumberland's plot. Thinking only of himself Cranmer knew without doubt that he would meet his death in the fires of Smithfield. The prisoners were within sight of the Guildhall when a single voice shouted 'Shame!' This cry was taken up until it became a scarcely suppressed roar. The guards moved in, separating the prisoners one from the other, and the halberdiers turned menacingly to face the vocal but otherwise undemonstrative onlookers.

Because of her rank Jane was the first to enter the Guildhall. She was followed in single file by Cranmer, her husband and her two brothers-in-law. And then, when the judge had entered and taken his place, they stood facing him in a little group at the bar. The edge of the axe carried by the executioner was meanwhile turned away from them. The charges were read out and one by one the prisoners pleaded guilty. It was thus a trial of shorter duration than any in recent memory. The judge accepted their pleas, the edge of the axe was turned upon them and sentence was pronounced. Cranmer was to die at the stake; the three Dudley brothers were to die by hanging, drawing and quartering; Jane herself was to suffer death by burning. Nevertheless, if they pleaded humbly for mercy all, because of their rank, would go to the block.

There was another and louder demonstration during their walk back to the barge, and yet another from the banks of the river as they were rowed to the Tower to re-enter it as they had left it by way of Traitors' Gate.

'Jane . . .' Guilford said, speaking to her for the first time.

'Guilford?'

'You stared the judge out of countenance. I saw his look of unease.'

'I am innocent and he knows it, but I should not have accepted the Crown.'

'To be hanged, torn down while still alive, then drawn and quartered,' he said with a shudder.

'Shall you not plead for the speedier death by the axe?'

Guilford brightened visibly. 'The trial was a mere formality. That was expected, and that was why we pleaded guilty. The Queen is free now to pardon us, and pardon us she will.' He touched her arm lightly. 'Take heart, sweet Jane.'

'I want to live,' Jane said, a feeling of tension gripping her. 'I want to resume my studies. There is so much yet for me to learn. At fourteen I thought myself the wisest woman in Christendom. Now, at sixteen, my ignorance appals me.'

'Take heart,' Guilford repeated.

During the week that followed the trial Jane was given greater liberty within the Tower and her grant from the Queen was increased by seven shillings a week. A hopeful sign, Jane could but think, until without explanation she was confined entirely to her lodgings and the once-privileged Mrs Eleyn was no longer permitted to leave the Tower.

'What has happened?' Jane asked fearfully. 'Is the Queen's pardon to be withheld?'

*

'London is seething with anger and indignation,' the Gentleman-Gaoler remarked, holding his spoon in mid air.

Jane, who was dining with him and his wife, asked in surprise: 'Because of the sentence passed upon me, Mr Partridge?'

'No, my lady, because of the Queen's astonishing announcement. She is to marry the Prince of Spain. Her Council has urged her to marry an Englishman but she will have none of it. Gossip has it that the only eligible one, Lord Courtenay, has displeased her by making merry in the City.'

'In what way merry?' Jane asked, thinking Master Partridge as great a gossip as any in London.

'The stews have been reopened,' Partridge said darkly.

It was an unfamiliar word to Jane. 'The *stews?*' she questioned.

'Our English description, my lady, of Turkish baths.'

'A little cleanliness will do Lord Courtenay no harm,' said a still puzzled Jane.

'Madame,' Partridge explained, with an apologetic lowering of his head, 'not even in the old days was a Turkish bath other than a brothel.'

The Gentleman-Gaoler alone remained Jane's source of information concerning events in the world beyond the walls of the Tower. The Queen, he told her, soon after Christmas, was raising a new and special army and offering the volunteers the increased daily pay of tenpence. The reason for this? It was feared that there would be a rising in protest against the Spanish marriage.

'Not a rising in my favour, I pray God,' Jane said.

'Either in yours, my lady, or the Lady Elizabeth's.'

It was not until the end of January that news of an actual rising was conveyed to Jane. The principal leader was Sir Thomas Wyatt, a Catholic who had earlier supported Queen Mary. Now, as an Englishman before all else, he had raised an army in Kent and had issued a proclamation against the Spanish marriage. Meanwhile the Duke of Suffolk, a conspirator along with Wyatt, had hurried to Leicester to issue a like proclamation and raise a force of his own in Warwickshire.

'My father?' Jane gasped. She remembered the tearing down of the canopy; she remembered her father's many weaknesses; and now, out of those weaknesses, an act of boldness that bordered on madness. Either herself or Elizabeth? Not Elizabeth, as far as her father was concerned. Am I, she asked herself, to be a victim once again? 'Mr Partridge,' she said, 'is there any possibility of success?'

'Who can say, my lady?' he temporised, believing himself

that there was none at all, and thinking with pity in his heart that only success could now save Lady Jane Grey.

The rising, far more serious than first believed, was put down only after desperate fighting in the City itself. Wyatt was taken prisoner at Temple Bar on February 6th. On the same day the Duke of Suffolk, having been discovered hiding in a hollow tree, was brought to London and marched into the Tower. Two days later Jane was told by the Lieutenant of the Tower that she and her husband must prepare themselves for death on the morning of the ninth. They were to die, not by burning in her own case, not by hanging, drawing and quartering in Guilford's, but in both cases by the axe.

'The Queen, God bless her, is merciful,' the Lieutenant said.

27

FRANCES, Duchess of Suffolk was praying in the little private chapel at Suffolk Place. She had been told that Jane and Guilford were to die the next morning, also that Suffolk was imprisoned in the Tower and would, stupid fellow, lose his own head despite his frantic decision to return to the old faith. In a private communication Queen Mary had stated that the rising was an attempt to deprive her of a husband, of love, of happiness and of children. There could be no peace in England, Mary had further stated, while her poor little cousin remained alive. Frances herself, Mary had promised, need never fear for her own life.

For what, then, was the Duchess of Suffolk praying? She was, in a moment of concern for Jane, praying for guidance. If God would speak to her she would hasten to the Queen and say: 'Madame, can you destroy the life of one who is not your cousin but your half-sister?' But would Mary believe her story? And if she did would she not regard Jane as an even greater menace to her hold upon the throne? And worse, would she not feel it necessary to destroy Frances, Duchess of Suffolk as a means of stilling her tongue for ever?

'Dear Lord, what must I do, good Christian that I am?'

There was no answer, not even a flash of lightning or a distant clap of thunder.

Still on her knees, Frances found herself thinking of Adrian Stokes, her handsome steward. To secure him permanently, she who was beginning to age noticeably, she would marry him when all was over and Suffolk, poor weak fool, had suffered what would surely be a just death.

'Dear Lord . . .'

Still there was no answer.

She rose from her knees, sure now that she must carry the secret of Jane's birth to her grave.

'God, by his silence,' she said, her voice echoing in the chapel, 'has granted his holy approval.'

*

'My lady,' Sir John Bridges said, his voice gentle, 'the executions have been delayed. They will take place on the morning of the 12th, three days hence. Lord Guilford Dudley will die on Tower Hill; you, as befits your rank and royal blood, will have the benefit of privacy within the precincts of the Tower.'

That, Jane knew, meant Tower Green.

'What is the reason for this delay?' she asked.

The Lieutenant withdrew without replying and a few moments later ushered into Jane's presence Dr Feckenham, a monk who, seven years earlier, had been imprisoned in the Tower for daring to preach a pro-Catholic sermon. Released by Queen Mary he had become her chaplain and confessor and was held in high regard at court. Of solid yeoman stock he was in many ways a kindly man, sincere in his beliefs rather than fanatical.

'You have been sent by the Queen to attempt my conversion,' Jane said flatly.

'And through it, Madame,' he said courteously, 'to offer you earthly salvation as well. Embrace the old and true faith, not in the manner of run dog, run devil, as others have done, but by the innermost promptings of your heart, and a haven of peace and safety will be found for you in Spain.'

Jane looked at him unsteadily. Exile instead of death. She told herself that she was not afraid of death itself, only of the manner of it. She had escaped death by burning but many were the stories she had heard of clumsy executioners. Not one sure blow but sometimes several agonising blows. She felt the now familiar churning in her stomach, the beast of terror finding no escape. Arm me, she prayed, that I may stand fast. Mary had said that she would die for her faith; she had said the same herself.

'It cannot be,' she said at last.

'Madame, it can and must be,' Feckenham urged, 'by which I mean I cannot see you die a heretic.'

'In Christian charity,' Jane retorted, '*I* cannot contemplate your dying, when your own time comes, a papist.'

Feckenham could but smile. 'You would convert me, Madame, when it is my duty to convert you.'

'With all my heart, Dr Feckenham.'

'This suggests, though incorrectly, that we have reached a deadlock at the outset.'

'Incorrectly? I stand fast by my beliefs.'

'As I do by mine, and all the more strongly because of the admiration you inspire in me. Let us begin, Madame, by referring to the sacraments, the correct number thereof.'

They argued, but quietly, Jane adhering to the two sacraments of the Reformed Church, Feckenham urging her to recognise the seven of his own Church. Making no headway he put forward the dogma of transubstantiation about which they argued for an hour. His admiration, sorrowful as it was, increased while Jane, for her part, moved by the human warmth of the man, felt strongly drawn to him. But they both remained adamant.

'I admit defeat,' Feckenhamd said sadly. 'It grieves me that we shall never meet again.'

Jane reminded him of these words when he came to see her again on the eve of her execution, not to resume the arguments but to ask if he might accompany her to the scaffold.

'Ah,' he said, 'I meant that I would never see you again in the next world.'

'Indeed you will,' Jane said softly, 'if it should please God to open your eyes.'

On the morning of the 12th Jane rose at seven o'clock. It was still dark. Mrs Eleyn lit the candles but before she could begin to dress her mistress three matrons presented themselves and on Queen Mary's order submitted Jane to a probing examination.

'A pity,' said the stouter of the three. 'Pregnancy would have brought a temporary reprieve.'

Jane laughed hysterically. 'Would a child of mine have been allowed to live?'

Mrs Eleyn dressed her in the clothes she had worn for her trial and then, with Jane refusing breakfast, prayed with her and repeated Jane's favourite psalm, the fifty-first. Partridge entered a moment later and told Jane that she had the Queen's permission, if she wished to avail herself of it, to see her husband before he was marched to Tower Hill.

'Does he wish it himself?' Jane asked.

'No,' said Partridge, 'he fears it would be too great a strain.'

'As do I,' Jane said.

'The Duke your father,' Partridge continued, 'is full of remorse and begs you to forgive him.'

'That I do readily,' Jane said, tears springing to her eyes, 'but he must ask forgiveness of God, not of me.'

At nine o'clock Jane forced herself to go to the window. Mist was swirling about the Tower but through it she recognised Guilford Dudley as the guards led him across Tower Green. His shoulders were hunched, his head was bowed and he was weeping. He glanced up momentarily at her window, seemed not to see her and passed from sight on his slow, dragging march to Tower Hill. She heard then the tolling of the chapel bell, and glancing beyond the place where she had last seen Guilford saw the newly erected scaffold. Mine, she thought dully.

Sir John Bridges waited on her thirty minutes later and for the moment unable to speak indicated with a gesture that it was time for her to leave the Gentleman-Gaoler's lodgings. Finding his voice before leading the way, he asked her for a keepsake.

'Your position is a difficult one,' Jane said, offering him a velvet-covered prayer book. 'You are the same Lieutenant who welcomed me to the Tower as Queen.'

She found the guard of halberdiers drawn up and waiting below. Sir John took his place on her right, Dr Feckenham his on her left. Mrs Eleyn, weeping unrestrainedly, stationed herself behind them. Sir John gave the signal to proceed but before he could be obeyed a hand-cart was trundled across Tower Green in the direction of the chapel. 'Dear God in heaven,' Mrs Eleyn moaned. Jane too had seen the uncovered body and severed head of Guilford Dudley. Well, she thought, her eyes brimming with tears, he is beyond all weeping now.

'Why the chapel?' she asked the Lieutenant in a choking voice.

'Madame, he is to lie there with Anne Boleyn and many another . . .'

'Victim, Sir John?'

The Lieutenant bowed his head. 'Come, Madame, I beg of you.'

But once again the procession to the scaffold was impeded,

this time by the executioner and his assistants fresh from their duties on Tower Hill. Jane watched them pass and then, trying desperately to still the beast of terror in her breast, gave the order herself.

'Come, Sir John.'

To her utter amazement she found herself walking firmly. Only when she had climbed the steps of the scaffold and stood facing the executioner, a huge masked figure dressed in scarlet, did she falter. She saw that the platform was covered in straw, and the sight of it caused an old memory to come flooding back. She saw herself at the age of nine in the presence chamber at Whitehall, she facing Great-Uncle Henry for the first time and shuffling her feet in the straw which covered the floor. And she heard the old King's voice: 'Laughter drives out fear. I pray that laughter, for you, will always drive out fear, however grave the circumstances.' Laugh she could not, but neither, remembering him, could she weep. The beast of terror had been stilled at last.

The executioner approached and, as custom demanded, begged her to forgive him.

'That I do willingly,' Jane said. 'I pray you, dispatch me quickly.'

He stood aside and pointed out the block. Mrs Eleyn stumbled forward with the handkerchief but so distressed was she that Jane was obliged to take it from her and with it blindfold herself. Then standing there, feeling the soft touch of the river mist on her cheeks, she repeated her favourite psalm again, beginning: 'Have mercy on me, O God, according to Thy loving-kindness . . .' Feckenham, his voice hoarse, echoed her words in Latin. Jane turned to him when she had finished. She reached blindly for his hand, found that he was kneeling and guided by his hand kissed him lightly on the brow.

'Are there not, in heaven, many mansions?' she said, astonished at her sudden wave of tolerance.

Blindly still she found her way to the block and knelt, and after a moment of groping placed her head in the curve.

'Madame, you must give the signal,' the headsman said.

Knowing what was expected of her Jane stretched out both hands and sensed that he had raised his axe.

'Dear Lord,' she said, 'into Thy hands I commend my spirit.'